JAIMIE ADMANS is a 35-year-old English-sounding Welsh girl with an awkward-to-spell name. She lives in South Wales and enjoys writing, gardening, watching horror movies, and drinking tea, although she's seriously considering marrying her coffee machine. She loves autumn and winter, and singing songs from musicals despite the fact she's got the voice of a dying hyena. She hates spiders, hot weather, and cheese & onion crisps. She spends far too much time on Twitter and owns too many pairs of boots.

She will never have time to read all the books she wants to.

Find out more on www.jaimieadmans.com or find her on Twitter @be_the_spark

Also by Jaimie Admans

The Post Box
at the North Pole

JAIMIE ADMANS

ONE PLACE. MANY STORIES

HQ
An imprint of HarperCollins*Publishers* Ltd
1 London Bridge Street
London SE1 9GF

www.harpercollins.co.uk

HarperCollins*Publishers*
1st Floor, Watermarque Building, Ringsend Road
Dublin 4, Ireland

This paperback edition 2021

2
First published in Great Britain by
HQ, an imprint of HarperCollins*Publishers* Ltd 2021

Copyright © Jaimie Admans 2021

Jaimie Admans asserts the moral right to be
identified as the author of this work.
A catalogue record for this book is
available from the British Library.

ISBN: 978-0-00-846693-0

MIX
Paper from
responsible sources
FSC
www.fsc.org   FSC™ C007454

This book is produced from independently certified FSC™ paper
to ensure responsible forest management.

For more information visit: www.harpercollins.co.uk/green

Printed and Bound in the UK using 100%
Renewable Electricity at CPI Group (UK) Ltd

For everyone who still looks to the skies on Christmas Eve and hopes to see something magical.

Chapter 1

Dear Santa,
I wish I could believe in magic again.
From,
Sasha Hansley, aged 12

What's the best thing that can happen a month before Christmas? Well, it's definitely not losing your job.

'Of course I understand,' I say to my friend Debra on the phone. 'I'll find something else. It's *fine*.'

And I do understand. I've been helping out at her dog grooming parlour on a casual basis, and now her sister-in-law's been made redundant and needs the extra income so she's going to help out instead.

'Family comes first,' I say cheerily. 'Especially at this time of year. No worries. I appreciate you keeping me on for as long as you have.'

She hangs up with another apology and thanks me for taking it so well, and I'm glad she can't hear my gritted teeth through the phone line.

Great. Yet another thing to be joyful about. Where on earth am I going to find another job at the end of November? Even the temporary Christmas positions will have been filled by now.

I drop my phone on the coffee table and throw myself back into the sofa where I'd perched awkwardly on the edge when Debra rang saying she had some news. And I get it. If family need help and you're in a position to help them out, of course you're going to. But I'm gutted too. I've been working there for a year and a half, and I *love* it. I get to spend my days hanging out with dogs. Washing dogs, drying dogs, brushing dogs, playing with dogs, distracting dogs while Debra clips their nails and cuts their hair. Walking dogs.

Christmas cheer was already in short supply this year, but losing a job I love is the icing on top of the dried-up fruitcake. Now I'm going to have to be extra careful with money, so I can't even drown my sorrows in copious amounts of mince pies, mulled wine, and tubs of Christmas chocolates like I usually would.

I'd say it's been one of those days, but really it's been one of those years. I open my eyes and blink up at the ceiling. How much worse can things get? I'm probably tempting fate by even thinking that.

At the ripe old age of thirty-six, I'm feeling so old and jaded that I'm ready to give up on life and move to a remote Scottish island where there's only one house and a few sheep. And maybe a watchtower with a cannon that automatically fires at approaching boats. Unless that was more Viking-era and might be frowned upon in this day and age . . .

It would be less isolated than I am now. I don't even have a pet to eat my corpse if I died. I'd be one of those cases where no one realises I'm missing until the neighbours start noticing an odd smell four months later.

I groan out loud. Working at the dog grooming parlour was just about the only thing that was going well for me. I *should* pick up my laptop to update my CV and upload it onto job search sites, but instead I pull the TV remote over and switch it on.

Cheerful Christmas songs. I switch channels and land on an ad break full of festive adverts, showing laughing families sharing jugs of gravy, singing children, and sentient snowmen. I switch the TV off again. The adverts do nothing but drive home yet another year of being alone for Christmas.

I look at the empty corner beside the TV where my tree used to go. I looked forward to putting it up every December, in the hopes that *this* December would be the one when Dad finally fulfilled his promise of coming home for the festive season and we'd have a proper family Christmas. As a child, I remember sitting under it, disappointed he'd broken yet another promise. Now I've gone from a disappointed little girl to a disappointed adult who gave up on seeing her dad for Christmas years ago and doesn't even bother to put up the Christmas tree anymore.

I don't even know where he is in the world. He's always off, here, there, and everywhe— My phone buzzes on the table and cuts off the thought.

'Speak of the devil,' I say out loud when "Dad" flashes up on the screen.

He's early. He usually leaves it until December 23rd at the earliest to tell me he won't be coming home for Christmas after all.

'Let me guess,' I answer the phone, ready for yet another excuse. 'A spacecraft landed in the middle of the road to the airport so you can't get home? Maybe aliens have taken over the population of Morocco or wherever you are, and you simply *can't* abandon them in their time of need? Perhaps a giant squid has invaded the village and you're the only one who can save them? Pirates? Dinosaurs? Man-eating jellyfish?' I've certainly heard more outlandish justifications over the years for why he's missing yet another dad-and-daughter Christmas.

'Sasha?'

I sit up straight. His voice sounds shaky and frail, and there's a wobble in it that I've *never* heard before. 'Dad? What's wrong?'

'Now I don't want you to worry . . .' He speaks slowly, almost a whisper, like he's struggling to get the words out.

It instantly sets alarm bells jangling. No one ever says that unless there's something to worry about and my mind jumps

3

into overdrive about all the accidents he could've had on his latest crazy adventure. Kicked by a camel in the desert? Fallen down a mountainside in Asia? Stampeded by a herd of elephants on the African savanna?

'I've had some health trouble . . .'

His voice is so quiet that I have to press the phone closer to my ear to hear him.

'The thing is . . . I've had a heart attack. I'm absolutely fine and you mustn't worry about me—'

'Dad! A heart attack? That's *serious* serious!'

My mouth goes dry and I can't hear myself think over the rush of blood in my head, like I've stood up too fast even though I'm sitting down. I definitely jinxed things by wondering how much worse this year could get.

He never takes anything seriously, but even he can't ignore a heart attack.

'When was this?'

'Two weeks ago—'

'You had a heart attack *two weeks* ago and you're only now telling me?'

'I didn't want you to worry. I feel fine—'

'You don't sound fine.'

He gives a weak cough as if on cue. 'I thought the doctors would send me straight back to work, but they're telling me – quite sternly, I might add – to take it easy.'

I scoff. Take it easy. My dad doesn't know the meaning of the words. He's nearly eighty but he acts like he's in his twenties. To be honest, twenty-year-olds would look at him and wonder where he gets his energy from.

Plus, taking it easy could be difficult depending on his location in the world. Taking it easy on a beach in the Bahamas, okay. Halfway up Mount Kilimanjaro might not be so okay. I clench my teeth again and ask the dreaded question. 'Where are you?'

I brace myself for the answer. It's always different. All answers

4

are equally worrying. He's never in the same place twice, and he never does things that most seventy-nine-year-olds would do, like pottering in the garden or doing crosswords with a nice cup of tea. He's always got to be scaling mountains or wrestling crocodiles or sailing across some previously un-sailable body of water where forty-eight boats have sunk in trying.

'I'm in Norway.'

Norway. Okay. Norway sounds like it might be a reasonably safe and calm country. What kind of scrapes could he get into in Norway? Ice fishing? Fjord crossing? 'Doing what?'

'I'm running a reindeer sanctuary.'

'Of course you are.' Reindeer. Why didn't I think of that? At least the word *sanctuary* sounds quiet, a world away from my dad's usual activities. 'Is that a difficult job?'

'Well, that's why I'm phoning . . .' Dad gives a weak cough again, and I wait while he takes a few breaths, and even though I'm trying to tell myself that he's *had* a heart attack and he's still alive so that's got to be a good sign, I'm panicking because his breathing sounds laboured and his voice sounds so feeble that he can barely form words.

'I need your help.'

Those are words my dad has never said to me before. He never asks for help with *anything*, and the fact he's asking now might be the most worrying part of this conversation so far. 'With what?'

'The reindeer. The doctors have forbidden me from doing any strenuous work, and I'm struggling to manage on my own.'

'Come home,' I say instantly. 'Move back in here. You know I have room. Let me take care of you. This has to be a sign, Dad. You can't keep running off around the world on these hare-brained adventures. Come back to the UK.'

'I was thinking more along the lines of . . .' He gives another cough and has to catch his breath. 'Maybe you could come out here? I'm on my own, Sash. I can't abandon my reindeer – there's no one else to look after them. I can't come home.'

Home. He still thinks of Britain as home then, despite the fact he hasn't lived here for a couple of decades. He hasn't even visited the country since I met him at a London train station when he was inter-railing around Europe three summers ago.

'I don't know who else to turn to,' he says quietly. 'I need someone stable who I can rely on.'

I never knew my dad thought that about me. It might be an insult really, like he thinks I'm an actual building. Me being "stable" and always staying in one place is usually something he criticises – he's constantly disappointed by my lack of adventurous spirit and refusal to visit him whenever he stops in one place long enough. He once invited me to meet him in Japan and climb inside an active volcano, and was surprised when I didn't fancy it.

'I'm struggling, Sash. I need your help. The reindeer need a lot of care, and it's not so easy for a man of my age to get around with all the snow.'

'It's snowing there?'

'It's Norway. It's been snowing for weeks.'

'That sounds cold.'

'Oh, no, not at all. It's only minus-fifteen today.'

'*Only?*' I say in horror. I love snow, and we don't get nearly enough here in Oxfordshire, but surely a pensioner who's just had a heart attack shouldn't be roaming about in those temperatures? 'Dad, that's madness. You have to come home.'

His breathing is harsh down the line, but I can tell he's not particularly enamoured with my plan. And I'm still struck by the idea of my dad actually asking for help. It leaves me with no doubt that this really *is* serious.

My dad is a larger-than-life character who will always be there. Despite his love of travelling and his daredevil spirit, it's never before crossed my mind that he *isn't* immortal. That one day, and one day soon given how frail he sounds on the phone, he won't be there. We might not always see eye to eye, but he's always been in the background of my life, off on his adventures,

6

nothing more than the occasional postcard dropping through my letterbox. A phone call every few months. A Christmas card with a few banknotes inside it every year. A birthday card that invariably arrives two weeks late.

'I know you can't take time off from your job at the drop of a hat, and I know you must be owed loads of holiday time because you never go anywhere or take any holidays.' He gives another wheeze. 'And I thought it might count as a family emergency . . .'

The word "emergency" sets my alarm bells ringing again. Does he think . . . is he really *that* close to death's door?

'And I thought . . . after all these years working at that fancy hotel . . . and you *are* the boss, after all . . .'

Ah, yes. That. There's the small matter of how my dad thinks I work at the Hotel Magenta, and that I not only work there, but I'm actually the manager. He got the wrong end of the stick a few years ago, and I never had the heart to set him straight. So whenever he asks me how work's going, I mumble something about it being great, and don't tell him that the management position never went to me, or that I've been through several dead-end jobs since he thought I became the manager of a posh hotel.

'We— I . . . I could really use your help and expertise. Not many . . . sanctuary owners would get a chance to consult with one of the top hoteliers in the country.'

'For the reindeer?' I ask in confusion. 'Are reindeer in regular need of caviar and champagne via room service, breakfast in bed, and five-star dining every night? Do they need a concierge to attend their every whim?'

'Well, they probably wouldn't complain.'

I don't laugh at his attempt at a joke. No matter how much he tries to brush aside the heart attack, this isn't funny. 'You have to come home,' I try again. 'You can't stay out there alone in snow and below-freezing conditions. You're clearly not well.'

'Don't write me off yet, Sasha. There's still plenty of things I need to do with my life. Space tourism, for a start. I've seen a

7

lot of the world, and now I insist on living long enough to get a place on the next rocket to the moon.'

'No! No space tourism! Terra firma is bad enough!' I say, even though the idea of him *not* living long enough makes my stomach roll.

I should tell him I've lost my job, even though it wasn't the job he thinks it was. The most exciting thing I do in my life is curl up in front of the TV with a cuppa and a packet of biscuits. I've never done anything my dad would consider "fun". I've never even left Britain. The only time in my life that he's ever been impressed by anything I've done is when I got that job. I don't want to disappoint him more by admitting I've been fired from a totally different job *or* that I never got that one in the first place. 'Maybe I could come out there for a little while . . .'

Even as I say it, I wonder what I'm thinking. Am I really saying I'll get on a plane to Norway to help my dad out with his reindeer sanctuary? It's not the most unusual thing my dad has ever asked me, but it's got to be in the top three, after the volcano climbing, and possibly that time he asked if I'd like to visit the wreck of the *Titanic* for my sixteenth birthday.

'Fantastic! I'll email you the flight info. I've booked your tickets for tomorrow.'

'Tomorrow? How did you know I'd . . .' I trail off. His voice sounds so animated now that I'm forgetting this is a man who's just had a heart attack. He's lucky to be alive. He might not have long left, and I haven't seen him for over three years. I'm not going to turn down what might be my last chance to see him, no matter where he is in the world.

'It'll be fun, Sasha. It's been too long since we saw each other. And finally a chance to spend Christmas together!' He sounds remarkably less close to death's door than he did a few minutes ago. He sounds normal now, like he's not even on death's garden path.

'Christmas? That's four weeks away. You need me for that long?'

'Well, it's a busy season. Reindeer and Christmas, they go hand in hand. And we're not keeping on top of things . . .'

'Who's this "we"? I thought you were on your own?'

'Me and the reindeer, obviously. They can't wait to meet you. I've told them all about you and your fancy job. They were very impressed.'

'The reindeer?' I ask, wondering if the incredulity is coming across in my voice. Should I feel guilty that there's now a bunch of reindeer somewhere in Norway who also think I'm the manager of a posh hotel?

Dad starts telling me about what wonderful animals they are, but this conversation has spiralled out of my control – a common feeling when talking to my father. It's like he's pre-decided how this phone call would go. 'Where exactly is this place?'

'We're in the northernmost part of Norway. It's lovely here. You'll love it. Two hundred miles north of the Arctic Circle and—'

'Two *hundred* miles north of the Arctic Circle?' I shiver involuntarily. 'Surely that's not . . . habitable?'

'Oh, yes, it's charming. You can survive quite happily up here.'

'Survive . . .' I repeat. 'Why is everything you do about survival and not just being happy where you are and having a quiet life?'

He doesn't answer and I feel the need to claw this conversation back around, to do something that wasn't already determined before he picked up the phone. 'Dad, I have a condition. If I'm coming out there, it's to help you sell the place. You might not have realised it, but you're an elderly man and you've had a heart attack. This cannot continue. You can't keep living like this. And you can't stay somewhere that's two hundred miles north of the Arctic Circle completely alone – that's not safe. You have to come back to a quiet life here in the UK with a doctor's surgery ten minutes up the road. You've been lucky to survive this, but you have to take it as a sign. It's time to give up the mad life and be normal.'

'And do what? Jigsaw puzzles while drooling into my slippers?'

'Yes! Exactly that! There are plenty of classes you can join to keep active, but you cannot stay out there by yourself running a flipping reindeer farm.'

'Sanctuary, not farm. We help injured and abandoned reindeer.'

He's deliberately ignoring me. 'I'm serious, Dad.' I squeeze the phone a bit tighter, even though the harsh breathing and coughing ceased since the moment I agreed to go. 'We'll get it market-ready, get a valuation and a survey and whatever else we need, and then get an estate agent to put it up for sale, and you come home with me in January. Enough is enough now. You've been living the wild life for too long. Your body is telling you to slow down. I'm not coming unless it's to help you sell the place and come home for good.' I give a sharp nod to the wall. He can't see it, but it makes me sound more confident than I feel.

He doesn't reply. Are all parents this frustrating or is it just my dad?

'Look, we both know you'll have moved on and bought a beach hut in Hawaii by Easter. You never stay in one place for more than a month or two, but this has to end *now*.' I sigh and try a different tactic. 'If you expect me to be able to shirk off work and leave all my colleagues in the lurch at my fancy, important job, then it *has* to be for a good reason.'

'Well, you never know, when you see it, you might fall in love with the place like I did.'

I do a deliberately sarcastic laugh. 'Oh, I don't think that's going to happen.'

Neither of us speaks for a long while. Dad usually fills any silence with tales of people he's met in random corners of the earth, and I usually recount the plots of TV dramas like they're events that happened to friends of mine in an attempt to make my life sound more interesting. My dad is a global traveller who's seen every inch of the world twice over. I don't even take the scenic route home from work. The most exciting place I've visited in recent months is the dentist. But I don't try to fill the silence this time. He has to realise that you can't have a heart attack and carry on as you were. Something has got to change.

'All right,' he says eventually. 'Maybe you've got a point.'

He sounds grudging and unconvinced, and I feel a little bit guilty for trying to make him do something he doesn't want to, but someone has got to be the sensible adult between us, and it's definitely not going to be him. 'So you agree? I come out there and help you, and then we put it in the hands of an estate agent and you come home with me in January.'

He doesn't confirm his agreement. 'It'll be fantastic to see you. I've booked you on flights for tomorrow, and I've arranged a taxi to collect you in the morning and take you to the airport. You're on a flight into Oslo, and then you get a connecting flight to our nearest airport, and I'll meet you there. I've emailed all the info over.'

It's so far off the beaten track that I can't even get a direct flight there. Brilliant. I try to ignore the wave of anxiety that washes over me at the thought of flights and travel and packing. I can't explain that to someone who flies more regularly than the local sparrow population.

'Pack warm!' he says cheerily. 'But don't worry too much – we have plenty of extra clothes here for anyone who arrives unprepared.'

'How many people arrive at a reindeer sanctuary, prepared *or* unprepared?' My face screws up in confusion. 'Is it somewhere people visit? Like a dog shelter or something?'

'Something like that. I must dash! See you tomorrow! Merry Christmas to all and to all a good night!'

I'm pretty sure I hear the chortling of a "ho ho ho" as he hangs up, and I sink back against the cushions and stare at the blank screen of the phone in my hand. Typical Dad. I have no idea how worried I should be. My immortal, effervescent, full-of-life dad has had a heart attack, and yet as soon as I agreed to go, he sounded like his old self again.

Maybe I'm being too hard on him. Maybe he just genuinely needs help and was relieved that I'd agreed. I'm sure once he's had a chance to think about it, he'll realise that selling up and coming back to England is for the best.

And it would be nice to be needed. My dad has never needed anything from me. No one ever really needs anything from me. Even the birds I feed every morning are indifferent to my existence.

And I do love working with animals. Helping sickly reindeer doesn't sound like the worst way to spend a December. I've never even seen a reindeer in real life before.

And the idea that it could be my *last* chance to see my dad wheedles its way in again. The sort of thought that no one likes to think, but if you've got elderly parents, you can't avoid it crossing your mind occasionally. It's scary enough to make me push myself upright and climb the stairs to find a suitcase I've only got because my dad sent it as a Christmas present last year, pack my warmest clothes, and dig out the passport I've never used and only have because Dad paid for it and insisted I'd need it one day.

'Okay, enough wallowing,' I say to the empty room. 'I'm going to Norway.'

And that's a sentence I never thought I'd say.

Chapter 2

Dear Santa,
What would you wish for? I bet no one ever asks you that.
From,
Olivia

After a long, long, long day of travelling, I'm exhausted by the time I get off a rickety plane at a tiny airport inside the Arctic Circle.

There is snow everywhere, and although I've not seen a lot of runways in real life before, I'm pretty sure none of them are meant to be this small.

It's only 7 p.m. but it's pitch-dark and freezing. Even though I've got a big coat on, the cold bites at my arms and hits my chest like a sheet of ice. My feet plunge into ankle-deep snow, and the two pairs of socks I've got on inside my trainers do nothing to keep it out. The air is so cold it's like breathing razor blades and it feels like shards of ice are hitting the back of my throat every time I inhale.

But it doesn't take away how grateful I am to be back on solid ground. I'm kind of impressed with myself for ... I don't know ... getting here, I guess. I've never done anything more complicated than take a train before, and somehow I've made it

13

to Norway and this is the third airport I'll have had to negotiate today. I didn't even have a panic attack mid-journey, which really *is* impressive considering the plane felt like it was going to fall apart in mid-air.

The wing gives an ominous creak as the pilot directs me and the two other passengers into a derelict-looking airport building that not only looks like it's about to fall apart at any moment, but also looks like it *has* fallen apart several times and been patched up with stray bits of wood haphazardly nailed on. My suitcase wheels give up at the sight of snow, and we clomp towards the ramshackle building down a snow-covered path. It looks like someone cleared it this morning, but more snow has fallen since and they've given up trying to keep up with it.

I'm shivering as I go through security, which is a woman behind a desk who peers at our passports and nods us through, and inside the building is an information desk, a vending machine, and a row of seats. I walk into the reception area looking around for my dad. I've spent the whole journey thinking about how good it will be to see him, and I can't help thinking he'll be a little bit proud of me for being brave and actually making it here, and that's without knowing how many times I nearly told the taxi driver to turn around and take me home on the way to the airport this morning. I don't know how people do this on a regular basis. Travel is *daunting*.

The feeling of being brave lasts until my eyes fall on a man standing in the reception area, facing the gate we're entering through, and holding up a sign reading 'Sasha Hansley'.

My heart is instantly pounding and I can't hear anything above the sound of blood rushing in my head. My suitcase clatters into the row of chairs and makes such a noise that it shakes the whole building as I rush across to him. My dad said *he'd* meet me at the airport. What if something's happened? What if I haven't made it in time?

The run across the tiny room leaves me breathless and I'm not sure if it's the exertion or the panic. I point at the man's sign. 'Is he okay? Where is he?'

He turns the cardboard sign over in his hand, looks at it, looks at me, and holds it out questioningly.

'I'm Sasha,' I say hurriedly. 'He was supposed to meet me. Has something happened?'

'He's fine. He delegated,' the man says. His voice is deep and has a slight accent.

I put a gloved hand on my chest and will my heart to slow down. Despite the freezing temperatures, warm relief floods me. 'I thought I was going to be too late.'

The man doesn't say anything, but I can feel his eyes on me.

'Are you a friend? Neighbour? Boyfriend?' I'm not sure the last one is likely, but with my dad, nothing is beyond the realm of possibility.

He raises a dark eyebrow. 'Employee.'

'You work for him?' I don't hide the double take. 'I thought he was on his own out here.'

'*We* are on *our* own out here.'

'Oh.' I take a step back and realise I have to strain my neck to look up at his truly colossal height. 'He left that key nugget of information out when I spoke to him yesterday.'

He once again doesn't respond, and I stand there staring at him in surprised silence. He is an absolute mountain of a man, taller and wider than some actual mountains. He must be six-foot-six at least, if not taller. He's wearing a red and white Fair Isle knitted hat with clear ski goggles pushed up onto it, and enough layers of padded clothes that he looks like a sexier version of the Michelin Man. Why didn't Dad mention him? Did he think I wouldn't have come if I'd known he's got an employee who looks like he could bench-press the entire building *and* the plane we came in?

'Taavi.' He gives me a nod that's probably meant to be a greeting.

'Is that a name or a location?' I say as a joke.

15

He's got a knitted scarf pulled up far enough to cover the lower half of his face, but he doesn't laugh, smile, or react in any way. Instead, he turns around and deposits the cardboard sign into a nearby bin.

Maybe he doesn't speak much English and he's out of his depth trying to have a conversation with someone who doesn't speak a word of Norwegian. So far we seem limited to single-word answers and the odd stilted sentence.

Instead of asking if I'm ready to go, he leans across and removes my suitcase from my hand. I go to protest that I can carry my own suitcase, but his huge hand, made even huger by the padded gloves he's wearing, simply closes around the handle and lifts it away from me like I'm completely inconsequential, leaving me grasping at thin air as he lifts it up and across the row of seats as if it weighs nothing. I've been hauling the thing around all day with both hands and a few choice swearwords in its direction.

When he reaches the door, he opens it and steps back to let me go through first, and I nod a thank you to him, hopefully translatable in all languages.

Outside, it's dark, and the air is sharp and cold, momentarily shocking me again as I inhale and look around. There are modern square-angled LED streetlamps shining down on snow that looks even deeper out here than it did from the runway, and the airport is in a small clearing in what seems to be the middle of a forest. Across the road, tall snow-capped evergreens rise up on spindly trunks.

There's a small car park with only four cars in it to my left, and to the right, there's a row of husky dogs tethered to a sled, all barking and howling, eager to get going.

'Oh wow.' I look at them in surprise. 'How charmingly Arctic. People don't really get picked up from the airport by dog sled, do they?'

Taavi doesn't respond so I start walking towards the cars, and it takes a few steps to realise he's not following.

When I turn around, he's loading my suitcase *into* the dog sled. 'Oh, come on. Those are your dogs?'

'No, they are not my dogs.'

'What are you doing with them then?'

'They're not my dogs, but they *are* my mode of transportation.'

'Are you serious? *That's* how we're getting to the reindeer sanctuary?'

'Unless you would prefer to walk, in which case, it's only two hours in that direction.' He gestures towards the trees. 'I'll send the coroner back to find your body in the morning. If there's anything left to find, that is. You'll probably have been completely devoured by starving wild animals by then.'

My eyes go wide. 'Are you serious?' I repeat, going for a world record on how many times you can ask someone if they're serious in a sixty-second period.

He doesn't speak or smile or do anything to suggest he *isn't* serious. Walking in this weather didn't sound appealing anyway, but even less so when you bring wild animals into the equation.

'Who travels by *dog sled* though?' I say apprehensively. 'Is it safe?'

He pulls his goggles down from his hat and fits them over his eyes with a pop. 'You'll find out.'

I look between him and the dogs. Getting pulled along in a sleigh that looks like it's made from strips of wood and held together with garden twine, by nine huge, excitable dogs was not on my to-do list *ever*. I know people come to this part of the world for experiences like this, but . . . not me. The most exhilarating experience I've ever wanted is the feeling when Netflix adds a new boxset and you've got a whole weekend free. And for *not* the first time today, I wonder what I was thinking of in agreeing to come here. This is not a place for someone like me.

Taavi is standing beside the sleigh and gesturing for me to get in. I can't see much of his face between the scarf and goggles, but I know there's an impatient look on it. I glance back at the airport. I suppose it's too late to turn back now.

The dogs start wagging their tails and barking louder as I step closer. I like dogs; I'm not out of my depth with them. I let the nearest one sniff my hand, but they're so eager to start running that the grey and white husky isn't interested in me and quickly goes back to yowling with the others.

Taavi holds an open hand towards the sleigh again, and when I hesitate, he leans across it and holds his arm out, offering me something to hold on to as I step over the side. Taking hold of his arm is like holding on to a tree trunk, solid and strong, and padded by however many layers he's got on under the thick coat. I lower myself down onto the red canvas lining so I'm sitting back. There's a pile of blankets next to me and I pull one over and spread it out across my body gratefully. I thought I was well wrapped up until I got here, but this cold is so bitter that it's no match for any of my clothes. As he steps onto the back of the sled, I look behind us to the road that leads out from the car park in the opposite direction. It doesn't seem like we're going to be able to turn around in this space.

He shouts something to the dogs to ready them, and then they take off, pulling us towards the forest.

'Where are we going? There's a road right there . . .' I shout up at him, struggling to be heard over the excited woofing.

'I don't do roads.'

Brilliant. Heading into the woods with a gigantic stranger of a man and nine dogs. I'm pretty sure horror movies have started with more promising opening scenes than this.

I squeal as we pick up speed and the sled veers from left to right as Taavi shouts commands to the dogs, snow spraying up behind us as we come dangerously close to trees when we round corners of the snowy forest. We shave past a tree with such force that the branches shake and deposit snow from the boughs unceremoniously on my lap.

I screw my eyes closed. If certain death is coming my way, I don't want to see it arriving. This is *horrible*. That plane felt safer than this.

I'd say I can feel the wind whooshing past my ears, but my ears are so cold that they've gone numb. I can hear the speed and the splatter of snow as we slosh through it. My entire face has started to tingle with the cold. I *really* hope Dad doesn't travel like this – it's no wonder he had a heart attack if he does.

I don't know how much time passes before there's a big hand on my shoulder. 'Look up.'

I open my eyes at Taavi's touch, and as soon as I do, a streak of green splashes across the sky above.

'The Northern Lights!' I squeak in surprise. The green ribbon dances across the inky darkness and disappears, only to be followed by a wave of yellowy-gold, which quickly disappears too.

I can't believe I'm seeing the Northern Lights. I've always wanted to see them, but never enough to be worth travelling to somewhere they'd be visible, and they're just . . . here. 'This is incredible!'

Even with most of his face covered, his blueish eyes are visible behind the ski goggles and I can tell he's smiling. 'This is a polar region – they put on a show most nights here.'

Most nights? That's insane. People have lifetime ambitions of seeing the Northern Lights, and my dad lives somewhere that they're a regular occurrence.

The sky has taken on a green glow and streaks of pink hover above, and I lean my head back as the sled continues moving.

And I realise something. It's not actually that bad.

There's another blanket folded up beside me and I pull that one across my chest and up to my chin, and I watch the sky change colour through the snow-covered branches of trees as we pass underneath them.

The dogs know exactly where they're going, following a well-worn path through the forest, and there's something about Taavi on the back of the sled behind me that's reassuring. He calls commands to the dogs constantly and uses his body weight to direct the sleigh, seeming well familiar with the route.

It's so still out here. There isn't a sound apart from the noise of the sled gliding through the snow and the excited noises from the dashing dogs. The lights in the sky skim a multitude of colours, and everything else feels distant and faraway. It's just us out here in the trees. It's like being inside a picture-perfect postcard. I'm living a dream that so many people would *love* to experience.

This is by far the scariest thing I've ever done, and it's also kind of . . . exhilarating. And fun. And incredible. I don't want to take my eyes off the sky because I don't want to miss a moment of the aurora that's come out to greet me, but I look down at the dogs and how much they're enjoying it, nine wagging tails in front of me as they tear along, and I glance back at Taavi again, who commendably doesn't take his eyes from the way ahead.

The lights above are the most beautiful thing I've ever seen, and I have an overwhelming feeling of emotion. This is something I never, ever imagined I'd get to see in my lifetime, something I hadn't even thought about when I was nervously waiting to get on my first plane this morning, and maybe . . . it was worth it. Netflix cannot compete with this.

And if it wasn't for the underlying fear about my dad's health and what exactly he's doing out here in the Norwegian wilderness, then this could be the most perfect moment I've ever experienced.

The two-hour journey evaporates in a blur of snow and Northern Lights until we pass a road sign. It's white with red lettering and a red border, and it looks like any average British street sign, but it says "North Pole".

Crikey, I know we're up north, but we're not *that* far north, are we?

I think I must've imagined it until we pass another one. I look back at Taavi questioningly, but the dogs drag us into a particularly thick area of forest where the trees are closer together and the track is so narrow that there's not a centimetre for error on either side, and he doesn't look down.

When we emerge, there's another "North Pole" road sign

standing between two tree trunks, and the Northern Lights have dimmed to nothing but a vague golden glow in the sky.

After a little while longer, the trees start to thin out, and Taavi calls a command to slow the dogs. There's a flash of different lights in the distance – twinkling Christmas lights. The trees disappear completely and we're going uphill, towards an open area of the woods.

'Welcome to the North Pole Forest,' Taavi shouts as we approach what can only be described as Santa's village. The clearing intersects with a tarmac road coming from the other direction, and there's a low red-brick wall surrounding a tall gate with "North Pole Forest" etched in fancy metalwork through the arch above it. There's another huge "North Pole" sign and an oversized red post box with "North Pole Mail" written on it, and a big metal stamp featuring a side profile of Santa, instead of the Queen's head we're used to seeing on British stamps. All along the wall and wrapped in a spiral around the gate arch are multicoloured Christmas lights, which are twinkling and flashing in patterns.

What the heck is this place? This can't be the reindeer sanctuary, can it?

The arched double gate is open and the dogs pull us uphill through it. There are trees everywhere, row after row of thick evergreens that must be twenty to thirty feet tall, their boughs heavy with snow. The road edges are piled high with snowdrifts, so close that I could reach out and run my fingers through them if I wanted to.

Around a bend in the road, Taavi shouts something that halts the dogs and they stop alongside two steps leading up to wooden decking outside a mansion-like house. It's painted white with red window frames and a red door, guarded on either side by two life-size red nutcrackers wearing Santa hats. There are lush green garlands wrapped around every wooden fencing post that surrounds the porch area, glimmering with warm white fairy lights, and a twinkling wreath on the door that looks nothing like the threadbare artificial ones you get at home. Icicles hang from the eaves, and above the door is a red and white sign that reads "*Julenissen* – Santa's House". Parked at the side of the house is a shiny red pick-up truck that I'm pretty sure you only see in Christmas movies. It's also decked out with garlands and twinkling white lights and has a wreath on the front.

The upper floor of the white house has got a clock-tower at the front with a big red clock-face looking down on us and a balcony running from front to back. The wooden railings are wound with the same twinkling garlands, hung in perfectly even scallop shapes and finished off with red ribbon bows.

Taavi's arm appears beside me, offering me a way to lever myself out of the sled. My legs are shaky, and as I step over the side, my feet plunge into calf-deep soft snow. I'd say it makes my feet go numb, but there's not a part of me that *isn't* numb already. Even my internal organs have frozen. My lungs are tingling with pins and needles, something I hadn't thought it was possible to feel *inside* your body until now.

'Where are we?' I ask as Taavi carries my suitcase up the two steps and strides across the decking to put it outside the door.

'North Pole Forest,' he says again, his tone suggesting he's already told me once.

'Yeah, but . . . where's my—'

At the thought of Dad, there's a noise of clattering hooves and a yell of 'Rudolph! Come back here!'

We both look up at the sound of jingling bells, and there's a swoosh as a reindeer canters past, followed in close pursuit by my father.

'Dad!' I shout. 'What are you doing?'

'Oh, Sasha, you made it!' Dad stumbles to a halt when he sees me and blows two air kisses. 'Mwah, mwah. Can't stop, Rudolph Number Three has escaped!'

'Again?' Taavi responds with a groan, making me look round at him. He pulls the ski goggles off and drops them on the doorstep too.

'Dad! You can't be chasing reindeer around . . .' I trail off.

Dad's taken off after the reindeer before I have a chance to ask what he's playing at. Almost-eighty-year-old men who have just had heart attacks shouldn't be chasing runaway reindeer in the snow. And then there's his appearance, which is *quite* different from the last time I saw him. He had a hat on, but the rest of his hair was long, white, and curly, with a bushy white beard touching his chest. He looks like Father Christmas. When I last saw him, he was clean-shaven and had short cropped hair, dyed dark to hide the greys.

Taavi steps beside me and I look up at his imposing height. I've never realised I was particularly short before, but I come up to barely above his elbow. 'The heart attack scared me more than it scared him. Since that first moment, I've been terrified for him, but he acts like nothing happened.' He looks down at me, eyes that are somewhere between blue and brown meeting mine. 'It's good you're here. I think.'

'He sounded so frail on the phone. I didn't think I was going to make it in time to say goodbye, and now he's chasing reindeer around the woods?'

'I'll go after them.' He gestures towards the line of trees and steps from the top step and across one of the huskies who are now having a sit-down and he runs after my dad yelling, 'Percy! Rudolph Number Three!'

I stand there looking around and feeling utterly bewildered. Dog sleds, Northern Lights, Santa's House, runaway reindeer apparently named Rudolph Number Three, and a man with quite possibly the most unusual eyes I've ever seen. What a night.

The dogs look at me in sympathy.

'This is madness,' I say to the nearest husky. 'I feel like Alice after she drank the potion and followed the white rabbit.'

I look out at the treeline which they've all now disappeared through and then back at the house behind me. The lights are on inside, and there's smoke pouring out of the chimney. It looks inviting, but not with my dad out in the cold.

I step gingerly over the reins lying on the snow and give the nearest dogs a quick head rub as I pass, and then I walk towards the trees too. 'Dad!' I yell. 'You shouldn't be out here!'

No response.

I wrap my gloved hand around a tree trunk, leaving a handprint in the frost that's covered the bark. There are two trails of footprints and one of hoofprints and I follow them further into the wooded area.

This is quite possibly the most surreal night of my life, but with my dad, nothing surprises me anymore.

Chapter 3

Dear Santa,
I've included a photo of my dog. He's a very friendly dog
and he won't bite you when you come down the chimney . . .
Probably.
From,
Elijah

The forest is vast, and I can't get a feel for quite how big this place is. The trees are close together, and I'm only following one set of footprints now; Taavi's, judging by the enormous size of the boots that made them.

'Dad!' I yell again.

This is ridiculous. I've gone so far past the point of being cold that I'm numb all over and the silence out here is deafening. Everything is dulled by the snow, but it's so different from being back at home. There's no traffic, no noise from cars passing on a distant road, no neighbour's kids screaming with delight as they build snowmen. This is *real* silence.

I come to a path between two trees, and the footprints I'm following go in one direction, and there's a set of hoofprints that go in the opposite direction. I look up at the sky like it might provide some form of divine inspiration but even the flashes of light are a distant memory now.

I shake my head and follow the set of hoofprints. I trudge through the trees, sinking into the snow with every step, using the thin tree trunks to pull myself along.

It doesn't take long to find the reindeer – he's got himself trapped in a small clearing between the trees, and although he's only got one antler, it's so wide that he can't fit through any gaps other than the one I'm standing in.

'Hello.' I'm ninety-nine per cent sure I'm about to be stampeded by a reindeer. He's only about waist-height, but the single antler looms above him, and I kneel down so I don't frighten him.

The reindeer looks edgy, like he's well aware he's trapped and I'm standing in his only exit route. He watches me with wide brown eyes.

'Rudolph, is it?' I ask. 'Or would you prefer Mr Reindeer? Sir Reindeer? Do reindeer have titles? Am I offending you by not referring to you as Sir Rudolph? Shall we stick with just Rudolph? Why the heck am I rambling about reindeer names in the middle of a Norwegian forest?'

My nonsensical babbling seems to convince Rudolph that I'm not a threat and he looks away, gives himself a shake that makes all the bells on his harness jingle, and starts poking his nose through the snow and eating something he finds underneath it.

'I'm Sasha. Percy's daughter. You probably know him as the old man who looks like Father Christmas who was chasing you earlier.'

He ignores me.

He's a beautiful animal. Thick fur in shades of grey and brown, a marble-like mix in some places, a patch of white below one ear, and a stump where one antler should be.

He's got a halter around his neck and across the top of his nose, but the end of it is dangling loose on the snow, and if I can get hold of it, then I can start leading him back. He seems calm as I shuffle closer on my knees.

'Why are you running away?' I keep talking as I approach him slowly. Once he notices I'm not blocking his exit anymore, he might make a dash for it. 'Or are you just trying to keep warm and everyone's misinterpreted your reasons?'

Rudolph glances up at me but carries on munching whatever he's extracted from under the snow and doesn't look like he's going to trample me or impale me with his antler.

'I must say your nose is a lot less red than I expected. Is that why you're running away – because people are disappointed by the lack of red nose?' I inch a bit closer. 'I guess any reindeer named Rudolph has a lot to live up to. But you have to be your own man . . . well, reindeer . . . And I know the feeling. People are usually disappointed when they meet me, and I spend a good chunk of my life wanting to run away too. I quite fancy a remote island somewhere, don't you?'

He's a reindeer, I say to myself. I doubt he's given much thought to emigrating to a remote island.

'But look, here's the thing, the longer you're out here, the longer my dad is chasing you, and it's flipping freezing. You probably don't notice it because you're a reindeer, but this is making winter in Britain feel like a weekend on the beach in Maui. I assume so anyway. I've never been to a beach in Maui. This is the first time I've been anywhere, actually.'

Another shuffle closer, close enough that I can reach out for the end of his harness. I hear movement behind me and in my peripheral vision, I see Taavi sidle up beside a tree trunk.

I expect him to take over, but he doesn't make any movement, and I don't want to risk Rudolph running again, so I carry on.

'I wouldn't worry too much about the red nose. Visitors probably don't even notice. My nose must be red enough to rival yours anyway now. I haven't been able to feel my face for the past few hours. You know when you go to the dentist and they numb your mouth for a filling? My whole face feels like that. Oh wait, you're a reindeer, you've probably never been to the dentist, have you?'

27

Behind me, Taavi lets out a laugh, and it makes Rudolph look up. While he's distracted, my hand shoots out and closes around the dangling end of the halter. I go to do a victorious shout, but think better of making any sudden movements.

I back out from under the reach of Rudolph's antler and stand up, wrapping the lead around my hand a few times.

'Good job.' Taavi steps out from behind the tree and enters the small clearing. 'I've never seen a reindeer lose the will to live before, but you obviously have a talent for it.'

I should probably be insulted but it's the nicest compliment I've received for a while.

He rustles a hand in the pocket of his coat, deliberately making noise to get the reindeer's attention, and then holds out a handful of what looks like the same stuff Rudolph's pulling up from under the snow.

'I caught up with your dad and sent him back to the house to get warm,' Taavi says as the reindeer snuffles the moss-like stuff from his hand.

There's something about his accent. He's got a reassuring voice that makes you think things will be okay. The kind of voice you'd want to hear on a pilot flying your plane or a doctor performing your life-saving surgery.

'Thanks.' I offer him Rudolph's lead but he shakes his head. Instead, he pats the reindeer gently, says something to him in Norwegian, and starts walking away. The reindeer trots after him, and I have to rush to catch up with them as the lead I'm holding pulls taut.

'Got to admit that's not how I expected to spend my first five minutes here.' I dodge around a tree.

'You came to help; you helped.'

You could have a more rewarding conversation with a nutcracker.

My feet sink into the snow as we walk between the trunks, but everything from the knee down is deadened with cold. The only sound is the crunch of Taavi's boots and the huffing of the reindeer. Even though we can't be far from where we started, the woods feel like they could go on forever. 'What kind of place is this?'

He screws one eye up and looks at me like he can't work out if there's something wrong with me or if I'm just a complete numpty. 'Not obvious?'

'Well, yeah, but . . . my dad said it was a reindeer sanctuary.'

'It is.' His eyes swivel towards Rudolph like I might not have realised that he is, in fact, a reindeer. 'It's also a North Pole themed Arctic resort. We have log cabins that guests rent out, glass igloos that people book overnight to view the Northern Lights, and Santa's House is open to the public for tours from 10 a.m. to 4 p.m. every day.'

'Ah, so it's not a real house! That makes so much more sense. No one actually lives in a place *that* picture-perfect.'

The look on his face says I've truly lost the plot. 'There's a grotto by the main entrance for children to visit Santa, and post boxes for them to post their Christmas letters. We used to have more, our elf workshops where toys were made are legendary, as were Mrs Claus's Kitchen baking classes, but it hasn't been the best few years.'

'Do you know my dad well?' I try to keep the conversation going because when it's silent, my mind wanders to what could be living in these woods and I'm convinced I hear a branch snapping and something hunting us.

'We've become close since he took over last year.'

My double take frightens Rudolph and Taavi has to murmur something reassuring to him. 'He's been here for a *year*?'

'Didn't you know?'

'No, I didn't . . . I didn't know where he was. My dad is not the sort of person you can keep up with.' I suddenly feel ridiculously awful. What kind of daughter doesn't know where her dad is in the world? How many times have I spoken to him this year?

29

Maybe three phone calls and a handful of emails. It's easier to avoid the topic, because talk of his travels always inevitably leads to him asking me to go on some trip with him and me saying no and disappointing him yet again. 'Are you sure? He's never stayed in one place for a whole year before.'

'He took over right after the Christmas season last year, at the end of December. He loves it here. He doesn't want to sell, no matter how much you come in throwing your weight around and bullying him.'

'*Bullying* him? Are you serious?'

He doesn't reply.

'He's going to be eighty in March and he's just had a heart attack. He can't possibly stay out here alone. Even with you here, which I *didn't* know about, this place looks huge. And *he* asked *me* for help, so it's obviously too much for him, even if he hasn't admitted it to you. I'm trying to do what's best for him. Am I the only person who notices how insanely cold it is?'

'No, you're the only person who's dressed inappropriately.'

That makes me feel like I'm a teenager wearing heels that are too high and a skirt that's too short, not the jeans, thick jumper, and coat I'm actually wearing. 'I was *boiling* in Britain. I felt like a right wally getting dressed this morning.'

'Wally?'

'Eejit. Moron. Plonker.'

'None of those definitions help, but I get your drift.'

'Look, you said you were worried about him after the heart attack; surely you see that it's not in his best interests to stay here? Where's your nearest doctor's? Nearest hospital?'

'Eighty kilometres south.'

I'm so caught up in the conversation that I walk headfirst into a tree and Rudolph stops to look at me disapprovingly. 'I don't know what that is in miles, but it sounds far.'

He doesn't say anything.

'He needs to be at home. To live a quiet life.'

'This *is* a quiet life. He's an adult. He's older than both of us put together. He has a right to make his own decisions.'

I can't argue with him there, but the problem with my dad is that his decisions are rarely sensible ones. Someone has to step in somewhere . . . don't they?

Silence falls again and an owl hoots somewhere in a distant tree and I rush to keep up with him in case it was something more sinister than an owl. 'Is that why you don't like me?'

'Never said I don't like you.'

'Are you this standoffish with everyone then? Because, if I've figured this out correctly, you work at a Santa resort and you get visitors here? You must be nice to tourists and children because I don't think they employ people as monosyllabic as you at a Santa village.'

He lets out a loud laugh and meets my eyes for just a second. 'You have a fair point and you make it well.'

Thankfully, the trees get more sparse and the twinkling lights of the house come into view, which saves me trying to make more awkward conversation. The dogs are still outside, but Dad has put down food for them and is standing on the decking outside Santa's House with his hands wrapped around a steaming mug.

'There you are!' He waves when he spots us. 'See, Tav? I told you we needed Sasha. She's making herself useful already.'

'Oh yeah,' he mutters, totally deadpan. 'I don't know how I'd have managed without a posh hotel manager to escort through the forest.'

I ignore the hotel manager bit, even though it makes me uneasy that yet more people know about this stupid lie.

'I can take it from here,' he says when we reach the house and my father is peering down at us from the top of the steps.

I unwind the end of Rudolph's halter from where it was wound surprisingly tightly around my glove and hold it out. The thick glove-covered fingers of his enormous hand brush against mine as he takes it with a nod of thanks.

31

'Thanks for the interesting arrival, Rudolph,' I say to the reindeer.

'Rudolph Number Three,' Dad corrects me. 'We wouldn't want them getting confused.'

I reach over and pat Rudolph on his shoulder, avoiding his antler as he turns towards me. His fur is immensely thick, so dense that you can barely get your fingers through it. No wonder they don't feel the cold. I stroke over it for a few moments.

'I don't know how he keeps getting out,' Taavi says.

'Maybe he can fly,' my dad says.

'Nah, don't be silly, Perce.' Taavi glances at me and then back at my dad. 'Only Rudolph Number One can fly.'

He's joking. Obviously he's joking, but neither of them do anything to confirm he's joking, and it's a little unsettling. The silence is uncomfortable while I wait for one of them to start laughing, but neither does.

Eventually one of the dogs starts ah-woo-ing, which sets them all off, and Taavi tugs on Rudolph's halter. 'I'll take Rudolph Number Three back and secure the paddock, and then return the dogs.'

'Where do they come from?'

'There's an outdoor activities centre seven kilometres west.' He meets my eyes and a smile twitches on his lips. 'Just over four *miles*.'

'How do you get back?'

He stares at me and then looks down at his feet like it's the most ridiculous question he's ever heard.

'You're going to *walk* four miles? In this weather? In the dark?'

'Of course.' He shrugs like it's the most normal thing in the world.

'Don't you want to come in and get warm? Have some food? You've been out here as long as I have; you must need to warm up.'

'I assure you, I've been out here a *lot* longer than you have.' He goes to walk away with Rudolph trotting after him, but stops

32

and turns back. He tilts his head to the side as he looks at me. 'Thank you, though. I appreciate the thought.'

'Ahh, so you *can* be friendly.'

He lets out that warm laugh again and his eyes are twinkling when they meet mine this time. 'I can, but I try not to do it too often. It unnerves people.'

He strides off with the reindeer and I stand with Dad on the wooden decking and watch as he follows the road we came in on, but instead of turning downwards towards the gate, he takes a narrow path left and disappears between the trees.

Dad's hand touches my arm, and even my coat must be cold, because he says, 'Oh, you're frozen – come in and have some hot chocolate to warm up.'

The door is open and my suitcase is now inside, and the dogs have quietened down again while they wait. I've gone past the point of no return with being cold now, because instead of following my dad inside, I can't help looking around for a moment.

Opposite the house is a wide hillside, clear of the trees that surround it. The hillside is dotted with little wooden cabins going all the way up and there's what looks like a ski slope in the middle. At the bottom, there's another huge red post box with "North Pole Mail" written on it, and there's another one at the edge of the house. We're on a snow-covered road that disappears into the distance, and even though there are Victorian-style streetlamps glowing at intervals along either side, it's too dark to see anything. I have no idea how big this place is or what exactly my dad is in charge of.

I eventually shake myself and hurry inside the door. I'm in a huge hallway with a log fire crackling in a hearth along one wall, and I rush over to it and pull my gloves off, rubbing my hands together and leaning as close to the flames as the protective grate will let me. I breathe a sigh of relief as the warmth filters through. It's toasty inside, the complete opposite of the biting iciness outside.

Along one wall inside the door, there's a mahogany reception desk with a computer monitor on it and in front of me is a mantelpiece over the fire, with nutcracker candlesticks holding flickering taper candles, and a huge portrait of Santa hanging on the wall above the fireplace. He bears a striking resemblance to my dad. The mantelpiece is decorated with another twinkling garland of evergreen branches interspersed with pine cones, berries, and sparkly poinsettia flowers. There are a couple of big rooms off the main hallway, and at the end, there's a grand staircase, also decorated like something you'd see in a magazine, not in real life. The wooden banisters are wrapped with twinkling garlands and wreaths are hung at intervals going up the baluster posts and finished with big red bows.

No wonder it's only a show house. It feels more like walking onto a film set than into someone's home. Even the air smells like cinnamon and freshly baked vanilla cookies.

'I'm so glad you came, Sash.' My dad reappears from what must be a kitchen with a steaming mug in one hand and a plate of . . . freshly baked cookies in the other.

Does my dad bake Christmas cookies now? Of all the things that have surprised me today, this is probably the biggest of them. Dad could barely find his way around a tin opener when I was young.

He puts the mug and plate down on a table beside the fire and takes my freezing hands between his warm ones. 'It's so good to see you.'

'It's good to see you too,' I mumble as he wraps me up in a hug, and it makes me realise it really has been far too long. I haven't hugged my dad in three and a half years. It's normal not to see him from one year to the next, but when something like this happens, it makes you realise how important hugs are, and my arms automatically tighten around him.

'How *are* you?' I ask as he squeezes me tight enough to make the breath leave my lungs. 'Seriously now, Dad. What did the doctors say about your heart?'

'Oh, nothing for you to worry about. It was just a warning – telling me that I need to take it easy.'

'I want to know everything. What happened that day? Where did it happen? How are you feeling now? *Are* you taking it easy? Have you got any follow-up appointm—'

He releases me and steps back before I can finish insisting on accompanying him on his next doctor's visit. 'You look cold. Take your shoes and socks off and leave them to dry by the fire. We've got underfloor heating – that'll warm your tootsies up in no time.'

I do as he says, even though I'm annoyed at him for trying to change the subject, and also keen to know what part of chasing a reindeer around a frozen forest constitutes "taking it easy".

I pull my wet trainers and damp socks off with a squelch of melting snow and leave them by the fire, and Dad disappears and returns again with a pair of fluffy socks, which he waves in my face until I take them from him, roll the frozen bottoms of my jeans up, and pull them on. I breathe a sigh of relief when my dry feet touch the warm floor.

I shrug my coat off and finally pick up the mug of hot chocolate, which looks like something you'd buy in a Christmas film, complete with whipped cream dotted with pink and white marshmallows and sprinkles, and a stripy candy cane hooked over the edge of the Santa-shaped red mug. I take a brightly iced bauble-shaped cookie and look over at my dad, who seems to be assessing me too.

He's wearing a white T-shirt and red braces holding up a pair of black trousers, and his feet are in thick red and green striped socks, like the ones he's just given me. I can't get to grips with the hair and beard, and without meaning to sound judgemental because I could do with losing a few pounds and a chin or two, but my dad is quite literally twice the man he used to be. He's on the go so much that eating is an inconvenience in his busy schedule, and he's always been so active that he's been slim and muscular without even trying. But now . . . he looks like the personification of Santa Claus in *every* way possible.

'I appreciate you taking time off work for me. I know your job is so important and it can't be easy to take off at the drop of a hat . . .'

Oh, that. I should tell him. I'm *going* to tell him. 'About that . . .'

'I'm so proud of you. I know I haven't been the best dad, but to see you strike out on your own, work hard, and get such a prestigious job . . .' He pats under his eyes like he's about to tear up. 'Your mum would've been so proud.'

The words die in my throat. He's so proud of my job that he's nearly in tears, and he's brought up Mum as well. How can I disappoint him now?

I bite the cookie instead and a multitude of flavours burst in my mouth. The sweetness of the icing, coupled with vanilla and cinnamon and an after-hint of some homely spice that turns warm in your mouth. 'These are *amazing*. You made these?'

'Tav made them. He's an incredible cook.' He takes a biscuit of his own and picks up his mug and beckons for me to follow him. I glance back at the fire longingly, but the whole house seems as warm and snug as this hallway.

Outside, the dogs start howling again and there's the sound of boots crunching on snow and a deep voice talking to them, and then the swish as they take off and their excited barking echoes into the distance.

I go over to the window in the living room, both hands wrapped around the mug as I sip the pepperminty hot chocolate. There's snow piled in drifts along the window ledges outside, and it's so quiet that I imagine the twinkling of all the lights on Santa's outside veranda is audible. I look upwards again, hoping the Northern Lights might make a reappearance, but cloud has drifted in now. 'You could've mentioned it was a Santa village, you know.'

'I didn't think you'd come. I know you like animals and thought

36

you might be swayed by the reindeer, but you're not really a big Christmas fan.'

'Dad, I would've come to help you, no matter where. Even halfway up a mountain in Outer Mongolia.' I hold a warning finger out. 'And don't go getting any ideas about mountains in Outer Mongolia; that wasn't a suggestion.'

My voice sounds joking, but I wouldn't put it past him to be actively planning his next trip up a mountain in Outer Mongolia. 'I'd go to the ends of the earth if you needed me.'

'Oh, now there's an idea. I've yet to see an end of the earth. I wonder where you might find one.'

'No,' I say warningly, but he's laughing when I turn to look at him. 'Speaking of things you didn't tell me, what's with the Big Unfriendly Giant?'

'Oh, Tav? He wasn't unfriendly, was he? I'll make sure he gets nothing but coal in his stocking if he was.'

I expect him to laugh, but his face is serious. How much has this place got to my dad? Coal, seriously? 'Not unfriendly, as such. Just . . . unexpected. I thought you were on your own. As you repeatedly told me on the phone despite saying "we" a lot,' I say to myself more than to him. It's making me question every aspect of my relationship with my dad. He's asked me to go many places with him – I've never said yes. Did he really think he had to hide so much just to get me to visit him when he's had a brush with death?

'He's a good lad.'

'Lad? He looks like he lives at the top of a beanstalk. I don't think "lad" is quite the right word.'

'Well, he's a lad to me. He's thirty-eight, you know, only a couple of years older than you. Single too.'

'That's very interesting and *very* irrelevant information. I'm *not* looking and he thinks I'm such a witch that I must have a folding broomstick in my suitcase.'

Dad laughs. 'You mustn't take him seriously. He's just being protective of me.'

'I'm your daughter! He doesn't need to protect you from me.'

'He knows how much I love it here. This is the first place I've ever been that feels like home.'

'Your home is in Oxfordshire. I've spent my whole life waiting for you to come back. To be a family again. You can't—' I go to repeat that he can't stay here, but it's falling on deaf ears.

'He's the best friend I've ever had, Sash. Do give him a chance.'

'I will, but it doesn't matter what he thinks. I'm here to help you, and that includes doing what's best for you, even if neither of you agree. You remember our deal, right? I'm here to help you get everything under control and sell up.' The words do sound a bit bullyish as they come out of my mouth, but what else am I supposed to do?

'I know,' he says solemnly, and I have a feeling this isn't going to be as easy as I'd hoped.

'So do you have visitors now? There's no lights on in the cabins on the hill over there, but Taavi said something about glass igloos?'

'We're empty at the moment.' Dad looks sadly at his pristinely decorated tree in the centre of the room, ceiling height, and so perfect that it couldn't possibly have been decorated by a real person. 'We've been empty for a while now.'

'How long's a while?'

'I bought it because it was going under last Christmas. Things had been going downhill and it was the end of the line for the old owner, but I couldn't imagine a world without the North Pole Forest in it. I wanted to restore it, but with my health . . .'

My ears instantly prick up. 'Has your health been this bad for a whole year then?'

'No, no, not at all.' He hesitates. 'It's just that this place needs a lot of rejuvenation and it's a lot for a man of my age to take on.'

'So someone foisted it off onto you, you realised you'd taken on too much, and now you're stuck with this huge failing business, and it's your turn to palm it off onto someone else – someone much younger who can do the work it needs.' I cup one hand around my eyes to block out reflections and look through the window towards the cabins on the hill opposite. From a distance, they look picture-perfect, but at a closer look, I can see pieces of wood hanging from their eaves, gaps in the wooden posts surrounding their outside deck areas, and dips in the blanket of snow covering them where the roofs have caved in. 'Or bulldoze it completely and put everything out of its misery.'

Dad, unsurprisingly, ignores my cheery suggestion. 'It's not that big. Only thirty acres.'

'*Only?*' I choke on the hot chocolate. I have no idea what thirty acres looks like, but it sounds like a lot. And I'm once again struck by that prickling of guilt that my dad has been doing this for a year, and I didn't know.

My eyes fall on yet another shiny red post box further along the road, in the direction Taavi took the dogs. 'What's with all the post boxes?'

'They're for Santa mail.'

'Santa mail . . . Like when children write to Santa?'

He nods.

'Do they still do that?'

'Of course. You're thinking it should all be email now, but there's nothing like the magic of sending a real letter. For a lot of people, a letter to Santa will be the *only* letter they write that year. People don't even write shopping lists anymore – they put it on their phones. The excitement of sitting down to compose a letter, maybe drawing a picture with it, decorating the envelope, and then posting it . . . That's magic to a child. The whole world has gone digital, but Santa is one person who should *always* uphold tradition.'

'Does Santa get a lot?'

'About 500,000 a year.'

I'm going to have to stop drinking when he's talking because I've made the mistake of sipping my hot chocolate again and I promptly choke on it *again*. 'You're having a laugh.'

'It's a fair split between us and the Lapland Santa village in Rovaniemi, across the border in Finland – they get about 500,000 and we get a similar amount.'

'That's a million. Are you seriously telling me that a *million* children write letters to Santa every year?'

'Of course.'

'Well, Santa must be a multi-billionaire to provide that many presents. Don't kids just give their lists to their parents so they know what toys to buy?'

'Don't be silly. The elves make the toys in the workshop at the North Pole. Santa only has to pay for materials.'

I genuinely feel like I've arrived on a different planet. He must be joking, but he's definitely worked on his delivery because he didn't used to be able to keep a straight face when telling a knock-knock joke, and *no one* laughs at a knock-knock joke.

'Have you written to Santa this year?'

'No, I haven't, because I'm thirty-six.' I give him my most incredulous look. How many *more* times can I ask if someone's serious today? 'You're really into this whole Santa thing then?'

'It's magical. Our job is to make children believe in magic. Imagination is the most powerful thing any child has, and Santa's job is to preserve that.'

Well, when he puts it like that . . . It does sound magical, and exactly what Christmas should be like for a child.

It's just that I half-expect him to offer me a glass of reindeer blood and a spear carved from antlers for my initiation ceremony into the Santa cult.

Instead of anything quite so macabre, Dad goes into a big kitchen via an open doorway through from the living room. He makes us both another hot chocolate while I look around in awe.

The kitchen is the definition of somewhere you'd expect to see Mrs Claus pop up at any moment. A red and white tiled floor, dark wood cabinets, and a glittery marble worktop run around the perimeter of the room. There's a ribbon-wrapped silver cooker hood on one wall, above what looks like a line of several professional-style ovens.

'They used to run Mrs Claus's Kitchen workshops from here,' Dad explains. 'Mrs Claus herself used to teach people how to make festive staples – gingerbread, Christmas cookies, mince pies, a nice fruit cake . . . That all ended before I started.'

There's an island in the middle of the room with a few shiny red stools pulled up along one edge, and in the middle of the island is a tiny Christmas tree strung with micro fairy lights and decorated with gold chocolate coins. There's a jar of candy canes, and a delicately iced gingerbread house on display too. It's so perfect that it must be plastic, but on closer inspection I see that it's real, and I'm awestruck that someone can do such intricate work.

After another hot chocolate and a catch-up chat in which Dad dodges every question related to his health, we wander back into the hallway, and while I'm enjoying the heat of the fire again, Dad puts a hand to his ear. 'There's Tav now.'

He opens the door and I go over and stick my head out too, unprepared for the sudden icy blast. Taavi is trudging up the road, his hands shoved into his pockets, shoulders hunched against the cold, and his hat pulled down as far as it can go. He looks *frozen*, and I wish I'd been more insistent that he come in and warm up earlier.

My suitcase is still inside the door, and I have to jump out the way as Dad nearly runs over my foot as he hauls it outside.

'Where are you going with that?' I rush to take it off him because he shouldn't be lifting anything heavy.

'I didn't think you'd want to room with your old dad, so we put you in the Candy Cane Cabin. The furthest one at the top.' He points to the hillside opposite.

Tav lifts a hand in greeting as he clomps up the steps. 'Dogs safely returned.'

'I can't make it to the top of that hill, so Tav's going to take you up there now,' Dad says.

41

I glance at Tav, who's holding a hand out for my suitcase. A snowman would look warmer. When he lifts his head above the scarf, there's a hint of dark stubble on his face, and there is literally ice forming on it. 'No, *Tav* is going to go inside and stand by the fire.'

'Sasha, I've lived here for many years. I appreciate you thinking of me, but being cold is in my blood. I'm used to these temperatures.'

I step out onto the wooden bit of decking that's protected from the snow by the upper floor balcony above it, but still cold enough for the wood to start to freeze through my socks instantaneously. I put a hand on my hip and hold an arm out towards the house, and give him my sternest look. 'I don't care. You look cold. Go inside. Don't make me start shoving you because I will.'

I raise a threatening eyebrow. I imagine trying to manoeuvre someone of his size would be akin to a meerkat trying to push over a rhinoceros, but I don't let my doubts show on my face, until eventually my dad starts laughing.

'Don't argue with her, Tav. Women will *always* outsmart us, and this one takes after her mother, who was small but mighty.'

That's quite possibly the most my dad has said about my mother since her funeral, twenty-four years ago.

Tav looks between us, but then his eyes meet mine and I raise my eyebrow higher, until eventually he smiles and shakes his head in resignation. Dad steps aside to let him in, and while he's stomping snow off his boots on the red "Merry Christmas" doormat, I slip in and close the door gratefully behind us.

'I'll get you a hot chocolate.' Dad disappears to the kitchen again, having seemingly taken on self-employment as a hot chocolate waiter.

'Thanks,' Tav says to me, his voice low and sounding rough from breathing such cold air.

'You've just walked four miles in the dark in minus-fifteen. That's ridiculous, no matter where you come from.'

His strangely coloured brownish-blue eyes, a colour I've never seen before, are glinting when he looks at me, and after a few moments, I realise I'm leaning against the closed door and staring at him as he pulls off his gloves, loosens his scarf, and removes his hat, revealing mid-brown straight hair, messy from the hat.

'I'm glad you're here.' Dad comes back in, carrying another hot chocolate and yet another plate of Christmas cookies. 'We missed proper introductions. Tav, this is my daughter, Sasha. Sash, this is Taavi Salvesen – Tav to his friends – which you are now, whether he likes it or not. Don't let his grumpiness fool you, he's a reindeer whisperer extraordinaire and a lifesaver to this old man. He's my right-hand man, and he's here to attend your every need.'

Oh, doesn't *that* sound fun. 'I'm quite capable of taking care of myself, thank you all the same,' I say, quite horrified by the idea of him "attending" anything.

'Thank God for that because I have no intention of attending a thing.' He takes a sip of hot chocolate and sighs, the steam turning his cheeks red. 'I'll walk you up to the cabin in a minute. If you'll *permit* me, that is.'

'Not until your beard's defrosted,' I snap, completing today's list of "things I never thought I'd say".

He lets out another laugh and runs a hand over his stubble. It's not really a beard, he just hasn't shaved for a few days, and I find myself hypnotised by the way the dark hairs catch on long fingers.

'Do you actually live here?' I force myself to look away and turn to Dad. 'Tav said it was a show house.'

'It's open for tours, but that doesn't mean it's not a real house,' Dad answers. 'It's my home now. I can't imagine living anywhere else.'

And I'm here to try to sell the place. This is going to go absolutely swimmingly, isn't it? 'You have people going on tours through your actual house? Poking around in your drawers and private parts?'

43

It's Tav's turn to choke on hot chocolate.

'Only in December,' Dad says, oblivious. 'Interest in Santa's House depletes after Christmas.'

'Is the North Pole Forest open all year round?'

He and Tav exchange a look.

'It used to be,' Tav says eventually. 'But custom has fallen and we haven't had any interest outside of November and December in recent years. We used to be open year-round . . .'

'But?' I say when he trails off. 'How bad are things?'

'We're surviving on day trips now,' he says. 'School visits, and people who come back every year for nostalgic purposes. It's not a destination anymore. There's not enough things to do to encourage people to stay, and not enough time and money to add new things.'

'Or restore the old things,' Dad adds, sounding more upbeat than I expected.

'Some of the cabins need repair before we can rent them out again. Candy Cane Cabin is the only one I've done so far,' Tav carries on. 'We've got a few bookings in the Northern Lights igloos towards the end of the month, and a family coming in for the Gingerbread Cabin for five days before Christmas and I have to fix it up before they get here.'

'You do all that? Renovate the cabins as well as handle reindeer? Alone?'

'Other people will only let you down.'

'You have a fair point and you make it well.' I deliberately mirror his words from earlier.

It makes him laugh again and my cheeks heat up for no reason, especially when Dad looks between me and Tav with *that* look on his face.

This could be way more complicated than I imagined.

Chapter 4

Dear Santa,

Thank you for spreading joy and making so many people happy. Does anyone ever get you gifts? I made this bookmark for you because you look like the kind of person who enjoys reading, and maybe you can use it to keep your place in the naughty and nice list when you check it twice. My brother thinks you must get bored of reading it so many times, but I think you must enjoy it, like I enjoy reading my favourite books over and over again!

From,
Avery

'See, now it's even harder to go back out,' Tav says as we step outside the door and he yanks his knitted hat down over his ears. 'But I suppose I should say thank you for making me all warm and tingly.'

I choke on thin air and have to pretend the cold has got to the back of my throat. Maybe there is a language barrier after all, because that's not the sort of thing a gorgeous guy can say to a woman and expect her *not* to choke.

There's something nice about the idea of him being tingly as

I zip up my wholly inadequate jacket and the air stings at my face again. I pull my hat down and my scarf up so there's barely enough space to see where we're going.

Tav picks up my suitcase with the same one-handed ease of earlier, and when I go to take it from him, he lifts it out of my reach and gives me a self-satisfied smile.

Dad presses a button on a remote control and the cabin at the very top of the hill is instantly illuminated with red and white fairy lights showing its outline in the darkness. The same Victorian-style streetlamps give out a warm orange glow at intervals up the hill, but not all of them are working.

Dad follows us out onto the decking and gives me another hug. 'Thanks for coming, Sash. You're going to love this place.'

His cherub-like face looks so innocent and hopeful that I don't have the heart to protest. He releases me and waves us off as I rush to catch up with Tav who is already halfway along the snowy road with my suitcase.

He waits for me at the bottom of the hillside where the cabins are. It looks steeper than it did from the house. A *lot* steeper. I should have twigged when Dad said he couldn't make it to the top, really. When a man who's climbed the biggest mountains in the world has trouble with a hillside, *then* is the time you should figure out a cabin at the top of said hillside probably isn't the best place to stay.

One of the streetlamps flickers as if to reflect my feelings of horror. 'Oh, holy sh—'

'Night.' Tav frowns at me. 'No swearing at the North Pole. There might be children around, and it's a scientifically proven fact that an elf falls down dead every time they hear a swearword. "Oh, holy night" is what you meant to say, right?'

Just when you think things can't get much worse, you find out a good swearword is forbidden. 'I don't think "scientific fact" and "elf" are words that belong in the same sentence.'

He ignores me.

46

'Fine,' I mutter. 'Holy *night*, that is one *heck* of a hill.'

'Do you want me to carry you?'

'Good God, no!' I recoil so fast that my foot slips in the snow and I struggle to keep my balance.

'Steps, that side.' He points across the hill to the right-hand side. 'But I haven't had a chance to shovel them off lately, so they're too dangerous. Path, this side. Let's go because my tingle is rapidly decreasing.'

It makes me laugh again, so much that it takes my mind off the climb as we start walking up, and he doesn't rush this time, but stays beside me on the path that's barely wide enough for one person.

'This isn't really the North Pole,' I say, annoyed because a lady should be allowed to swear if necessary. 'The North Pole is much further north.' I point in a random direction.

'That's west. North is that way.' He points behind him, and then stops long enough to pull a compass from his pocket, looks at it for a few seconds, and holds it up to show me. 'See?'

Who walks around with a compass in their pocket? I give the contraption in his hand a cursory glance. 'I didn't mean it literally. No one has any clue which direction is which, nor do they care.'

'You should care. It's easy to get turned around and lose your way in these woods, but if you know which direction you came from, it's easy to find your way back. Besides, you'll need to know if you see a bear. Polar bears are more likely to come from the north.'

'If I see a bear, anywhere, believe me, my first thought will *not* be to determine which direction it's coming from.'

He laughs, which is all well and good until I realise what he's said.

'Wait . . . you have *bears* here?'

'Give me a shout if you see one; I'll shoot at it for you.'

'Shoot *at* it?'

'Well, I'm not going to shoot *it*, am I? That would be murder, and I'm in the business of saving animals, not hurting them.' He glances down at me and rolls his eyes. 'Generally if you fire a shot into the air, any bear will run away. No animal is going to stick around to find out if you're going to fire another one. Bears are more scared of—'

'*Don't* tell me bears are more scared of us than we are of them. They say that about spiders and, believe me, it's *not* true.'

He laughs again, and I'm *so* glad he finds my terror amusing. 'Generally it's very safe. Polar bears rarely venture this far south, brown bears hibernate through winter so they won't bother you at this time of year, and lynx almost never attack humans.'

'Comforting,' I mutter.

All this talk of bears has distracted me so much that I've barely noticed the incline changing as we climb higher. As I stop to look back at our progress, my foot slips in the snow and I squeal and squeeze my eyes shut as I envision plummeting back down to the bottom again, and I brace myself for the fall, but something as solid as concrete grips my upper arm and I open my eyes and realise Tav is holding me up. With one hand.

I feel like a kitten when the mother cat moves them by the scruff of the neck, just sort of dangling in mid-air, and I shuffle to get my feet back under me.

'What size are you?'

'Excuse me?' I go to give him an earful about being polite enough not to swear but not polite enough to *not* ask a woman her dress size and that I know I need to eat a few less mince pies, and so far this evening I've consumed three calorific hot chocolates and God knows how many Christmas cookies but I lost count at seven, when he nods towards my feet.

'You can't come here in trainers.'

'Oh! Shoe size!' I go red in embarrassment even though I only scolded him in my head. 'Six. I'm a six.'

'We have plenty of spare boots because there's always at least one idiot who comes unprepared. A guest turned up in flip-flops once, if you can believe that.'

I laugh at the absurdity of the mental image and look down at his feet – he's got on sensible black boots that go up to under his knees with a thick line of cream faux fur around the top. No doubt his feet are a *lot* warmer than mine.

Tav holds his arm out without a word, and it takes a few moments for me to realise what he's getting at.

'Oh, that's okay, tha—' As I'm about to refuse his offer and carry on walking, my foot skids again and I grab his arm gratefully, and the burnt almond and cedar scent of his cologne surrounds me.

I want to protest and tell him I'm not a damsel in distress who needs an arm to hold, and despite how pathetic I must look, my level of fitness is actually much better than it seems because I do a lot of walking with the dogs at Debra's grooming parlour, but I can't tell him that because I'm supposed to be a fancy hotel manager, and holding his arm is actually quite . . . nice. In a reassuring way. He seems to know exactly where to put his feet, and his boots have got thick treads to get a good grip on the snow.

'I didn't think you spoke English at the airport.'

'Just because you can doesn't mean you should,' he says simply.

'Indeed.' I'm surprised by the amused tone in his voice. 'The world would be a better place if some people didn't speak English. The prime minister, for one . . .'

'I was not aware that the British prime minister did speak English. It certainly doesn't seem like it in most speeches.'

I have no idea if he's trying to be funny or not, but I let out such a howl of laughter that it'll make the inhabitants of this forest think they've gained an extra wolf. Oh God, wolves. I hope there aren't wolves here. 'Never has a more accurate judgement of our country been spoken.'

He's laughing when I look up, and his scarf has slipped down enough that his breath appears in the cold night air. He must sense me looking because he meets my eyes and his full lips form into a smile.

'You were good with Rudolph Number Three tonight.' He

sounds begrudgingly impressed. 'He's a bit tetchier than the others.'

'How come?'

He looks around and then cups a hand around the side of his mouth like he's whispering a secret. 'Between you and me, I think it's because he's never allowed to join in the others' reindeer games.'

'Are you serious?'

'No!' he says incredulously. 'I was quoting the song.'

'I know, that's why I said it.' I roll my eyes. 'Only I wondered if it was because the others always laugh at him and call him names?'

He lets out an unexpected laugh. 'It's got to be one of those things, right?'

The laugh warms something in my chest. 'I like animals. A hell of a lot more than I like humans, anyway.'

'I hear you there.' The hint of bitterness in his voice makes me look up at him again. 'You don't live in a forest surrounded by reindeer if you like people.'

'No, I suppose you don't.' I hesitate for a moment. 'I was thinking of a remote island, possibly with a cannon to shoot anything that considers approaching.'

He laughs, a warm rumbling sound. 'Sounds ideal to me.'

I'm thinking about his laugh too much and have to distract myself. 'What's with Rudolph Number Three? What happened to Rudolphs One and Two?'

'They're still with us, but you haven't met them yet because they're not as *naughty* as Rudolph Number Three.' His voice rises on the last part of the sentence and he turns to the left, like the reindeer are still listening out in the forest and he's letting them know of his disappointment.

'How many Rudolphs are there?'

He looks up to the sky as he thinks about it, like he's mentally counting. 'Four.'

'Can you not call them something other than Rudolph?'

He shrugs. 'I don't have time for thinking up reindeer names. Once you've used the obvious ones of Santa's nine, you cycle round and start again.'

'Could you not just call them all Clive?'

'Clive?' He lets out that burst of laughter again.

I have to force myself not to think about his hearty laugh and look across at one of the log cabins on the opposite side of the hill. There's a wooden gingerbread man sign outside, but it's fallen over so its head is buried in the snow. 'Is that the one you've got to get ready for guests?'

'Yep. Fix the sign, fix the big hole in the roof, fix the electricity supply because that's gone dead as well, and there's a broken floorboard in the kitchen.'

'And you can really fix *all* that? You can't rely on other people so you do literally everything yourself?'

'Yes.'

That simple. No explanation, no need to call anyone in. There's a lot to be said for independence, but that seems overboard even to me.

'Are all the cabins themed?' I ask, instead of pushing him because that one-word answer doesn't make it seem like he's going to elaborate.

'They are. We've got a nutcracker one, a mistletoe one, a snowman one, a reindeer one, a Christmas tree one, a Mr and Mrs Claus one, and a Twelve Days of Christmas one.' He points out each themed cabin as he speaks. 'You name it, I've themed a cabin after it.'

'Why?'

'Fun? Guests like it?' He gives me a look that suggests it's a stupid question. 'I thought it was festive to name them, and then when it came to decorating, it was easy to play into the theme.'

I suppose it's a nice idea, really. And staying in a place called the Candy Cane Cabin in the North Pole Forest does sound idealistic and have a twee ring to it, if you're a person who likes Christmas, that is.

51

We're not far from the top of the hill now, and what I thought would be an impossible climb has actually been quite easy with Tav's arm to hang on to. The twinkling of red and white lights is tantalisingly close, and the exertion has warmed me up enough that my face can move again because it was frozen solid earlier, like Botox but cheaper. People should give up fillers completely and just walk around in minus-fifteen for a bit.

Tav nods to the middle part of the hill that looks like an icy ski slope. 'There's a snow saucer in the cabin if you want to slide down in the morning.'

'No, thanks. I like my limbs in the same number of pieces they're currently in.'

It makes him laugh again. 'Kids love it when they stay here.'

'I'm too old for that sort of thing.'

'You're never too old for fun.'

I go to protest, but he's got a point. I can't remember the last time I had fun.

We come to a plateau on the incline where the cabin stands, trees towering over it from behind and extending further up the mountain. Tav extracts his arm from my hand and goes up a few wooden steps to the small deck area surrounding the cabin while I glance down the hill doubtfully. There might be a distinct lack of fun in my life, but getting on a saucer and sliding down that is never going to end well.

'Welcome to the Candy Cane Cabin.' He opens the door and ducks inside to flick a switch, and the little building is filled with warm white light, illuminating the waist-high candy cane sign, striped with lines of darker wood and the words "Candy Cane Cabin" wood-burned in a semi-circle across the hook of the cane.

Tav stands back and holds a hand out, inviting me to go in first, and that feeling of him being a gentleman makes me smile again. I can't remember the last time a man held a door open for me.

I let my hand push snow off the wooden railings as I climb the steps, tread across the decking and peer in cautiously.

I expected it to be like a giant candy cane inside, but it's not. The walls are smooth wood with plenty of rustic knots giving it a natural look. There's a raised stone hearth with a black grate hiding an open fireplace. At one end, there's a double bed with a candy cane duvet cover, but even that is a tasteful dark red with tiny white and green striped candy canes all over it.

Tav ducks in behind me, sets my suitcase down by the door, and closes the door quickly, rubbing his hands together. He pulls off his gloves and drops them on a table. 'Let me make a fire for you.'

I look around as he goes to the hearth and sits on the grey brick edge, takes a couple of logs from the basket beside it and lights the fire.

There's a red sofa with a white throw over it, patterned with red candy canes, and a cushion on either end, red-knit with a fluffy candy cane in the middle, a dining table and chairs not far from the fire, and in one corner is a six-foot Christmas tree with a sparkling glass topper. It has a red skirt patterned with candy canes and red and white striped boxes stacked underneath it, and it's decorated with glittering candy cane baubles and red and white lights. A candy-cane-shaped wax warmer is plugged into the wall which is creating the pepperminty scent in the air. A candy-cane-shaped china lamp sits on the bedside table, and the window to the side has candy-cane-patterned curtains in the windows.

I want to make a sarcastic comment about overkill, but it's exactly what Christmas décor should be like. Understated, tasteful, and festive without being over the top.

'Bathroom, kitchen.'

I'm so busy looking around that don't realise the fire is crackling away behind the grate, and Tav is still sitting on the hearth but pointing out two doors, disguised as part of the wooden wall apart from the nameplates wood-burned into them. 'Minimal facilities; the main kitchen is down in the house, but you have a kettle, mini fridge, sink.'

'Thank you.' I don't know what I was expecting, but it wasn't this. After seeing Santa's House in its all-singing, all-dancing, all-twinkling glory, I thought the log cabins would be the same, but this is *gorgeous*.

'That's for you.' Tav points to a wicker basket on the dining table. It's large and has got a big curved handle that's wrapped with intertwined red and white tinsel and finished with an over-sized striped bow.

'What is it?'

'A gift basket. We welcome all guests to the cabins with one matching the theme.'

I go over eagerly and my hands part the never-ending goodies that are so nicely displayed in it. There are candy canes and peppermint swirl sweets, candy-cane-flavoured teabags and a jar of candy cane coffee, peppermint-flavoured popcorn, and a box of candy cane artisan chocolates. Then there are red and white striped fluffy socks, hand-knitted striped gloves and a matching hat, candy cane lip balm, scented shower gel, hand cream, soaps, and bubble bath.

'Thank you. You didn't have to do that for me – I'm not a proper guest.'

'All part of the service.'

'You didn't make these, did you?' I ask. It's a distinct possibility seeing as he seems to do everything else around here.

'All handmade by local sellers in the nearby village. We're proud to support local businesses and they support us in return. You'll find business cards and discount coupons in the bottom of the basket if you like anything and want to go Christmas shopping while you're here.'

It's a nice touch, something that gives a community feel and makes me realise there must *be* a village nearby and we're not completely isolated out here.

There's a framed painting on the wall behind the bed, depicting a little wooden cabin with smoke coming out of its chimney, in a forest full of snow-covered trees with the Northern Lights in the sky.

'It's beautiful. The whole cabin is perfect.' I wander around the little room, letting my fingers trail over smooth wood and candy cane accessories. It's so much larger inside than it looked from outside. The window at the right-hand side of the bed looks onto the forest, and when I look out, I have an uninhibited view of the sky.

'Does it meet your *very* high standards of the exceedingly posh hotel business?'

His voice is quiet but it still makes me jump in the silence of the night, and then cringe again at the idea of him thinking I'm a fancy hotel manager. I don't know why I thought Dad was the only one who'd know about my supposed job. I hadn't considered he'd tell other people.

I look around to see him still sitting on the edge of the hearth. He looks exhausted. He's so tall that he doesn't really fit there, and I'm not sure if the hunched shoulders are because of that, or because he's too tired to stay upright.

'If Dad can't get up here, that means *you* did all this? By yourself?' I ask, skirting his question.

He shrugs. 'It's a pleasure. I like having guests in and we haven't had many this year, and I love Christmas . . . Who doesn't, right? It's the most magical time of the year.'

'Yeah, if you're six. I've missed that by thirty years.'

'That's the saddest thing I've ever heard. You're never too old to believe in magic.'

I frown at him, but he grins up at me. 'Don't forget your wishing jar.'

'My what?'

He inclines his head towards the basket on the table, and I go back over and root through it until I pull out a tiny glass jar that's full of iridescent fake snow that reflects a rainbow of colours as I twist it under the light. The metal lid is also a lock, and the neck

55

is wound with red and white striped twine tying on a tiny metal key. I unlock it, and inside, buried in the fake snow, is a strip of white cardboard. I hold it up in confusion.

'You write your Christmas wish on the cardboard, lock it and keep the key, and stand it by the fire. When it disappears, you'll know Santa has granted the wish.'

'Seriously?'

'We don't joke about Christmas wishes.'

'When it disappears, what *I'll* know is that you've got a key to the cabin and you've let yourself in and taken it.'

He grins and points towards the door. On the back of it, a key is hanging on a hook with a large wooden candy cane keyring. 'Firstly, that's the only key – I don't have copies. And secondly, the jar itself doesn't disappear – the wish does. When you get a magical feeling, open the jar and see. If the cardboard is blank, the wish has been granted.'

'So you give me a special pen to write it in erasable ink that fades over time?'

'Nope.' He gives me that self-satisfied smile again. 'Write it in whatever you like. Your own pen. Permanent marker, if you want.'

I hold the jar up again and shake it, dispersing the snow inside. 'So there's some chemical in this that dissolves ink?'

'How did you get to be so cynical?' He meets my eyes and the smile he gives me this time is soft. 'It's magic, Sash.'

It's the first time he's called me that, and I know it's probably because it's what my dad calls me, but there's something quite nice about him being so overfamiliar. 'There's no such thing.'

'Anyone who thinks that will never see it.'

I bite my lip as I try to think of a suitable comeback, but typically, my mind is blank. It's a nice sentiment and kids must love it, and I *wish* I was young enough to believe in magic and go sliding down hills on a saucer, but I'm not.

There's something about a man in his late thirties talking about magic like it's real though. And yet, he doesn't seem insane. It just seems like he's forgotten I'm *not* a four-year-old guest here to visit Santa and his flying reindeer and enquire about my positioning on the naughty and nice list.

'I should go.' He pushes himself up off the hearth with a long groan and a few noises of pain that he probably doesn't realise are audible. 'See? That's the problem with sitting down – it makes it so much harder to get up afterwards, like going inside to warm up when you have to go outside and get cold again.'

He pulls his hat down and his gloves back on and points to the right. 'Shout if you need anything. I live in a cabin out there, but I'm never far away. Enjoy your first night at the North Pole.'

'It's not the North Pole,' I say again as he opens the door and steps outside, but I can't help smiling this time.

He turns around and grins at me. 'Isn't it?'

Of course it isn't, but I don't have the heart to say it. There's something nice about thinking it might be. Something that makes me feel like a kid again, giddy and unable to ignore just the tiniest fizzle of excitement.

'Come down to the house for breakfast in the morning,' Tav calls as he starts walking down the hill we came up, and I'm half-disappointed that he didn't grab the saucer that's stashed beside the kitchen sink and slide down on that. 'It'll be worth the trek, I promise.'

I go back inside and my eyes are drawn to the Christmas wish jar on the table. It's bollocks, of course. If it works at all, it'll be some kind of clever trickery, but I've got a biro out of my bag and I've sat down in one of the chairs before I've even thought about it.

If nothing else, I can prove Tav wrong about it being magic.

The bottle is only the size of my thumb and the cardboard strip is tiny when I pull it out. At first I don't know what to write, so I close my eyes and think about it. If there were any such thing as Christmas wishes, and any hope of mine being granted, I'd wish for the one thing I've wanted again since I was twelve.

I write "*a happy family Christmas*" in small letters on the cardboard, push it into the snow inside the bottle and lock it. I tie a knot in the twine holding the key and wrap it back around the bottleneck, and leave it on the edge of the hearth.

I wander around the cabin again, appreciating the attention to detail and consideration that's gone into every inch of it. It feels warm and cosy and safe, safer than I thought I'd feel in the middle of a forest inside the Arctic Circle anyway. The fire is going to dwindle before long, and there's a little space heater tucked under the table so I plug that into a socket on the wall, and when I pull the bed covers back, I'm glad to see there's a hot water bottle waiting for me – with a candy cane cover, obviously. I have a hot shower and make a cup of tea with the box of PG Tips I find in the kitchen cupboard and the milk in the fridge, which is a really nice touch. Probably Dad's influence. He used to take British teabags with him wherever he went. I re-boil the kettle to fill the hot water bottle, and while I'm drinking my cuppa, I have the urge to see outside again.

I get the oversized snuggly soft dressing gown I found hanging in the bathroom and shrug it on over the pyjamas I'd never been so grateful to change into when I dug them out of my suitcase, and I open the door.

The snow on the deck area has started to melt with the heat coming from inside, and I rest my cup on the wooden railing surrounding the cabin and lean on my arms as I look out across the land.

This far up, there are snowy treetops surrounding me from the wooded areas below. I've got a direct view down to Santa's House, and the multitude of multicoloured Christmas lights that illuminate it in the darkness.

In the distance in one direction, I can see the bend of the road we came in on that curves around the house and continues out of sight in the other direction, the way Tav went when he returned the dogs, and I get the impression that Dad's land goes a lot further than I'm imagining.

I watch the lights all over Santa's House chasing each other as they flash in ever-changing formations, and it makes me feel more Christmassy than I have in years. The red nutcrackers on either side of the door look back at me. I've always liked nutcrackers. They're comforting somehow, reassuring in the way they stand like sentries. Mum used to say they brought good luck and protected a house from harm.

It's idyllic here. The other cabins are spaced out and none block the view of the ones above. If they were all lit up like mine is, it would be a perfect little alpine Christmas village. If you have to spend a December somewhere, there are definitely worse places you could spend it.

The owl hoots from somewhere in the trees behind the cabin, sounding much closer than it did earlier. He must agree. Or be warning me that a wolf is on the way.

I ignore that thought, wrap both hands around my mug and sip my tea. There isn't a sound to be heard, the air is clean and fresh and smells of the evergreen trees all around, and the silence is like a blanket wrapping around me, and making me feel more peaceful than I can ever remember feeling.

Maybe this Christmas won't be so bad after all.

Chapter 5

Dear Santa,
What do you want for Christmas? Dad says Mrs Claus will
get you anything you desire and does something funny with
his eyebrows, and then Mum yells at him and tells him to
behave himself. What does Mrs Claus get you, Santa? Dad says
you must be too tired to unwrap her gift on Christmas Day.
From,
Lucas

I don't expect to get any sleep, not in the middle of a forest
surrounded by God knows how many different kinds of man-
eating predators, but when I wake up, I realise I don't remember
anything after putting the hot water bottle into the bed and
pulling the brushed cotton duvet over myself.

I must've been more exhausted than I thought after all that
travelling yesterday. Usually I'd lie awake for ages worrying about
one thing or another, but I don't even remember my head hitting
the pillow.

The light coming in the window has a blue-tinged twilight-
esque slant, and I have a brief moment of panic that it's the
following evening and I've slept the whole day, and then I

remember something about polar winters and it being dark a lot here, and reach over for my phone on the bedside table. Just gone 10 a.m., and Norwegian time is only an hour ahead of what I'm used to.

And then I remind myself that I'm in *Norway*. I never thought I'd go *anywhere*, and yet I got on *two* planes yesterday, rode in a dog sled, captured a reindeer, witnessed the Northern Lights, and saw my dad for the first time in three and a half years.

No wonder I needed a good sleep.

And my dad seemed in fine spirits and nowhere near as bad as I'd imagined health-wise. And I feel reassured somehow that Tav is around. There's something calm about him. The kind of person who'd be good in an emergency. The only emergency I've ever had to deal with is a dog pooing on an angry man's lawn.

Lying in bed thinking about dog poo is a sure-fire sign it's time to get up, and I stretch luxuriously and sit on the edge of the bed. I don't think I've ever slept in anything that comfortable before. My feet, snug in the fluffy socks from the gift basket, touch warm wooden floors, which must have the underfloor heating on a timer or something.

I force myself upright and decide a quick blast of cold air will be what I need to wake up, so I pad across to the door and pull it open, and my eyes fall on a box right outside.

There are pictures of people hiking up snowy mountains on the front and a big yellow "6" in the corner, and I crouch down to flip the lid up and fold back the tissue paper inside.

It's a pair of snow-boots, like Tav's but in white, with bright pink laces and pink-tinged white faux fur around the top. Tucked into the corner of the box is a compass.

It makes me laugh out loud, and I glance down the hill towards Santa's House, but there's no movement and no hint of how long ago he left them.

I pull on jeans, a thermal vest that was also in the gift basket, a T-shirt, and a jumper over the top of that, and I smile every time

I think about *not* having to put my feet back into my slippery and damp trainers that never dried out last night. I sit on one of the wooden chairs, lift the boots from the box and run my fingers over the fluffy lining and solid-feeling rubbery outside, and then tuck my jeans into thick socks and bend down to pull them on. They fit perfectly, and when I get up and walk across the cabin, they feel like much-loved familiar boots that are so comfortable you forget you've got them on.

I can't wait to get down to the house and thank Tav for them. I finger-comb my blonde hair and pull it into a side plait over one shoulder, wrap my cream and grey knitted scarf around my neck and brace myself as I step out and lock up behind me.

The air is crisp and the twilight-esque light is slowly turning to full daylight with a hint of brightness to the east as the sun peeks above the horizon. The steps to my left have been shovelled off, so I take those instead, a long line of wooden stairs passing every cabin on the way down. I can see why my dad wanted to restore this place as I pass weather-damaged roofs and broken signs.

The Christmas lights are still twinkling along every inch of Santa's House, and the main lights are glowing from the living room and hallway, so I let myself in and stomp snow off my boots on the doormat.

'Hello?' I call out. 'Anyone home?'

Someone's singing. And they're *really* good.

I follow the sound of "Joy to the World" along the hallway, past the crackling fire, and through the living room until I reach the kitchen doorway.

There's a buttery smell in the air, and Tav is at one of the stoves with his back to me, something sizzling in a pan in front of him. He's got a deep and warm singing voice that's as comforting and reassuring as his talking voice, but I'm surprised because he seems like the opposite of someone you'd expect to find singing Christmas carols first thing in the morning. He has no idea I'm here, so I lean on my shoulder against the doorframe and enjoy it for a moment.

He's wearing a Christmas jumper, but not an uncool one with tinsel or flashing lights on the front like you'd usually picture a Christmas jumper – this is a heavy and cosy-looking one with a zip neck and a high collar, knitted in cream with a pattern of red reindeer pulling a sleigh going around it in stripes, and even from the back, he looks hot. His mid-brown hair has chunks of lighter brown going through it like natural highlights. It's thick and longish, straight and shaggy at the same time. The kind of hair you want to run your fingers through.

If you were so inclined, which I'm not. Obviously.

But I can appreciate a nice-looking man as much as the next girl, and his voice really is lovely. Not in a professional singer way, just as a guy who's enjoying his day uninhibited, and I suddenly feel guilty for the intrusion. I should back away and pretend not to have heard, make some noise on my way in, but the floorboard creaks under my foot and it's too late. 'You did *not* strike me as a "Joy to the World" type.'

He lets out a wholly un-macho scream and the pan he was holding clatters onto the counter when I make him jump so much that he drops it.

'Oh holy *night*.' He puts such an intonation on the word that it sounds *worse* than the most abhorrent swearword. He clearly has a talent for making even the most innocent words into something unthinkable. Last night, I thought he was a bit of an idiot for telling me not to swear, but I've never heard the title of a song sound so sweary before.

He whirls around. 'Sasha! Warn a guy before you sneak up on him.'

'I'm sorry, I didn't mean to make you jump.'

'At this rate, Percy's not going to be the only one who's had a heart attack.' He puts a hand on his chest, making me appreciate the curve of what are clearly *huge* muscles under that jumper.

63

'I wasn't sneaking up, I was enjoying the entertainment. You don't seem like a guy who sings.'

'It's Christmas. Who doesn't sing at Christmas?'

'I don't. My neighbours and the remaining Great British Public have never done anything bad enough to deserve that inflicted on them. I might if I sounded like you though. You have a great voice.'

'Thanks.' He looks like he doesn't want to smile but he smiles anyway. And is he . . . blushing? 'I can't help myself when it comes to Christmas songs. I love the music at this time of year. There's usually only reindeer to hear me though.'

I think he is. He's definitely blushing.

'Thank you for the boots,' I say as I push myself off the door-frame and step into the kitchen. 'They're so comfortable.'

'What boots?' A look of confusion pops onto his face.

'The boots I'm wearing?' It comes out like a question instead of an answer. Surely he can't have forgotten already?

His eyes run down me, making me feel warm for an altogether different reason, until they land on my feet. 'I didn't give you any boots. Maybe it was the *nisse*.'

'The what?'

'The Norwegian equivalent of Santa Claus. We don't really have the traditional Santa that you do, instead we have *nisse* – small elf-like creatures who live in barns. If you're kind to them, they're kind to you and will bring you good fortune, but if you're not kind to them, they'll wreak havoc. You have to leave a bowl of rice porridge out for them to enjoy on Christmas Eve, and they'll be particularly angry if you don't, and it *has* to have a knob of butter on top.' He glances at me. 'Your dad tells me they've been commercialised in other countries in recent years. You probably know them as gonks – little gnomes you buy with a round body and just a nose and a big white beard showing under the rim of their tall pointy hat.'

'Elves?' I laugh until I realise he's not joking. 'Oh, come on. Seriously? There was a compass in the box. We talked about a compass last night.'

'All I said was that you need a compass. Common knowledge. GPS doesn't cover anywhere this remote so map apps on your phone won't help if you get lost. Anyone who lives in a place like this would agree.'

'You're telling me that although *you* asked me my shoe size and said I needed a compass last night, it was actually someone *else* who brought me boots and a compass this morning? And not just someone, but actual *elves*?'

'Answer me this – don't you think I'd have left footprints?'

I go to answer but nothing comes out, and I end up mouthing the air like a fish stuck on land. He's right. Despite the thick snow leading up to the cabin, I don't recall seeing *any* footprints on the decking or the hill down to the steps. 'And I suppose you're going to tell me that elves shovelled the steps too?'

'No, I shovelled them. It would've taken the *nisse* all day to do that – they're very small.' He's gone back to the pan on the stove and he answers without looking up, like this is completely normal.

Is he joking? *Is* he insane? Is he like an actor who refuses to break character even when they're not on set? Does he think there might be a five-year-old lurking nearby, ready to jump out at any moment and ambush him with questions about elves and flying reindeer? There is *nothing* in his voice that suggests which one it is.

The lack of footprints can be explained – fresh snowfall since he left the boots, although there was none covering the box. Some sort of shoe jiggery-pokery that prevents shoes sinking into the snow? Maybe he threw the shoebox from the top of the steps. Maybe there *were* footprints and I didn't notice them.

'Christmas pancake?'

I'm so lost in thought that it makes me jump when I realise he's turned to me and is holding the pan out in front of him and there's something Christmas-tree-shaped in it.

'What are Christmas pancakes?'

He holds his spatula out towards the island in the middle of the kitchen. 'Have a seat and you'll find out.'

'I don't put things in my mouth without knowing what they are.'

He considers this for a moment and then gives me a nod of approval. 'Generally a good life policy to have.'

His seriousness makes me laugh, and I sit down on one of the stools, and he slides a Mrs-Claus-shaped plate down the unit, spins around with the pan, stops the plate directly in front of me, and glides a pancake onto it in one swift movement. I raise an eyebrow, impressed. If I'd tried anything so dexterous, the plate would've smashed on the floor, along with the pancake, frying pan, spatula, probably a couple of limbs, and I'd have taken out half the floor tiles too.

He grins. 'Vanilla, cinnamon, nutmeg, ginger, with a hint of orange. Christmas in a tree-shaped form. Tea? Coffee?'

'Coffee, please.'

'Peppermint, gingerbread, mince pie, or Christmas pudding flavour?'

'Just coffee.'

'Gingerbread it is, then. Coming right up.' He presses a button on a coffee maker on the unit and ladles some more batter into the frying pan, presumably for his own breakfast.

I go to protest that I can get my own coffee, but I make the mistake of putting a bite of the pancake into my mouth, and it's so good that it stops all words and thoughts.

This is quite possibly the most festive thing I've ever eaten. It literally melts in my mouth in a medley of warming spices and buttery loveliness. 'Oh my God, Tav.'

'Told you it'd be worth the trek down,' he says with a smile, but there's something else in his face – that blush again, a hesitance, like he doesn't *quite* believe it himself.

I take another bite. 'Flipping 'eck, *that* is a pancake.'

He's still smiling to himself as he puts a snowman mug full of steaming coffee down in front of me and goes back to the pan on the stove.

Who knew festive homeware was such a thing?

I haven't taken my eyes off Tav's back as I eat, each mouthful of the pancake somehow tasting better than the one before. His wide shoulders flex as he moves, flipping the batter, things sizzling, and not just in the pan.

He catches me watching as he turns around, sipping a cup of coffee he's already got on the go, and eats his own pancake with a fork straight from the pan.

'Won't you sit?'

He lifts a hand to cover his mouth while he's chewing. 'Running late.'

I'm about to ask what for when a floorboard creaks upstairs and I use my fork to point upwards. 'Is that Dad?'

'Yeah, he's had breakfast and gone upstairs to get ready.'

I've almost finished my pancake, and as much as I could quite happily sit here and eat another twenty-nine of them, it's probably a good thing that won't be an option. There's a telltale creaking of the stairs, so I shove the last bite into my mouth and jump down from the stool. 'That was amazing, Tav – thank you. I'll go and say good morning.'

I go back through the living room and into the hallway, but when I turn to the stairs at the end, Santa is coming down them.

My dad is dressed as Santa. He's *dressed* as *Santa*. 'Why are you dressed as Santa?'

'I am Santa.'

'There's a school class coming in today.' I didn't realise Tav had followed me and is standing in the living room doorway until he speaks.

'To visit Santa?' I look between them and he nods, and I point at Dad. 'And you're *playing* Santa? And no one told me this?'

'This is Santa's House,' Tav says. 'Did that not give it away?'

'Well, yeah, but . . .' It suddenly all adds up. Dad looking like Santa. This house and how festive it is. The portrait above the fireplace. No wonder I thought it looked like my dad last night.

Tav's trying – and failing – to suppress laughter as he watches me figure it out.

'You're supposed to be taking it easy!' I say to Dad, who's hovering on the bottom stair.

'What could be easier than playing Santa? I get to sit in a lovely big chair all day and meet lots of wonderful children. The most strenuous thing I have to do is a swift round of "ho ho ho"s.'

'Dad . . .'

'All I do is sit there. Tav welcomes them, directs them, takes commemorative photos for the parents, organises anything else they want to do. It's the easiest morning for me. They treat me like a king.'

'Apart from the children who pee on you, spit on you,' Tav starts. 'Sneeze on you. You remember that kid who was eating chocolate ice cream and spat all over you? Santa had to go for a quick beard wash after that one.'

'That sounds awful!' I try to hide the shudder, but also want to giggle in horror. 'They come here?'

'No, at Santa's grotto, near the west entrance.' Tav looks at me and points to the left. 'That's that way.'

I barely restrain the urge to poke my tongue out at him, and in doing so, I see past his shoulder to the fireplace in the living room. There are three stockings hung on the mantelpiece that weren't there last night. They look hand-knitted, and one of them has my name on it.

I squeeze past Tav and go across to lift it off the hook. It *is* hand-knitted and my name is embroidered in glittering thread. 'Why is there a stocking with my name on it?'

'It's your stocking.' Dad is hovering in the hallway, looking like he's waiting to make a quick getaway.

'I only got here last night.'

'The *nisse* made it for you. They're fast workers.'

'Dad . . .'

'You'll still be here for Christmas. Santa needs somewhere to put your presents.'

'Okay, enough with the Santa stuff. I've not been here for twenty-four hours and I'm already fed up of hearing about Santa and elves. Do we need to have "The Conversation"?'

'The birds and the bees? Your very existence should signify that I know *all* about the birds and the bees.'

I roll my eyes. 'No, the Santa conversation. Usually reserved for children under the age of eight, but we can adapt.'

'Well, this is a Christmas village. You're going to hear Santa's name a lot. He's arguably the main attraction.'

Tav has stayed quiet until now, but he moves to step between us, effectively blocking the whole view from the living room. 'We're running late, Perce, we should go.'

'You're absolutely right, my friend. Have a good day, Sash. See you later.'

'Dad, you're not supposed to be—'

There's the sound of the front door slamming and a "ho ho ho" from outside.

'. . . working!' I call after him.

'He's been playing Santa here for four years, you can't expect him to stop now,' Tav says gently.

I sigh. 'He has to— Wait, four years? I thought he bought the place last year?'

'He did, after playing Santa here for the previous four Christmases.' He speaks slowly, like he's explaining quantum physics to a pigeon.

'He's been coming here for the past four years? He never returns to the same place twice. It's one of his things.' I put on a deep voice. '*There's so much world to see, Sasha, and I want to see all of it.* He's even offended when he has to fly through an airport he's been through before.'

'There's something special about this place,' Tav says with a shrug, clearly not grasping the enormity of this.

'I'm sure there is. I'm also sure it's some sort of hallucinogenic in the water supply, but let's not go there.'

'The water supply is well filtered, I assure you. No hallucinogenic could get in there.'

'I didn't mean it literally.' I groan, but his earnestness makes me start laughing. 'I thought you said you'd only known him for a year?'

'I've *known* him for four years – what I said was we'd become good friends in the year since he took over full-time. How come *you* didn't know this?'

I shake my head in bewilderment. 'He always says he's going to come home for Christmas, but he never does. There's always some outlandish excuse or another, but never once has he told me he's playing Santa Claus in some Arctic alpine village.'

'Have you ever considered that maybe, to him, he *is* home for Christmas, and where you live is not his home?'

I go to tell him not to be so stupid, but the words stop in my throat. There's something about his gentle voice, something that wheedles under my skin and makes it impossible to snap at him.

'I should . . .' He points towards the door.

'Tav, hang on.' I take a step towards him. 'Will you be honest with me? What have I walked into here? Is he just playing a part or does he genuinely think Santa exists? Because I thought he still had all his wits about him, but seeing this place, hearing him talk about Santa and elves and reindeer flying . . . He's seen doctors about his heart – they would've noticed if something was off mentally, right?'

Tav thinks about it for a few serious moments. 'Okay, answer me this – how do you know the *nisse* didn't knit that stocking?'

I should've known that a word of sense was too much to hope for. I look around the room, giving him time to laugh and tell me he's joking. He remains straight-faced.

'Because elves are fictional?' I say when I can't stand it any longer. It comes out sounding like a question that I already know won't be answered.

'Because you haven't personally seen something, that means it

70

doesn't exist? Have you ever held a million pounds? Enjoyed a cup of tea without being interrupted? Seen the Loch Ness monster?'

'Also fictional.'

'Are you kidding me? Nessie is *fictional*?' This time he can't keep a straight face, and seeing his lips twitch as he tries not to laugh makes me smile, even though I want to frown.

'All right, you're hilarious, but this isn't funny. We're both adults, Tav. Level with me, please?'

He's quiet again, and I think I'm finally, *finally* going to get some sense out of him.

'Why is it so impossible to believe that your childhood Christmases might be true? Has the world really been so cruel to you that you no longer have an imagination?'

I go to reply, but nothing comes out. The words hit me hard. I loved Christmas when I was younger. I believed in Santa for longer than most kids, and even when I knew the truth, I still *wanted* to believe that this magical man would come down my chimney on Christmas Eve, that there was some mythical being out there, watching over us all. Mum and Dad went out of their way to make Christmas feel magical, from when I was too young to understand it until I was far too old to appreciate their gestures.

'Tav, hurry up! You're the head elf and the class are supposed to be here at half past!' Dad knocks on the living room window from outside and makes us both jump.

'Aren't you the *only* "elf"?' I do the inverted quotes in case he was under any illusion that they're getting to me.

'I'm not an elf, I'm a human.' He ducks out into the hallway and lifts a red and green striped hat from a hook by the door, complete with pointy elf ears on the sides, and an abnormally long tip with a bell that jingles. He pulls it on and tucks his hair in, and even wearing that, he still manages to look sophisticated and . . . sexy. I've never thought a man in an elf hat could be hot before.

'Can I help with the school visit?' I ask instead of trying to pursue the conversation any further. It seems futile.

71

'No, thanks. I have it under control.' He pulls on a pair of red and green striped elf gloves to match the hat.

'What can I do? I'm supposed to be here to help.'

'Don't ask me, I don't need any help. No matter what your dad says, I'm on top of it.' There's a defensiveness in his voice that intrigues me.

Eventually he sighs and seems to soften. 'You can do whatever you want. Go and explore, look around, but be careful – we don't get much daylight at this time of year. The sun rises around 10 a.m. and it'll be dark by 2 p.m.'

It makes me feel a bit useless, and Tav seems offended by the implication that he might need help with anything.

'See you later.' He opens the door and turns back with a cheerful grin and a wink. 'May your day be merry and bright!'

It makes me laugh despite the underlying worry that my dad is a little bit *too* dedicated to his role as Santa *and* is working too hard, and I watch from the living room window as the two men walk off down the road together.

I look at the stocking again. Elves, indeed. One of them must be able to knit. Or know someone who does. I didn't think my dad was a knitter and Tav looks like he should be in the forest chopping down trees in a plaid shirt, not clicking needles together. They only knew I was coming forty-eight hours ago. Who has time to knit a stocking in forty-eight hours?

I wander into the kitchen and my eyes fall on the pile of washing up in the sink. I can't get my head around stockings and *nisse* and magical wishing jars, but washing up is something normal, so I roll my sleeves up and make a start. *No one* refuses help with the washing up, not even Tav.

Maybe he'll think the elves did it.

I keep thinking about what he said about imagination. Is it that simple? Is Christmas just supposed to be about childlike wonder and believing in the impossible? Am I really so old that I can't appreciate how much Christmas means when you're a kid?

I wish I could still look to the skies on Christmas Eve and expect to see a whoosh of light as Santa and his reindeer whizz by, but I can't. The world takes that away as we grow up.

The window above the sink looks out onto Santa's garden, and I look up when movement catches my eye, and there's a reindeer looking in at me. The shock makes me laugh somewhat hysterically, but the reindeer carries on chewing whatever it's eating and moseys on, not at all concerned by my presence in Santa's House.

Only with my dad could you find a reindeer watching you do the washing up. I'm probably lucky he hasn't given them the run of the house too. I wouldn't be even vaguely surprised to turn around and find a reindeer watching TV in the living room.

When it's done and mostly put away because there are so many cupboards that I can't find where everything goes, I take Tav's advice and go to explore because I still can't imagine the scale of this place.

I step outside and onto the road, and glance in the direction they went and I'm surprised to see someone coming towards me. She raises a hand and waves enthusiastically.

It's a postwoman! In a climate-appropriate red and grey uniform! I don't know why I'm so excited by the prospect of seeing someone delivering the mail. I certainly don't get excited at the thought of my postman at home coming – he usually only delivers bills and junk mail.

'*God morgen!* You must be Sasha! Percy has told me all about you. I'm Freya.' She shakes my hand vigorously when she reaches me. 'It's so good of you to leave such an important job and come to his aid.'

I'm so excited by the prospect of another human that I nearly hug her.

I'd half expected to run into an elf.

Or a reindeer, coming to critique my washing-up skills.

And I steadfastly ignore the part about my job. How can Dad

have told *more* people? Half the population of Norway think I'm the manager of a prestigious hotel, and even if I tell Dad the truth now, he'll be embarrassed about having told all his friends something that isn't true.

'It's so nice to meet you. Someone with your skill and experience is exactly what this place needs to perk it up.'

I blush at that, even though she's talking about my experience as a fancy hotel manager, which is limited to a short stint at the reception desk of a hotel before I got fired. 'And between you and me, Percy and Tav *really* need the help.'

'They do?'

She looks like she's in her sixties, with a long fringe and greying blonde hair down to her waist. 'It's *so* good you're here. Someone needs to stop lovely Tav working himself into an early grave.'

'Tav?' I say in confusion. Surely she means my dad?

'He never stops, that man. When I heard an ambulance had been called up here, I was sure it was going to be for him. Every time I see him, I tell him he's going to do himself a mischief by working so hard.'

'But he's like a giant untouchable giant,' I say, thinking I should really have better descriptive words for him by now. Even as I say it, I think of his hunched shoulders when he sat on the hearth in the cabin, the way he had no intention of coming into the house last night, the way he ate breakfast on the go just now.

'Look a bit closer – no matter how difficult he makes it,' she says, cryptically. 'He's too much of a gentleman to accept help from someone old enough to be his grandmother, but someone young and vibrant like you is exactly what this place needs.'

I almost snort at the suggestion of me being young and vibrant. It's not what most people would call me if they saw me snuggled up in my dressing gown in front of Netflix by seven o'clock most evenings. Young and vibrant suggests someone with rainbow-coloured hair who goes out partying every night and has a wide range of friends and a busy social life.

'Oh, sorry. I'm so excited to meet you that I'm forgetting why I'm here. Today's delivery!'

She hands me a bag with "*Posten*" printed on the red fabric and it's a true comedy cartoon moment as I take it off her, expecting it to be lightweight, and it's so heavy that it hits the ground, nearly taking my arm out of the socket with it. 'What on earth is this?'

'Santa mail.'

'Letters children write to Santa?' I hoist the bag up with both hands and heave the strap over my shoulder so the weight rests against my hip. I thought Dad was winding me up when he mentioned it last night.

'Of course. I used to take them to the North Pole Forest post office, but the pile of unread mail in there is so big that it's started posting them back out at me.'

The mental image makes me giggle.

'I've been handing them to Tav lately, or leaving them in the box for him.' She nods towards the post box on the roadside at the edge of the house.

I've flipped the top of the bag up and my fingers run across colourful envelopes in every shape and size imaginable. I pull one out and there's a dinosaur sticker on the front, and the return address is to Argentina. My dad gets letters from Argentina. I put it back in the bag and pull out another one. New Zealand this time, and the address on the front reads "Santa Claus, the North Pole". 'It's not even addressed here.'

'It doesn't matter what address is on it, the post office identify all Santa mail and it's split between here and Finland.'

I put the New Zealand letter back in the bag and rifle further through the masses of envelopes. 'There are hundreds of letters in here.'

'Only 1,057 today and nineteen different countries – a quiet one.'

I give a loud laugh and quickly realise she isn't joking. 'My dad gets letters from *nineteen* countries?'

'He gets letters from every country in the world, Sasha. There was even one from Mars once, although that might've been a joke, but who knows. Anything's possible at Christmas – even aliens wanting presents.'

'Every country in the world,' I repeat, staring at the layers upon layers of colourful envelopes in the huge bag. 'And this is a *quiet* day?'

'It's still early. Lots of children don't write until the first half of December. Santa can get thirty thousand letters a day at peak Christmas season.'

My mouth drops open in shock. 'He gets thirty thousand letters a *day*?' All I seem to be doing is repeating her words in a more disbelieving tone. Dad has a tendency to exaggerate and I took what he said about Santa mail with a pinch of salt, but . . . really? Am I the only person who didn't know writing to Santa was still a thing?

I did it myself when I was little, in the years between being old enough to write and still young enough to believe in Santa, but it was Mum who always took my letters and promised to stamp them and put them in the post box. In later years, I realised she never did. Those letters weren't to Santa – they were so my parents knew what I wanted for Christmas. Surely all letters "to Santa" are the same? Kids write a list of what they want, parents read the list and know what to put under the Christmas tree. Job done.

And surely things are too modern for actual letters these days? What kid wants to write a letter when they could send Santa an email, or text him, add him to a WhatsApp chat, or take a photo of their list and tag him on Instagram?

'Leave the empty bag tucked under here and I'll collect it tomorrow.' She backsteps to the post box at the edge of the house and retrieves yesterday's empty mail bag that was folded underneath it.

'Does my dad read all these letters?' I ask her. He can't do, can he? There aren't enough hours in a day to read over a thousand letters. And what difference does it make anyway? These are going to be full of lists of presents children want – expensive technology and must-have toys and probably some Argos catalogue pages with items circled on them. What's the point in Dad reading them? He's not going to buy stuff for these children and send it to them, is he? Despite his insistence, he isn't actually Santa.

'Probably not as many as he'd like to,' she says. 'He read every single one at first, but he and Tav have had too much on their hands lately, and when Tav had to let the staff go . . .'

There *were* staff here at some point then. It hasn't always just been Dad and Tav. 'Since then?'

'Things went downhill quickly. It was on the brink of going under last year when your dad bought it. The whole community was so glad when he swept in and saved it. It's unthinkable to imagine this area *without* the North Pole Forest.'

I get the impression she's wondering if she's said too much, and it doesn't seem fair to prod for any more information when she's clearly uncomfortable talking about friends behind their backs.

'Do you know where Santa's post office is?' I ask instead. I have no idea what I'm supposed to do with this huge bag of letters. The house is so crammed full of Christmas decorations that there's no possible place it could fit in there, and I still can't get my head around the idea of my dad having his *own* post office.

She points to our left, in the direction she's come from. 'There's a whole load of cabins near each other – the older parts of the Santa village gone to ruin. It's so sad. The post office was always their main attraction. People used to travel from all over to post their Christmas cards here with the "North Pole Mail" outgoing stamps on them. There's a tourist map that should help you find your way around too. Keep on down this road – you can't miss it.'

This place is big enough to warrant a "you are here" map. The thought almost makes me laugh. Of course it is.

'I'd best get on. I always linger when I come here and make myself late for the rest of my round. I'll see you again, no doubt,

I'm here every day with the next delivery. Keeps me fit in my old age.' She flexes a bicep. 'Nice to finally meet you, Sasha. Percy's said so much about you that I feel like I know you already!'

'Have a good day,' I call after her as she hurries off.

I don't want to walk that fast, so I wander in the same direction. The snow has been shovelled from the road and a fresh layer has already frozen on top because it's thin and crunchy under my boots and the iciness makes cracking noises with every step. It's still not quite daylight and I spot two reindeer grazing on something in the snow. I still can't believe I'm in a place where you randomly walk past grazing reindeer. One of the reindeer looks up at me, and the other one carries on munching without giving me a second glance. One of them is the one-antlered Rudolph from last night.

I can see why this place was special once. There's a tingle in the air that doesn't just come from being cold, although I pull my scarf a bit higher anyway. If I was a child who believed in Santa Claus, walking along here with drifts of snow and Christmas trees on either side, passing reindeer in the woods, Christmas lights twinkling all over . . . It would be magical.

The road slopes gently downhill and the sound of distant bells reaches my ears. A festive ring-ting-tingling that adds to the Christmassy atmosphere.

Unless polar bears come with bells now.

I walk a bit faster just in case. You never know what skills predators may have picked up this far out in the back end of beyond. Polar bears could be maestros of percussion instruments by now.

Eventually the trees thin out and I can see the edge of a clearing on the left side of the road. There's the most traditional North Pole signpost I've ever seen – on top of a red and white striped pole is a rectangular "North Pole" sign, complete with a red-breasted robin on top, and below are arrow-shaped signs pointing in different directions.

"Santa's House" and "Reindeer Runway" point towards the

direction I've just come from, and then smaller signs point towards the twisting cul-de-sac of log cabins that the clearing leads to, showing the directions for "North Pole Post Office", "Mrs Claus's Kitchen Diner", "Ice Cream Parlour", "Hot Chocolate Bar", and "Elf House".

A sign to "Santa's Workshop" points down into the forest on the opposite side of the road where there's what looks like the beginnings of an overgrown path between some bushes, and then there's a sign pointing further along the road that reads "Santa's Grotto" and "Main Entrance", and one elongated arrow that points out past the collection of little cabins that reads "Northern Lights Igloos". Each sign is red with white writing to match the striped post, and a layer of real snow enhances their traditional look. Whoever built this place was truly dedicated. So much effort has gone into something as simple as a signpost. I take my phone out and snap a photo of myself standing next to it, and go to send it to my friend Debra, but I stop myself. She isn't going to be interested in where I am. She's probably not given me a second thought since firing me the other day.

The map is next to the sign – a big glass-covered table that I have to brush snow off to see the 3D layout with a "you are here" arrow in the shape of an upside down Santa's hat.

There's a vague sound of chatter from the visiting school class in the distance, but I ignore it and wander into the clearing, a gentle incline that leads up to a winding cul-de-sac of log cabins that are much bigger than the guest lodges. A real hideaway in amongst the trees. The closest wood-constructed building has a ramp to a double door, and a large sign reading "North Pole Post Office" is curved above it in red and green. There's a wreath on the door that's made from tree branches and decorated with tiny wooden envelopes, and beside the door is the biggest glossy red post box I've ever seen, and I can imagine parents lifting excited children up to post their letters through the wide slot.

I go and look at the other cabins on a winding path that twists around the shallow hillside from one door to another, each one surrounded by overgrown holly bush hedges covered in glossy red berries. Mrs Claus's Kitchen Diner looks like it's seen better days. The tattered wreath that was once on the door now lies on the ground, half covered with snow, and the jagged edge of the broken hook is still attached to the door. I peer in the windows, but there's so much dust and grime on the glass that I can barely make out the silhouettes of a few tables with chairs that have fallen over. There's a "North Pole Ice Cream Parlour" and a "North Pole Hot Chocolate Bar" in the same condition, and some sort of elf house – a peek in the windows reveals a house full of miniature model things. It's like looking into a life-size doll's house, but it looks like the only things currently residing inside are spiders.

The post office intrigues me the most though. The thought of so much mail is unfathomable, and I crunch back towards it and try the door handle, surprised when it opens. Well, opens is the wrong term. It loosens in its frame, but giving it a push to get inside does nothing. It's pushing against something. I crouch down and open the letterbox, and a slew of envelopes come whooshing through it, making me jump back so fast that I land on my bum in the snow.

I gather up the stray letters and push harder against the door, feeling the resistance of what must be the most ridiculous pile of paper on the other side. It barely budges an inch, and I wonder if I'm going to find the previous postmaster in here, suffocated under a mountain of envelopes.

I throw my whole weight at the door until it starts to move, a centimetre at a time, eventually opening wide enough for me to edge my way around it. I've pushed so many letters aside that as soon as I let the door close, a heap of them slides down, blocking it again. I'm going to have to dig my way out.

I blink as my eyes adjust to the darkness. The whole room smells musty and papery, the cloying, inky smell of pens and the waxiness of fading crayons that a majority of the letters are written in, mixed with the clammy smell of a room that hasn't been opened for months.

I aim for the nearest window and climb over literal mountains of envelopes to reach it and undo the rusty latch. The hinges are stiff as I push it open until a blast of desperately needed Arctic air sweeps in.

My boots slip and slide over the letters as I wade through them to the other window and open that too, letting in daylight. I finally spot a light switch beside the door, and I start pushing letters aside with my feet to make a path and flip it on, blinking as the bare bulb hanging from the ceiling hesitantly flickers into life, like it's been off for so long that it's not quite sure what to do.

It illuminates a room that's absolutely *full* of letters. No wonder Freya hasn't been able to get any more in through the letterbox. At the other end of the room, there's a hefty wooden counter, and behind that, an open doorway to a back room of some sort.

Dad said half a million letters a year, and I'm pretty sure this is a few years' worth. So many letters feels overwhelming, but despite my urge to squeeze back out the door and pretend I never saw this place, something about it intrigues me. The idea that *this* many children still write to Santa, and that all those letters are actually delivered. I would've thought that if post offices got any Santa letters, they'd have gone straight to the recycling plant, but the idea that these letters come to a physical place, a real person, and that my dad actually reads them . . . I like it, somehow.

The building has the same Tardis-like feel of Candy Cane Cabin because it's much bigger inside than it looks outside. There are shelves around the walls that hold Christmas cards and North-Pole-themed postcards, along with festive gift boxes and wrapping paper, and stationery supplies for writing to Santa, but they're covered in a heavy layer of dust, and half of the shelves have fallen down at one side, so things are diagonally slipping into the sea of letters below.

It was obviously loved once. I can imagine people dressed as elves working here, happily singing as they went about their day. There's a feeling in the room, a sense of something so strong that I almost expect the envelopes to start fluttering at me of their own accord.

I start pushing them up to the walls on either side, making a path from the door towards the back room. When I finally reach the counter, the floor behind it is clear, apart from where a shelving unit on the side wall has collapsed, spilling the letters it was holding. The broken in-trays all bear the names of different countries. There are wooden shelves built into the underside of the counter, full of Santa postage stamps and stickers and pens, and all sorts of stationery you'd expect to see behind the counter of a real post office. I pick up a "North Pole Mail" rubber stamp – a circle containing a leaping reindeer and the words "delivery from Santa" running around the edge – and then put it back on the dried-up ink pad.

Through the open doorway in the back room, there's a solid oak desk that's almost empty, apart from a dusty desk lamp and the wooden chair behind it. I've still got the mail bag over my shoulder, and there's another chair in a corner – a comfy reading chair in red fabric with a couple of reindeer cushions on it, and I finally let the heavy bag slip off my shoulder, sending up a cloud of dust as it lands on the seat.

There's a window to one side so I open that too, and then look around at the office-like room. There are a few sets of shelving on one wall, containing what were once living poinsettias, and underneath them is a row of filing cabinets and document boxes. On the wall, there's a framed photo of my dad dressed as Santa sitting at the desk with a pen in his hand and letters spread out in front of him. It must've been taken a couple of years ago because his hair isn't as long and white as it is now, and below that are a few photos of other men dressed as Santa. A history of the Santas here over the years.

I open one of the desk drawers and find a pair of golden letter openers with initials engraved on them. PH . . . Percy Hansley? TS . . . Taavi Salvesen? I've never even used a letter opener before. It feels like something a posh lady with satin gloves on would use, but I select an envelope, push the letter opener in and slide it along, and pull out two halves of the letter I've just sliced clean through. Oops.

I put that one aside and pick up another one, trying to be more careful this time. I pull the letter out and start reading . . .

Chapter 6

Dear Santa,
I'll leave carrots out for Comet. Not the other reindeer –
I only like Comet.
    From,
    Jacob

'You found the post office then.'

Tav's voice makes me jump in the silence. How can I have been so absorbed in the letters that I didn't hear him come in?

I look up at him and it's only when tears drip off my face and land on the letter in my hands with a splosh that I realise I'm crying. And have been for a while.

Before I have a chance to be embarrassed, Tav reaches inside his jumper, pulls a packet of tissues from his pocket, and tosses them to me without a word.

'Thanks.' I scrabble one out and turn away to wipe my wet face and snot-filled nose. Always ideal in front of a *hot* stranger.

When I think I might be a bit more presentable, and I've got plenty of time to be embarrassed about being in floods of tears over letters children have written to Santa, I turn back towards him.

I notice two things – the light is much brighter than it was when I last looked up, and the way Tav is leaning in the doorway at an almost diagonal angle to accommodate his height. One hand is holding the doorframe above his head and he's got to duck to see in. It's a sight that could've come directly from *Elf*.

'You do not seem like the type of guy who carries packets of tissues about your person,' I say in an effort to detract from how embarrassed I am about needing said tissues.

'Kids with runny noses and Santa don't mix. Head elves have to be prepared for all eventualities and children have a *lot* of orifices for many unpleasant eventualities to emerge from.'

His seriousness makes me laugh and I let out another embarrassing wet snort.

'What time is it?' I ask when I can muster the courage to face him again post-snort.

'Half past one.'

'Seriously?' I say in surprise. It was before 11 a.m. when I came in. I've been here for over two hours, sitting on the floor, surrounded by piles of letters. 'How did you know I was here?'

'The *nisse* told me.'

I raise an eyebrow so high that he laughs and points behind him. 'Footprints leading up to the door but not away from it.'

'Ahh, the snow foils everything.' I'm glad he isn't maintaining the elf nonsense this time. 'And there was me thinking you were some master tracker or something.'

His weird-coloured eyes twinkle in the sunlight coming through the windows. He shifts awkwardly and switches arms holding on to the doorframe and quickly ducks when he nearly hits his head on the ceiling. 'Thanks for doing the washing up.'

'I didn't. Maybe it was the elves.'

'Maybe so, but the elves usually put everything away afterwards, and this "elf" wasn't sure where things went.' His tone is jokey this time and it makes me smile.

'I'm sure the new elf will find their way around in time.'

He seems to be lingering and it makes me smile to myself. I don't even know why. It's not like I need his help with anything, and asking him questions is as useful as a waterproof teabag when every answer is something to do with elves or Christmas magic.

I appreciate that he hasn't said anything about the crying though. He hasn't tried to ridicule me or make me feel silly, like some men would. Most men see a woman in tears and decide she's hysterical, but Tav is just . . . there.

'You met Freya?' He nods to the now half-empty "*Posten*" bag on the chair.

The thought of the letters make my eyes well up again. 'Oh my God, Tav. Are they all like this?' I gesture to the pile of opened envelopes behind me.

'Not all. Some of them are exactly what you expected – long lists of expensive toys from demanding children, but some . . . Santa is a special person in children's lives. He's a confidant, a year-round friend, someone who already knows their deepest secrets so they feel comfortable sharing anything with him. He's the only person some children have got to talk to.'

I'd never thought of Santa like that before, but most of these letters have been the opposite of what I expected when I delved into Freya's bag. 'I've just read a letter from a nine-year-old girl who's got cancer, and for her present this year, she wants Santa to leave something that will help her mum and dad cope when she dies. She's asking if Santa will make the extra effort this time because she'll be gone by next year and he won't have to worry about delivering to her after that.' My voice breaks again.

Tav gives me an understanding nod. There are tears streaming down my face again, but I can't pretend I'm not touched by the things I've read.

'Earlier there was one from a boy who's being bullied and he wants Santa to make it stop.' I reach behind me and rifle through the pile, trying to locate the correct letter in the rainbow piles of paper and envelopes that are scattered across the room. 'A brother and sister have written together saying their mum and dad have both lost their jobs and could Santa bring them enough food for a Christmas dinner this year.'

'We can send a food parcel if you've got their address.'

I look up at him in surprise and blink through the tears. 'We do that?'

'If we can. We ignore the lists of toys, but if a child shares that their family needs help and we can help, then we do.'

'Do we have the budget for that?'

He shifts on his feet and one hand drops from the top of the doorframe to wring his fingers together. He's still wearing the elf gloves from this morning, even though his hat is gone. He ums and ahs like he's trying to answer but can't find the right words, but I can see exactly what he's trying to say.

'By "we", you mean "you", don't you?'

'Too many "yous" in that sentence,' he mumbles, but his cheeks are red and he won't look up from the floor.

'That's really nice, Tav.' I feel like I've discovered a secret he didn't want me to know.

'I'm lucky in life. I have enough money to eat, heat my cabin, and feed the reindeer. I don't need much else.' When he finally meets my eyes, his are so sincere that it makes something flutter in my chest. 'If I can help someone who isn't that lucky . . . Surely that's one of the greatest privileges of working here.'

It's enough of a sentiment that it makes my breath catch in my throat and more tears form in my eyes. I'd never thought of it like that before, never thought Santa could be a way of helping people who need it, but he's clearly got a heart proportionate to his huge size, and I'm so touched that it makes me want to give him a hug, even though I can't remember the last time I hugged anyone besides Dad last night, never mind a stranger who I met yesterday and I don't think likes me very much.

'I'm not expecting you to do the same or anything,' Tav says quickly. 'I don't know your financial situation – I would never expect you to fund anything like that . . .'

'Good, because I've just lost my—' Oh God, of all the things I wasn't supposed to say, and of all the people I wasn't supposed to say it *to*. 'Can you pretend you didn't hear that?'

He gives me a soft smile. 'Hear what?'

I let out a nervous giggle, but there's something infinitely trustworthy about someone who would send a food parcel to a family after reading a child's letter to Santa, and I *know* he won't repeat it.

'If you come across anything like that, anywhere we can help, there's a website I use to put together care packages for people all over the world. I'll give you my login details and you can use my account to send something.'

'My dad doesn't know you do this?'

'He knows I used to, it *was* part of the service here, but the North Pole Forest's budget ran out long ago, and he'd yell at me for continuing without it.'

I can't help smiling at the idea of this *at least* six-foot-six guy scared of being admonished by my five-foot-four father, who actually looks like he's shrunk since I last saw him.

There's something incredibly disarming about Tav. I feel like I've known him much longer than I have, and I lose track of time as I sit there without losing eye contact until another tear drips off my chin and lands with a cold splat on the back of my hand.

I sniffle and turn away to take another tissue out of the packet he gave me and blow my nose. I don't know why this is making me so emotional. 'Sorry.'

'Don't apologise.' He goes to duck into the room but misses and clonks his forehead on the doorframe.

In the middle of the sadness, it makes me laugh as he rubs it and looks accusingly at the doorframe itself. The wooden floorboards creak under his boots as he crouches down on the opposite side of the pile of letters, read and unread getting muddled where the bag has tipped on the chair and envelopes have started pouring onto the floor.

My face is still wet and I turn away and swipe the backs of my hands under my eyes. There's not much I hate more than showing vulnerability in front of other people.

'I know what it's like reading those letters. You wouldn't be human if they didn't get to you.' He reaches out as if he's going to pat my knee comfortingly or something, but he pulls his hand back quickly.

Instead, he takes his red and green striped gloves off and picks up the letter opener from the floor where I've discarded it, takes an envelope and flicks it open with the expertise of someone who's done it a million times.

He holds it up to show me a crayon drawing of a boy driving a big bus with a bird flying above it. 'For Christmas, this lad wants a double-decker bus and an eagle as a pet. Whoever he is, he's going to go far in life.'

It makes me giggle. 'Do children really think Santa can provide that?'

'Imagination is the limit. Nothing is impossible when you're young. It's growing up in this world that takes that away and makes people old and bitter.' He opens another letter and his eyes skim over it. 'This kid wants iPads, and iPods, and various other things with an "i" in front of them that make me glad I grew up before these things existed. Santa can't help with that kind of request.'

He puts the letter back in the envelope and chucks it on the pile. 'I should go. I need to check on the reindeer.' He puts both hands on his knees and pushes himself to his feet, having to duck even at the highest point of the ceiling. He takes a couple of steps away and then turns back. 'Do you want to come? There's plenty of reindeer you haven't met.'

'I'd love to.' I thought he was eager to get away, but the fact he's inviting me makes me go warm all over because I didn't want him to go yet.

And reindeer. Despite my close encounters of the antlered kind so far, it would be nice to see the reindeer sanctuary part of this place my dad talked about on the phone.

Tav holds a hand out to pull me up and I slip my hand into his without thinking. Ridiculously long fingers close around mine. His palm is hot, hotter than I thought it was possible to be in this climate, and his skin is rough, catching on mine, creating friction that feels like it could spark a fire. It's the first time either of us haven't been wearing gloves and the skin-on-skin contact makes me go fluttery all over.

What is wrong with me? It might've been a while, but a simple chivalrous gesture has never been responsible for such a wave of feeling before, and it seems like forever before he hauls me to my feet with very little assistance on my part.

I've been sitting on my knees for so long that pins and needles shoot through them and he keeps a strong enough grip on my hand to hold me upright, and I cling on as I stamp my feet and jiggle my legs to get rid of the numbness. He must think I'm a total muppet not to be able to get to my feet on my own, but handsome men always catch you at your most embarrassing moment, don't they?

I can feel my palm rubbing against his, a pulsing beacon of heat as I wobble around like a magpie that's been at the fermented fruit, not quite certain that it's *just* the pins and needles causing the unsteadiness.

I have to distract myself somehow. I wave my other hand towards the photo frames on the wall. 'I expected to see you up there. You've never played Santa?'

'I'm too young. And that's something I don't get to say very often.' He laughs. 'Santa has to be genuine. That's a hill I'll die on. He cannot be played by a thirty-eight-year-old in a fake beard and a wig. Children know these things. No one is going to believe in Santa if they can pull his beard off.'

His dedication to making children believe in Santa is admirable,

I'll give him that. Mum and Dad took me to visit Santas in supermarket grottos when I was young, and I have absolutely no idea whether their beards were real or not. I'm pretty sure that in my Christmas-filled young eyes, I didn't know or care either way, but it's nice that he does. The small details seem to be Tav's thing.

I stopped stamping my feet ages ago, but he's still holding on to my hand, and he watches me for a moment before he lets go and stands back to let me walk out first.

I glance at the pile of letters. I want to come back here. I want to read more of them. I've put the one that needs a food parcel on the desk, but surely there's something we could do for more of them. Something to help these children feel like they're not alone.

I pull the door open and step out into falling snowflakes.

'Snow!' I say in delight.

Tav looks at me in confusion as he ducks out the door. 'Were you not aware that it snows here? Quite regularly, in fact. Or did this general covering of white not give it away?'

I give him a scathing look because he knows exactly what I mean. The snow cloud is above us, but the rest of the sky is blue and the low sun is glinting over a mountain to the west, soon to sink below the horizon and into darkness. For now, the snowflakes falling from the sky are so white and fluffy that it's like someone's tipping a bucket of crocheted ones directly over the top of us.

I skip down the ramp and spin around with my arms out, watching the snowflakes land on the sleeves of my coat, and like any adult in the snow, I stick my tongue out and catch some. When I spin back in Tav's direction, he's watching me with a raised eyebrow.

'Snow is falling,' I say like it explains everything.

Instead of making fun of me like I expected, he sings the first line of "Merry Christmas, Everyone" by Shakin' Stevens, complete with finger-clicking arm movement.

This was always my mum's favourite Christmas song, and it's a well-known fact that no one can hear it without singing along, and I wish I was brave enough to join in. I'm too self-conscious to sing in front of anyone, but he continues the song as he walks down the ramp.

I'm breathless from spinning, but I feel young and carefree for a moment. Snow always makes me feel like a child on a snow day when the schools unexpectedly close and you run outside to build a snowman or slide down a hill.

'Thank you for the boots,' I say, appreciating the traction they give me on the freshly fallen snow. 'They're the most comfortable things I've ever owned.'

He glances down at my feet. 'You're welcome.'

In my head, I do a victory punch. Who knew an adult conversation with no mention of elves would be a cause for celebration?

'You said you live in the woods?' I have so many questions for him that I'd make even the most hard-hitting journalist jealous, but I get the impression he doesn't talk much and won't answer if I don't tread carefully.

'In a cabin to the west. Just beyond your dad's land border, with the reindeer I'm responsible for.' He gestures in the general direction we're walking, to the left of the sinking winter sun. 'To be honest, I've been staying at the house for the past couple of weeks. Since the heart attack, I've been scared to leave Percy in case something happens, y'know? And the reindeer are all doing well at the moment. We don't have any that require round-the-clock care right now, so I felt it was better for me to be close by for a while.'

'Tav . . .' I take a deep breath. 'What happened when he had the heart attack? He won't talk about it. You were here, I take it?'

He looks at me again and I keep my eyes fixed firmly on the horizon. I have no doubt that he can hear every ounce of fear in my voice, and I can see the kindness of his eyes without looking, but I'm a fraction of a second away from tears again, and there have been more than enough tears in front of gorgeous men today.

'I came in one morning and started making breakfast, thought it was odd that he wasn't around, because usually you'd hear the floorboards creaking if he was upstairs getting ready, or he'd have left a note to say where he was going. You know when things feel off and you can't put your finger on why, and you think you're just being a doom-monger, but you can't shake the feeling that something's wrong? I did a quick check of the house to make sure he hadn't overslept, then I realised there was a track of fresh footprints leaving the house, so I followed them, and found him face down in the snow.'

I can't help the intake of breath at the thought of my dad being so . . . vulnerable.

'It was near the Northern Lights igloos.' Tav turns and lifts his arm in the direction we've come from. 'I made sure he was breathing, called the ambulance, and then carried him back to the house to get him warm. He didn't regain consciousness until he was at the hospital.'

The thought of Dad being in that position makes my heart skip a beat. And the thought of what would've happened if Tav hadn't found him . . . My breath does that shuddery thing it usually saves for after a good cry. 'You saved his life.'

'I did what anyone would do if they came across someone in trouble.'

'No, I mean, you being you. Being tall and strong enough to carry a grown man. And trusting your instincts that something was wrong. If you hadn't been here, if you hadn't followed those footprints . . .' It's too late to stop myself crying again as tears spill down my face.

Tav steps closer and drops a heavy arm around my shoulders, tugging me loosely into his side.

'He's okay, Sash.' His lovely voice is soft above my ear.

The kind, comforting gesture makes me cry harder. I've never been good with people being nice to me when I'm upset. I half-heartedly push at his side, but it's as ineffective as I thought it would be. 'Don't, Tav. People don't hug me.'

'That's convenient because *I* don't hug *people*, but new experiences are good for us. Character building and such.'

It makes me laugh through my tears, but it's also comforting somehow. I feel like Tav understands.

Like he can sense it too, his arm tightens and he pulls me closer as we walk, but it feels protective, not pushy. I have no doubt that if I stepped away, he'd do the same.

I'm also really glad I had the forethought to shove the packet of tissues into my pocket, and I surreptitiously wipe my face. 'I didn't realise how scared I was of something happening to him. He always does all these crazy things, and all my life, we've joked that he's going to be eaten by a crocodile or swallowed up by a volcano or something, but it's never seemed like something that will actually happen. The thought of him having something as ordinary as a heart attack really makes it hit home.'

'Yeah. It shocked me. He's so young at heart and vibrant and full of life. He makes me feel old and decrepit and I'm forty years younger than him.'

It makes me giggle again because it's so relatable. Dad could make a five-year-old after ten tubes of Smarties look like a hibernating tortoise. 'How is he now? He says he's fine, but I don't think he'd tell me if he wasn't.'

'I don't know.' Our eyes meet again. 'If he's affected by it, he doesn't mention it to me. He acts like nothing happened. When the hospital discharged him, he couldn't understand why I'd been worried. You'd think it was the equivalent of breaking a fingernail. He's not someone who easily admits vulnerability.'

'You really do know him well.'

He's quiet for a moment. 'I did try to get him to call you before, but he was adamant that he didn't want to worry you.'

That makes me feel better somehow. I thought I was just an afterthought, that maybe if Dad hadn't needed my help, he wouldn't have told me at all.

'I was surprised when he did. He hadn't said anything about

needing help. It was a surprise to see "pick Sasha up from the airport" on my jobsheet yesterday morning.'

'*That's* when you knew?' I say in surprise. I'm clearly not the only person my dad doesn't share things with.

Tav seems to suddenly realise his arm is around my shoulders because he jumps and yanks it away. 'Sorry,' he mumbles. 'Percy's told me so much about you that I feel like I know you and keep forgetting you don't know me.'

I shake my head to clear it. 'He has no intention of selling this place, does he?'

'I don't know what he intends.' Tav's blueish copper eyes meet mine again. 'I know he doesn't *want* to sell.'

'It's not about what he wants, it's about what he needs, and he needs to live somewhere normal with a doctor's practice nearby and ambulance access. These temperatures are stressful on the body as it is, and if you *hadn't* been here that morning . . .' My voice breaks again and I force myself to take a couple of deep breaths and get a grip. There are only so many times in one day you can burst into tears in front of the same gorgeous stranger and I'm quickly approaching the upper limit.

I try a different approach. 'What happens to it for the rest of the year? What do you both do in the months when he's not being Santa? How does it earn money?'

'It doesn't – that's the problem.' He looks at me for a long moment and seems to decide he trusts me. 'We need a buyer who wants to restore it, but that's never going to happen, is it? It's got to the point of needing too much work. As soon as you fix one thing, four more things fall apart. Whoever you force him to sell to will be a developer. They've sniffed around before and been sent swiftly on their way, but this time, I don't see another way out . . .'

I glance up at Tav. He *is* gorgeous. I'm still wearing my bobble hat but snowflakes are settling in his hair, which is pushed back and the sun reflects off a couple of blond strands mixed in with the light and darker brown.

'Unless you have any suggestions with your hotel expertise . . .'

There's a faint tone of mockery that makes me wonder if he suspects the truth about my job, but I'm so distracted by the way his longish hair tickles the back of his neck and how I'm almost positive I can make out the silvery marks of scars on the skin there that it takes me a while to realise what he's said.

'I wouldn't know where to start,' I stutter eventually. I feel like I have to prove myself somehow. God knows why. I'm *not* the manager of a fancy hotel, and the last thing I want is to convince him I am.

'Everything has to come to an end eventually, and if I'm brutally honest with myself, things *have* been a struggle lately. Maybe it's time to say goodbye.' He's unable to hide the depth of gloom in his voice.

We pass Santa's House and crunch down the curve of the main road, and then Tav takes the same narrow path through the trees that he took when he led Rudolph back the other night.

Was that really only last night? It feels like I've been here for weeks, but it's barely twenty-four hours.

'Have you worked here long?' I rush to catch up with him. He's not intentionally hurrying, he just doesn't realise my legs sink into the snow a lot deeper than his do.

'Since time began. Since the year dot. Since cavemen roamed the earth and Alexander the Great rode through on Bucephalus.' He turns back to grin at me, and when he realises I'm lagging behind, he stops to wait. 'Or about fifteen years, give or take.'

'How long's it been going?'

He tilts his head side to side. 'About fifteen years, give or take.'

'You've been here from the very beginning?' I say, surprised again.

'Well, it turned up on the doorstep of my reindeer sanctuary. What else could I do?'

'Oh, so you ran a reindeer sanctuary *before* the North Pole Forest was built here?'

'Something like that,' he says with the familiar tone of not wanting to talk about it, and I can't work out *what* it is that he doesn't want to talk about. 'When your dad took over last year, he let me keep my job, and now he puts jobsheets through my door every Monday morning that I ignore and get on with my own work.'

'It's like someone bought up the forest and pulled bits of it out to put cabins in.'

'That's exactly what someone did.'

'Really? Who?'

'Santa, of course.'

Here we go again. 'Yeah, but who built it? Who put it here?'

'Santa.'

'Right. Of course he did. Because I was thinking more along the lines of a construction company seeing as Santa isn't particularly known for his DIY skills, and I can't imagine his team of reindeer being particularly good with hammers and nails.'

'You'd have to ask him that.'

Of course I would. 'And I suppose it was Santa who gave you the job here?'

'Obviously,' he says, but there's a teasing tone in his voice, like he wants me to know he's winding me up now.

'Well, whoever sold this place to my dad really saw him coming.' We've been walking for ages and we *still* haven't reached the property line. This place is unimaginably huge.

'Saw him coming?' Tav glances back at me with a confused expression. 'Because he's colourful when he wears his Santa suit?'

'No, because he's a vulnerable old man and whoever owned this place clearly knew that and set out to take advantage.'

'What do you mean? He *wanted* to buy the North Pole Forest. *He* wanted to restore it. It was his idea, not the old owner's.'

'Yeah, but an almost-eighty-year-old man can't cope with all this on his own. They clearly knew that and shafted it off on him anyway.'

Tav looks like he only understands fifteen per cent of that sentence. 'He's not on his own.'

He's stopped at the edge of the path to wait for me again and I wait until I reach him to speak. 'You're only one person, Tav.'

'I've got it under control. I don't like people implying that I haven't.' His tetchiness intrigues me because he doesn't sound annoyed – it sounds more like an explanation.

'It evidently needs more than two people. For him to even think this is a sensible thing for a man of his age to take on . . . Between you and me, I'm seriously wondering if he's starting to lose his marbles.'

'Marbles?' Tav looks even more confused. He looks at the ground like someone's genuinely dropped some marbles. 'I don't understand. We don't have any marbles here.'

His non-understanding of my British slang is so adorable that it makes me burst out laughing. 'Believe me, I can *see* that.'

He looks yet more confused.

'It means . . . Oh, you know what, maybe I should just stop talking entirely.'

'I think that would be a very reasonable plan.' That teasing tone is in his voice again.

Another clearing has sprung up amongst the trees, and we come to a wooden three-slat fence with a wide path around it. A reindeer is trotting across the paddock towards us.

'Welcome to the North Pole Forest reindeer sanctuary.' Tav goes to the fence and pulls a handful of greenery out of his pocket and offers it to the approaching reindeer.

'Do you *always* have some form of plant life in your pockets?'

He laughs. 'As I said – all eventualities. You never know when you might need to win over a reindeer.'

'No antlers?' I ask as I watch the reindeer gobbling the plant from Tav's hand.

'Males drop them by this time of year and the females keep them until May to protect their calves. Factually, all of Santa's reindeer would be female to still have antlers on Christmas Eve.'

'I can honestly say I've never thought of Santa's reindeer and the term factually in the same sentence before.'

When Tav's hand is empty, he brushes them together and leaves the reindeer chewing as we walk along the path towards a wooden cabin. It's exactly what you'd dream of for a log cabin in the forest. There's a low fence with strings of glowing white lights strung through the posts, a wooden gate and a snow-covered path up to the door, and a small potted Christmas tree on either side. It's so different to the loud and colourful decorations of Santa's House. This is understated and classy, and it reminds me of the cabins on the hillside. 'You live here?'

'Yeah. This has been home for many years. It was just the cabin at first; I added the stables and paddock later.'

'Don't you get lonely?' It feels like we've walked about a mile, maybe more. My voice is swallowed up by the seclusion of the trees. The only movement is a few of the reindeer making their way towards us.

'Lonely?' His Adam's apple bobs when he swallows. 'I've got twenty-three reindeer.'

'And you don't like people and can't rely on anybody?'

'Exactly.' The smile he gives me doesn't look genuine as he opens a heavy gate and lets us into the reindeer pen.

'They're amazing. When I was little, I didn't think they were real animals.'

'A lot of people have never seen one in real life before, and the astonishment on children's faces is magical to behold.' His eyes light up when he talks about it, and it's clear in every millimetre of his body language that he *loves* this job.

I'm so distracted by watching him that I have to duck out of the way fast when a reindeer mooches up and nearly takes my eye out with an antler.

Tav laughs. 'That's Vixen One. They won't hurt you, but keep an eye out for errant antlers. Here.' He pulls out another handful of plant life and offers it to me. 'The way to a reindeer's heart is most definitely through their stomachs.'

'What is it?'

'Cladonia lichen. It grows all over the northern forests. On trees and under the snow. I grab handfuls when I see it.'

Quite a few reindeer are heading towards me, and I hold the lichen out to Vixen One who's coming closer to sniff out my pockets, but most of them change direction and follow Tav where he's gone into a storeroom behind the cabin and comes back out with a bag full of the stuff.

While Vixen One is chewing, Tav shows me where to rub her nose and I let my fingers trail over her coarse hair. 'This is a real sanctuary for them?'

'Yes. Reindeer are and always were my main priority. A way of combining my passions. Helping reindeer and helping children believe in the magic of Christmas.'

'The tourists must love them. Do you take people on sleigh rides?'

'No.' He seems offended by the suggestion. 'They are *not* here for entertainment purposes. Some of them are recovering from injury and trauma. I let them be part of the North Pole Forest because they love to meet people and socialising is good for them, but I don't agree with using animals for entertainment. If they're fit and healthy, I walk them so tourists can stop and chat and feed them, but I don't allow unsupervised visits, and their paddock is out of the way because I don't want tourists wandering off and finding it.'

There are signs all along the fence saying "Do NOT feed the reindeer", and an explanation saying that reindeer can die from being given the wrong food, written in many different languages.

'Some of them are working animals. They pull sleds that I take to go down into the village and collect supplies, and they take me on journeys whenever I need to go elsewhere.'

Another one comes over and pushes his big, furry nose into

my hand and I let him have a bit of lichen and stroke across the thick beige fur at his shoulder.

'Donner Four,' Tav says.

I'm impressed he can recognise them. They all look so alike.

'When you want to go into the village, the reindeer sleighs are kept in the stable. I'll show you the ropes the first time, but it's very simple.'

The idea of going somewhere by reindeer-drawn sleigh is so absurd that it makes me laugh a mildly demented cackle. He can't be serious. 'Can't I walk?'

'If you want to carry heavy shopping for three kilometres in thick snow and anything from minus-ten to minus-twenty-degree temperatures.'

'So, let me get this straight . . . so far, for modes of transportation, you recommend dog sled and reindeer-drawn sleigh. There's a truck outside Dad's house – can't we use that?'

He does something that's not a laugh at all, more like a scoff. 'I don't drive.'

'Me neither.' It's unusual to meet someone else who doesn't, especially a man. 'Never learned?'

'I just don't.'

There's something defensive in his voice, and I can't help noticing the tension that's squaring his shoulders and the finality in the tone of his terse answers. 'My mum died in a car accident when I was younger,' I say as an explanation.

'I know.'

Dad must've told him then. I'm surprised because Dad has *never* talked to me about the accident they were in. 'Are people ever disappointed that they don't actually fly? Or that Rudolph doesn't have a red nose?'

He looks over at me like he understands the change of subject for what it is and his lips curve upwards. 'They only fly on Christmas Eve. And Rudolph's nose only glows in the fog. Everyone knows that.'

I laugh, but it makes me smile too because he switches from serious to children's entertainer at the drop of a hat, but you can hear the joy in his voice when he talks about Christmas magic.

I bite my lip to stop myself smiling. 'This really means a lot to you, doesn't it?'

'It's something that was sorely missing from my childhood. My parents are very sensible people, always too serious to let me and my brother and sister believe in anything as whimsical as Santa Claus, and when I was older, I saw how other families bolstered this belief and how magical it must be for a child to grow up believing in the impossible, and I wanted to be part of that.'

'So that's why you do it? That's why you're so dedicated? Making up for lost time?'

'No. I just like seeing people happy, and I think children should grow up thinking there's something wonderful in the world.' He meets my eyes. 'And it's never too late for adults who have lost that sense of wonder to get it back. Santa is a symbol of hope, a sign that things will always get better. Christmas is something to look forward to. A joyous end to the year – a celebration of a good year or good riddance to a bad year, but always a moment to measure your life by, whether adult or child.'

His eyes are burning into me and I can't look away. I'm so distracted that I'm still holding a piece of lichen in mid-air and I jump when another reindeer comes over and helps himself from between my fingers.

'What about you? I can't imagine Percy raised you to *not* believe in Santa.'

'No. My mum and dad always made Christmas special and went to great lengths to stoke my belief in Santa. There were always snowy footprints leading from the fireplace to the Christmas tree on Christmas morning, mince pie crumbs and an emptied glass of milk and half-chewed carrots on the plate by the fire, glittery hoofprints in the garden, noises from the roof on Christmas Eve, bells jingling from above.'

I don't realise I'm smiling at the memories until Tav points at my face. 'See that? That smile right there? *That* is why children should grow up believing in Santa. Because when they're old and cynical, they can still look back and recall a time when they believed in magic.'

Again, it's a nice sentiment, but my childhood Christmases make very little difference to my adult life.

'Are you a vet?' I ask to change the subject, because it feels so peaceful out here, and being around animals has always been calming for me. These creatures are truly majestic in the middle of this gorgeously natural forest, and it makes me want to breathe deeper and be still for a moment.

'No, I'm self-taught.' There's a hesitancy in his voice that says he clearly expects ridicule. 'Through experience and through courses I took for the knowledge, not the qualifications. I work with a vet down in the village because, obviously, there are things I can't do and problems I don't always know how to fix, but I've been looking after reindeer for nearly twenty years now.' There are three around him as he talks and he expertly dodges antlers and gives them all a handful of lichen and a bit of a fuss. 'Injured reindeer come here for rehabilitation. I get a lot of orphaned reindeer calves. Then there are wild animal attacks, traps, hunters, people who chase them for sport.'

'You're so good with them.'

'Better than I am with people.'

'You know where you stand with animals. I miss the dogs I used to work with. People are unpredictable, but a dog never is. They always want a walk and a belly rub, no matter what's going on in the world.'

'Dogs? Is this before or after the fancy hotelier job?'

I freeze mid-reindeer-stroke. What is *wrong* with me? I've barely known this man a day and I forget myself completely in front of him. I am the *worst* at keeping secrets.

'It's all right,' Tav says. 'I'll pretend I didn't hear that too.'

I give him a grateful smile, and feel even more grateful when he doesn't push for more info even though he *must* have worked it out by now.

Instead, he looks out across the paddock. 'Rudolph Number Three is missing again.' He glances at me. 'Or Clive, as he'll now be known.'

It shouldn't make me laugh as hard as it does. '*Clive* was in the forest earlier with another reindeer, a small one with big antlers.'

He does a headcount. 'That's odd. We don't have another reindeer. You definitely saw two? And it wasn't one of this lot?'

I look over the animals in front of me. Am I really supposed to recognise them?

Tav must clock the look on my face because he laughs. 'It seems impossible now, but they all have different antlers, markings, and personalities. You'll get to know them in time.'

'Not with all the numbers after their names, I won't. You can't seriously expect anyone to remember those. You could use the time you spend memorising numbers to think up actual names for them. Right, this one.' I nod to the non-antlered chap who's now snuffling across my palm in search of more lichen and Tav holds the bag out for me to take some. 'From now on, he's Mr Bean.'

'Why?'

'It was my favourite TV show growing up.'

'No, I mean . . .'

'The least you can do is give them the honour of having their own name, not another reindeer's recycled name with a different number. And for God's sake, haven't you heard of creativity? There isn't a reindeer in the world *not* known as Rudolph. Think outside the box. Look, those two, Ant and Dec. Those two, Richard and Judy.' I point at two pairs of reindeer on the opposite side of the clearing. 'Holly and Phil. Mary Berry and Paul Hollywood. And that one, look, he bears a striking resemblance to Martin Clunes. That one with orangey-brown fur has got David Dickinson written all over him. Look at the messy fur on that one's head – it's definitely Boris Johnson.' I keep pointing to individual reindeer. 'This one, Richard Madden. That one, Oscar Isaac, and look, there's Pedro Pascal.'

I make a clicking noise with my tongue to attract the attention of the three reindeer who are pawing at a bale of hay. 'Come on, Oscar Isaac. Come and have some lichen. Oh, look, Oscar Isaac seems quite interested in Richard Madden's back end . . . Oh, now Oscar and Pedro are having a playfight over who gets to stand nearest to Richard Madden. And . . . they're back to comparing antler sizes. Honestly, men are all the same.'

Tav is laughing so hard he can barely breathe. 'I don't know who any of those people are, but Reindeer Namer has just become your job. Even after you leave, I'll send you photos of new arrivals and you can send me names back. It's your job for life now.'

I swallow hard. I've been here a *day* and I don't even like Christmas, but the thought of Tav sending me photos of reindeer while I'm at home in miserable Britain makes a rock settle in my stomach. The thought of being back there with Dad, of having made him miserable too . . . And what if Tav's right about the property developers? What would someone want to build here? Some state-of-the-art outdoor sports centre? An Arctic Circle novelty ice hotel? A luxury spa? All sharp angles and concrete and stone and glass? What if they want to bulldoze it completely and put in a ski resort? He'll be trying to run a reindeer sanctuary on the edge of a building site, looking after reindeer recovering from injuries or poor orphaned calves being lost without their mums, and all around them are pneumatic drills and excavators and trees being felled.

I don't realise my eyes have welled up again until Tav asks if I'm okay.

'Cold air,' I mutter, turning away to take some deep breaths.

Mr Bean follows me and pushes his furry nose right into my face and it distracts me from the sudden and overwhelming sadness at the thought of this forest being spoilt.

I give Mr Bean a head rub and distract him with another mouthful of lichen and look over at Tav, who's watching me with intense eyes.

'You're different than I thought you'd be,' he says eventually. 'I expected posh and pristine. All business and not wanting to get involved. But I can tell you like it here, and you've made me laugh more in the last twenty-four hours than I have in the last month put together.'

I blush because he makes me feel like laughing too. There's an honesty about him, a sense of ease and candour, the kind of guy who makes it okay for me to be myself without judgement. 'Well, everyone needs more laughter in their lives.'

'Maybe some people need more magic in their lives too.'

He's not wrong there, but I don't give him the satisfaction of admitting it. There's a sense of joy here that pervades the whole forest. It's the kind of place that makes you happy.

Chapter 7

Dear Santa,
Can you bring me a penguin for Christmas?
From,
Matteo

After dreams of reindeer surrounded by diggers and their hooves click-clacking across concrete jungles and endless car parks, I wake up early the next morning. Usually I'd lie in bed, obstinately refusing to get up a second before the alarm goes off, but I'm excited to see what the day brings.

It's still dark outside as I shower and change into another pair of jeans, a thermal T-shirt Dad gave me, a normal T-shirt, a black jumper, and pull my coat on over the top. There. That should do it. I pull my hair into a side plait and go out the door. It feels much earlier than it is when I start walking down the steps towards Santa's House, hoping Dad and Tav won't have left yet. The thought of Tav makes my pace quicken and there's a little fizzle inside me.

It's only for the pancakes, I tell myself as I knock and let myself in.

'Hello?' I call, disappointed not to walk in on a rendition of a Christmas song this morning.

'In the kitchen, Sash,' Dad calls back.

The underfloor heating is on so I step out of my boots and leave my hat, scarf, and gloves by the door as I walk through the living room and into the big kitchen. I can't help smiling at the sight that greets me. The air is heavy with the scent of cinnamon, ginger, and butter. Dad is sitting on a stool at the island in full Santa regalia, and Tav's at the stove again.

'Good morning.'

Dad's jumped down before I can stop him and he comes over to envelop me in a hug. He squeezes approximately three-quarters of the life out of me, and doesn't release me until I'm moments away from suffocation.

'You're early – you must've been eager to see one of us.' He chortles a perfect "ho ho ho" as he climbs back onto the stool and carries on with his breakfast.

I go red even though there's no reason to.

'Well, who doesn't want to see Santa on a cold December morning?' I'm quite proud of myself for saving that so well, even though my cheeks are still tingling with redness that's not *just* about coming in from the cold.

When I risk looking at Tav to see if he's got the implication, his cheeks are red too, and his lips curve into a smile.

I can't help smiling back. The chill in the air from the walk down has left something feeling clenched in my chest and it instantly defrosts and leaves me so warm that I start undoing my coat.

He's wearing another cosy-looking wintry jumper, navy with a line of white mountains around the chest, and black snow-proof trousers with lighter stripes down the sides. His stubble is even more unkempt than yesterday. It looks like it should be perfectly shaped but he hasn't had time to shave for a few days, and his brown hair is pushed backwards and not-quite-dry from a morning shower.

Thinking about Tav and showers was not a good plan because

my face goes even redder than it was before, and I may as well be carrying a placard that reads "I am thinking naughty thoughts".

'You wouldn't be doing pancakes over there again, would you?' I say to distract myself.

'Gingerbread waffles today,' he says cheerfully. 'Brown sugar, flour, butter, cinnamon, ginger, nutmeg . . . Just so you know what it is.'

'You can stop making fun of me anytime now.'

'I'm not,' he says with a grin. 'I'm going to adopt it as my own life policy. Don't put things in my mouth without knowing what they are. People live by life policies like "make every day count" or "do something each day that makes you smile", but I think *this* is where people are going wrong. Putting things in their mouths without knowing what they are can lead to all sorts of trouble.'

He inclines his head towards the stool next to Dad's, and I hop on and watch him do that dexterous thing of sliding a plate across while simultaneously pouring a mug of coffee and placing the waffle in front of me with chef-like precision.

'Does anyone ever make you breakfast?' I ask as he turns back to ladle his own waffle into the griddle pan.

'I don't like people doing things for me.'

That independence again. I look over at Dad but he carries on cutting up his waffle obliviously.

'How are you this morning?' I ask him.

We had dinner together last night, but the conversation stayed on a strictly superficial level. Dad didn't mention the heart attack, and any attempt to get him to open up about his health was met with: 'I'm fine, Sash, you don't have to worry.'

Which, obviously, makes me worry more.

'You're dressed up so you're planning on working again today, but you're supposed to be slowing do—'

'I'm fine, Sash, you don't have to worry about me,' he repeats like a broken record with its mouth full.

I roll my eyes and cut off a corner of waffle and inhale the steam rising as I take a bite and soft and fluffy gingerbread flavour melts in my mouth.

'Oh my God, Tav.' I let out an orgasmic noise. '*Are* you a chef? Because if you're not, you *should* be.'

'No, don't say that.' Dad slaps his hand onto the table. 'Don't give him ideas – we can't afford to lose him round here.'

Tav laughs. 'My cooking is limited to unhealthy comfort food, but thank you.'

'Thank *you*.' I take another bite. 'I didn't know it was possible to enjoy breakfast so much.'

Tav does what he did yesterday and turns around to lean against the unit and eat standing up. I watch him for a moment and then nod to the island. 'Won't you sit?'

He mumbles something unintelligible around his waffle.

'Sit, Tav.' I point my fork at him threateningly. 'It's earlier today; you can't be late for anything yet. The place isn't going to fall apart if you're off your feet for a couple of minutes. Don't make me come round there.'

'And what? Poke me with a fork?' He's laughing as he takes a seat, but the stools that are a struggle for me to climb up on are actually too small for him and he's hunched over.

'What do you think of our fine establishment, Sash?' Dad asks. 'You're the expert. How would you improve it?'

'I'm not an—' Oh, right. He means with the hotel. Apparently I *am* an expert.

'No need to be modest,' he barrels on. 'You've turned the fortunes of Hotel Magenta completely around. Wave your magic wand and we'll be back up and running in no time. You're the brains, Tav's the brawn, and I'm Santa Claus. Between us, we'll have guests back by Christmas, right?'

'Advertising?' I glance at Tav. His hair flops forward as he gives me an encouraging nod. 'No one knows about this place. I'd never heard of it.'

'You don't travel,' Dad interjects.

'Well, no, but . . . I mean, places like Finnish Lapland are super busy at this time of year. They're real destinations . . . dream holidays. We should be doing the same for northern Norway. This place is amazing. You're saving reindeers' lives and living under the Northern Lights . . . People have lifelong dreams of seeing them and they put on a show for me within ten minutes of arriving. That's special – something people would want to visit if they knew it was here.'

'Can't guarantee the Northern Lights,' Tav says.

'Budget's too low for advertising,' Dad adds. 'What did you do at the hotel? I didn't think you had a huge budget there. Anything can succeed if it's got enough money behind it, but it takes real innovation to be a success with a small budget.'

'Non-existent budget,' Tav corrects.

Dad sounds so different here. Even his voice is different – a deeper, rounder tone to it, and his British accent is milder than it used to be, and the other thing that's missing is any hint of the frailty I heard on the phone. 'Dad, I don't think you should be worrying about things like this in your condition . . .'

'Oh, pish-posh. Fit as a fiddle, I am.' He's watching me expectantly and I'm struggling to think of what to say. I *haven't* single-handedly saved the hotel I'm supposed to work at. I didn't even know it *had* been in trouble. I um and ah for an embarrassingly long time, trying to come up with something vaguely competent.

'Maybe Sasha needs to look around more.' Tav evidently takes pity on me. 'She can't be expected to be a miracle worker when she hasn't seen it all yet.'

I look up at him and try to show my gratefulness in my eyes. He's obviously clocked that I don't work where my dad thinks I do by now, and instead of dropping me in it, he's trying to change the subject.

'Ah, for inspiration.' Dad claps his hands together. 'An excellent point. Have you seen my workshop yet?'

'Your workshop?'

'Well, Santa's workshop, but you know, we're one and the same.' He does another "ho ho ho". 'Where the elves make the toys.'

'Where the elves *used* to make the toys,' Tav corrects him again.

'Yes, but all we need is an upswing in bookings and enough visitors to increase our budget and let us bring some much-needed staff back, and we'll be right on track. And you're an expert at that sort of thing with the way you've pulled Hotel Magenta out of the doldrums.'

When choosing to lie about working in a hotel, why couldn't I have chosen one that had gradually faded into obscurity and closed down instead of becoming one of the busiest in England? No one would expect me to be an expert then.

'You must see it. Tav can take you there after breakfast.'

'Can't you show me?' I ask, because showing me a workshop might be less strenuous than another day of work for him.

'No, no. It's Santa's busiest time of the year.'

'I know, but you're not meant to be busy, Dad.' I sigh and try to change tack. 'I wanted to spend time with you and I'm sure Tav's got better things to do than show me around.'

'Nonsense, Tav's priority is to take care of our guests and you are currently our only guest.' He looks between us. 'And it's a tad overgrown for me with my health at the moment.'

'I really don't mind. I do whatever I'm told,' Tav says.

'You don't have time to name reindeer, but you have time to show me Santa's workshop?' I raise an eyebrow at him across the island countertop.

'Priorities,' he says with an easy shrug.

Priorities. Something inside me freezes at the word. It's been a long while since I felt like a priority in anyone's life.

'What can I do to help? You asked me to come here and so far all the pair of you have done is insist you don't want my help.'

'The elves tell me you were at the post office yesterday – that's a great help. The post office is a much-loved and much-neglected

112

part of the North Pole Forest,' Dad says. 'It needs someone to give it some attention again.'

'Yeah, but reading letters isn't helping you to take it easy. I came here to do the physical stuff so you could rest.'

'What we need most is your expertise in the industry, and your love of Christmas.'

'I hate Christmas.'

Dad and Tav do a gasp of horror in unison.

'For goodness' sake, Sasha, don't say things like that around here!' Dad cries. 'An elf drops dead every time someone says that, like the fairies in *Peter Pan* when people say they don't believe in them. Next you'll be telling me you don't believe in Santa Claus.'

When I look up, Tav's biting his lip so hard that the skin has gone white where his teeth dig in and he's clearly about to burst into uncontrollable laughter.

'I would never say anything so abhorrent.'

My sarcasm goes straight over Dad's head because he nods sagely. 'Thought so. And how can you say . . .' his voice drops to a whisper and he covers his mouth with his hand '. . . the *unsayable* thing? You loved Christmas when you were little.'

'Yeah, when you and Mum used to do the fake-snow footprints and hoofprints, and all the sleigh bells and noises from the roof.'

His forehead furrows in confusion. 'Sash, we never did anything on the roof. That would've been Santa himself.'

'We must've had some very festive bats living in the attic then,' I say flatly, determined not to enable him any longer. I still don't know if he's playing the role or if we're in serious delusion territory, and I haven't spent enough time with him to find out yet. And his complete ignorance annoys me. Does he really not understand why I'm not the biggest Christmas fan? 'Besides, Christmas is a time for family, and when you're alon—'

'Don't forget to take pictures for social media while you're out and about.' Dad doesn't let me finish the sentence, and I sigh in resignation. He's never going to listen or care enough to understand what Christmas is like when there's a father-shaped hole in your life.

I deliberately avoid Tav's eyes as I paste a smile back on.

'You're on social media?' The surprises keep on coming. Last time I checked, Dad didn't know how to access his voicemail, never mind navigate Twitter.

'Santa needs to be accessible to all in this technological era. It's a wonderful way to connect with people.'

'We're @NorthPoleForest on Twitter, Facebook, and Instagram,' Tav says as I get my phone out and send Dad a couple of the photos I took yesterday.

With the waffles gone and Dad engrossed in his phone, Tav grunts as he gets off the stool. 'See? Now I've sat down, it's harder to get up.'

I think about what Freya said about Tav working too much and how tired he looks when he's not trying to hide it. 'That's no reason to keep going like an Energizer bunny that's just plugged itself in.'

He ignores me. 'Ready to go?'

I glance at Dad, who's now "ho-ho-ho-ing" over a comment online and clearly has no intention of *not* working today, and then back at Tav resignedly. 'I guess so.'

Outside, it's still not daylight, but the sky is starting to brighten and lighter wisps of cloud drift across the blue-black darkness.

Tav steps out the door behind me. 'It's going to be a beautiful day.'

'How can you tell?' I look up at the sky but it doesn't give anything away. 'Some "pink sky at night" thing?'

He looks at me like I've lost the plot. 'Every day is a beautiful day.'

'Oh, right. You meant metaphorically.' I simultaneously want to make vomiting noises and wish I had his attitude. Thankfully I'm saved from having to decide between the two when we see Freya coming towards us, an LED lamp shining from a strap around her head to light the way.

'Sasha! Tav!' Her breath puffs out into the cold morning air. 'Nice to see you together. I knew you two would hit it off.'

I have many questions, considering she knows next to nothing about me or what kind of men I get on with, and so far, standing on the same road seems to constitute "hitting it off".

I don't know why I'm so pleased to see her again, but the sight of her makes me smile, even though she looks like she's listing to one side under the weight of today's bag. When she reaches us, she shrugs it off her shoulder and the heaviness yanks her arm down.

'There are 1589 letters from twenty-two countries.' She holds the bag out to me. 'It's going up as the December days go by.'

I go to take the bag but Tav intercepts it and swings it over his own shoulder like it weighs nothing.

'Always such a gent.' Freya winks at me, and I like the way he blushes at the compliment.

'Any collections today?' she asks and he shakes his head.

'Collections?' I ask.

'Your delivery contract with *Posten Norge* is fully paid up until next September.' She nods towards the red post box beside the house. 'We get such a large volume of mail for you that we signed an agreement that's beneficial to both you and the postal service. You can send out anything you want at no cost. It's all part of the North Pole Forest deal. We have a lot of mail for you and you have a lot for us, it's in both our interests to make the most of that partnership. Leave any outgoing mail in the bags for me to collect, no extra charge.' Freya looks around as if she's searching for someone. 'No guests this morning?'

'None at all,' Tav says. 'You know I've got my eyes open. If anyone even vaguely matches his description, I'll accost him on sight.'

Freya says her goodbyes and hurries off, and Tav and I start wandering down the same road we walked up yesterday.

'What was that all about?'

'She had a random encounter with a guest here last year.

115

It was a "love at first sight" thing, you know? He was with his grandchildren, their eyes met across a snowy road and sparks flew . . . and then a bus full of tourists pulled up between them, visitors piled out, and by the time the crowd dispersed, he was gone. It was over there.' Tav points to the bottom of the hill where the cabins are. 'He was crossing from the cabins towards Santa's House at breakfast time, so we assumed he was a guest, but we never found him.'

'That's so romantic. That's the kind of thing that happens in movies, not in real life.'

'It's not *that* romantic because they didn't find each other. She's looked for him every day since, but it's been almost a year now, and he never came back. And she's instantly recognisable in her uniform, and no guests ever asked after our postwoman, so I can only assume he didn't feel the same. There aren't any guests on the books for this year that sound promising either, but I haven't had the heart to tell her yet.'

'Aww.' There's something about this that's so sweet, and yet Tav is the unlikeliest person to be in the middle of it. 'Do people regularly share their romantic woes with you?' He seems like a nice guy, but not really someone I can imagine being the confidant of a sixty-something-year-old woman.

'She wrote to Santa.'

'She's in her sixties!'

'I didn't realise there was an age limit on believing in magic.'

I'd laugh if it wasn't for the seriousness in his voice. He's such a conundrum. One minute he's serious, cynical, and distrustful, and the next minute, he'll be going on about *nisse* and helping little old ladies with their love lives.

'I read her letter and put two and two together. I went through the guest register in the hopes I'd find him, but nothing matched a grandfather with two young grandchildren, so I had to tell her I'd opened her letter and needed more info, but we could never piece together enough to find out who he was.'

'Beneath that gruff exterior, you're a soppy old romantic, aren't you?'

'The guy could've been anyone. He could've been a creepy weirdo perving on women while his grandkids were in tow. I wanted to make sure she wasn't going to be his next victim if he turned out to be a serial killer.'

This time I can't help laughing. It's much more fitting with what I know of Tav so far.

We pass the clearing to the post office and Tav stops at a gap in the bushes on the opposite side of the road. He holds his hand out and I slip mine into it without a second thought. Neither of us have gloves on, and I hadn't realised how numb my fingers had gone until his hand closes around mine, and his warmth makes my skin tingle.

Tav stares at our joined hands for a moment and then shakes himself. 'This way. There was a minor landslide a couple of years ago so the path isn't what it used to be.'

For the second time in as many days, I follow this man down an overgrown path into a mysterious wooded area and he seems completely unfazed by anything that might be lurking there.

The path is narrow and sharp holly leaves catch on my jeans, branches spring out at all angles, and the ground is uneven and steep in parts. As we move further down into the forest, the snow-covered roof of a building comes into view amongst the trees, hidden in the middle of the woods, and I feel like Jack Skellington seeing Christmas Town for the first time.

'Why is it so far down?' I ask as Tav stops and holds up a preventative hand. He lets my hand drop as he jumps down a gap in the path, and even though I'm quite capable of doing the same, he turns back and holds both hands out to me, waiting until I give him the okay nod, before his hands touch my body.

It isn't intimate, and with the number of layers I'm wearing, there's only the vague pressure of his hands touching my sides as he lifts me down effortlessly. I feel like Baby in *Dirty Dancing* in those few seconds I'm suspended in the air, like a gazelle, weightless and free, or a ballerina dizzy after too many pirouettes, as he transfers me from the narrow path to wide-open space next to a tree trunk, the post bag banging against his side like it weighs nothing. God knows how he can lift me *and* that without breaking a sweat.

The closeness brings his cologne into sharp focus, and I breathe in crisp leaves and it's only the hint of almond that makes me realise it's actually him and not the forestry around us.

My hands are on his arms and it takes a few moments for me to come back to the present and realise I'm on solid ground and Tav is patiently waiting for me to let go of him.

I step back guiltily, banging into the tree trunk and bringing an avalanche of snow splattering down all around me.

'Because it's Santa's workshop.' Tav answers the question I asked seconds ago, but my brain is so frayed by being close to him that it takes me a while to catch up. 'It's secret. Only very few children get to see behind the curtain and watch the elves making toys. It's one of the most mysterious things about Christmas. It's supposed to be shrouded in secrecy and magic.'

At the top of the path back up to the main road, a reindeer's head appears over the holly bushes and peers down at me. 'Is that Rudolph-slash-Clive again?'

Tav looks up from fiddling with a bundle of keys and grunts, and when Rudolph sees him looking, he dashes off, the sound of his hooves echoing into the distance.

'See? You're already starting to recognise them. I have no idea how he keeps getting out – none of the others do. It's strange because he never goes far, and he always comes back.' He unlocks the wide double door, etched with elegant scrolls and panes of red and green stained glass. "Santa's Workshop" is carved over the entrance, and the outside is surrounded by a wooden fence with train carriages carved atop each post, now chipped and faded compared to the bright colours they once were. The doors grind and stall as Tav drags them haltingly open. The only thing missing is a flock of moths flying out of the dark, damp building, disturbed from years of slumber.

He steps back to let me through first, ducking at the last second before he clonks his head on yet another doorframe, and he lets the post bag slip off his shoulder and onto a wooden chair inside the door, sending up a cloud of dust that I wave my hand to disperse.

'This is where the magic happened.' Tav indicates the two rows of desks lined up next to each other like a conveyor belt, and I can instantly imagine them filled by a factory line of workers. At the moment, they're mainly filled with cobwebs.

'We had a married couple on staff who made all the elf costumes themselves, and running the workshop became their pet project. We used to have enough elves to fill these seats, and when children would come to visit, they'd see them sitting here painting train carriages or wooden dolls.' He walks to the end of a desk and plunges his hand into a box. I half-expect him to come out with something responsible for all these cobwebs, but he pulls out a little train and a couple of carriages, the plain wood waiting to be painted by elves who no longer work here.

You can tell the room was once done up in primary colours, but the walls are faded and scuffed now. There are other parts of the building too, closed doors with signs on them. One reads "Presents", the other reads "Storage", and on the right of the room is a door with "Elf Workshop" on it, the wooden sign held up by only one corner now.

That level of detail hits me again. I've never visited a Christmas village before, but surely they don't all stage actual Santa's workshops so children can *see* their toys being put together?

'This is exceptional,' I murmur. It's another of the many things that make the North Pole Forest seem out of this world.

'Exceptional? Really?' He doesn't hide the surprise in his voice. 'I thought you hated Christmas.'

'Well, yeah, but the thought that's gone into this . . .' Something hovers at the edge of my mind about Tav's attention to small things and eye for detail.

He smiles to himself and throws the wooden carriages he's still holding in the air, and catches all three of them with one hand and deposits them back into the box.

'Tav . . .' I start, unable to take my eyes off his deft movements. 'Why?'

'Why what?'

'All of this just to convince children Santa exists? Why so much effort?'

He watches me for a minute and then lifts his chin. 'Go back outside and look in a window.'

I stomp back out into the snow and cup my hands around my eyes to block reflections and peer in a clear gap at the bottom corner of a stained-glass window depicting colourful presents.

'You'll have to use your imagination,' Tav says. 'Close your eyes.'

I roll them instead, and then do as he says.

'Imagine being young again.' He speaks louder so I can hear him from the outside but his voice stays soft, his Norwegian lilt coming out in his slow words. 'Imagine tiptoeing up to that window and peeking through the only corner you were tall enough to see in. Imagine seeing row after row of elves working. The air smells of peppermint and the scent of freshly sanded wood, and the colours are bright and exciting and you don't know where to look first.'

His voice is hypnotic and I have to blink a few times because I'm lost in the vision he creates.

'Imagine you're an older child on the verge of realising Santa is a fairy tale. It's a significant moment in any child's ageing process when they find out Santa isn't real, and at that point, they lose a piece of their innocence and become one step closer to being a cynical adult like us. And you peek in this window and there can be no explanation for it other than Santa's workshop, so you start to question all the things you've heard about Santa being a myth and you wonder . . . Could he be *real* and anyone who thinks otherwise just isn't lucky enough to have seen a place like this yet?'

I feel like I'm waking from a trance when he stops speaking. His voice is so calming. Listening to it is like lying on your back in a tranquil lake while a gentle breeze nudges you slowly towards the shore.

I go back and lean in the doorway. 'I don't get it.'

'You wouldn't be smiling like that if you didn't.'

My smile gets wider. 'Okay, why Santa? Why not a room full of teeth to prove the existence of the tooth fairy?'

He laughs. 'Firstly, that would be a remarkably macabre and disturbing sight, and secondly, *everyone* knows it's the parents who put the coins under the pillow, and thirdly, Christmas is the best time of year. Everything feels more magical at Christmas, like the universe is already primed to help. Seriously, Sash.' He shakes his head, his shaggy hair flipping sideways. 'Santa is the most important thing anyone ever believes in. The most magical. The most impossible. Children need that sense of wonder in their lives. Every child deserves to think magic is real. Every adult deserves to have that to look back on. And for me, because it's the most life-affirming thing in the world to see that wonder on a child's face, to see children literally realise that magic is real, knowing it's something they'll remember forever, and I'm a part of that.'

He crosses the room and pushes open one of the other doors. It sticks, swollen with dampness, and when he shoves his entire weight against it, it opens with a sudden slide and crashes hard against something behind it, the bang reverberating through the floorboards. 'This is one of the elf workshops.'

This room has workbenches and child-friendly tools hanging on hooks around the wall. It's like being back in school and looking into the technology classroom all over again.

'We'd have the wooden blanks of a few basic toys, and children could choose what they wanted to make, and the elves would help them put it together and sand it and paint it. We also had elf art classes where kids could come and draw.' He nods to the far wall, which displays a number of yellowing drawings with curled edges, showing children's depictions of Santa and his reindeer.

The amount of effort that was put in here really is exceptional. I've never realised there are people in the world who care *that* much about children believing in Santa. And it makes me wonder something else too. 'What about other families?'

A dark eyebrow quirks up as he looks at me.

'You're all about making the children who come *here* believe in magic, but I'm guessing this is quite an expensive trip. So many families aren't able to afford it, or can't take time off work or don't want to travel . . . What about underprivileged children? The children who write letters like the ones I read yesterday? Arguably the children who need to believe in magic most of all?'

He's quiet for a while before he answers. 'I can't change the world. All I can do is make my little corner of it the best it can be.'

I don't know what I expected the answer to be, or what I'm getting at by asking. It just seems odd to put *so* much effort into making one place magical when there are thousands of letters from children who could *really* do with believing the world is a better place than it is.

Tav's phone buzzes in his pocket and he pulls it out, looks at the screen, and then holds it out to show me. 'He didn't waste any time in posting those.'

On the screen is a Twitter post by my dad showing the photos I sent him – the selfie I took with the signpost yesterday, one as I walked towards the post office, and one I took from my cabin looking down onto Santa's House. The accompanying tweet reads: "*It's December and Santa's daughter has arrived to save Christmas! #NorthPoleForest #KeepingItInTheFamily #SantaClausIsComingToTown*"

'Save Christmas?' My fingers brush his as I take the phone out of his hand.

The tweet makes a chill creep down my spine. 'Did he only invite me here because he thinks my knowledge of hotels will somehow save this place?'

I appreciate that he doesn't make any comment on the hotel bit. I've slipped up so many times that he's obviously realised I'm not being honest about my job, and this is a perfect opportunity to confront me, but he doesn't. 'He invited you here because you're his daughter and you hadn't seen each other for three and a half years, and he had a brush with death.'

'And this place just happens to be on its last legs and I just happen to be responsible for "turning around the fortunes of one of the biggest hotels in Britain".' I repeat Dad's words from earlier. 'Is that all he wants from me?'

'I think . . .' he says slowly, 'he just wants you to love it here as much as he does.'

I've got to admit there's something about a man who thinks before he speaks and doesn't blunder in blindly offending everyone.

'It's okay to admit you like it here, you know. I get why you're worried about Percy – I am too – but it's just us here. You can say something nice with no consequences. I won't tell him.'

There's a hint of mischief in his voice that makes me smile despite myself. 'It's a beautiful place, Tav. Perfect, even, back in the day. But budgets run out for a reason, and my dad's plans to do the place up have been foiled by his health. That isn't going to change. If anything, after a heart attack, it's going to get worse . . .'

I sigh and step away from Tav. Despite the sawdusty smell of the workshop, his fresh almondy cologne is still in my nose and it might be clouding my judgement. 'Maybe there's a solution that doesn't involve selling it. What about renting it out?'

'Unfeasible.'

'Why? If we could get tourists back, get a loan or something to cover the repair work and a new marketing campaign, and then it could pay for itself on a monthly basis. What about you? You obviously love it, you don't want to see it sold, and you practically run the place anyway. If it made more money, enough to cover a rent fee every month, why couldn't you rent it? Dad would be happy leaving it in your hands – someone he trusts and knows will keep it as it is. That could be a good compromise.'

'It's not that simple.'

I stare at him but I have absolutely no doubt that he isn't going to elaborate on *why* it isn't that simple. 'Because you're not as gullible as Dad?'

'What?'

'What I said yesterday about how the old owner saw him coming. Whoever it was must've set out to take advantage. He's a nice man – too nice. Too gullible. He'll believe anything. He's a nightmare with phone scams and those fake phishing emails. Whoever owned this place really unloaded a deadweight. Manipulated him into buying it then jumped ship at exactly the right moment, and let my dad foot the bill of watching it sink.'

Tav scoffs. 'If anything, he coerced the old owner into selling. They thought he would save it and above all else, they wanted it saved.'

'You knew them then?'

'I've worked here for fifteen years.' His tone is cold and clipped again, and he shoves a hand through his hair. 'Come on, we should go.'

He goes to pull the wooden door shut, but it gets stuck again. He yanks it and it crashes into the frame with such a bang that it shakes the whole building. From inside the room, there's the unmistakable clatter of something big and heavy falling over. Tav uses his shoulder to shove the door open again, and we peer back into the room. The heavy wooden cabinet the door crashed into earlier is on the floor, its cupboard doors open and bent backwards and its drawers have slid across the room and all manner of supplies are spilling out.

'What is all this stuff?'

'Leftover stock from the elf workshops.' He lifts the cabinet back upright like it weighs nothing and shifts it further along the wall. 'I ordered too much and visitors stopped coming long before the stock ran out. So it's just here, waiting I guess, in the hopes people will come back one day.'

His sadness is audible again at the sight of the chaos that's spilled out. There are sets of paints and brushes, packets of colouring pens and pencils, and Christmas colouring books. Blank wooden craft shapes ready to be painted in festive designs. Boxes of what look like Christmas cracker toys.

Tav's already started gathering them up, and I crouch down to help, but he holds a hand up. 'I've got it, Sash. I know where everything goes. Won't be a minute.'

He sounds embarrassed by the fact I've seen all this, and it doesn't seem like I'll do any good by insisting on helping, so I wander back into the main workshop. I peer into the box at the edge of the desk that Tav got the carriages out of earlier, and it's overflowing with wooden trains. There's an excess of everything here.

I go over to the door and take breaths of air so cold it feels like my tonsils are being frozen on contact. My hand brushes against the "*Posten*" bag on the chair where Tav dumped it, and I take out a random envelope.

I tear it open and read the letter from a little boy in the UK who politely requests that Santa give his present to his little brother because his mum has told him they don't have much money for presents this year and he thinks his little brother deserves two gifts.

A feeling tingles at the back of my neck that has nothing whatsoever to do with the ice-cold breeze stealing in, and everything that's happened this morning clicks into place.

'Tav!' I run back across the room and into the workshop. 'Can we send some of this stuff out?'

He's standing wide-legged and bending down to gather up packets of colouring pencils and sketchbooks and he looks up when I stumble in.

'We have all this stuff we don't need, we have a treaty with the post office that allows us to post anything free of charge, there's a load of packaging materials behind the counter in the post office, and we've got letters from kids whose families haven't got money for presents.' I wave the letter around. 'It won't cost us anything, and it'll make use of stuff that's just sitting here.'

Tav pushes the armful of art supplies back into the cupboard and takes the letter from my hand. I can't tear my eyes from him as he reads it, mesmerised by the way his smile starts out small and gradually grows until his whole face is lit up.

'Coming here is the holiday of a lifetime,' I say in a rush. 'Parents who are struggling to put food on the table can't even contemplate going on holiday, but their kids still write to Santa. They still share their thoughts and feelings and secrets with Santa. They have as much right to believe in magic as the children whose families can afford to take trips to Norway in December. We can reach people who can't get here. Kids who need something to make Christmas special. Kids who need to be reminded there's good in the world. That someone's reading their letters. That someone cares.'

'You want to start replying to the letters?'

'Yes!' I'm surprised by how excited my voice is. 'Not all of them, obviously. Not the ones that are demanding lists of toys. But some of them, the children who send these heartbreaking letters and you feel so helpless reading them because there's nothing you can do . . .'

He's watching me with a bemused smile and I don't know if he's impressed or thinks I'm two ants short of a picnic, so I carry on. 'I know we can't do much, but what if we sent a little box of goodies to children who need it? A Christmas care package from the North Pole? Something that might be the only gift they get this year. Nothing extravagant – just some of that stuff.' I point to the cupboard. 'Something to let kids know someone cares about their lives. That letters to Santa actually mean something – they

126

don't disappear into the ether of the post office never to be seen again. There's people like you in this little corner of the Arctic Circle who work really hard to make kids believe in magic. We can do a lot of good with stuff we've already got . . .' I trail off when I realise I'm practically hopping from one leg to the other and gesticulating with my hands like I'm trying to ward off a swarm of particularly lively bees. 'For God's sake, Tav, say something!'

He finally lets the laugh burst out and the deep, warm sound ricochets around the small room.

'What?' I demand.

'Nothing. Just you, being so determined that magic doesn't exist, but being so keen to help children believe in it.'

'It's nothing to do with magic. It's just . . .' That feeling tingles over me again. Every inch of me is buzzing with excitement. The overwhelming feeling from yesterday of how much I wished I could help the kids who shared their deepest secrets in those letters, and the thrill that this might be the way. It won't change people's lives, I know that, but it's important for children who are lonely or struggling to feel that they're not alone. That, somewhere out there, someone cares.

I don't think I breathe again until Tav says, 'I love it. I actually kind of hate myself for never thinking of this. Not that you need my permission, but you have it in full. Go for it.'

I squeal in excitement and before I realise what's happening, he's stepped across the pile of debris between us, and my arms are around his shoulders and his are around my middle, his hands splayed wide on my back, his whole body encasing mine. I'm not sure which one of us hugs the other first. Did he step across to hand me the letter back and I accidentally assaulted him? Did he slip on a colouring book and stumble into my arms? Did he actually mean to hug me?

'This is a fantastic idea, Sash,' he murmurs in my ear. At least, I think that's what he says because I'm so lost in the warmth of his body and his voice so close that his breath stirs the hairs on the back of my neck and the way his stubble catches on my hair that I've forgotten my own name.

His cologne is all around me again, and I'm drifting in a haze of that Christmassy almond scent. I can't believe I'm hugging a man *this* gorgeous, and my fingers curl into the knitted material of his jumper because I don't know where else to put them.

'I'm glad you came.' He releases me and steps back 'I'm sorry, I don't know why I did that. It's been so long since we had guests that I've forgotten how to act around fellow humans.'

'I'm glad I came too.' I deliberately ignore his apology for the hug. He has nothing to apologise for and trying to explain that is going to get awkward and rambly.

His cheeks are red and he crouches down again, continuing to gather up the stuff that's fallen from the cupboard. 'This won't take a minute and then we'll go.'

'I'm not a kid, Tav. I can make it up the path on my own.'

'I know.' He looks up at me from his position on the floor. 'Maybe I just want an excuse to hold your hand again.'

I fix him with a dubious look, but inside, every part of me starts flittering.

He looks at the ceiling and forms his hands into claws like he's frustrated with himself. 'Again, I'm sorry. I've literally forgotten how to act around people my own age. Everything I say sounds flirty and cringeworthy and wrong, and I'm just trying to be friendly and not as harsh as I was on the first night.'

'It's okay,' I say, because I know *all* about being awkward around members of the opposite sex, as evidenced by not being able to think of an even vaguely funny or flirty comeback to that. 'I need to take some of this stuff back to the post office.'

I trail my hand along the storage shelves until I find an empty cardboard box, and as he's putting things back, I start piling them into the box instead.

He tilts his head to the side and rests it against the cupboard, smiling as he watches me. Pieces of his hair fall forward and I once again realise he looks so tired he could fall asleep standing up. I'm pretty sure he's been up working for most of, if not *all* of the night, so I take my time over selecting what to put in, just to give him a few minutes' rest.

When the box is full, Tav lifts it out of my arms and rests it on his hip. I go to protest, but he gestures to the door for us to go. As we walk out, he grabs a few handfuls of train carriages and drops them in too.

I go to pick up the post bag, but with one flick of his wrist, it's over his shoulder instead, along with the box under his right arm.

'I can carry it, Tav. You don't have to do everything.'

'Yes, I do.' He sounds cheerful and easy-going, but I meet his eyes, and for one flicker of a second, there's something else there.

He looks away before I have a chance to think about it, and he's already outside, waiting for me so he can close up.

'Thank you,' I say as we walk across to the path back up to the road. I'm not sure if his chivalry is gentlemanly or outdated, but there's something old-fashioned about him in a good way. I can see why my dad likes him – he's more like a true gent of my dad's generation, rather than the image-obsessed men I've had the misfortune of meeting in recent years.

I've been alone for a long while. Relationships have been few and far between and rarely progressed further than a few dates. The guys I've met lately are immature even in their thirties and things like carrying a bag wouldn't even cross their minds. I don't need anyone to carry bags for me, but it's nice when someone does.

At the top of the path, my hand feels numb with the chill when it drops out of his, and I go to take the box from him but he sidesteps easily and walks towards the post office. I'm certain he's going in the opposite direction to collect wood for a cabin roof repair, but he won't even let me take it for a couple of minutes.

He puts the box and bag down outside the post office door and stands back. 'I should leave you to it.'

Why do I feel so disappointed? I have 1589 letters to be getting on with in that bag, and I don't know what his daily to-do list looks like, but I suspect it's longer than the neck of the world's tallest giraffe. 'Thank you. It was magical seeing that, even as it is now.'

'I wish you'd seen it before.' He bumps the toe of one black boot against the other. 'In its heyday, the North Pole Forest would've made even the Grinchiest Grinch believe in sugarplum fairies.'

'Somehow, I can believe that.' I smile and he smiles back, his eyes reflecting the shine of the sun.

We're lingering. There's no reason for him to stay, and I can't think of any excuse to keep him from his work much longer, and yet, we're just standing in the snow, waiting for the other to say something.

Right on cue, the clock on Santa's House chimes eleven times across the forest, and we stand there listening until the last dong.

'Eleven o'clock. I should go.'

'And I should get reading.' I hold my hand out towards the bag by the door.

He nods. 'May your—'

'Day be merry and bright?' I finish for him.

He grins. 'May you find many moments that make you smile today.'

'Are you always this cheerful?'

'It's Christmas,' he says with a parting shrug, like that explains everything.

He's singing "Let It Snow" as he walks off down the road, lines of which still reach me as he disappears into the distance and I find myself humming along as I open the post office door and haul the bag inside.

Maybe Christmas isn't too bad after all.

Chapter 8

Dear Santa,
I am ten years old and I know the truth about you now, but
I wanted you to know how much I enjoyed believing in you
for the past ten years. It wouldn't be Christmas without you.
From,
Isaac

It's a few days later, the end of a long day that's involved wrangling families to visit Santa Claus, taking a group on a tour of Santa's House, and I then got to take two reindeer for a walk down the main road to meet visitors. I've barely seen Tav – trying to repair a hole in the roof of the Gingerbread Cabin turned into replacing the whole roof, and he's been lugging planks of wood up and down the hill all day and there's been a lot of sawing and banging.

I'm more knackered than I can ever remember being, and sleep should come easily, but it isn't happening tonight. I roll onto my back and stare at the ceiling. An owl hoots outside, and from a distance away, another owl hoots back a reply.

I roll over and tuck the hot water bottle against my back instead, but it's no good. I can't sleep. My mind is racing with thoughts of my dad and how excited the kids were to see him today, and how happy *he* was to see *them*. It was the first time I'd got to see him interacting with children and spreading Christmas cheer, and it made him seem like a young man again. Jolly, happy, and full of life. Not three weeks post heart attack and unable to do most of the things he used to do. It was like he's always belonged in his little wooden grotto.

The thought of somehow forcing him to give it up burns in my mind and I roll over and pull the duvet and blanket further over my head, but the image doesn't go away.

The first care packages went out a couple of days ago, and I took a bag of 3290 letters to the post office this morning, but I haven't had a chance to read any of them yet, and I actually *miss* doing it. I feel like I have a duty to read them, and by tomorrow there will be more. It's probably not going to be long before it'll be like Tim Allen receiving the naughty and nice list in *The Santa Clause* via a fleet of FedEx trucks.

Well, they say it's best to get up and do something if you can't sleep, so I pull my snow trousers – a gift from Dad – on over my pyjamas, wriggle into my coat and wrap my scarf around my neck a few times, slip my boots on, and grab my torch.

The night air bites when I step outside. It feels like the coldest night so far, and I briefly reconsider my plan in case I literally turn into a snowman before I reach the post office, but the idea of lying here staring at the ceiling for another couple of hours is arguably less appealing than freezing to death.

I glance up at the sky, consistently disappointed the Northern Lights haven't made another appearance yet. I find myself sky-watching all the time, like if I look away for too long, I'll miss them. And there's a constant urge to stay up late in case I miss them while sleeping. I can sleep after Christmas – the Northern Lights are something I'm unlikely to ever see again when I go home.

I ignore the pip of darkness that thought sets off inside me. Going home is good. It's still the plan for me *and* Dad. It has to be.

There's a light on in the back of Santa's House, and I debate going in for some company, but if it's Dad then he'll worry about me being up late, and if it's Tav then he's unlikely to want my company in the middle of the night, so I turn and carry on, sweeping my torch across the road in front of me, lest an angry wolf jump out from behind a tree.

Maybe I'm not as brave as I thought.

An angry wolf would surprise me, but not as much as opening the post office door does. So much that I have to step back outside and look up at the sign to make sure I've entered the right building.

Inside, it's not the post office. I mean, it *is* the post office, but it's not as it was yesterday. Instead of letters fluttering down to greet me as the door disturbs them, the floor is clear, and there are huge boxes on either side of the room, which the unread letters from years gone by have been piled into. The wooden flooring is recently polished and the whole room smells of a festive pine scent.

Even the door sounds surprised as the click of it closing behind me echoes through the newly empty room, and as I walk further in, I find another gigantic box full of the toys from the workshop. The counter – previously covered in dust and debris – is clean, polished, and empty too, and the mail organisation shelf that was in pieces has been mended.

Tav. Inexplicably, my eyes well up. He's the kindest person. Nothing is too much trouble, even though he's got a million things on his plate already, he still made time to do this. For me. And at least it explains where he disappeared to when he wasn't working on the cabin earlier, and it flits across my mind that Dad's request for my help today was to purposely get me out of the post office so Tav could do this.

Behind the counter, the shelves of packing materials have been cleaned and organised, and added to. There are now sheets of giftwrap, coloured tissue paper, and ribbons, along with flat-packed boxes and padded envelopes and reams of "North Pole

Mail" stickers and stamps, a pot of Christmas pens in a variety of colours, with balls of tinsel, bells, and North Pole signs on top. It's a stationery lover's dream.

In the back room, the desk has been polished, the comfy chair in the corner has been cleaned and there are a couple of extra blankets and cushions on it, and down beside it is a space heater, and I'm so grateful that I want to cry again.

The shelves have been strung with Christmas lights, the dead poinsettias replaced with living ones with glittered red leaves and, like he knows what my favourite decorations are, there are a few nutcrackers staring down from the shelving too, and in the middle of the desk, there's a tiny living Christmas tree in a festive pot, covered with lights and decorated with mini candy canes.

No one has ever done anything this thoughtful for me before and I debate walking back up to the house to thank him, but I tell myself I can thank him in the morning. I don't *need* to see him now.

I switch on the space heater and leave my coat and scarf on the counter before I sink into the chair and plunge my hand into the bag of letters and lose track of time. I file the letters I read into piles. A pile for demanding lists of presents to ignore, a pile for ones that deserve a response, and a pile for ones that need something more – food parcels or clothes vouchers or something. One boy asks Santa for new shoes for him and his siblings because their toes are hurting but their parents can't afford new ones. Another child asks Santa to make Mummy and Daddy love each other again.

I get so caught up in each letter, enraptured by these strangers' lives, from places I've never even *heard* of, and touched by the amount of effort that goes into each letter. Children send Santa paintings and drawings they've done of him, they write him poems, they tell him stories. One little girl writes a monthly update and although I don't have any of her previous letters to hand, she writes to him every month telling him about her life, her friends, what they've been doing at school, and includes photographs of her pet guinea pigs and a hamster.

I'm so wrapped up in her life that I jump when there's a soft knock on the door, and Tav's voice filters through. 'It's just me. Polar bears don't knock, I promise.'

My heart pounds for an altogether different reason as he comes inside. I don't know why I was so desperate to see him tonight, but the fact he's come here, he's sought *me* out, makes me want to throw my arms around him. I can't stop thinking about that hug in the workshop the other day, the strength of his body and the way his arms encased me.

My face is aching from how wide I'm smiling and he beams back at me. Although if I'd have known a gorgeous man was about to walk in, I wouldn't have got so comfortable that the chair has almost swallowed me.

He's wearing his usual padded dark grey coat, carrying a flask, and he's got a blanket draped over one arm. His hair looks mussed up and pillow-creased, like maybe he's been trying to sleep and couldn't either.

'Tav, I—' I go to thank him, but he holds up a finger to stop me and then slowly turns his hand and does a "come here" gesture.

I unplug the heater and cross the room, and he picks up my coat and hands it to me, and then deposits my scarf into my hands too. I shrug my way into them and his chest brushes against my body as he leans past me to pull the door open and let me out first.

'All right, what are we doing?' I ask as I walk down the ramp. My voice sounds like a thunderclap in the silence.

'Look up.' His hand touches my shoulder and pushes gently, urging me to look to the sky above the post office building.

And there they are. The Northern Lights. The entire sky has taken on a purplish hue, and there's just one faint ribbon of green billowing through the darkness. There are more stars than I've ever seen in my life and they somehow look bigger than they do from the UK.

I don't realise I've grabbed Tav's hand where it was on my shoulder until his fingers wriggle out of my grasp and I snatch my hand back in embarrassment. If I'm not fantasising about touching this man inappropriately then I'm *actually* touching him inappropriately. I lose the ability to think straight around him.

'It's so beautiful,' I say, wanting to look at him but unwilling to take my eyes from the sky for even a nanosecond.

'I think it's going to get stronger.' His voice is a whisper. 'I thought you'd like to see.'

'How'd you know where to find me? Footprints to the door again?'

His laugh is warm and right above my ear where he's still standing so close. 'I appreciate your faith in my tracking abilities, but no.' He nudges his elbow towards the building behind us. 'Light's on.'

It's so simple that it makes me laugh out loud, and then clamp a hand over my mouth in case the noise will scare the lights away. It feels like we're seeing *real* magic and it doesn't seem right to speak in a normal voice.

Behind me, Tav moves, softly draping the blanket around my shoulders, waiting until I clutch it over my chest and hold it on, snuggling into the extra warmth gratefully. He pulls one mug and then the other from the top of the flask and he somehow manages to hold them both while unscrewing the lid. The scent of rich, decadent hot chocolate fills the air as he pours it out and nudges one of the mugs into my hand.

I wrap both my cold hands around it, the heat of the drink making the plastic flexible, and I breathe it in, letting the steam rise up and warm my nose. 'You didn't have to do that in there, you know.'

He knows what I'm talking about without needing to say it. 'It's been on my list for months. You gave me the jolt I needed to get on with it. It's no big deal.'

'Yes, it is, Tav. I know how busy you are but you made time

to do it anyway.' I step back into his space and look up until he meets my eyes. 'Thank you.'

His smile looks involuntary and like he couldn't stop it if he tried and it makes something heat up in my chest.

'You're welcome.' He mouths the words but no sound comes out.

My neck is bent to look up at him, and he lowers his head minutely, and I realise how easy it would be to kiss him. His tongue touches his lips and my fingers twitch with the urge to brush them over his stubbled jaw. His pupils are blown wide and my toes move to push myself upwards, and . . . he steps back and rams his hand through his hair and I snap my head back down so fast that my heartbeat throbs in my ears.

'At least I know why you disappeared earlier.' I say it so fast that it comes out as a singular word rather than a sentence. 'Did my dad really need my help today or did you just want me out of the way?'

His laugh sounds as awkward as the weird tension between us after that . . . whatever that was. 'I wanted it to be a surprise. Plus, I *wanted* you to see your dad in action. You can't hide in the post office *all* day.'

He's clocked what I'm doing then. I haven't even admitted that to myself, but when Tav says it, it becomes true. Every day, I get lost in other people's lives through their letters, and I don't have to think about how the days are going by and I still haven't confronted Dad about having to do the sensible thing and give up the North Pole Forest, nor have I succeeded in getting him to slow down and take it easy, or made any attempt to contact an estate agent.

'I'm not hiding.' I don't take my eyes off the sky because the faint strip of green seems to be fading in front of us.

He doesn't respond, and for as much as it annoyed me at first, I like that Tav doesn't fill the air with pointless platitudes.

I can't tell him I've barely stopped thinking about my dad being

Santa since I left the grotto. Dad's been running away for most of my life. This is the first time I've ever seen him stop somewhere. And what Tav said on that first night whispers in my ear again. For years I've been telling him to "come home". What if Britain *isn't* his home anymore?

The whole sky bursts into life and it feels so fragile that even a breath too strong would blow it away.

'You never get used to it,' he whispers. 'No matter how long you live here, you never take it for granted. It's always new, always different, every night. Never any less awe-inspiring. In the millions of years this has been happening, it's never once been the same as it is tonight.'

I don't doubt that for a second. This is the kind of thing that you can never see enough of. That thought of going home flickers at the edges of my mind again, like a flame growing stronger. I didn't realise how much I'd always wanted to see the Northern Lights – it's something that was such an impossible dream that I put it out of my mind, locked tightly in the box labelled "things I'll never be brave enough to do" and now I can't imagine never seeing them again. And when I go home, I never will, will I? The southern, built-up county of Oxfordshire isn't exactly known for the Aurora Borealis.

Every star in the universe must be out tonight, twinkling down on us, the movement of the curtains of green gives the illusion that the stars are dancing in time with the lights. Shades of pink creep into each green splash and turn yellow before fading away completely, only to be replaced with more flowing streaks of light, and just watching them makes me emotional. When I blink and let my eyes close for a moment, tears form along my eyelashes and I have to scrub them away before they freeze to ice.

'I grew up in a city further south. The Northern Lights were never seen there. When I first moved here, it stopped me in my tracks. I spent so many nights outside, unable to tear my eyes away in case I missed even a glimpse.'

So he's not local. Despite spending more than a week in his company now, I still know barely anything about him. I'd assumed he was born and raised here. 'How long have you lived here?'

'A long time.'

And he's back to being his usual wordy self. I glance at him and he looks awkward and red-faced. Even that one sentence seems like more than he intended to reveal.

I look away when I feel his eyes on me too, like one of those ghosts in Super Mario games that hides whenever you look directly at it. I self-consciously fiddle with my hair. It was in a loose plait when I went to bed, but all the tossing and turning has pulled it half out and there are bits hanging around my shoulders that say "unkempt scarecrow" rather than "effortlessly sexy". I don't think I've ever said "effortlessly sexy" in my life, but if I'd expected to see him tonight, I'd have at least stuck a band around my hair or pulled a hat on.

Without realising it, my gaze has drifted from the sky to Tav again.

'What?' he whispers without looking at me.

I think about what Freya said about him working too much. I don't know what time it is, but it was past midnight when I last looked at the clock on the cabin wall and that was at least an hour ago. Even in the dark, I can tell there are shadows under his eyes. 'Are you as tired as you look?'

He lets out a short burst of laughter. 'I'm fine. But thank you, I wasn't self-conscious before but I am now.'

I can tell he's joking, but it's another evasive answer that doesn't tell me anything either way. 'How'd the roof repair go today?'

His head snaps down from looking at the sky, and when he meets my eyes, he looks like no one's ever asked him that before. 'You have *that* to look at and you want to talk to me?'

'Yes.' I do the best equivalent of crossing my arms defiantly that's possible while still holding a plastic mug. 'There's this phenomenon where you can use your eyes and mouth independently of each other and have actual conversations while looking at things.'

The thought of Tav and mouths makes me come over all hot – a truly impressive feat in these temperatures, but at least it gets a laugh out of him.

He doesn't answer for a while, and I think he's not going to, but eventually he says, 'I got there in the end. With you helping Percy, I didn't have anything to drag me away from it.'

Apart from clearing up the post office for me, I finish for him in my head.

'How about you? Read any gems tonight?' he asks, clearly wanting to change the subject.

'Children are really nice, aren't they?'

'That surprises you?'

'I . . . don't know. I guess I don't meet many children, but I didn't expect Santa letters to be what they are. I was just reading one from a girl who says she doesn't want a present this year because she's worried Santa works too hard and she wants to give him one less house to go to. And there's one girl in a right tizz because she doesn't know if Santa would prefer cookies and milk or a mince pie and sherry, and she's going to put out cookies and milk *and* a mince pie and sherry so Santa can have a choice, and she's read somewhere that reindeer prefer red peppers to carrots, but she doesn't have any and wonders if they'd accept a turnip instead. This is so real to children. I want to write back and tell her not to get so wound up over a fictional character and if anyone's eating anything on Christmas Eve night, it'll be the parents.'

'I don't have to tell you that you're not allowed to do that, do I?'

I give him such a scathing look that he laughs.

'There was one from a girl who says her mummy is in heaven and all she wants for Christmas is for Santa to get a message to his friend, God, to tell her mummy she loves her because she didn't have a chance to tell her before she went to heaven—' I didn't realise how much it had affected me until my voice breaks and tears spring to my eyes again.

His huge hand splays on my back, his fingers and thumb rubbing gently at five different points, nothing more than a soft pressure through the layers I'm wearing.

His silent support is something I've never felt before. He knows what happened to my mum – my dad has probably talked to him about it more than he's ever talked to me – but no one knows how alone I felt in my grief. Dad disappeared after Mum died, and was replaced by my nan, who moved into the cottage to look after me, but she was stoic and strong, of a generation that didn't show emotion, and she was mourning the loss of her daughter too. We existed in our grieving solitudes while Dad was off having the time of his life on his amazing adventures.

I have to stop thinking about it. 'I wanted to reply but I haven't got a clue what to say.'

'Just say you're sure her mum knew how much she loved her – mums always know. You lost your mum at a young age – of all people, *you* are the one person who *can* answer that letter. What would've helped you to hear when you were young?'

I look up. 'Go outside and whisper it to the night and trust that Mum will hear it. I had an appointment with a grief counsellor the school set up. It was pretty useless. The woman was stuffy and didn't seem to have ever lost anyone in her life, but one thing I did take from it was to write Mum letters telling her all the things I wished I could say. I did that for a couple of years, and it helped.'

'So tell her that. Don't pretend to be Santa responding. Be you.'

'Who would want a letter from me?'

'Who *wouldn't?*' He gives me a smile when I look at him disbelievingly. 'It's about knowing someone cares. Knowing someone read her letter and connected with it. Hearing from an adult who went through what she's going through and came out the other side. You can't underestimate the value of that – kids often feel like they're the only person who's ever dealt with what they're dealing with. And there are letter writing sets under the counter – you

141

could send her one of those as a gift. It might help.' His fingers rub minutely against my back where his hand is still splayed out. 'This is exactly what I wanted to achieve by accepting so much post, but I ran out of time, money, and if I'm honest, motivation. Seeing you get involved in this is inspirational. You don't realise how much of an asset you are to this place, Sash.'

'I don't think anyone's ever said anything that nice to me before,' I say carefully, trying to hide the wobble in my voice.

'Ah, come on. You've single-handedly turned around the fortunes of one of Britain's best hotels; you must be a massive asset to them.'

Oh, bollocks. *That.*

There's something playful in his voice and I'm once again sure he knows the truth, and when I don't say anything, he takes his hand away from my back. I try not to read into it, and look up at the lights instead, rivers of green, pink, and gold flashing through a purple sky.

'The Finns call them *revontulet*. They believe they're caused by the spirits of fire foxes running across the snow and sweeping the sky with their tails, sending up sparks when they brush against the mountains. The Sami people believe they're a bad omen and think it's dangerous to talk to them because they'll come down and take you away, but some cultures whistle to encourage them closer, believing they can pass on messages to the dearly departed.' He doesn't take his eyes off the sky as he speaks, and I realise I haven't taken my eyes off him for quite a while either. He looks down and meets my eyes and a shiver goes through him.

'Here, have half of this.' I've still got the blanket round my shoulders and I go to shrug it off, but he holds a hand up.

'I'm fine.'

'No, you're not, Tav. You're already tired and you're using extra energy to stay warm. You don't need to be all macho and chivalrous.' I hold one corner around me, and try to throw the

142

opposite corner over his shoulders, but it's as useless as trying to give a handkerchief to an elephant might be.

It's got to be minus-twenty out here tonight, and honestly the blanket probably isn't doing much to improve matters, but he doesn't need to be quite so stubborn.

After ineffectively throwing one side of the blanket at him a few times, he accepts that I'm not giving up and ducks enough to let me slip it over his shoulders. He refills our plastic mugs with still-warm hot chocolate, then his hand curls into the blanket and holds his half around himself, stooping so he doesn't pull it away from me, his arm pressing against mine.

'Do you want to walk out and see the igloos?' He inclines his mug in the direction of a small path past the post office building. 'It's the best viewing spot for seeing the lights.'

I glance up at him. The dark smudges under his eyes suggest he should be going home to bed, but I can't bring myself to let this night end so soon. 'I'd love to.'

'We're going to have to . . .' There are a few awkward steps as we try to negotiate walking with the joined blanket, our arms banging into each other, jostling the hot chocolate. Eventually he holds his arm out, inviting me to slip mine through and I do so gratefully. It's the only way this can possibly work.

The path leads up a gentle slope through a few sparse trees, so thick with frost that they block the view of the lights and I no longer have a distraction to look at, just the charged silence between me and Tav.

'I need to tell you something,' I blurt out as our feet crunch over frozen snow.

'Could it be that you're not a fancy hotel manager?'

'So you *do* know then?'

'I was curious when Percy kept talking about you. Intrigued to see this massive turnaround in your hotel's fortunes. He told me where you worked and I googled it. They have a staff list on their website and your name wasn't on there.'

'When was this?'

'Back in the summer, when he first started saying you were the person we needed to help us with this place.'

'Months ago?' I say in surprise. 'And you didn't tell him?'

'It's not for me to tell.'

Warmth floods my belly. That little feeling of him being on my side. 'Thank you.'

'It's none of my business. What's between you is between you. People often have reasons for telling a little white lie, and it's not for me to bluster through the middle of that.'

'Thanks, Tav,' I say again. I don't know why I'm so touched, but I've never felt like anyone was on my side before, and if he knew, I expected him to be running straight back to my father to tell him everything, and there's something really nice about the fact he isn't. 'Wait, you've known for months and you're just now telling me? I've been here for over a week and you've let me carry on lying by omission.'

'I was intrigued by how far you'd go with it, and I wanted to understand why. Besides, you've slipped up enough times in front of me that I'd have guessed by now anyway.'

I go so red that steam must start rising from my cheeks.

He squeezes my arm with his inner elbow where mine is still hooked through it. 'Don't be embarrassed. I'm honoured that you let your guard down in front of me. Because I don't. I can't let my guard down in front of *anyone*.'

I've definitely gathered that much. I glance up at him but he keeps his eyes on the snowy ground we're adding the first set of footprints to.

'It wasn't meant to be a lie,' I start and his arm holds mine a little tighter. 'I did work at the hotel as a receptionist, answering the phones, taking bookings, that sort of thing. When the job opening for a manager came up, I applied. I didn't have any managerial experience, but I'd worked there for a couple of months, I was good with customers, and the other staff all thought I had

144

a great chance of getting it. Dad phoned as I was rushing out the door to the interview and I quickly garbled that explanation, and he assumed the job would be mine. And then I didn't get it. And I couldn't bring myself to tell him. He was so pleased that I was finally going somewhere with my life, and I didn't want to disappoint him yet again. And then he saw something online about this hotel's change in fortunes, and he was so proud of me, and he'd never been proud of me before . . .'

'Who wouldn't be proud of you?'

It makes me blush. 'He's never been proud of me. I've never been what he wanted.'

Tav nearly stumbles over his own feet and the movement yanks me to a halt. His hand reaches out like he's going to tuck my hair back, hovering in mid-air in front of me. 'I'm sure that's not true . . .'

The blanket drops off his shoulders and his arm gets tighter around my arm, and I relish in it for a moment. 'He wanted a daughter who'd go on adventures with him, and I don't like to leave the house unless it's absolutely necessary. I don't want to go river rafting down the raging Nile or go on a walking safari through the lion-infested grasslands of Zimbabwe. Every time I speak to him, he asks me to go to some far-off place and I always say no, and he can't hide the disappointment.'

He looks at me for a long moment, and I get the feeling he wants to say something, but eventually he sighs and looks away. 'Yeah, well, I'm with you when it comes to disappointing family.' He gathers up the blanket again and strides off, and I have to dash to keep up.

It intrigues me, but like with everything else, I expect pushing him will cause him to clam up entirely. He's practically running away from me already. So far tonight, I know he's not from here originally, and he's disappointed his family at some point, and it seems like those are two very small pieces in the jigsaw puzzle that is Tav.

I can see the silhouettes of glass igloos spread out across an open space, and as we step out of the trees, there's a panoramic view of the whole horizon. I spin around, trying to take in the 360-degree view all at once. Tav was *not* kidding when he said this is the best spot.

'This is unreal.' It feels like I can see every inch of the Northern Lights. The mountains are low and the sky is all-consuming, and nothing encroaches on it. You see places like this on TV, but this is *real*, and I'm *really* here.

'It's one of our most popular areas. The idea was to diversify from *just* Christmas and appeal to different kinds of people, adults without children who otherwise wouldn't want to come here, and I also wanted to tap into the privilege of living here and having such an incredible view of the Northern Lights each night. It's something that deserves to be shared.'

I walk over to an igloo and cup my hands around my eyes to peer in. Each one has got a double bed in the centre with enough room to walk around it, and then the arched doorway leading in is made of covered glass that conceals a tiny kitchen area and bathroom. They're small enough to look inviting even though the idea of sleeping in a greenhouse at minus-twenty shouldn't be appealing. 'They're not very private, are they? It gives a whole new meaning to that Christmas song – Santa can, quite literally, see you when you're sleeping. And so can anyone else who happens along. That's not creepy *at all*.'

He lets out such a hard laugh that he leans a hand on the glass to keep himself upright. 'Do you want to go in?'

He pushes the door open, holding it for me to step inside, and then he ducks through the doorway and closes it behind him. His hands touch my shoulders as he urges me further in until he can get to a control panel on the wall and press some buttons. A row of lights illuminate around the bottom edge, and warm air instantly starts filtering in from an inbuilt heating system.

'Sit?' Tav indicates towards the bed, and I perch on the edge and lean forwards to hold my hands over the vents where warm air is coming in. My hands tingle with pins and needles as the numbness dissipates.

'You must be freezing too.'

He looks at me with that soft smile. 'I'm fine.'

I don't think he's ever given any *other* answer to that question. He's still holding the mug like it's warm, even though the contents have almost definitely turned to ice by now.

When I can feel my limbs again, I shuffle backwards on the bed until I'm sitting against the headboard, and have got a soft headrest to lean my head on.

When he's decided I'm comfortable, he turns the light off, shrouding us in darkness that makes it easier to see the lights above. Instead of sitting like I thought he would, Tav stays at the edge of the igloo, leaning against the frame, his fingers red from the cold, still curled around the empty plastic mug like it can somehow warm him.

'Aren't you going to sit?'

'If I sit down, I'll fall asleep.'

'Ah-ha! So you *are* tired.'

Even in the low light, I can see his raised eyebrow. 'It's a little strange how happy that makes you.'

'I meant because I was right, not because I'm happy you're overworked.' I roll my eyes. 'If you fall asleep, I'll carry you to bed.'

He bursts out laughing. 'You couldn't carry one of my *legs*, never mind the rest of me.'

'We're in an igloo. You'd be sitting on a bed – there are worse places to fall asleep.'

He flashes his eyebrows at me.

'Sit, Tav. Please,' I say after a couple of minutes. 'And don't tell me it's easier not to sit down because it'll be harder to get back up. All that shows is how much you need to rest.'

He shakes his head with a tight smile.

'Right, I'm not above brute force.' I vault myself back up and stalk

147

around the igloo to him. I remove the cup from his hands and put it down on a shelf, wrap both my hands around his forearm and pull.

He raises an eyebrow but doesn't budge an inch. Time for a different tactic.

I go up the entrance step so I'm approximately two centimetres taller than I was before, which obviously makes *so* much difference, get both hands on his upper arm and start pushing.

He raises the other eyebrow.

'For God's sake, Tav. It's too cold to go back outside yet, so we're stopping here for a bit. You're not just going to stand there. If you need to fall asleep that badly then your body is trying to tell you something. Sit down.' I fold my arms and raise an eyebrow, giving him the sternest look in the history of the world.

He holds my gaze, his eyes not hiding his surprise, and I think he's going to refuse, but eventually his shoulders droop and his arms sag. Even his head drops and he shuffles over and perches on the edge of the bed, and the whole thing tips towards him under his weight.

'Good.' I give him a "so there" nod and go back around to my side.

'Do you know how long it's been since someone bossed me around?' he says as I wriggle around to get comfortable, kicking my boots off and sitting back against the headboard again.

I cross my ankles over each other on the bed. 'What I want to know is how long it's been since someone realised that being six-foot-six doesn't make you invulnerable.'

The hitch in his breath is sharp and audible in the otherwise silent night. He looks over his shoulder and meets my eyes before he swallows and looks away. 'Last time a doctor checked, it was six-foot-seven actually.'

My ears prick up. Why would he be measured by a doctor? His shoulders were tense anyway, but from the way they've gone absolutely rigid, I don't think he meant to say that much. Maybe he is capable of letting his guard down after all.

We sit there in silence for a while, his shoulders never losing their tension, his head tilted upwards, but I get the feeling he's not really watching the lights, and even though his back is to me, I'm struggling to take my eyes off him. I *know* I shouldn't say anything else, but I can't help myself. 'People don't reach your level of hyper-independence without being hurt, Tav. Refusal to rely on anybody and being so determined to do *everything* yourself is a result of your ability to trust being so badly damaged that you don't think it can ever recover.'

'That's a very generalised assumption.'

'Yes it is.' I look over at him. 'I also think it's true.'

As is tradition, he doesn't give anything away. 'You're missing the lights.'

I force my attention back upwards, but his shoulders sag after that. His hands come up to his knees and he rests his chin on them, watching the lights straight ahead instead of above like I am, and I hope my reflection in the glass doesn't give away how often my eyes flick to him, or how often his head keeps jerking up like he's dozed off and woken up sharply.

Eventually I can't take it anymore. 'Can I touch you?'

'People don't touch me, Sash.' His voice is deep and rough with exhaustion.

I've got a choice to make here. I think he'll bolt if I touch him without permission, so I can either leave it at that or push him even though I don't know him well enough to know which way he'll react.

'Well, new experiences are good for us.' I turn his own words from the other day back on him. He's too tired to have his walls fully up and I can't help picking at the tiny cracks that are showing through. 'Character building and such.'

He laughs. 'I brought that one on myself, didn't I?'

He considers it for a moment and then toes his boots off and pushes himself back on the bed so he's sitting nearer, cross-legged instead of perched on the edge, his back still to me, and I shift over and touch my hands to his shoulders.

He's still got his coat on and a thick jumper underneath, and God knows how many layers under that, so it's not exactly an intimate massage, but I rub his shoulders, trying to ease out some of the tension that's clear in every angle of his body.

'Oh, ho-ly night.' He puts a *long* extension on the O. 'It should be illegal how good that is.'

It makes me laugh out loud and my hands tighten on his shoulders. It *isn't* a good massage – it can't be with so many layers between us, but it confirms I did the right thing.

His elbows slip off his knees and his arms fall down limply, and his head drops forward. He grunts and groans, making little noises of pleasure with every movement. I can feel his shoulders loosening with every press and push and his moans get so risqué that I'd blush if this wasn't the least intimate setting and we weren't both done up like Michelin men.

'Is masseuse your regular job?' His words sound like they're already slurring into one.

I laugh again. 'No.'

'Seriously.' After a few moments, he lifts his head and looks back at me through heavy-lidded eyes. 'I want to know. If you don't work at a hotel, what do you really do?'

I use the angle of his head to move further up his neck, being careful not to stray off the coat, and his eyes close while I'm holding his gaze.

It's my turn to groan. 'At the moment I don't do anything. My friend owns a dog grooming parlour and I've been helping out there, but her sister-in-law lost her job so she let me go. I'll start job-hunting again in January when we go back.' A cold shiver slides down my spine that has nothing to do with the temperature. The thought of going back to normal life after spending Christmas here seems so much more impossible than I ever expected. The North Pole Forest is like a little glowing gem in the middle of the woods and once you know it's here, you can't ever un-know it.

'Do you want to work with animals again?'

'Honestly, at this point, it's any job that will have me. I've got the cottage to look after, and if Dad's with me . . .' The image of him in his Santa grotto floats across my mind again. He's never going to get that in the UK. What is he going to do back there? Draw his pension and join one of those Santa agencies that send Santas out to supermarkets or shopping centres? Give it up entirely? What about all the Santa mail? He won't be able to get any of that in the UK . . .

'But what do you *want* to do? Isn't that important?' Tav's Norwegian accent sounds stronger as he relaxes and his long, long spine curves forward.

'I don't know. I've never known. I worked from dead-end job to dead-end job, until I got fired or the companies downsized or went into administration. I'd just lost a supermarket job a couple of years ago and Debra asked if I wanted to take some dogs on walks and it morphed into being her general assistant.'

'Only to throw you away as soon as someone better came along?' He's quiet for a moment. 'Sorry, I didn't mean someone *better* than you, I meant . . .'

'It's okay. It's the truth. I'm never a priority in anyone's life. I'm just there, existing on the sidelines. I come in useful when someone needs something. I don't think the people I call my friends would even notice if I disappeared. I didn't tell anyone I was coming here. How sad is that? There's no one *to* tell. No one who will notice I'm not there. No one to wonder where I've gone.'

'That's impossible. I've only known you a week and I can tell you're going to leave a gigantic hole in my life when you leave.'

For just a second, I stop breathing. It's like there's a lump in my throat and I'm not sure if I'm going to cry or throw my arms around him. Or possibly both.

'It must be quite an event for you to have a conversation with someone who's not a reindeer,' I grate out eventually.

My emotion must be audible because he looks over his shoulder at me again before he answers. 'Something like that.'

I squirm under his gaze, because the idea of *not* knowing him, of going home and pretending I never came here and never met him, leaving him to deal with whatever the consequences of selling this place will be . . . It prickles at me worse than the pins and needles of earlier.

I use the different angle of his neck to rub at a knot I can *see* under his collar and his eyes close again and he lets out a debauched moan and faces front, his chin dropping onto his chest.

The long and straight front parts of his hair have fallen forward and my fingers twitch with the urge to tuck it back. He looks dishevelled and softer than usual. He's usually so sarcastic and barbed, and I know just from how relaxed he is that I've got at least one brick out of his wall tonight.

They are scars on his neck. I thought I could see them the other day but I wasn't sure. Barely visible marks and silvery lines in the thin skin. His hair is long enough to cover them, but I catch a glimpse when his head drops forward. I want to reach out and touch, pretend it's part of the massage, but I keep my hands firmly on his coat-covered shoulders. And I definitely don't have the urge to lean forward and press my lips to the back of his neck.

I have absolutely no doubt that if I asked about them, he'd bolt upright and run away, so I steadfastly ignore how anyone gets scars like that on the back of their neck or how many more his thick hair hides. It isn't my business. I shouldn't have to keep reminding myself that I barely know this man. Whatever scars he hides are nothing to do with me.

I don't realise my hands have stilled on Tav's shoulders until he reaches back, slips his fingers around mine and lifts my arm over his head and away, and without letting go, lies down and shifts until his head is resting on the pillow. He tugs at my hand until I do the same.

'My limbs feel like blancmange after that,' he says as I get comfortable, keeping a space between us even though his fingers are still curled around mine. 'I don't think I could walk if I tried.'

He must be being sarcastic because a quick shoulder rub through layers thicker than the earth's core does *not* have that sort of effect on anyone, but we lie there in comfortable silence for a while, watching the phenomenon of Mother Nature above. The stars have moved across the sky since we got here, and lying here looking up, it's like we can see the world turning. I've never known anything like this before.

And I feel ridiculously lucky. I never dreamed I'd ever get to see the Northern Lights, and now getting to fall asleep under them is a normal part of my life.

'He *is* proud of you, Sash.' Tav's voice is barely a whisper.

'Yeah, for a job I don't even do.'

'No, for *you*.' His hand squeezes mine to punctuate his words. 'It isn't my place to get involved, but he has huge regrets about how things have gone between you two. He talked about it a lot after the heart attack. Something like that makes you think . . . a life flashing before your eyes thing . . . He wasn't proud of himself. He knows he's let you down. I think that's the main reason he asked you to come – because he was terrified of dying without making things right between you.'

His words make me feel emotional for a multitude of reasons – my dad thinking that, Tav being kind enough to tell me, and the fear of losing my dad. It's dissipated since I got here, seeing him happy and a far cry from how ill he sounded on the phone, but hearing that brings back how close his brush with death was and how easily he could have another one. I nudge my elbow into his arm on the bed. 'Not because he wanted my help as a fancy hotel manager then?'

Tav lifts his head and fixes me with a look that says he can see right through my false attempt at humour.

I sigh as he settles back again. 'I was seventeen when my nan died. It was the first Christmas I'd been alone for. He promised he'd come home for it. It would be the first time I'd seen him in nearly five years. I was so excited. My nan had been anti-Christmas and neither of us felt like celebrating with Mum gone and Dad away, but that year because he was coming back, I went all out. I couldn't afford it, but I put up a huge tree with all our old family decorations, I got a turkey, all the trimmings, festive food, crackers, silly jumpers, Santa hats, mince pies, the lot, and he rang on Christmas Eve to say his flight had been cancelled. The following year, it was because snowfall had closed the road to the airport. One year, he rang me on Boxing Day because he'd been out of signal up a waterfall in Thailand to tell me he wouldn't be able to make it home for Christmas, which I'd pretty much worked out for myself by Boxing Day. Every year, there's some outlandish excuse or another. He can't just admit he doesn't want to come back. That would be easier to take.'

'That's why you're not a Christmas fan?'

I nod, our heads so close he can feel it. 'Christmas isn't fun when you're on your own. It reminds you of the people who aren't there.'

His fingers tighten around mine. 'You're not on your own this year.'

I have to blink fast to stop my eyes filling up. There's something about Tav. I don't know if it's his size or his competency at just about everything, or the sense of protectiveness that comes from being near him, the fact he saved my dad's life or what Dad's said about him being a good friend. He's the sort of person who I wish there were more of in my life. 'What is it about you? Why do you make everything seem better than it is?'

'I don't know what you're talking about – there's nothing about me.' He's smiling as he says it.

There's definitely something about him.

'You should talk to him, Sash.' His whispered voice is serious again. 'I know Christmases have been difficult, and a huge part of that is his fault, but an accident like the one your parents had, losing your mum like that . . . It changes a person. Maybe it's not that he hasn't wanted to see *you*, but he hasn't been able to *face* the past. And right now, he misses you as much as you miss him. That has to count for something.'

I don't reply. I know he doesn't expect me to. The sky shimmers and changes as we watch it. The stars twinkle through the stripes of green light, making it look like someone's up there brushing glitter paint across the universe.

I can feel Tav's breathing evening out, feel his pulse slowing down where it's beating against my fingers, and when I shift my head far enough back to see his face, he's blinking long and slow, and with every blink, I think he's going to fall asleep right there.

His eyes are barely open, but he can obviously sense me looking at him. He pulls his hand out of mine and stumbles upright, goes to a chest at the bottom of the bed and pulls out an armful of fluffy blankets and tosses a couple to me, which is an impressive feat for someone who's ninety-five per cent asleep already.

He flops back down beside me, stretching a blanket over himself too, and wriggles around to get comfortable.

'Sash,' he murmurs. He holds his hand out from under the blanket and I slip mine into it again. 'Thank you.'

He curls towards me and snuggles down, his forehead nearly on my shoulder, my hand still in his as he drifts off.

'Goodnight, Tav,' I murmur, leaning to the side so my cheek presses against his hair.

He takes care of everyone else, but doesn't allow anyone to take care of him, and it's about time someone pushed that wall down, brick by brick.

Chapter 9

Dear Santa,
For Christmas, can you get the teachers to stop giving us homework? And an Xbox to use up some of the time now there won't be any homework?
From,
Dylan

Tav's gone when I wake up, and the blanket that was covering him is now over me as well. It feels like so many hours have passed that I expect it to be late afternoon, but the clock beside the bed shows it's only half past eight. Any hint of the Northern Lights is long gone, and on the bed beside me is Tav's compass and a piece of paper, and when I pick it up to decipher, it's a map of the path to follow to get back to the main part of the Christmas village.

He must've thought I wouldn't recognise it because it was dark last night. I smile as I fold up the blankets and return them to the storage chest. My thumb rubs over the face of his compass when I pick it up. He's the most thoughtful person. He seems to think of everything. It makes him seem caring in a way that no one else in my life is. It was good of him to say what he said about Dad last night. I know he doesn't want to get involved; I get the feeling he's the type of guy who stays far away from conflict of any sort, but he knew I needed to hear it.

Thankfully the control panel I saw him open last night is simple to operate and I turn off the heat and step out the door. A fresh dumping of snow has obliterated his footprints already, and I follow his map and emerge next to the post office we left last night.

It won't be daylight for hours yet, and the lights are on in Dad's house but I go up to Candy Cane Cabin for a quick shower and change, put my hair up in a neat ponytail, and get back down the hill in record timing.

'Good morning!' I call as I open the door and pull my boots off.

'Didn't expect to see you so early.' Dad steps out of the living room with his hands wrapped around a cup of coffee.

I give him a morning hug. 'Is Tav here?'

'Not yet.' He gives me a knowing look. 'But that explains why you're so eager. And I did happen to see Tav doing the "walk of shame" this morning.'

I go red even though there's nothing to be ashamed of. 'There is no walk of shame. We fell asleep in an igloo under the Northern Lights. That's it. Nothing happened, certainly nothing like what you're hinting at.' I think for a moment. 'It's the most romantic thing I've ever done with someone I'm not romantically involved with.'

'And—'

'And never will be,' I interrupt. There are enough problems around here without my dad trying to imply something between me and Tav.

'Ah, so I made it before him . . .' I realise what that means. 'For a change of pace, I'm making breakfast today, and Tav . . . isn't.'

'He won't like that.'

I give him a curious look.

'Tav doesn't like people doing things for him. He's very independent.'

157

"Very" is *very* much an understatement. 'Well, Tav is going to have to like it or lump it. He's got enough to do as it is and I didn't come here to be waited on.'

'I knew you'd be the tonic we needed.' Dad sips his coffee. 'What are we having?'

'Mum's mince pies,' I say without thinking about it. There isn't much I can make, but the things that have stayed with me over the years are the things Mum showed me how to make when I was little.

Dad swallows and looks down. 'Been a few years since I had them.'

Tav's right about needing to talk to him, and this seems like a good opening. 'I make them every year. Maybe if you'd come home more oft—'

Dad turns his head sharply towards the snowman-shaped clock on the wall. 'Tav's going to be here any minute; you'd best get a move on.'

I sigh again. He closes down any conversation that strays too far towards the past, but he *has* got a point about the time.

'How long ago did you see him?' I ask as Dad directs me around the kitchen to find ingredients.

'About half hour ago, not long before you walked back.'

'Good, that means he slept,' I say to myself, and then turn to Dad. 'Do you sit here spying on your staff all morning or what?'

'I like to watch the world go by. It's so beautiful here, Sasha. Like living in a Christmas card. I can sit in front of that window all day watching the snow coming down.'

'But you can't . . .' I see an opportunity to bring up the topic of staying here, but I trail off and it jangles unsaid through the atmosphere between us.

Dad clonks his mug down loudly on the counter. 'You've noticed that he doesn't, then?'

'Doesn't what?' I'm distracted by the change of subject. I should've said something. We keep skirting around my reason for coming here, the idea that somehow, at some point, I'm going to *have* to follow through on my plan of getting an estate agent involved, but every time I think about it, I put off bringing it up just a little bit longer.

'Sleep.' Dad's gone back to my earlier comment. 'He's always so busy. He struggles to switch off at night.'

'Or he's got so much to do that he *has* to work twenty-four-hour days to even make a dent in his to-do list. You need some help around here, someone to look after you. Both of you.'

'I thought I needed to sell up?'

I look at him across the kitchen and it's like there's an ice-cold thread winding between us. 'Er, yeah. That.' I drop his gaze, annoyed at myself for still not broaching the subject. That was the perfect chance, but every time I even *think* about suggesting we call someone to survey the place and put a value on it, a stone of nausea settles into the pit of my stomach.

I take my frustration out on the pastry mixture as I rub the butter into the flour and sugar. Dad slurps from his mug, deliberately making noise to fill the silence. I know I should talk to him and not let him get away with changing the subject, but it's a nice morning and it feels wrong to create an atmosphere between us.

'What's his story, Dad?' I ask when I press the shortbread-like dough into tins and spoon the filling in.

'I don't think I'm the person you want to hear that from, do you?'

I'm impressed that even after so many years apart, my dad can still read me so well. What I want is for Tav to open up to *me*, not to hear second-hand information from someone who wouldn't betray his trust anyway.

'And honestly, Sash, I don't know what his story is. I've known him for a fair few years now, and he's never shared much. He makes life so much harder for himself though. Like how he always insists on going everywhere by reindeer-pulled sleigh. My truck is right outside, the keys are by the door, I'm always telling him

159

to use it but he refuses. The way he insists on doing absolutely *everything* himself. And it's not just him being protective because he's young and I'm old – he's always been like that. He's half-inspirational-quote and half-Grinch. He's bright and sunny and yet dark and distrusting. There's nothing he doesn't know about the land and he's an absolute whizz with reindeer. The height hides the gentlest soul. Do you know he sends food packages and clothing vouchers to families who are in trouble out of his own pocket, and he thinks I don't realise he's doing it.'

It makes me burst out laughing as I close the oven door on the mince pies. Maybe my dad and I aren't the only ones miscommunicating around here. 'He thinks you'd be mad at him—'

I stop at the sound of the front door opening and Tav's voice calls out. 'Good morning.'

I rush through the living room and into the hallway where he's pulling his boots off in the doorway. 'Good morning.'

He looks up mid-boot-pull and smiles, and we hold each other's gaze until he overbalances and has to grab the doorframe to stay upright.

I hover in the living room doorway, unsure of how to greet him after last night.

Once free of the boots, Tav walks over to me. He's wearing his usual snow trousers and a heavy winter jumper in deep burgundy with cable-knit lines of white running through it. His dark hair is windblown and he shakes it back and pulls off his gloves.

'Good morning,' he repeats, and we seem to be in a competition to see who can repeat those words the most times in the shortest period.

His hand lifts, reaching out towards me hesitantly, and I'm not sure if we should hug or if he's trying to politely move me out of the way so he can get past. My hand automatically reaches out too, my fingers brushing his forearm, and he bends down, and it turns into an awkward one-armed half-hug thing where we're both using the wrong arm and there's far too much distance between us for it to be a hug. He's so uneasy, the opposite of how relaxed he was last night, and I've gone from being confident in bossing him around to unsure of how to act around him, when all I really want to do is pull him down and wrap him in a tight hug.

Like he can sense this, he pulls away and stands up so sharply that his head collides with the top of the doorframe with an audible bang.

He doesn't react, but I wince on his behalf. 'Okay, serious question – how many times have you knocked yourself out on doorframes around here?'

He laughs out loud. 'Enough times that I don't even notice anymore. My forehead is full of dents. Here, feel.' He bends low enough that I can easily reach, and without thinking about it, my thumb runs across his forehead and my fingers slide through the long front of his hair, stroking it back. I was probably only supposed to do it once, but his eyes close and his head grows heavy in my hand, like the touch has eased the tension between us.

And then I realise that in the middle of a joking conversation, I've reached up and touched a complete stranger's head, and I pull back so quickly that it makes him jump.

He shakes himself and points towards the kitchen. 'I should . . .'

'Yeah.' We do the dance of awkwardly squeezing past each other in the living room doorway, and he goes to walk across the room, but I stop him. 'Hey, Tav . . .'

I hold my hand out and scrunch my fingers to make him do the same, and then fish his compass out of my pocket. 'I believe this is yours.'

I place it in his open palm and he looks down at my fingers holding the polished sliver disc against his hand.

He swallows and his tongue wets his lips. 'Maybe the *nisse* left it.'

'Maybe they did.' I support his hand with one of mine and use my other to close his fingers around it one by one. 'They're very thoughtful elves.'

A smile twitches his lips, and when I go to pull away, his thumb catches my index finger and closes over it, holding it against his palm, and I get lost in his eyes. In that moment, there is nothing but Tav's blue-brown eyes, a mix of two colours that change with the light and reflect the multicoloured twinkling coming from the Christmas tree, and I lose all sense of time passing.

Until Dad clears his throat from the kitchen and we yank our hands back so sharply that there's a good possibility I've just dislocated my wrist.

'Now go on.' I shoo him towards the kitchen where Dad's already back on his stool at the kitchen island. 'I'm making breakfast. Have a seat.'

Tav looks like he's going to object, but I fold my arms and raise my sternest eyebrow. 'Don't make me start shoving you because you know I will.'

'Oh, not again,' he says with a laugh, but sits on the stool next to Dad. 'Help me, Perce, your daughter's bossing me around again.'

'Ah yes, something as unspeakably evil as trying to make you sit down,' Dad says with a laugh.

Tav's eyes are on me as I move around the kitchen. 'Can I help? Make the coffees or something?'

'It's all under control,' I say. 'Dad's already had his and I'm fairly sure people who have had heart attacks are meant to be on limited caffeine, so he's not having another one no matter how longingly he looks at the machine.'

Dad sulks so hard that I can *hear* it.

'Let me get the plates out, at least.' The stool scrapes the floor as Tav moves and I spin around and point a pastry brush at him, flicking it downwards so he sits again with a sigh.

I lean my elbows on the island directly opposite him and duck my head until his eyes meet mine. His hands are balled on the counter and I reach across and slide my fingers over the top of them. 'Taavi.'

He raises an eyebrow. 'No one calls me that.'

I glare at him for trying to change the subject. 'Tell me

162

something. What's the worst that can happen by allowing someone to cook breakfast? Have you previously been poisoned by someone cooking you breakfast? Do you think I'm going to accidentally mix in bits of broken glass instead of flour or something? Do you think a misplaced gecko is going to leap out of your mince pie and attack you?'

He slips one of his hands out from under mine and rests his chin on it uninterestedly. 'Burning.'

'Someone's burnt your breakfast in the past?' I say in confusion.

'No.' He inclines his head towards the oven. '*Burning*.'

I turn around at the exact moment the smoke alarm starts shrieking and black smoke fills the kitchen. I let out a string of swearwords that are definitely *not* "Oh, holy night" as I dash back to the oven and rescue the tray of mince pies, and lean over the counter to throw the window open, narrowly missing the reindeer in the backyard again.

Tav's jumped up to reassure the smoke alarm it's under control and impressively, sat back down again while I flap around a tea towel to disperse the smoke. He's laughing so hard that the stool nearly topples over.

Even the reindeer has stuck her head in the window to have a look, her furry nose twitching as she sniffs the air.

'Hello, lovely,' I say to her. Without a word, I step backwards until I can reach across the island, and Tav deposits the lichen I knew he'd have in his pocket into my hand, and I go back and hold it out to the reindeer, waiting for her to take it from me, her antlers banging against the open window.

'Hold on, who's that?' Tav's voice makes me jump, and my jump startles the reindeer, who takes off running across the garden and disappears between the trees. He's suddenly behind me, his body pressing against mine as he peers out the window. 'That wasn't one of ours.'

'She's around often. Seems friendly enough. You have loads. How can you possibly tell?'

163

'You can tell.' He nudges his arm against mine and nods to the smouldering mince pies. 'Now I'm up, can I help?'

'You're incorrigible,' I tell him and point him back to his seat in no uncertain terms. One culinary disaster doesn't change things. At all.

'Well, that was the most interesting breakfast I've had for a while,' Tav says as we step out the door half an hour later. It's still dark but the sky looks lighter than it was, like the winter sun isn't far below the horizon.

Dad's gone to set up his grotto, and Tav's insisted on walking me to the post office.

'See what I mean about sitting down and giving in to it?' he says as soon as we get a few steps away from the house. "If I'd stayed standing up, that wouldn't have happened last night.'

'Does it matter? You slept well, right?'

'Yeah, but . . .'

'Then I regret nothing.' I cut him off before he can finish that sentence. 'And neither do you, in case you were wondering.'

He laughs and knocks his arm against mine. 'Thank you for breakfast. It wasn't bad at all. When you cut off the burnt bits.'

The jokey tone in his voice makes me laugh. 'I'm out of practice. I don't cook for other people very often.' I don't add that in terms of cooking for other people, the most that could be counted lately is opening tins of dog food at work.

'And I don't let other people cook for me, but . . .'

'New experiences are good for us.' We finish the sentence in unison, meet each other's eyes and burst into laughter.

I like how easy he is to be around. I feel like I've known him for much longer than the week or so I have, and walking along with him, laughing with him, teasing each other a little bit . . . It feels like something I didn't know was missing from my life.

I'm walking fast because I'm excited to get to the post office, and it's had the counterproductive effect of cutting down the walk with Tav, because we're at the door before I know it, and Tav looks up at it like he didn't expect it either.

We stop at the bottom of the ramp and kind of hover. I don't want him to go yet, and he's lingering like maybe he doesn't want to go yet either.

He ducks his head and his hair falls forward, hiding part of his face, but not hiding his smile. My nails dig into my palms as I fight the urge to reach up and tuck it back. His hair naturally looks like he's just pushed it back with his hands, but he doesn't seem to use any product so it falls and flops every time he moves, and I really want to brush my fingers through it again.

'I should . . .' He points back towards the Gingerbread Cabin that he's still repairing.

'You didn't have to come out of your way for me.'

'It's dark.' He ignores the fact that it's almost always dark and I'm quite capable of carrying a torch and there are loads of streetlamps. 'And I wanted . . .' His voice cuts off and he has to swallow and start again. 'I wanted to say thank you for last night. It's been a long time since I slept like that or since my shoulders had the range of movement they've got this morning.'

'Good.' I go to reach up and touch his shoulder but stop myself at the last minute.

He notices, and then holds his arms open, inviting a hug. 'C'mere.'

If I had time to think about it, I'd probably be nervous of getting close to him, but it's automatic to step into his arms and let them circle around my waist and draw me to him.

He's so all-consuming that it's like being swathed by his body. His bitter almond cologne fills my senses. His arms could probably wrap around me three times, even in this puffy coat, but they tighten to the perfect degree – warm, safe, and protective.

I let one of my hands trail up his arm, stroking across his shoulder, my fingertips skimming the back of his neck over the edge of his coat collar. I don't want to make it obvious I saw those

165

scars last night, and a shiver goes through him but he doesn't pull away. He holds tighter, curls further around me, folds me in closer, and all my worries melt away in his arms. His stubble scratches against the side of my neck where he tucks his head into my shoulder, his soft hair tangling with mine, and I finally give in and let my other hand come up to blindly brush it back, and instead of doing that once and letting go, my fingers curl into the strands and grip it to hold him in place.

His breath is against my neck as he lets out a long, slow sigh, and his shoulders sag so much that he nearly stumbles and has to plant his feet firmer on the ground to keep us both upright.

I should probably pull away, *definitely* pull away, but everything is so peaceful that I can't bring myself to move. All I can hear is the steady thrum of my own heartbeat, overexcited by this closeness, Tav's breathing, and the chirrup of birds in the trees around us.

It starts snowing again, and it's so quiet that I'm sure I can hear the sound of the snow itself drifting down. A snowflake lands on the back of my neck and makes me shiver, and Tav goes to pull away but I make a noise of disappointment and every part of me clings on tighter, and I feel his lips shift into a smile against my neck and he holds me closer again.

I don't know what's got into me. I've never thought I was a particularly huggy person, let alone the kind of person who doesn't want a hug to end, but I can't persuade myself to pull away, not even after we've stood there for an abnormal length of time.

I don't think there's ever been a better hug in the history of the world.

Eventually, he groans like he's waking up from sleep and slowly starts unfurling himself from my body finger by finger, and then one limb at a time, and I find myself shivering at the coldness seeping in after the body contact had blocked it out.

I laugh at the sight of the snowflakes that have settled in his dark hair, especially when he goes to shake them out, the long front of his hair pulled forward and whipping side to side, and without

166

thinking, I reach up to brush them out and he bends to let me, even though it's coming down so fast that more have already settled.

Eventually he pushes it back, pulls a Nordic-patterned knit hat out of his pocket and jams it onto his head.

'See you later?' He takes what I convince myself is a reluctant step away.

I garble out something that bears no resemblance to the calm, dignified, 'Yes, that will be lovely, see you later too,' that I hear in my head.

His grin says he didn't hear what I heard either. 'May you have a downward road all the way to your door.'

'Have you recently escaped from a Christmas cracker with your motivational sayings and bad jokes?' I call after him and his laughter echoes back to me as he walks away.

I shake my head to clear it and have to blink a few times to remind myself of where I am and what I'm doing.

If you've ever imagined hugging a mountain, that's probably what it would be like. If the mountain was gorgeous, funny, kind, and really, really warm. I've never known anyone who hugs like Tav does.

It's cosy in the post office and I'm still reading through the impossible backlog of letters when Freya knocks with over 6000 more.

'Never seen Tav with such a spring in his step,' she comments, peering in the door at the newly cleared post office. 'You happen to look like the Arctic air is agreeing with you too, Sasha.'

I feel different too. I hadn't realised it before, but something about this place *is* agreeing with me. I thought I'd hate it, I thought it would be freezing and scary and uninhabitable, but it's the opposite of all those things. Apart from when you hear a rustling in the trees late at night.

On cue, my dad "ho ho ho"s his way past with a group of children in tow. He waves when he sees us, and the children all turn in our direction, and my dad tells them we're the post box elves.

167

'I just met Tav bringing the reindeer out,' Freya says. 'Kids get more excited about them than Santa sometimes.'

'One of yesterday's letters was from a little boy wanting to know *everything* about them. What they like to eat, what they do when they're not flying, how long it takes them to learn to fly and if they have reindeer runways and need a licence like pilots do . . . It's so sweet. I never knew this whole Christmas thing mattered so much to kids. I thought it was all just circling things in the Argos catalogue for the parents to get . . . Well, I suppose it would be adding things to an Amazon wish list nowadays, wouldn't it?'

'Exactly why handwritten letters are so important. Any to go out today?'

'Plenty!' I drag today's delivery inside and return with yesterday's bags full of outgoing mail – letters I've replied to, and packages of little gifts, something from Santa's village to make children smile.

As Freya leaves, I notice she's looking around like she's searching for someone – probably the man Tav mentioned. That brief encounter must've meant so much to her to still hold out hope even so many months later. We'd need a Christmas miracle *and* an overflowing vat of Christmas magic to find him again.

Back inside, I finish off my reply to a young girl who's having trouble sleeping and is worried Santa will see she's awake and not come, and then I make a start on today's bags.

The first few letters are lists of presents so I drop them into the box for things we can't help with, but then the next one is from a ten-year-old boy.

> *Dear Santa, we have everything we need this Christmas, and my mummy and daddy always get us lots of presents, so don't worry about us, but for my Christmas present this year, could you please keep the homeless man and his dog who live under the bridge by my house warm, safe, and healthy?*

It makes tears prickle my eyes again. I never knew children could be so thoughtful and so observant of the world around them. At first I file it as a letter I can't do anything about, but then an idea dawns on me.

The boy has put a return address on the envelope, and I open Tav's laptop and put the postcode into Google Maps, locate the house, and then virtually walk around until I find the bridge near it. It's the only bridge in the vicinity. It's got to be the right one.

Delivering to a bridge can't be the strangest request a courier's ever received, can it?

There's a website Tav uses to send care packages that require more than we've got in the village, so I log onto that and fill my virtual shopping cart with food that will store, blankets and pillows, and throw in some dog treats, a toy, and a large-sized coat because I have no idea what kind of dog it is, but the boy has drawn a picture and it looks like it might be quite big. I add a gift note that says this is a friend's Christmas wish and that I hope some of this stuff will be useful, and then add delivery instructions asking the courier to deliver to the homeless man with a dog under the bridge and hope it will get there safely.

I write back to the boy to tell him Santa has sent his friend a care package and thank him for his kindness.

It isn't much. I don't know what the man might actually need, but all I can do is take a stab in the dark and hope it will make both the boy, the man, and the dog smile.

It feels good. It's the first request I've solved that's required any detective work, and the feeling of doing something good is addictive. It makes you realise how lucky you are to have the basic things in life that are so easy to take for granted.

I get lost in more and more letters, full of the exuberant joy that always pours out of Santa letters, along with glitter, sparkly confetti, and drawings of reindeer. They remind me of all the Christmases I've looked at the night sky and wished to see Santa zipping past on his sleigh. All the times I've struggled to pay bills and wished that life was like it was when I was young, when Christmas was magical and not the stress-filled rush it is nowadays with the annual panics that my Christmas cards will be late or a gift I wanted to give is out of stock. When I've looked at glittering Santas on Christmas cards telling me all my Christmas wishes would come true and wished I still believed. Don't we all, at some point, wish we believed in magic again?

As if the letters can hear my thoughts, I read one that simply says she doesn't believe in Santa, and I write a simple reply. *But I believe in you, Nicole.* I sign it from Santa. Maybe it'll give her a smile when she opens it. I drop it into the outgoing mail bag and carry on opening envelopes.

There's a crunch of hooves from outside, and I get up and walk across to the window. The cold air nips, but the sun is shining down, reflecting on the snow and making it sparkle.

'What are you doing out there?' I say to the reindeer who's walking past. It's Rudolph-slash-Clive again. I never thought I'd be able to recognise any of them, but his singular antler gives him away.

'Running away from me,' Tav's voice calls, unseen from the forest.

The reindeer's big furry snout twitches in my direction, and he takes a few steps towards me.

'Hello, darling,' I say as he comes over and I pull the window fully up and lean out until I can stroke his downy nose.

'Aww, hello, sweetheart,' Tav quips as he appears from the woods. 'I didn't know you cared.'

'Not you, you wally,' I say fondly. I know he's joking as much as he knows I meant the reindeer. He pulls lichen out of his pocket and holds it up to me, wordlessly asking if I want to feed Rudolph Number Three-slash-Clive, and I nod and hold out the hand that's not rubbing over the reindeer's fur.

Tav approaches carefully from the side, like the reindeer is liable to run away at any moment, and deposits the plant life in my outstretched hand, his fingers brushing over my palm.

'You're like a walking greenhouse – do you know that?'

He laughs so hard that tears form at the corners of his eyes. 'I can honestly say no one's ever complimented me like you do before.'

While the reindeer is eating, Tav inches closer until he can gather up the loose ends of Rudolph's halter and wrap it twice around his palm.

With me in the post office and him outside, I'm taller than him. 'Never seen you from this angle before.'

He leans against the building and smiles up at me, and my heart thuds harder in my chest because his smile is so easy-going and laid-back, and if I just leant out a bit further, I'd be able to pull him to me and . . .

No.

'He likes you,' Tav says, jolting me out of the daydream of kissing him.

'He likes lichen.'

'Nah. From that first night in the forest, he's been different around you. More relaxed.' He pushes his hair back and rolls his head until he's facing the sky. 'Same could be said of me if last night's anything to go by.'

It makes that fluttering start in my chest and I have to distract myself. 'What are you up to?'

'Apart from trying to catch rogue reindeer?' He turns back to me. 'This guy had been good today so I brought him out to meet one of your dad's tour groups and he outfoxed me and got away again.' He points in the direction he's come from. 'There's an unsafe fence that belongs to the outdoor pursuits place. I keep asking them to fix it, and they keep saying they will, but it never gets done. Don't want any reindeer getting tangled up in it.'

I don't know if it's the reflection of the sunlight or the glare from the snow, but when he looks up at me again, he's got a twinkle in his eyes that makes my knees feel weak. He leans on his shoulder against the building and crosses one boot over the

171

other. Taking my eyes off him shouldn't be this difficult, and I have to force myself to concentrate on the reindeer instead.

'How come Rudolph-slash-Clive has only got one antler?' I rub his head as he carries on chewing. 'I thought you said males lost them by this time of year.'

'He'd been in an accident when he came here. I think he was hit by a car, probably head-on – that's why his antlers are in bad shape. One doesn't grow; one doesn't drop. He's long since recovered now, but his antler burrs are damaged for life.'

'You're amazing with them. Amazing to do what you do.'

Judging by his red cheeks, I've embarrassed him, and he tightens Rudolph's lead and pushes himself upright. He goes to walk away, but then stops. 'Do you want some help?'

'Haven't you got enough to do?'

'Yes. Yes, I have.' He takes another step and then turns back. 'But I can't tear myself away from this place. The letters were the most important part for me and that's got lost over the years. I can spare a few minutes.'

'In that case, I'd love some help.'

The winter sun is nowhere near as bright as the boyish grin that lights up his face. All the stress lines and pinched frown lines that sometimes play around his forehead disappear and he looks years younger. 'Let me take this chap back and I'll be there.' He jogs away and the reindeer runs alongside him, like a giant dog walking to heel.

I sit back down and continue going through the letters, but Tav makes it back in record timing. He knocks as he comes in, carrying two mugs of steaming hot chocolate and sits down cross-legged on the opposite side of today's post bag. He makes the best hot chocolate I've ever had. There's something in it, a touch of cinnamon or nutmeg or some other spice that warms you from the inside out.

'Any interesting ones today?' He pulls an envelope out of the bag and splits it open with practised ease.

I'm beaming with pride as I tell him about the homeless man, and Tav's smiling even wider than I am. The letter is still unread in his hand because he hasn't taken his eyes off me. 'Think you might've found that Christmas spirit after all.'

'Nah.' I tap the letter in my hand. 'This kid wants a huge list of things that mainly begin with the letter "i", and who knew they even *made* this many versions of Xboxes and PlayStations? And he's included a checklist for Santa to tick off and send back to him, and if Santa doesn't comply with his wishes, he's going to tell all his friends Santa's a fraud and leave sharp pokers in the fireplace. Nice lad.'

I put it back in the envelope and aim it for the box, but it flies away like a paper aeroplane and Tav catches it.

'Doesn't that bother you?' I say when he reads his own letter and deposits it in the same box for letters to ignore.

'People view Santa in different ways. Some see him as nothing more than a toy vending machine, and some really care about him and see him as a grandfatherly figure who's a big part of their lives. When you get a bad one, you'll always find a good one to balance it out. It's the law of the universe. Something good always follows something not-so-good.'

As if by karma's hand or Tav's words, the next letter I pull out is from a little girl asking how Santa is. She wants to know if he's had a good year and if he's in good health, and how Mrs Claus and the reindeer are, and says she keeps hearing about global warming and worries about them living so far north. She includes a picture she's drawn of Santa feeding his reindeer, and doesn't ask for anything at all. I hold the letter up. 'Okay, how did you do that?'

That grin again. A wide, unprotected, open smile that changes his face from severe to joyful. I can't help watching thick dark eyelashes as he looks down, a strong, pointed nose with a cleft in the tip, reading letters much faster than I do and filing them into the labelled boxes.

'Nothing surprises me working here,' he says without looking up. 'There's magic in the air. Sometimes things happen that you can't logically explain.'

'*Everything* can be logically explained.'

This time, he looks up and meets my eyes. 'Can it?'

It's more of a challenge than a question, and I want to find an answer, but he looks back down at the letter he's reading and I can't bring myself to say anything. 'What can't be logically explained is how you have time for this.'

'You're worth making time for.'

My breath catches for a different reason and he looks up at the choked-off sound I make. It's just a sentence, but those are words I've always wished someone would say to me. Always wanted someone to *feel* about me. I'm on the periphery of most people's vision – there but unimportant. Tav makes me feel like his number-one priority, and it's a good thing I'm already sitting down because it makes my knees weak and my chest all quivery.

He's looking at me curiously and I realise I'm staring blankly into space and he probably thinks I'm staring at him. I flap the letter in my hand around. 'Sad one.'

He accepts that and goes back to flicking open letters and I get so caught up in watching his long fingers easily split envelopes that when I come back to myself, he's humming Christmas songs and I hadn't even noticed.

The deepness of his voice is even evident in his gentle humming to the soft tune of "Silver Bells".

'You can sing if you want. It's highly encouraged at the North Pole.'

I don't bother trying to argue that this *isn't* the North Pole. 'Nah. The nearest hospital's too far away when both your eardrums burst.'

He laughs. 'Christmastime is made for singing.'

I shake my head, even though I always used to sing with Mum when I was little, especially when it came to Christmas carols, but as a self-conscious adult, Christmas is only made for singing when you have a voice like Tav's, not mine.

'Hum along then.' He shrugs one shoulder. 'No one can go wrong with humming.'

Debateable, but there's something about Tav that makes me want to be young and carefree again, and I wish I could forget myself and go back to being full of childlike wonder and believe in magic again.

Even so, as I read the letter I'm holding from a little boy asking for a robot dog and saying that he and his mum are going to bake cookies on Christmas Eve especially for Santa, I realise I'm humming along anyway.

And judging from the smile playing on Tav's face, he's noticed it too. He doesn't look up, but his smile gets wider as he starts singing the song softly under his breath.

I steadfastly ignore him and read another letter from a girl who wants Santa to make her grandmother better so she's well enough to come for Christmas, but it's like he knows this was another one of Mum's favourite songs, and I don't realise I remember the lyrics until I'm singing along too.

I forget my self-consciousness in front of him. I worked with Debra for months and she would always sing to the dogs in the parlour, but I could never let myself go that much. Tav makes me feel free and at ease. It doesn't matter what my voice sounds like when it's so easy to just *be* with him, to embrace the madness of the North Pole Forest and lose myself in the joys of Christmas.

The absurdity of this situation makes me start giggling.

'You okay?' Tav looks wary enough that I must look slightly deranged.

'Do you realise how weird this is? Two weeks ago, I never even knew writing to Santa was still a thing, and now I can't wait to respond to some of these.' I wave the letter around. 'This is the opposite of everything I've ever done in my life. I've never been *anywhere* and suddenly I'm reading letters from all over the world, from countries I didn't know existed and in languages I can't even identify.'

'An opportunity to open your eyes to different walks of life?'

'Yeah, I guess.' I shake my head and open another envelope. 'No wonder my dad connects with you. You must be like a son to him. You're my age and you're outdoorsy and adventurous – exactly what he always wished I was.'

'Whatever gives you that idea about me?'

'You're always, I don't know, doing stuff.'

'Outdoorsy, yes. Taught myself to do everything so I never needed to rely on other people, yes. Adventurous, no. I stay here. I talk to the same people, and the visitors we get. I trust no one. The furthest I ever go is taking my reindeer sleigh to pick up injured reindeer.'

'Really? You don't go on Great White shark feeding expeditions or base-jumping from the top of Angel Falls at any given opportunity then?'

His face screws up in confusion. 'Why on earth would I do that?'

'I don't know why anyone would, but my dad enjoys it. Everyone wants to be adventurous these days and I don't get it. I'm the odd one out for being happy to stay where I am. There are things and places I'd like to see, but the thought of getting to them . . . Planes, trains, and crowds of tourists. I'd rather see photos online and live vicariously through them.'

'I'm with you. I'm happy here. Safe here. I like a quiet life. And I don't like travelling. Why would I *not* be happy to stay where I am?'

'Exactly.' Our eyes meet across the pile of letters and the understanding in his makes me smile, even though something prickles at me about his use of the word "safe". It seems an odd word choice for someone who is so good at making other people feel safe.

He watches me for a moment and then goes back to another letter.

'Don't you ever feel like there's something wrong with you?' I blurt out.

'Plenty of things wrong with me, but why should that be one of them?'

'Because *everyone* wants to travel and take holidays, and I don't. People look forward to their holidays all year. My friend Debra used to count down to her holidays and which hot, beachy country she was going to would be planned out for the next three years.'

'And, let me guess, she's one of those people who call them "holibobs" and come to work in flip-flops, do no work in the week leading up to it, *and* make you suffer through holiday snaps.'

I burst out laughing. 'Okay, *how* did you know that? Oh, wait, don't tell me, the *nisse* told you?'

'Use of the word "holibobs" puts anyone on the naughty list.'

I laugh so hard there are tears running down my cheeks, and Tav's smiling, making me feel like we have an inside joke about a situation that always made me feel like an outsider at the dog parlour.

'When I had time off work, I sat in the garden reading or caught up on Netflix. She made me feel like a real weirdo for not booking flights to a Greek island to laze around on the beach for two weeks and spend the evenings drinking Ouzo and pole dancing.'

'While that mental image is one to treasure . . .' He laughs and then turns serious again. 'People like different things. That's okay.'

'Doesn't my dad ever tell you that you should visit this-place or that-place?'

'All the time, but I don't want to, so what difference does it make? That isn't *me*. I'm not going to do something because someone else thinks I should. I don't like travelling; other people do. That's fine.' He looks up and catches my eyes again. 'It's okay to be yourself, Sash. Your "friend" might judge you for it, but I won't. And I don't think your dad means any harm with his comments – he's just trying to find common ground between you. He wants that to be through something he likes, but he'll have to try a bit harder, won't he?'

There's something about his . . . what is it? Confidence? Self-belief? Knowing that he's *enough* just as he is, and he doesn't try to gain other people's approval by being more like them.

I like that about him. I wish I was more like that.

'Or you could isolate yourself in a forest surrounded by reindeer and never make a connection with anyone,' he says. 'Reindeer don't care where you go as long as you have lichen in your pockets.'

It makes me laugh again, but he keeps his eyes down as he rifles through envelopes, and there's a tinge of sadness to his words, and I can't stop thinking about it, even when the "few minutes" Tav could spare turns into a couple of hours, and today's post bags are almost empty. We're both lost in snapshots of other people's lives, and I can almost forget that one day soon, *this* isn't going to be my life anymore.

Chapter 10

Dear Santa,

How do you get into my house? We don't have a fireplace. Did you know that breaking and entering comes with a prison sentence? My dad installed a burglar alarm this year, so don't think we won't catch you.

How much do you get paid? Who employs you and pays for the elf factory and your house at the North Pole? Do you pay the elves fair wages or are you in the slave labour trade? How old are you? Shouldn't you have retired by now? Do you not drink or smoke – is that why you're still alive? Do you eat all the cookies at once or save some for later? Do you share them with the reindeer?

From,

Jackson

Unusually, Tav's behind the reception desk in the hallway of Santa's House when I get to the bottom of the hill a few mornings later. He's got the phone between his shoulder and ear and is scribbling something down on a notepad and alternately jabbing at buttons on the computer in front of him.

'That's fine, it'll be a pleasure to have you. The Nutcracker

Cabin is ready and waiting for your family's arrival.' He speaks into the receiver but grimaces at me, even though his eyes are smiling.

'Was that a booking?' I ask when he puts the phone down.

'That was the third booking this morning.' He moves over so he can type details into the computer. 'Two cabins and another igloo, all before Christmas, and I've had a coach company confirm full seating for a group of day trippers. The Christmas spirit must've crept up on people this year.' He doesn't sound as overjoyed as I'd expected him to.

'But it gives you more work to do?'

His eyes meet mine and he looks surprised that I've understood. 'I've only just fixed the roof of the Gingerbread Cabin, the inside still needs fixing up, and now we've got a booking for the Nutcracker Cabin, and that needs cleaning and getting ready and—'

The phone rings again and I toe off my boots and take off my hat and scarf while Tav takes another booking for two nights in one of the igloos.

'Does trade usually pick up like this?' I ask when he hangs up.

'No. We're usually booked months in advance. Sometimes we'll get an uptick if I've got an advert placed in a tourist magazine or something, but none of this last-minute stuff. I don't know what's going on.' He shakes his head and smiles at me. 'Also, good morning.'

He steps out from behind the desk and awkwardly wraps one arm around my shoulders and bends to hug me, and I slip one arm around his back and clumsily pat his forearm through the heavy knit sleeve of his brown and cream zip-up cardigan. Whenever I have time to think about it, I forget how to act around Tav. If I hug him on the spur of the moment, it works, but if I have time to overthink it, I swiftly develop the limbs of an octopus and the brain of a goldfish who can't work out what to do with them all.

'This is why!' Dad shouts, waving around his tablet as he jumps out of the living room in full Santa outfit, and Tav and I leap apart like we've been caught doing something that would make Rudolph's nose glow even redder.

'We've gone viral! Well, *you* have, Sasha. Look at what you've done!'

We gather around the tablet and he presses play on a video onscreen. It's a group of children in an African school tearing into shoeboxes I filled with little goodies – colouring books and pens, fidget spinners, stickers, cracker toys, festive bows and ribbons, and candy canes. It was one of the first packages I sent out. Their letter had been a class project – their teacher wrote to Santa and each child added a wish. There wasn't much I could do about their actual wishes, but the idea of a whole class of children going to so much effort, and the juxtaposition between their world and mine was something I hadn't been able to shake off.

In the video, the children are screaming and laughing and running around barefoot on the beach under a scorching December sun with their gifts, the total opposite of freezing and snowy Norway, then they're throwing tinsel and ribbons at each other, and then it ends back in the classroom. 'Three cheers for Santa!' the children all shout at the end and unroll a banner between them that reads #ThankYouNorthPoleForest.

The video has 12,987 views so far, and there are loads of comments.

'Look at this one.' Dad points out a comment from a parent saying her daughter got a personal reply from the same people and it made her year. The comment finishes with, "*She'll always believe in Santa now, even when she finds out the truth.*"

There's a link to Twitter, and someone else has posted a photo of a little boy playing with a wooden train I sent, and used the hashtag #ThankYouNorthPoleForest.

'This is phenomenal,' Tav murmurs.

I reach out and press the play button again, and the children's delighted cries echo through our bedazzled hallway. 'Look at how happy they are.'

My eyes fill with tears and I turn away and take a few deep breaths. This is ridiculous. Why am I getting so upset over a few happy children? I didn't expect to ever *see* the results of the letters and parcels I've sent. Some of those letters are so poignant that you'd need a heart of stone not to be touched, and this video has hit me like a thump in the chest. We can make children *this* happy by spending five minutes packing up a box with stuff we don't need.

Tav's hand closes over my shoulder and squeezes, a comforting gesture, just being *there*. 'Look at how happy *you* made them.'

It makes my eyes water even harder. I don't think I've ever made anyone happy before.

'I knew you could do it!' Dad claps me on the shoulder and then addresses Tav. 'See? I told you she was just what we needed.'

Something bristles at that, and I wipe my eyes and turn back. 'It wasn't meant to go viral. I wasn't *trying* to generate publicity; I was trying to help.'

Dad's reading through the comments now. 'People are saying they've been on our website and it looks like a lovely place. Someone else says they don't live far and they're going to bring their kids here solely because of this video. Someone else asks where they can make a donation to the nice people who do this. Someone says this is exactly what they needed to see today, and just the sort of content the world needs. Ooh, I've just checked our Twitter account and Santa's got five hundred more followers than I had last night. Let me share this video . . .'

'It's Tav as much as me,' I say as Dad presses a few buttons and types something.

'Nothing to do with me.' Tav's hand is still on my shoulder. 'This was your idea. Credit where it's due, because I'm guessing you never got much of that from "Ms Holibobs" even though you did a vast majority of the work.'

I laugh loudly to outshine the prickle of unease because he's not exactly wrong.

'I might congratulate myself actually,' Dad says. 'It was me who knew you two would make a wonderful team, and now look, we've got guests booking and people talking about us. This is exactly what we need to turn our fortunes around.'

'It wasn't meant for that though. I didn't know this would happen.' His insistence that the viral video was somehow planned makes me feel underhanded.

'Good people doing good things will always find the right audience.' Tav says it so softly that I don't think Dad even hears it. 'And this is just one parcel. You've sent out *hundreds*, and there's plenty of stock left. Think of how many children you can make a Christmas wish come true for.'

It makes a lump jump into my throat again, and I turn around, and Tav sidesteps until he can catch my eyes. He gives me a silent nod, a wordless "you okay?" and I nod in response. Seeing that video has given me the warm fuzzies like nothing ever has before, and I want to rush to the post office and start replying to children's letters *right now*, but Dad's busy with his Twitter comments and the business email account is open onscreen on the desktop computer and it's pinged with the new email arrival sound six times in the last ten minutes.

'Have you two had breakfast, I can—'

'No!' Tav cries out. 'We've suffered enough. I've got a pocket full of lichen, please let me eat that instead.'

I laugh so hard, complete with squiffy-pig-style snorting, that it drives me away from the edge of tears. 'It'll be Mum's cinnamon rolls today.'

The phone rings yet again and I push Dad into the kitchen and leave Tav to answer it.

'I knew you'd be good at this, Sasha.' Dad puts his tablet on the counter and climbs onto his usual stool at the kitchen island.

'What about you, Dad? You're supposed to be taking things easy, and with more guests coming, that's—'

'Yes, yes, I knew you'd see exactly what this place needed.' He's not even going to listen, but this feels like the opposite of the gentle retirement I was *supposed* to help him accept.

The deep lilt of Tav's voice reverberates through the downstairs as he takes another booking. 'It's barely 8 a.m. and he hasn't stopped. The last thing he needs is to come in here and cook breakfast for all of us.'

Dad lets me clatter around the kitchen, getting ingredients out and making a dough. 'You really care about him, don't you?'

'No, not at—' I was going to tell him not to be so silly, but I can't get the words out.

'You've been good for him. He's different with you here. A bit fuzzier around the edges.'

This time I do tell Dad not to be so daft, but I can't help smiling to myself as I move around the kitchen, rolling out dough and adding the sugary cinnamon filling. I don't realise I'm humming "Silver Bells" until Dad joins in.

'Another igloo gone for New Year.' Tav comes into the kitchen and surveys the scene. 'I'm going to back out slowly and you two pretend you never saw me. There's some charred remains of last night's fire in the hearth. I'll eat that instead.'

'The mince pies weren't *that* burnt,' I say incredulously.

Tav's laughing as he sits down next to my father, seemingly willing to be fed despite his teasing.

Dad's still engrossed in replying to Twitter comments, and Tav folds his arms on the counter in front of him and lays his head down on them.

His tousled dark hair has flopped forward and I have an overwhelming urge to brush it back. And I can't help thinking he *has* changed lately. I can't imagine the guy I met a couple of weeks ago letting his guard down enough to do that.

I put a cup of coffee down and slide it across the island towards him, the backs of my fingers nudging the thick jumper covering his forearms. 'I'll help getting the cabins ready.'

'I can't let you do that.' He lifts his head and meets my eyes. 'You're here for your dad, Sash, not for me. We both know he's *meant* to be resting.' Tav's comment is aimed at Dad, who steadfastly ignores him too. 'You're loving the post office and you're doing something wonderful there. I can't take you away from that.'

'All right. Answer me one question.' I lean my elbows on the countertop and reach one hand across until I can slide my fingers over the top of his fist. '*Can* you do this by yourself?'

He goes to open his mouth but no words come out. He stares down at my fingers touching his and his tongue peeks out to wet his lips. 'Yes, of course. I've never backed down from a challenge before and I don't intend to start now.'

All right, maybe not *that* fuzzy around the edges.

'Okay, another question. Can you do this by yourself and still have time to sleep at night?'

After the serious answer to the last question, his smile makes dimples appear at the edges of his mouth. 'No.'

I grin even though he isn't joking. 'It's settled then. The letters can wait – paying guests cannot. You can do the structural stuff and I can sort out the inside.'

'Sash . . .' His other hand closes over mine where it's still on top of his. I assume he's going to protest so my fingers tighten, and we smile at each other for a few long moments.

He lifts his chin towards the oven. 'Burning.'

'Now you're just teas—' The smoke alarm starts shrieking, making Dad look up from his tablet.

'Oh, holy night,' I mutter as I get the *slightly* chargrilled cinnamon rolls out and Tav gets up to calm the smoke alarm down.

'At least if Santa runs out of coal for the naughty list's stockings, we can use these instead and no one will know the difference.'

I thwack at him with a tea towel and he laughs as he sits back down, and I can't help giggling too as I move around the kitchen, teasing, laughing, and joking, and it feels good. This weird little makeshift family, a home at the top of the world that I never expected to find.

'This is perfect.' I peer around the door of the Nutcracker Cabin and Tav leans around me to switch on a light, which flickers once and makes a pinging sound as the bulb dies and plunges the room back into darkness.

Tav brushes aside a cobweb and goes to poke at the hearth. We both stand and watch, my shoulder pressing against his arm, as the firelighter crumples and the flames take hold, filling the room with the scent of burning logs and the crackle of wood, and giving just enough light for Tav to find a bulb in a cupboard and replace the main light.

'Right.' I put down the bucket full of cleaning products I'm carrying and pull my sleeves up. 'Let's get to work.'

I've never minded jobs like cleaning, and I get on with it happily while Tav surveys the building for structural damage and construction needs. He swears when he finds a broken window at the back.

Freya comes up to say she's left today's mail delivery in the post office, and that Santa's grotto looked busy. When we left, Dad was at the living room mirror, perfecting his beard curls with tongs, but he insisted I come up here instead of helping him, despite my protestations that he can't manage the grotto on his own.

'I've always thought these cabins were so romantic,' Freya muses when Tav has gone down to check on him. She picks up one of the wooden nutcracker soldiers that decorate the mantelpiece above the crackling fire.

'I'm told you had a moment of romance . . .'

She sighs. 'It's silly really. Just a foolish old woman trying to convince myself I'm still young enough for there to be someone out there for me. Tav indulged me too much. I should've forgotten about the mystery man.'

'It's so romantic. Eyes meeting across a busy road. Chance encounters. Things like that happen for a reason. He could come back. He could be looking for you too.'

'No.' She strokes the long blonde ponytail hanging over her shoulder. 'It was a fairy tale. My husband of two decades left me for a younger woman a few years ago, and since then, I've been alone and better off that way, but that moment, it . . . I don't know . . . made me think there was a chance that love *could* happen for me again. It was a nudge from the universe. After my husband left, I thought that was it for me, that I'd grow old and die alone, but feeling that little flutter, butterflies like I was a teenager with my first crush again . . . It gave me hope.'

'He must've felt it too. Maybe he'll be back this year. He could've been a day visitor and not a staying guest. We'll keep an eye out,' I say, even though no one but Freya has any idea what he looked like.

'I keep looking. It's why I always bring the bags up to the house, just in case.'

'You'll see him again. Christmas is the time of year for magic, after all. If we can't believe in the impossible then, when can we?'

'I see Tav's rubbing off on you.'

'It's not just Tav. It's everything. The whole world feels different since I got here.'

'The magic of the North Pole Forest.' She gives me a knowing nod before she leaves.

'He's busy but managing.' Tav ducks as he comes back in the door with two mugs of hot chocolate. 'I passed Freya on her way out and she's going to come back after her round, don an elf hat, and help for a bit.'

'That's really good of her.' I take the mug gratefully and sip it before I run back down the hill to Santa's House to find the linen closet and collect the spare nutcracker-themed soft furnishings.

When I get back, Tav's started rehanging the misaligned bathroom door, and for the first time, he's taken his jumper off and is only wearing a hunter green T-shirt and I have to stop in the doorway and adjust to the sight of all that muscle on display. Even though it's a thick, thermal T-shirt, his rugged back muscles and solid shoulders go on forever, and I might be drooling as my fingers twitch with the urge to find an excuse to touch him.

'Okay?' Tav asks over his shoulder, and I'm grateful to have an armful of bedding to hide my red face behind, embarrassed at being caught ogling him.

It's the first time I've seen him without heavy layers on, and I swallow hard because my mouth has gone dry. 'I didn't run into any *nisse*.'

He laughs. 'I don't think you need to now, Sash. You've been singing along with me all morning.'

'No, I haven't.' I think for a moment. 'Have I?'

He makes an affirmative noise around the screw he's holding between his teeth and starts humming again, loudly over the whirr of the electric screwdriver he's using, and it takes me a few moments to realise I'm still staring at him, appreciating the way every little movement makes strong shoulder muscles flex under his T-shirt, and I need to have a strict word with myself and get on with the task at hand. I start putting on the fresh bedding with an enthusiasm usually reserved for when someone offers me chocolate.

It's been a while since I found someone physically attractive. At thirty-six, you're past the age of crushes and most men you meet are married or otherwise taken, and on the rare occasions I have dated, it's more about making a connection with someone than what they look like, but *oh, holy night*, Tav is *gorgeous*.

Within a few minutes, I've realised why he took his heavy-knit zip cardigan off. It's roasting in the cabin with both the fire and an electric heater going and the added aspect of doing physical work. By the time I've got the bottom sheet on the mattress, sweat is prickling at my forehead. It's the first time in the two weeks I've been here that I've wanted to take clothes *off*.

I feel Tav's eyes on me as I dump my outer layers on the sofa, and when I glance at him, he averts his eyes so quickly that he hits his thumb with the hammer he was using to flatten the hinge. It's been a *long* while since I felt physically attractive to someone else. All my relationships in recent years have been lacklustre and never progressed past a few disappointing dates, but I can't help sneaking glances at him as I squeeze pillows into nutcracker pillowcases and wrestle plump cushions into nutcracker covers, and every time our eyes meet across the cabin, it makes the butterflies in my stomach feel so big that they could be reindeer flying inside me.

And that's when I notice the scar. A thick white line in otherwise smooth skin. It runs from under the sleeve of his T-shirt, around his elbow and down the top of his forearm before disappearing underneath. Most men have hairy forearms, but his are smooth and muscular and I can imagine them with a tan in the summer.

I don't realise I'm staring until he notices me noticing. He looks between me and his elbow, and quickly moves, turning around so the scarred arm is on the other side and his body blocks my view.

Within two minutes, he's mentioned being cold and put his cardigan back on, even though with the fire and the heater going, sauna designers could use our current room temperature as a blueprint.

I feel like I've done something wrong by noticing it, and I want to apologise and explain that I was looking at his forearms rather than the scar, but I get the feeling that even bringing it up will cross a line that's not mine to cross. His clear hiding of it intrigues me, and I want to ask about it, but scars are personal and usually the result of something traumatic, and someone who so obviously hides one isn't going to want to talk about it.

He's visibly too hot, and I want to tell him to take his jumper off again, but I can't say it without drawing attention to the scar I'm pretending I haven't noticed. Instead, I unplug the heater and walk across to wedge the door open with a nutcracker doorstop, and when I turn back, Tav's resting his head against the frame of the door he's fixing and his eyes are on me.

I give him a smile. 'Hot work.'

He holds my gaze for a long few minutes, and a couple of times I think he's going to speak but he stops himself. Eventually he mouths a "thank you" and goes back to work on the door hinge, and I go back to changing the bedding, when what I really want to do is go over and hug him, because I don't know what causes scars like that, but like the ones on his neck the other night, I know he didn't intend me to see them, and I know he dropped his guard long enough to let me, and that makes me feel warmer than the crackling fire.

It's the end of a long day but the cabin is finally looking presentable. I fiddle with the garland on the mantelpiece while Tav lines the gift basket with tissue paper and starts piling nutcracker-themed goodies in. I smooth out the red nutcracker-patterned throw folded at the end of the bed and stand back to survey our work. 'Looks good.'

'One more thing.' He pulls a bunch of mistletoe out of the box he's using. 'Finishing touch.'

He winds a red ribbon around the stems and into a loop to hang it, then gets out a tiny plastic nutcracker and clips it onto the middle of the bow.

The fresh green scent of the mistletoe combines with the cinnamon sticks I've tied to the tree, and there's a scent warmer on the edge of the hearth, ready to be plugged in with a cube of sugarplum-scented wax in it to fill the room with fragrance before the guests arrive.

'If it's a couple staying, I always put a sprig of mistletoe up for an extra touch of romance. It reminds people to stop and take a moment for each other.'

'That's very romantic for someone who doesn't strike me as the romantic type at all.'

'It's for good luck more than romance.' He grins when he catches my confused look. 'We have this story in Norway about the origin of a kiss under the mistletoe. It starts with Frigga, the goddess of love. Her son was killed by an arrow made from the mistletoe plant, and as she sat underneath the tree where the mistletoe grew and cried over his body, the tears dropped onto the arrow and turned into little white berries that took away the poison and brought him back to life. She was so happy that she started kissing everyone who passed, and she declared that from then on, no one who stood under a mistletoe branch would come to any harm, and would instead receive a token of love – a kiss.'

In one swift move, he's hooked his foot around one of the chairs at the dining table and pulled it over, and he's holding the bunch of mistletoe out towards me. 'You do the honours.'

Despite the fact Tav could reach it easily, it feels special that he wants me to do it. He keeps the chair steady with his foot and holds his hand out, his arm as rigid as granite, letting me use it to push myself up until I'm standing on the chair. One of his hands is curled around my hip to steady me, and when I take the mistletoe bunch, his other hand closes on my other hip, keeping me secure as I reach up and slip the red ribbon over the unobtrusive hook in the wooden ceiling.

Even though I'm quite capable of standing on a chair without assistance, the atmosphere is charged between us. I *love* the feeling of his hands on my body, and I get the sense it's nothing to do with keeping me steady and, in fact, is probably having the exact opposite effect, because my whole body is running with tingles. His fingers press into my back, and I slide my hands over his where they're on my hips. I let them drift down his arms, running the length of them from his wrists up to his shoulders, and further, giving in to the urge to skim across his neck and upwards to brush his hair back. His eyes drift closed and his head drops into my hands.

I'm leaning on him as his hands slide up and tighten around my waist, lifting me down with ease.

I barely register that I'm standing on the wooden floor again because with Tav this close, the whole world feels as unsteady as a boat on a stormy sea.

'Sash,' he murmurs, his tongue wetting his lips. He's blinking slowly and his eyes are on my mouth.

I let my gaze shift upwards to the mistletoe and have to swallow a few times before words will work. 'We can't disappoint the goddess of love.'

He laughs, easing some of the tension. 'No, we can't.'

His head lowers and my eyes drift shut as his lips press against my cheek. I hadn't realised how cold my skin was until I feel the burning imprint of his lips against it. It's soft, gentle and lingering, right on the edge of my cheekbone. His nose is cold where it presses against my skin, and someone lets out a whimper, and to be fair, it was probably me.

His hands are still on my ribs and they tighten as my hand curls into his hair and my body presses against his. The few days' worth of stubble peppering his jaw is tactile against my skin, and I float on his almond and gingery cologne. My other hand curls into his arm, and I'm glad he's got a thick jumper on because my nails would've definitely made crescent shapes in his muscle.

He stays there, his lips against my cheekbone, breathing against my skin. His nose rubs the side of my face, and then he presses another kiss and stands back up to full height, although he doesn't move away, which is definitely good because he's the only thing holding me upright.

I don't open my eyes for a few long seconds because I don't want to lose the moment yet. My only experience of mistletoe until now has been ugly plastic branches hung in doorways at office parties, nothing more than an excuse for married drunk men to attempt a pervy kiss. But *that* is how you do mistletoe.

Tav runs a hand through his hair and flicks his head like he's trying to clear it. 'Best mistletoe I've ever hung.'

I burst out laughing, possibly hysterical from the closeness to this man I barely know. I've had less intimate kisses than that with men I was actually dating.

One of his hands is still on my ribs and he squeezes gently. 'Thank you for your help today.' His voice sounds as shivery as mine undoubtedly will.

I let my other hand come up and slide over his forearm until I'm inadvertently gripping the elbow of his left arm, above the scar I saw this morning. 'Thank you for letting me. I know it's not something you accept easily.'

His cheeks redden and he tugs his sleeve down even though it was already down to his wrist, but he doesn't move away.

'What happened to you, Tav?' I feel brave for asking. I *think* he might be starting to open up to me, but I'm unsure if asking so straightforwardly will push him away.

'Why are you so sure something happened to me?'

'I can see your scars.' I gently squeeze his elbow. 'Not the physical ones. There's something in your eyes. A vulnerability. An absolute terror that someone's going to suggest you can't do something.'

'I'm six-foot-seven. I'm *not* vulnerable.'

'If you think it has anything to do with your height . . .' I move my hand from his elbow, going to reach up and touch his face, but this time, he pulls away sharply.

I think he's going to stalk out, but he backs across the room until his legs hit the sofa and he sits against the arm. His breathing has gone sharp and shallow, and I don't dare to move because I'm sure he's going to speak.

'I was in a car accident,' he says eventually, the words whispered to the floor instead of to me. 'When I was twenty. Pretty bad one. At the scene, technically I was dead for longer than anyone should be dead. Then I was in a coma. In the ratio of bones in my body, I had more broken than unbroken. Every part of me was damaged. That's where the scars come from – the physical ones *and* the emotional ones.'

He hasn't looked up once and I haven't taken a breath since he started speaking. I take a step towards him, desperate to hold him, touch him, hug him, but he puts both hands up to keep me away and vaults to his feet. 'I need some fresh air.'

I *need* to know more, but he's totally closed off now. I can hear the wood creaking under his feet as he paces outside, and I have no doubt that if I went out there, he'd race off down the hill so he didn't run the risk of me asking any more questions. I plump up a nutcracker cushion and force myself to leave him alone, because I don't think he intended to tell me that, and I'm not sure which one of us is more surprised by this small start at letting his guard down.

All I know is that it takes a lot for Tav to open up, and I'm certainly not going to let him stop now.

Chapter 11

Dear Santa,

I tried really, really hard to be good this year, but it's so difficult. I managed half an hour. I'm sorry. Will I still get a present?

From,

Penelope

Things are usually quieter on a Sunday, but today was the exception. It's the 12th of December and bookings have steadily increased, and most of the day has been spent in my dad's grotto, ferrying children in and out to visit Santa. Even Freya came by on her day off and donned her elf hat to help out again, and now it's evening time and neither Tav nor I can tear ourselves away from the post office.

I stamp an envelope with our "North Pole Mail" stamp, go over to drop it into the outgoing bag, and then come back to look at a fraction of the 7882 letters that were delivered yesterday.

'Did you ever write to Santa?' Tav asks as I sit down opposite him with the bag between us.

'I did when I was little. Mum used to do it with me every year until I was old enough to realise what she was actually doing was finding out what I wanted for Christmas so she and Dad could get it for me and put it under the tree "from Santa". I look up at him, unsure if I want to tell him one of my childhood secrets, but his eyes find mine and he gives me an encouraging smile, like he knows I was going to say something else.

'I did one other time too. After she died and Dad had been away for a few months. I was far too old to be writing to Santa, but I was still writing letters to Mum after that therapy session with the school, and writing to Santa somehow fitted with that. It felt like things would never be normal again. My nan hated Christmas and I so desperately wanted something to feel like it used to. I wished that Santa could make me believe in magic again.'

I expect him to laugh at the idea of a twelve-year-old writing to Santa, but he takes his usual time in thinking before he speaks. 'What *would* make you believe in magic again?'

'Being somewhere so beautiful, so unspoiled, so *good*. Seeing the Northern Lights. And you . . . meeting someone who didn't fall for the traps of growing up like most people did, who talks about elves and flying reindeer like they're normal and doesn't try to be something you aren't. The amount of effort you put into this place. And reading letters from children all across the world who put so much time and energy into making every letter special, and it isn't just about getting stuff. Seeing my dad happy. I don't think he's ever been a happy person, not since Mum died. A kiss under the mistletoe.'

'All I can say about that is next time I fix up a cabin, you're hanging the mistletoe at the end.' His teeth pull his lower lip into his mouth and he smiles at the same time. 'And it's never too late for a Christmas wish to come true, you know.'

My instinct is to tell him not to be silly. I'm thirty-six, well past the age of Christmas wishes coming true, but I *wish* I believed it was still possible.

'I've never told anyone that before,' I say instead.

His smile is slow this time. 'That makes two of us. I've never told anyone . . .'

I hold my breath because I'm sure he's going to mention the accident again, but he hesitates and then finishes the sentence in a rush. 'Some of the things I've told you. What did you used to do with your mum and dad at Christmas?' He drops my gaze and goes back to the letter in his hand, but the abrupt subject change leaves me feeling off-balance.

I want to scooch across the floor and squeeze his hand or something, but I force myself to stay still. 'Write to Santa, visit his grotto at the supermarket, when it snowed we'd go for walks and build snowmen, come home for hot chocolates, make mince pies, decorate the tree, sing Christmas songs . . . All the things I've been doing here, actually.' I think for a moment. 'It's almost enough to make someone believe in Christmas magic again.'

He goes to smile but I stop him. '*Almost*. How about you? What were your Christmases like?'

'Christmas is different here. We celebrate on the 24th, not the 25th. We eat rice porridge for lunch on Christmas Eve and an almond is hidden in it, and whoever finds the almond wins a marzipan pig – it doesn't sound like much, but the marzipan pig is a big thing. The neighbours always want to know who got it in each household. The main Christmas meal is in the evening, and then *Julenissen*, our version of Santa, doesn't come down the chimney but knocks on the door with his sack of presents. And then there's the period of *romjul*, the time between Christmas and New Year, which is for cosying up with your family and enjoying the holiday. That's what I grew up with, but my parents were never big on Christmas. In recent years, especially with your dad here, we do a mix of Norwegian and British traditions.'

I'm looking forward to Christmas. For the first time since I realised every year would bring another excuse for Dad not to come home, things will be different this year. I'll get to spend Christmas with Dad and Tav, and not for the first time, I think about this weird little makeshift family I've found here. It makes me think of the wishing jar that's on the mantelpiece in Candy Cane Cabin, the one he gave me on the first night. When I get back later, I'm going to check it. I mean, I'm *sure* the writing will still be there, but I'll check it anyway. Just in case.

Tav looks like he can tell what I'm thinking. I smile at him, but a familiar coldness settles back in my chest as the words "what then?" float through my mind. Because when Christmas is over, we'll *have* to decide what to do about this place, and I'll have to go home. We've been so busy that I haven't really thought about anything beyond the next day, but once Christmas is gone, everything else will have to be faced.

I push it out of my head and try to concentrate on the letter I'm reading from a girl who wants a pet squirrel.

Tav laughs at one of his. 'This little girl wants to know if the "little donkey" was okay after the song, and for Christmas, could she please have some donkey food to give to him.'

'Aww.' I push my bottom lip out and open another envelope. 'This one says her cat ran away earlier this year and now her other cat is sad, so could Santa bring her a mouse to cheer her up.'

'We'll be sure to put that one in the stocking. Her parents will be *thrilled*.'

It makes me laugh out loud again as I slice open another innocuous-looking letter. Usually they're addressed to "Santa Claus, North Pole", but this one is addressed directly to the North Pole Forest, and it doesn't look like a child's writing.

'Tav . . .' I hold the letter out in front of me like it's made of glass. 'Listen to this. *Hello. This is probably the stupidest thing I've ever done, but here goes. If anyone's reading this, I'm sure you've never had a letter from a seventy-year-old man before. It's a long shot, but I visited the North Pole Forest with my grandchildren last year. The date was December the 8th . . .*' My eyes flick to the date he's written in the upper right-hand corner. It's the same date. '*I remember it to the exact minute because the clock on Santa's House showed eleven minutes past eleven . . .* That's got to be significant. You have to make a wish if you see a clock with those numbers.'

I glance at him and continue reading. *'I locked eyes with a woman on the opposite side of the road. I felt what I believe young people call "a connection". I'm writing today because even though a year has gone by, I still can't get her out of my mind, and it feels significant. With so much time having passed and the fact I still think about it, maybe it's something I should chase up? I don't know why I'm writing this or how I expect you to help me. Maybe you know who it was. My granddaughter said the lady was wearing some sort of uniform, but I'm afraid my focus was only on her eyes. The feeling that passed between us obliterated all else. I'm planning on bringing my grandchildren to visit Santa once the schools are on their Christmas break, and I don't even know what I'm hoping for really. Maybe that the fates will align and she'll be there again.*

'Think you can send me a little festive magic, Santa? Seasons blessings, Osvald.'

'It's Freya,' I say, stating the obvious. 'It has to be.'

He holds his hand out for the letter and I pass it over and watch as he reads it. 'That's amazing. It was *really* real. When Freya told me, I've got to admit I thought she was probably imagining it, but I didn't want to be discouraging. Eyes don't meet across a crowded road and strangers don't make an instant connection. But the fact that she's still thinking about it a year later, and so is he . . .'

'And they both wrote to Santa at different times,' I add. 'So they have things in common like ways of solving problems and belief in Christmas magic.'

'See? Anything is possible at Christmas.'

'What are we going to do?'

He folds the letter up and hands it back to me. '*We* are not going to do anything. You found that letter for a reason. You believe in love. Make a little magic yourself. What are *you* going to do?'

'Well, we have to write back, don't we? We have to find out

when he's coming and make sure Freya's here as well. Get them together somehow.'

'And you say you don't believe in magic.'

'I don't. I didn't . . .' I trail off because I suddenly want to cry. I believe in *anything* when I look into Tav's eyes. 'It's nothing to do with Christmas magic. It's common decency. She's looking for someone and we now know he's looking for her too. No one would just ignore it.'

'But it's only because of Santa that we do know it. Because of their belief that magic can happen at this time of year . . .'

I scramble to my feet, taking the mystery man's letter with me, and plonk myself at the desk as I pull out some North Pole Forest stationery and start composing a reply.

'Dear Osvald,' I speak in disjointed sentences as I write. 'We were so pleased to get your letter because our friend has been looking for you all year too. We know exactly who you mean, and your granddaughter is right: she was wearing a *Posten Norge* uniform. Santa and his elves are keeping an extra special sprinkling of fairy dust for you this year. Please let us know when you're intending to visit and we'll set up a meeting.' I finish off by giving him the phone number and telling him to ask for me or Tav.

'Perfect.' Tav's looking up at me from the floor, chewing his lip without taking his eyes off mine.

It does feel perfect. It's the kind of thing that only happens in movies, and I can't imagine it happening in real life too, and as I stamp the letter shut with a wax seal, it fills me with butterflies on Freya's behalf.

'We can't tell Freya,' I say as I squeeze past him and slip the envelope into the outgoing mail bag, even though I'm fizzing with excitement. When she collects this bag tomorrow, I don't know how I'm going to stop myself blurting it out. 'It has to be a surprise. We'll need to get our stories straight and make sure we know exactly when he's going to be here.'

'It would be great if we could set it up like it was before so their eyes meet across the road . . .'

I let out a low, longing sigh. 'Oh, can you imagine . . . That would be so romantic. We have to do that. Between us, we can make sure they're both in the right place at the right time.'

He grins at me and I grin back at him. 'I've never been involved in anything like this before. These letters are . . .' That feeling of not wanting to leave flickers across my mind again. Being here and reading these is the biggest privilege I've ever felt in my life. 'Special. An insight into the world around us and how much Christmas matters to people. I wouldn't even think of turning to Santa with my relationship woes, but here we are, creating romantic Christmas miracles.'

'We should celebrate,' Tav says after a moment, and I sure he can read each thought that flashes in every corner of my mind. 'I was making a batch of fresh *gløgg* before I left the house so we have something to give the Gingerbread Cabin couple as a welcome gift.'

'I don't know what that is.'

'I love how British you are.' He rolls his eyes and gets to his feet in one swift movement. 'It's the Norwegian equivalent of mulled wine, except we add our own potato-based spirit, more spices, and raisins and almonds. It wouldn't be right not to taste-test it before giving it to paying guests. Wanna bunk off work early?'

'It's eight o'clock!'

'Is it? Sorry, you make me lose track of time, Sash.' He blinks for a long moment and then shakes his head. 'Let me rephrase that – wanna bunk off work ridiculously late to do even more vitally important work?'

The idea of making Tav lose track of time makes me feel flushed and fluttery. I get the feeling he's highly scheduled and time is something he doesn't have *time* to lose track of. 'I rarely say no to anyone offering me wine.'

He holds his hand out as we leave the post office and I take it automatically. The streetlamps are glowing, their orange tinge like Christmas lights strung all the way along the road back to Santa's House, and it's a good thing I am clinging on to his hand because I'm looking skyward so much in the hope of a glimpse of the Northern Lights that I stumble over my own feet a few times.

'It's too cloudy.'

'There are patches between the clouds. You can see the stars.'

'You're optimistic, you know that?'

'No.' I stare at him. 'No one's ever called me that before. My life is sad and miserable. It means nothing to anyone. I'm pessimistic and always think the worst of people.' The words burst out before I can stop them. I didn't mean to say any of that to Tav, but he sees me in a way I'm just . . . not, and he makes me feel better than I am. Things are easy here, festive and magical, but the more time that passes, the closer the countdown ticks to having to go back to a reality *without* reindeer sticking their noses in your window every five minutes.

'Maybe you're just in the wrong place.'

I've never thought that before and I'm sure he can hear the hitch in my breathing. I can feel his eyes on me but I keep mine steadfastly focused ahead and don't speak again until we reach Dad's house because I'll end up crying if I do.

'Ah, my two favourite elves,' Dad says when we walk in. 'My grotto has been hectic and my Twitter notifications have gone through the roof. People keep tweeting about the letters and gifts they've got.'

The thought of the letters I've written being online makes me feel edgy. I replied because I thought the children deserved a response, not because I was trying to make something go viral and benefit *us* in the long run. 'That's not a good thing, Dad. You're not supposed to be worki—'

'Your hotel is so lucky to have you,' Dad interrupts, and Tav excuses himself to the kitchen. 'I could've hired a world-class

202

publicist who couldn't have done what you've done for this place. You've put us on the map. I had several enquiries for next year and I've booked them in provisionally because, well, we don't know where we're going to be, do we?'

The lump moves from my throat to settle as a stone of unease in my stomach. It's another perfect opportunity to broach the subject of what we're going to do, but I can't make myself face it.

'He said something about *gløgg*,' I say to change the subject and point in the direction Tav went, even though I'm not sure if men who've just had heart attacks mix with alcoholic festive drinks. 'Do you want . . .'

'Oh no,' Dad cuts me off quickly. 'That's for you *two*. I'm going to have a shower and an early night. I've got a lot of bookings for tomorrow. And tell Tav another two igloos have been booked for the *romjul* period, and I've hired a cleaner to come in and sort them out so he doesn't have to.'

'He won't like that.'

'That's exactly why it'll be better coming from you than me.' He gives me a cheery pat on the shoulder. 'But I realised that I'm the boss and I can overrule Tav and we've taken more than enough in the past few days to cover the expenditure. Nighty night.'

'Night, Dad.' I watch him go up the stairs, taking them fast, like a man with knees belonging to a fifty-year-old. He *loves* this place. He loves being Santa. He glows brighter than the street-lamps every time he talks about it. How can I be responsible for taking that away?

'Dad said . . .' I say as I walk through to the kitchen.

'I know, I heard.' Tav looks up from the stove where he's stir-ring a saucepan.

'And that doesn't bother you?'

'He's right, he is the boss.' He shrugs. 'And honestly, you *forcing* me to share some of the work has been . . . nice. Made me realise that maybe I can't do it *all*.' He draws out the last word.

'I'm sorry, was that Taavi Salvesen admitting someone else

203

was right?' I take a step backwards, pretending to be so shocked it nearly knocks me over.

He grins. 'Doesn't mean I can't try though.'

'How am I going to get him to slow down, Tav? He's supposed to be taking it easy.'

'He *is* taking it easy. You didn't see him before the heart attack.'

'We need to take on staff or something. He needs more help than me and you and Freya when she's got a bit of free time. This isn't on.'

'I know,' he says quietly.

The entire room smells of cinnamon and cloves and star anise, and he ladles a spoon of the festively scented drink into two glasses set out on the kitchen island, and I go around it to stand nearer to him.

'*Skál.*' He picks up his glass and clinks it against mine, and I take a sip.

'Mmm, that's nice.' The sweet and fruity taste melts across my tongue, a far cry from the cheap mulled wine at office parties, and I'm once again I'm struck by how much Tav really knows how to *do* Christmas.

'Thanks.' He crouches to clatter around in a cupboard under the kitchen island until he retrieves two bottles and a funnel and ladles the steaming liquid in, and screws both lids on tightly, ready to be delivered to the Gingerbread Cabin.

He picks up his glass and clinks it against mine again. 'Happy Christmas, Sash.'

'Happy Christmas,' I murmur back.

This is what Christmas *should* be like, and for the first time ever, Christmas feels like something worth celebrating.

Chapter 12

Dear Santa,
If my Christmas presents are made by elves in the North
Pole, why do they all have "Made in China" written on them?
From,
Milo

It's colder and darker by the time we get back outside, and sure enough, there are flashes of green in the night sky, hidden by curtains of cloud and only peeking out once in a while.

'Your optimism wasn't misplaced.'

'I don't want to miss any. You get to see this every night and I have to . . .' I stop myself finishing the sentence, like if I don't speak the "go home" aloud, I can somehow avoid it.

'It's been nice to see it through your eyes again. You've made me realise how weary I've become. Since you arrived, it's the first time I've stopped to look up in a while.'

I bite my lip as we stop at the Gingerbread Cabin door and he lets us in, the scent of gingery spices greeting us even though the scent warmer is off. I hover outside as he goes to the kitchen table and nestles one bottle into the gift basket, and then comes back with the other one. 'For you.'

'What am I supposed to do with this?' I ask even as my gloved fingers curl around the neck of the bottle.

'Generally people drink it . . .' He sounds so confused that it makes me burst out laughing.

'No, I meant . . . alone? Do you want to walk up the rest of the way and share it?' I incline my head towards the top of the hill. 'It's not right that you make it and then don't get any.'

His smile spreads like he knows full well it's not about the wine but the fact I don't want to say goodnight to him yet.

Once we reach Candy Cane Cabin, Tav goes inside to start the fire while I take the bottle to the kitchen and pour it out into two glasses, and when I turn to look for him, logs are crackling in the hearth, but the door is open and he's gone back out.

I stand next to him and lean my elbows on the wooden railing surrounding the decking at the top of the steps up to the cabin and hand his glass over. His arm presses close to mine as he takes it, and we both stand there in comfortable silence, looking out across the forest, waiting for a splash of green light between the clouds. It's so quiet that I can almost hear the sound of the Northern Lights zinging above us.

'Will you tell me what happened?'

He automatically knows what I'm talking about. I feel him look over at me, hear him sigh, and he sinks down to lean on the railing too. I'm certain he's going to think up an excuse and run away at any moment, and I don't think either of us realise he's going to speak until the words spill out.

'A lorry hit me. My car burst into flames, flipped over a few times, and plunged two hundred metres into a frozen lake. The last thing I remember is seeing the lorry veer towards me, although for many years, that didn't stop the flashbacks and nightmares. So I'm not sure if they're my actual memories or my imagination of what people told me had happened. I only remember waking up in hospital and choking on the breathing tube down my throat, and it had gone from winter to spring when in my mind, I'd been driving across that bridge the day before, not two months earlier.'

He drops his head onto his arms and I can't stop myself reaching out to brush his hair back where it's flopped forward. His eyes close, but he's so quiet that I'm convinced he's not going to say anything else, and it surprises me when he does.

'It was completely the other driver's fault, and it made me *hate* people. When you survive something like that, you're supposed to be overjoyed and thankful to have a second chance at life and embrace it with both hands, but I . . . I went the opposite way. I withdrew from everything. I hated everything. I was angry with the whole world. When I eventually left the hospital, I got compensation for the accident and I used it to buy a cabin out here and . . . never left.'

'Far away from your family?' I remember what he said about being from much further south, my fingers still brushing through his choppy hair.

'I needed to be alone. I needed to recover at my own pace. I couldn't deal with cheerful nurses telling me how well I was doing like a puppy at obedience class. I couldn't deal with my family's worry for me. Looking back, I realise it wasn't the healthiest response, but it was what I needed at the time.'

'Like an injured wolf going to ground to lick their wounds?'

'Exactly.' He does a soft mocking growl and it sends a tingle down my spine.

'Are you okay now?'

'I'm fine.' He lifts his head and smiles at me, making my hand slide out of his hair. 'It was a long time ago now. Nothing left but lifelong aches and pains and a body with enough pins in it that I set off any metal detector that comes within a five-kilometre distance, and I have enough scars that I'm glad you'll never see me with my clothes off.'

What a thought. Thankfully it's too cold to even consider removing a glove, never mind anything else.

'Everyone kept telling me how lucky I was, but I felt the opposite. This thing had completely changed the course of my life. I resented normal, uninjured people. I resented people going about their daily lives when my world had stopped. I was so angry with every pain, every movement that hurt, every *thing* I couldn't do. I resented my stupid broken body. I resented that I *didn't* feel this amazing sense of second chance that *everyone* told me I should feel. I thought there was something wrong with me as a person, that my entire psyche was corrupt because I didn't feel that. I resented the other driver because he'd been fiddling with his radio and he walked away uninjured. The assumption was that I was to blame because I was young and he was fifty-something with decades of driving experience. They put out an appeal for witnesses, and there were a *lot* of people on the bridge that day, and not one of them came forward for me.

'The police eventually proved it through the skid marks and the damage to the road barrier and the vehicles . . . but it showed me that you can't rely on anyone. People are inherently selfish. They only care about themselves. The driver never admitted fault. He got a couple of years for negligent driving, but I still couldn't walk by the time he got out of prison.'

The hand that's next to his has gradually crept over his arm until his fingers squeeze mine and I realise I've got a death grip on his hand.

'I'm in touch with my family again now, but I never even told them where I went. I just disappeared. I wanted to get back on my feet myself. I didn't want to be an imposition on anyone else's life. I didn't want them to pity me or have to worry about the helplessly pathetic invalid I'd become. It had ruined my life; I didn't want it to impact on my family's too. It took most of my twenties to get back to where I am now, physically. And to stop hating people. I like to think I'm a well-adjusted fellow human now, but it took a few years.'

I put my glass down on the wooden railing and slide my other hand over his, holding it between both of mine, hoping he can tell how hard I'm squeezing it through the gloves.

'Can I say something?' He opens his arms, silently asking if he can hug me. I nod, and he bends down and pulls me tight against him, his head dropping until he can speak the words into my shoulder. 'I've never, ever, *ever* told anyone that before. And never *ever* thought I would, either. And if anyone asks, I'm drunk.'

I shift enough in his embrace to look at the full glass on the railing. 'You've had, like, two sips!'

'I know, but I don't share stuff like this, so if anyone asks, I must be drunk.'

The thought of Tav being this open with me makes a fizzle run through my entire body, and even though I'm fairly sure it's impossible to hold him any tighter, it doesn't stop me trying.

'Okay, it's got to the point where I need to tell you something, and it's going to change things, and I can't do it sober.' He releases me, picks up his glass and knocks the drink back in one. He inclines his head towards the cabin door. 'Can I come inside?'

It's toasty in the cabin and I go over to pour us another drink each and shrug off my coat and gloves, and when I turn back from the kitchen area, Tav's done the same and is sitting on the cream faux-fur rug by the fire, his back against the wall beside the fireplace.

I hand over his glass and he puts it on the stone bricks of the hearth and pats the space between his legs. It could probably be misinterpreted, but it just seems like he wants a bit of human comfort, and I can't bear the idea of *not* sitting as close to him as physically possible.

His arms are around his knees and I sit down so my back is against his chest, and his arms close loosely around me too. 'Okay. When I first came here, I was alone. I was in constant agony. I could barely move, casts and splints and wounds that wouldn't heal, and I hated the whole world and everything in it – we've established that, right?'

I nod. It sounds horrific, but I can't help the smile at his self-deprecating way of talking, and I wriggle back until he curls further around me.

'What I learnt about myself was that there was one thing I didn't hate, and that was Christmas. That first year, it brought me comfort. I was a mess. The strongest painkillers didn't touch the pain. I drank myself into oblivion every night because it was the only way to get any sleep, and that was plagued by nightmares, and every waking moment was agony, but I somehow managed to lose myself in those soppy made-for-TV Christmas movies. They were a ridiculous escape. For two hours, I could forget everything and believe in happy endings and festive magic.

'And the following year, I decorated the cabin, more as a challenge than anything else. I had to train myself to walk again, and by that point, I could stand up for a few minutes at a time and I could walk a few steps but I never knew when my legs were going to give out, so I reasoned with myself that even if I did one thing a day, one staple in a set of lights around the roof, one string of tinsel somewhere, I was getting somewhere. And seeing it come alight in front of me made me smile for the first time in forever. And then the year after that, a little girl from the village came up the path and I froze because I hated people coming near the cabin.'

I'm sitting against him with my head leaning back on his shoulder. It's impossible to imagine him struggling so much when he's so strong and capable now.

'I never went out. I had everything delivered and answered the door like a crazy pair of eyes looking through the letterbox and telling the delivery guys to leave it outside and go away. I never let anyone see me because I was such a wreck. And this little girl simply put a Christmas card and a candy cane through my letterbox and left, and when I opened it, there was a crayon drawing of a reindeer, and it read, "*To the lonely man in the woods, thank you for bringing us joy every time we see your house.*

We hope happiness finds you this Christmas." It was signed by a few kids from the village. I didn't think anyone even knew I was living there. It was like a dam burst inside me. It touched a part of me that I thought had died in the accident. I sat on the doormat in floods of tears. I'd never cried, I'd never felt any emotion other than anger and frustration since the accident, and that moment . . . I changed. I realised there was still good in the world and being angry was taking away the life I had left.

'Things got better from there on. I don't know if it was psychosomatic or the shift in my attitude or what, but I got stronger. I walked further. Lifted heavier things. Don't get me wrong, I didn't run outside and embrace life again, but I started talking to my family on the phone, drank less, started walking outside, even answered the door to a food delivery once. Another year went by, and then the most Christmassy thing you can imagine happened to me on Christmas Eve.'

His arms are draped around me so his hands are in front of us, and if he's noticed the vice-like grip I've got on them, he doesn't say anything. And if he wanted to be drunk for this, I haven't let go of his hands long enough for him to pick up the glass yet.

'I was walking in the woods and I found an injured reindeer calf. Her foot had been caught in some kind of a trap and been pulled free, but the wound was horrific. And it was like meeting a kindred soul. She didn't run away from me – it was like she could sense I knew a bit about injuries. She let me pick her up and take her home. And she came to live with me, and she recovered, and she changed my life. I called her Dancer because if you find a reindeer on Christmas Eve, you *have* to name her after one of Santa's reindeer, and because dancing seemed like something I'd never be able to do again at the time. She became my confidante, my only friend, and also my mode of transportation. I couldn't drive – physically *or* emotionally, but you can get anywhere you need to go around here by sleigh.'

So much suddenly makes sense. Why he's so fiercely independent and averse to accepting help. Why he doesn't drive. Even why my father has such a strong connection with him.

'I built a sleigh out of pallet wood from old deliveries, trained her to pull it, and I started pushing myself to go out, to go further, to venture into the nearest village, and people were so kind to me. I thought they'd run away like I was some kind of monster, but they treated me normally. They loved Dancer, everyone asked about her. Word started getting around that I was good with reindeer and someone found an abandoned one and sent her to me, and then someone had an old one they couldn't bear to have put down, and I ended up as this cabin in the woods with reindeer all around me, and it brought so much joy back into my life. I got stronger through helping them get stronger, I met new people, children came to visit my reindeer, I put up more Christmas lights and people were wowed when they looked at my cabin, and I started thinking about what I could do to give something back.'

I can't stop thinking about how looks can be deceiving. Who would ever look at this huge, hulking, strong guy, and imagine he'd been through something like that in his life? I make sure one hand stays clasped around both of his, but I let the other one slide up behind me, stroking through the long hair at the back of his head, my nails brushing the scars at the nape of his neck.

He lets out a long breath and his body gets heavier with relaxation, and inside I do a little victorious dance. Getting Tav to relax is no easy task.

'This is the part you're not going to like, Sash,' he murmurs, sounding blissful and dreamily far away.

'Try me.'

'I bought the forest around the cabin.' He pauses, like he's waiting for me to understand.

To be honest, I'm so relaxed sitting with him that I can barely focus on what he's saying.

'I wanted to share Christmas magic. I started building one

plank at a time. It was my recovery project. I named the first one after the candy cane that little girl put through my door all those years before . . .'

'This place?' It suddenly hits me and I understand all at once. '*You* built this place?'

He nods, his head so close to mine that I only feel it.

'That means . . . you owned this place. *You're* the old owner? *You* sold it to my dad?'

He nods again. 'I know you think the old owner was trying to take advantage of him, but it wasn't like that. We'd been friends since he started playing Santa, and when he arrived last year, I told him it would be the end, and he *asked* if he could buy me out.' He's suddenly not relaxed at all, rushing to get the words out, stumbling over them in his haste. 'I hadn't been intending to sell, I was going to let it fade out of existence, because the budget was gone and the list of required repairs was getting longer, but he *wanted* to take it on. He had all these plans for it, and I felt he would breathe new life into it.'

'He's nearly eighty years old!'

'Yeah, but he loved the place as much as I do. He lit up when he saw it. Like you do. Full of childhood wonder. That's what was important to me.' He sighs and his head drops against the back of my shoulder. 'I know I should have told you earlier, and even though I'm so comfortable that I don't think I could move if I tried, you can throw me out. I'll go if you want me to.'

I let my hand fall away from his hair and trail back down his arm until both of mine are wound around his hands again. I should probably be angry, but it doesn't come as much of a surprise really. I knew Tav was heavily involved in this place and has always seemed like much more than an employee, and the fact that he's just opened up the way he has makes me want to do nothing but hold on to him as tightly as possible.

'It's okay,' I murmur, and his arms tighten around me. I'd thought badly of the old owner, but knowing it's Tav does change things, because he isn't the sort of guy who'd take advantage of an old man, and I know how persuasive my dad can be when he wants something.

I let my head rest back against his shoulder, and feel his breath against my neck as he exhales and relaxes again, and I wish I had the courage to tilt my head and kiss his jaw.

'Are you really okay now?'

He lets out a laugh of relief when he realises I'm not going to throw him out. 'I'm fine. It's eighteen years past. I keep active. I build muscle strength. I know you've noticed my displays of dexterity – that was a way of recovering, of teaching my body to work in sync again. You'd never know anything had happened now, apart from the scars.'

My hand drifts up to graze over the nape of his neck again, and his whole body goes boneless around me and his arms pull me even tighter against him, and I lose track of time as we sit there, wrapped around each other, surrounded by the warm glow of the fire and his cologne, almond, cinnamon, and something earthy like tea, and it's the most contented I've ever felt.

'I should go.' It feels like hours later when Tav eventually disentangles our bodies and pushes himself up to his feet. He bends down to pick up the now stone-cold drink and downs it in one.

'Stay?'

'It doesn't work that quickly, you know.'

I laugh. 'I know. Besides, that's two glasses. It'd take about six bottles to bring down a guy your size. I just meant . . . I don't know. Stirring up memories and stuff like that. Stay, Tav. Please.'

He meets my eyes and a smile hints at his mouth. 'I'd like that.'

It's soft and vulnerable and makes me *wish* there was a sprig of mistletoe nearby so I'd have an excuse to kiss him.

He's quiet as we get ready for bed, skirting around each other in the small cabin. There's something comforting about his presence, but by the time I'm lying in bed, I'm *really* missing the closeness of earlier. 'Tav?'

'I could've been asleep, you know.'

'Yeah, I know. But you weren't.'

We lie there in the darkness just listening to each other breathe.

I close my eyes and say the words into the room, like if I can't see them coming out, they won't be so forward. 'When I wanted you to stay, I didn't want you to stay on the sofa.'

He lets out a burst of laughter. 'When I agreed to stay, I didn't want to stay on the sofa.'

'Will you come over here?'

'You know I shouldn't, right?' He says, despite the fact he's vaulted off the sofa before I've finished the sentence.

'Oh, come on. It's cold. We need to huddle for warmth. You're providing a service to a guest.'

The bed dips under his weight as he sits beside me, and I turn onto my side to give him space.

He runs a finger from the base of my back up to my neck though the duvet, and without a word, he lies down beside me. He's on top of the duvet and I'm underneath it, and it's thick enough to feel like there's a few feet between us.

He pulls his own blanket over himself and spreads it out so it covers me as well, and then his arm drapes across me over the duvet, and his lips touch my shoulder through my pyjama top.

'Just a little while,' he murmurs, his voice sounding slurred and half-asleep already.

His huge arm is across my body, his hand resting on top of the blanket on top of the duvet on my other side, and I want to pull my hand out and slide it down his arm and intertwine my fingers with his, but the idea of having a limb outside the duvet is horrific, so I fit my palm underneath where his is resting, and I can't help the giggle as his fingers squeeze mine back through the duvet.

I'm warmer than reasonably possible given the Arctic temperatures, and it's the cosiest way I've ever fallen asleep.

Chapter 13

Dear Santa,
For Christmas, can I have – a skateboard, new trainers, a
Nerf water blaster, a PlayStation, and £63,567.
From,
Giovanni

Even though I didn't expect anything different, Tav's gone when I open my eyes in the morning, but everything he said last night is still ringing in my ears. Like so many mornings lately, I'm rushing to get dressed because I can't wait to see him, and I race down the hill in record timing, so eager that I *almost* consider pulling out the saucer and sledging down. But I'm not quite that brave. Yet.

I barrel into the house and skid to a halt in the living room doorway, having forgotten to take my boots off and tracked snow through the hallway.

'Good morning.' Tav sounds bemused at my hurried appearance. He's sitting in an armchair with both hands wrapped around a mug of steaming coffee, and looking far too tired for this early in the day.

'Oh, good, you're here!' Dad looks up from his tablet, almost bouncing in his seat. 'We're trending on Twitter! Something about

216

a little boy and a homeless man. One of the national newspapers back in the UK has picked up the story, and people keep commenting about how their children have got letters from us and are begging their parents to bring them here because this is where the *real* Santa lives. The dog looks very fetching in the coat you sent him.'

'We're not giving up on this place,' I blurt out.

Tav raises an eyebrow.

'I understand now, Tav. This place is *you* and we are *not* going to lose it. *You* are in every corner, every plank of wood – it's your love for Christmas and your attention to detail. *That* is what makes this place so special. I've noticed it from the very beginning but I only understood it last night.'

Dad's ears prick up at the mention of last night.

I glance behind me at the reception desk and I can see the visitor book open and covered in Tav's handwriting. No wonder he looks like this is the first time he's sat down all morning.

He notices me looking. 'Yes, we're busy at the moment, but interest in Santa nosedives off a cliff on December 26th.'

'No it doesn't. Kids love Santa all year round. They write to him often, not just at Christmas. This could be a destination twelve months a year. The reindeer are here all year round. People would come to see them outside of Christmas. And it's not just that. How many months a year are the Northern Lights visible?'

'September to April.'

'Okay, so after Christmas, we rebrand. The North Pole Forest becomes the Northern Lights Forest. How about the summer? What's good here then? Fishing? Hiking? Bird-watching? Any fjords nearby? How about the opposite of the near-constant darkness in the warmer months – the midnight sun? That would be a pretty amazing thing to see too. And this place embodies the idea of "getting away from it all" – people need that at any time of year. And some people love Christmas and would quite happily celebrate it all year round, so there could still be an aspect of that. This is a winter wonderland for months on end. There is so much more we can do here. You have one hill for sledging, but the place is surrounded by hills. All the snowdrifts, so deep you could literally dive into them. There's so much space. Why aren't we having snowman-building contests and snow slides and all the other fun stuff that kids don't get to experience in the UK and other warmer countries? Back at home, we're lucky if it snows once a year. This is the complete opposite of the singular day of sleet and the mud-tinged thin layer of snow we're lucky to get at home. People would come here for so many reasons – not just to see Santa Claus.'

'I know how Hotel Magenta must've felt when you came on board,' Dad says.

I force myself to ignore that. 'I don't think you realise how much of a world away this is from the UK. The only thing we need to do is get people to know about it.'

Dad taps his tablet. 'I can't keep up with my notifications. I'm perpetually five hours behind my mentions on Twitter and I haven't been brave enough to open my Facebook page yet.'

'Exactly. People are talking about the North Pole Forest. A *lot* of people who didn't previously know it existed. Those letters were never meant to go viral, but now we have to make the most of it and engage our followers in other things. Naming the reindeer, for instance. I've read so many letters asking about the reindeer. We could run a competition on social media to name them. We could take photos and post facts about them. We could take pictures of the cabins and offer a prize for correctly guessing the theme to each one. We can keep interest going after Christmas *and* showcase this place for how beautiful it is. You've already got bookings for next year. Holidays like this aren't booked on the spur of the moment; they're planned months in advance. We have to offer more stuff, because all we've got at the moment is Santa and some reindeer. You've mentioned Mrs Claus's cooking lessons and elf workshops – we have to get those restarted because they're so unique. And there's that outdoor pursuits place over there.' I point in a vague direction that's probably nowhere near where the outdoor pursuits place actually is. 'They offer the husky dog sledding, snowshoeing expeditions, hiking trails . . .'

'Skiing, ice fishing, snowboarding,' Dad interjects.

'Us and them are the only two places around here – I'm *sure* we could get into some sort of cooperation with them. We could be a stop-off on their trips, a destination to get to, stop at for a hot chocolate and a homemade mince pie, and in return, we advertise their expeditions to our tourists, and vice versa. It would benefit both places, and you borrow their dogs so you must get on with the owners; surely they'd be up for a discussion? There is so much more we can do here. The ice cream parlour, the hot chocolate bar, Mrs Claus's diner and bakery need to be reopened.

'And I was thinking about those coupons in the bottom of the gift baskets. You make the nearby village sound like a little craft market with people making and selling homemade goods. They already support us by offering our guests discounts, but what if they got more involved? What if we repaired those unused cabins and asked local crafters if they'd like to sell their bits and pieces here? Visitors *love* a gift shop and we haven't got one, and there's no on-site bakery anymore, nowhere to get a cuppa, but if we could add something like that, it would make it like a year-round Christmas market and add non-seasonal interest.'

I realise it's been a while since I stopped talking, but instead of saying anything, Tav looks out the window and sips his coffee.

'Why aren't you excited?' I try to quell my enthusiasm as I take a step towards him. 'You've got the most can-do attitude of anyone I've ever met, but you seem to have given up on this place entirely. Make me understand, Tav.'

'I've seen it fail once.' He looks me directly in the eyes. '*I've* failed it once. I had this many ideas when I started. I had this much energy. It didn't do any good in the end. You're right – this place means *so* much to me, and I *can't* see it fail again.'

'It won't. Not while I'm around.' I give him my best grin, feeling confident because I'm more excited about this than I have been about anything in a really long time. From the moment I set foot here, something clicked into place, and what I thought would be an awful experience has been magical from start to not-yet-finish. 'This is a passion project for you, but you have no expertise in marketing. You're amazing at building, decorating, and boosting the Christmas spirit, but you have no experience of the holiday industry and what tourists would be drawn to.'

'Neither do you!'

Dad looks between us curiously and Tav backpedals. 'I mean, you didn't, before the hotel . . .'

I smile at him for still trying to protect my lies even when he's annoyed at me. 'What I mean is, you're seeing this place as a Norwegian. Snow for six months a year is normal to you. It's not normal to me – it's exceptional. You advertise as a Santa Claus village rather than a winter destination. There's so much untapped potential here, and you can't see it because you're too close to it, but I have an outsider's perspective. Plus, staff, Tav. A huge part of why this place is on its last legs is because you *cannot* do everything yourself and your insistence on trying leads to you sounding as burnt out as you sound right now.'

'People stopped coming, Sash. Christmas doesn't mean what it used to anymore. People are frazzled and stressed out. Most parents can't wait for Christmas to be over. They don't want to add a Christmas-themed holiday to their already frantic lives. To most adults, Christmas is an inconvenience, something they have to put up with to please their kids.'

'Then we need to do something that shows the true meaning of Christmas. To the kids who write those letters, Christmas hasn't lost its meaning; it's the old and jaded adults who need to believe in it more than anyone. Like me – you've made me believe anything's possible at Christmas. No, I don't believe that a mince pie addict in a red suit is going to pop down my chimney on Christmas Eve and leave presents under the tree, but you *have* made me see Christmas in a whole different light. It can change people's lives. It can make a bad year better. It can give you something to smile about all year through . . . What?' I trail off when I realise they're both grinning at me.

'I wish your hotel didn't need you back, Sasha,' Dad says. 'You're exactly what we need around here.'

'Maybe I could wrangle a few extra weeks . . .' I know I should tell him, but what if he's only listening to my ideas because of the respect he has for my job? He thinks I'm talking with this wealth of expertise behind me, and things will change if he knows I'm not.

'It'd be worth it just to see that smile on his face.' Dad nods to Tav. 'Don't think I've ever seen you smile like that, mate.'

Tav blushes and springs to his feet so fast he nearly spills what's left of his coffee. 'C'mon, we've got work to do.' He disappears into the hallway and the front door clatters shut behind him, and all that's left is the echo of the clonk as he banged his head on the doorframe.

'When you built this place, you really could've sized the doors better,' I shout after him.

I'm debating whether I should stay with Dad or go after Tav when Dad holds his tablet up. 'Sash, can you have a look at this? I've got a message from a mum who says her son is on the verge of not believing and can we do something special for him? She thinks it'll be his last year and she wants him to remember the magic. Can you do something about that?'

I nod as I take a photo of the screen so I've got all the info, and in my head, I'm already composing the letter I could write to him.

'I'm really glad I came here, Dad,' I say as he closes the cover on his tablet and gets up.

'So am I. I knew you'd love it.' He comes over and gives me a hug. 'You and Tav are doing something that money can't buy with those letters. You talk about doing something to show the true meaning of Christmas but you've already started without even realising it.' He steps back and his watery grey eyes meet mine. 'I know I haven't been the father you wanted at Christmas, but this season meant so much to your mum that it was impossible without her. I'm glad you and I have had this chance to reconnect. She'd be happy if she's looking down on us.' He blinks for a moment and I'm not sure which one of us is going to cry first, but then he exclaims, 'Beard curls!' and grabs his tongs from the mantelpiece and "ho ho ho"s his way out to the mirror in the hallway.

I stare after him, surprised by his hasty departure and by the mention of Mum. That's the most he's ever spoken about her. And that's *still* all there is. Even after all these years, that's *still* the best explanation he's willing to give. Yes, Christmases were hard without Mum, but he still won't look me in the eye and tell me why he thought they'd be easier to cope with alone rather than together.

Same old Dad, and not in a good way. In the past couple of weeks, I've felt like we might be getting somewhere, but we're clearly not. I call a goodbye over my shoulder as I go outside and scream in fright when Tav pushes himself off the wall of the house where he was leaning.

'Sorry,' he says, trying not to laugh at how much I jumped. 'I was going to stomp off down the road and then I realised I'd rather talk to you instead.'

It makes me smile and a warmth settles over me, soothing the unease of Dad's abrupt exit. Even standing next to Tav is like being wrapped in a snuggly blanket. Him being close warms some part of me from the inside out.

'Which bruise did you add to this time?' I incline my head so he ducks down and I reach up to let my fingers stroke gently at the side of his forehead.

'All of them,' he murmurs, his eyes drifting closed and his head growing heavier in my hand. 'Although if this is the response, I might have to start deliberately walking into doorframes.'

While I could stand there tucking his hair back all day, eventually Tav stands back up to full height and my hand falls away. He offers me his arm as we step off the porch and start walking down the road.

'You okay?'

'Yeah, just . . .' I sigh. 'Just Dad. He seems to be limited to one sentence about Mum before he overloads and rushes off. I thought we were reconnecting and moving forward since I've been here, but he still acts like he's the only one who lost her. I've spoken about her more to you than I've spoken to my own father.'

He squeezes my arm against his ribs. 'An honour I'll never forget.'

I roll my eyes, but it makes me smile when what I really want to do is shake Dad and beg him to tell me something *real*.

I can hear noise in the distance, a vague chatter-like sound. 'What's that?'

He takes his phone out and pulls up the Wi-Fi link to the security cameras. 'The car park's full.' He holds it out to show me the live image on screen. '*That* is the noise of about fifty families lining up to see Santa and the reindeer.'

'And it's not even nine o'clock.' I nudge my shoulder into his arm. 'This is going to work, Tav.'

'It's been years since I saw the car park like that.'

'And that's just people who live within driving distance. Others will come too. You'll see.'

'Thank you.' He squeezes the arm that's slotted through his and holds it tighter against his side. 'I don't mean to sound so negative, because I really appreciate your help, but I got my hopes up last year with your dad. He had so many plans. He had the money to invest in what we needed. And obviously I know his health is far more important and the fact he hasn't been well enough isn't his fault, but that elation of selling it to someone who loved it as much as I did, and then the soul-crushing crash of realising it wasn't to be . . . This place means so much to me – too much,

223

probably – and I've spent the past few months coming to terms with letting it go, and now I can feel your excitement building in me too, and I don't want to go through that again.' He looks down at me and looks away as soon as our eyes meet. 'And what about you? You're leaving. Are you still going to force your dad to sell up?'

My fingers curl tighter into his forearm through his coat sleeve. 'I don't know,' I say, because I honestly don't. Seeing how happy he is does change things, but the facts remain that he'll be eighty in a couple of months and he's had a heart attack. It's only minus-ten at the moment – pretty balmy for a December day here. It can't be sensible for him to stay.

He makes a noise of approval, and while I'm sure he's itching to push the matter, he doesn't. 'And you're really going to stay a bit longer?'

A lump springs to my throat because the thought of delaying my departure brings to mind the thought of leaving and somehow having to go back to normal life in the UK and carry on like I don't know the North Pole Forest exists. Or Tav. I glance up at him. I can't imagine carrying on with life like I *haven't* met him.

Even without an answer, he smiles but keeps his eyes on the road ahead. 'Good. Because I'm starting to wonder what the hell I'm going to do without you.'

I hold his arm so tightly that he'd probably have bruising if it weren't for the protective padding of his coat. I'm about to choke out some garbled response when I catch sight of two people walking towards us looking very . . . bright. 'Who's that?'

'That's Anja and Nils. They're a married couple who used to work here. They used to run the workshop, but after what you said about staff last night, I asked if they'd come in to help out until Christmas. Because I'm not a complete idiot and I know we can't manage on our own.'

'That's good, right? I mean, if *you* realise you can't do something alone, things must be going well.'

'Ha ha,' he says sarcastically, except when I meet his eyes, there's a softness in them that makes me want to pull him to a halt and forcibly hug him.

Thankfully we reach the pair coming up the road before I have a chance to do anything stupid. They're both dressed in red and green striped trousers under their red coats, with matching plastic points on their ear tips and stripy hats on their heads with bells jingling from the tip. Tav introduces us and we all shake hands and they quickly go to warm up with a cuppa before the gates open.

If Tav notices I'm holding his arm tighter as we carry on towards the post office, he doesn't say anything. Bringing two members of staff back, even temporarily, feels like a huge step in the right direction.

'What would you do about a kid on the cusp of not believing?' I ask, thinking about the message Dad showed me. 'Assuming an animated Tom Hanks *isn't* going to turn up at midnight and offer him a ride on *The Polar Express*.'

'Given your expansive knowledge of Christmas films for someone who supposedly hates Christmas, you and I need to have a festive movie night one of these days. I make a good cinnamon popcorn.'

One of us lets out a wanton moan of pleasure. It was probably me again.

He laughs at my noise. 'I'd write him a letter saying Santa does exist, but not in the way he's always thought. He exists in the hearts of everyone who keeps the spirit of Christmas alive, and *that* is true Christmas magic. Add that the spirit of Christmas is never lost for good and you hope he rediscovers it when he most needs it, and gets to share it with his own children one day.'

And just like that, I'm choking up again as we reach the door of the post office and Tav stops at the bottom of the ramp.

'You know you came in the wrong direction, right?' I say, assuming his first task is to get the reindeer ready for visitors.

'Walking with you is never in the wrong direction.'

'Oh God, Tav.' I do another guttural groan. 'Are you trying to melt me or what?'

He laughs and holds his arms open. 'Can I?'

I nod and go to hug him too, but he bends until his arms slide around my waist and stands back up, lifting me completely off the ground.

I squeal and wrap my arms tightly around his shoulders, clinging on for dear life. I can feel his face shifting into a smile against my shoulder and I bury mine in his gorgeous tousled hair. His arms are so tight and make me feel so safe that I risk unfurling one hand and letting it rub over his shoulders, and this time it's him who makes a noise of contentment. I can't stop myself turning my head to the side and pressing a kiss to his earlobe, and it feels like his knees buckle because he wobbles and sets me back down quickly, but he doesn't pull away.

After we've stood there for an abnormally long time, his stubble scratches across my cheek as his lips press a kiss there and he pulls back, but his hands stay on my waist and mine stay on his arms, holding on for a moment longer.

'I should be helping,' I whisper because it feels like speaking at full volume would be wrong.

'You are.'

Two simple words, but that genuine feeling washes over me again. I feel valued here, like I'm doing something that makes a difference.

'None of this would be happening without you, Sash. And I . . .' He trails off instead of finishing the sentence. 'I'd better go.'

The familiar feeling of being bereft comes again as his hands drop and he steps away, and I have to have a stern word with myself about being so silly. 'Shout if you need anything.'

He stops in the middle of walking away and turns back with a grin. 'You know what, I actually will.'

I do a victory punch into the air and the corners of his eyes crinkle up as he laughs. 'May the magic of Christmas twinkle throughout your day.'

'Yours too, Tav,' I say as I watch him walk back up the road and I find myself staring into the distance long after he's out of sight.

Being around him makes me feel giddy and excited, like a child on Christmas Eve night, lying awake listening for the sound of reindeer hooves on the roof, and I know one thing – going home is going to be more impossible than I thought.

Chapter 14

Dear Santa,
No cookies and milk for you! You need to go on a diet. I'll be leaving out some celery, a glass of water, and a Joe Wicks DVD. You can do this! Diet and exercise! Do you have gyms at the North Pole? If not, don't put so much work on the elves and do some yourself. My nan says all those cookies aren't good for you and you'll get diabetes like her.
From,
Savannah

It's a Saturday afternoon a few days later, December 18th, and as I approach the bottom of the hill, Tav is outside the house, loading supplies into the back of a sleigh with a reindeer harnessed to the front of it.

'Are you going somewhere?'

'An injured reindeer has been found about fifty kilometres north. The person who found it thinks it might've been hit by a train. I've got to go and find it and see what we can do. Sorry, Sash, this is my job first and foremost. It has to take priority.'

'Of course,' I say, even though I hate the idea of Tav going away for any length of time. I have a limited number of days left here and I don't want to lose any time with him, and judging by the amount of stuff he's got packed into that sleigh, it'll be a while. 'How long will you be gone for?'

'Just until tomorrow. If I leave now, I can stop overnight, find the reindeer first thing and be back by tomorrow afternoon. Monday is the start of Christmas week, we're going to need all hands on deck so I don't want to be gone longer than necessary.'

I go over to talk to the reindeer harnessed to the front of the sleigh, enjoying a pile of lichen Tav's put down for him. He doesn't have any antlers and I think he's the one I named Mr Bean. Maybe it's a sign that I'm starting to recognise them. 'Is it safe?'

'Of course. I've done it thousands of times.' He looks over and we hold each other's gaze for a few long moments. 'I'll miss you, you know.'

Before I have a chance to process that or admit I'll miss him a truly ridiculous amount for someone I've only known for a few weeks, the front door opens and Dad bustles out with a picnic box in his hand. 'Oh, good, are you all packed too?' He says when he sees me. 'I've put more than enough food in for both of you.'

'I'm not going with him.'

'Of course you are. I'm not sending him out into the forest on his own.'

I laugh out loud at the idea of me being able to somehow protect Tav. 'You do realise there are mountains smaller than him, right? If he ran into a polar bear, *it* would run away in fright.'

'It's fine, Perce,' Tav says. 'This is the only way I travel. You've never worried about me before. You need Sasha here because neither of us are going to leave you on your own overnight.'

'Oh, don't you worry about that. I'm going to my friend's house in the village. There's a football match on. We'll have a few beers and I'll stop on his couch for the night; save toddling back up here after a nightcap.' He turns to me. 'So if you stay here, you'll be completely alone. Apart from the wolves. And the polar bears. And the brown bears. Oh, and I saw footprints this morning that almost definitely belonged to a lynx.'

I gulp.

Tav looks between us. 'You can come if you want, Sash. It'll take me five minutes to hitch up another sleigh.' He must be able to sense my apprehension because he says, 'I'll be right in front of you. We can tie together. My reindeer are well trained; you only need to know a few simple commands.'

On the one hand, going off into the wilderness in a reindeer-drawn sleigh sounds terrifying, but so does staying here alone, and the promise of more time with Tav is enough to outdo all of the doubts.

'Are you sure you'll be okay?' I say to Dad, and I don't miss the huge grin that breaks across Tav's face and his valiant attempt at stifling it.

'I won't be here. I'm busy in my grotto for another couple of hours and my elves, Nils and Anja – that couple you met the other day – are here to help. They're going to give me a lift down to my friend's house when we close for the night, and tomorrow's Sunday so we don't open until late and things will be quiet.'

Tav gives me an encouraging nod.

'Okay. I'll go and pack some clothes,' I say, a bit bewilderedly. How do you go from barely leaving your house to heading out on a reindeer rescue mission with someone who might possibly be the favourite man you've ever met?

Despite being nervous, travelling by reindeer-pulled sleigh is amazing. It's slow and steady and gives me a chance to look at the frozen world all around.

Tav's in front of me, following the map and setting the pace, and his sleigh is tied to mine so we don't get separated. The reindeer themselves are expert sleigh pullers because they mosey along like it's no bother at all. The one I named Pedro Pascal doesn't seem to notice the extra weight he's pulling as he trots along the snow, his hooves spreading as each foot touches the ground, like a built-in snowshoe.

It's only four o'clock but it's as dark as the dimmest night, and it really is the wilderness out here. We're climbing north, and the trees are bare snow-covered branches rather than the evergreens around the forest, but they're still dense as we slide between them and overgrown skeletal bushes on well-worn but narrow paths.

'Do you really travel like this all the time?' I call to Tav.

'I don't drive, Sash. I haven't got back in a car since . . .' He abandons the sentence and I wish I'd asked when he was within hugging distance.

At first I thought he was mad when he mentioned travelling by reindeer sleigh, but I can see how it's the kind of lifestyle you could get used to, and it fits Tav's laid-back persona perfectly. He doesn't rush or get stressed about anything else; why should his mode of transportation be any different?

The stars are twinkling above us, and the sky is so clear, I'm pretty sure I can see the entirety of the Milky Way. The air is so pure, it's crisp and cold, but instead of biting at my lungs like it did at first, they feel clearer than they did at home.

I don't realise how quickly the hours pass. It's the most peaceful thing I've ever done, being pulled along by the gentle trotting of a reindeer with only the sound of their hooves on snow, so quiet I can hear Pedro Pascal's stomach gurgles and the clicks and grunts as he walks along.

'Your dad set up the route.' Tav has got out and is walking Mr Bean and following a map on his phone. 'Our overnight stop is on a frozen lake that's one of the most perfect places for seeing the Northern Lights. We should be coming up to it now . . .' He trails off as he looks into the distance. 'I can see the *lavvu* poles leaning against that tree.' He halts both the reindeer and holds out a hand to pull me up from the sleigh. 'We'll have something to eat and settle down for the night, and then get off early in the morning so we've got a hope of making it back by tomorrow afternoon.'

'That was amazing, Tav. Talk about the way to travel.'

He smiles as his eyes meet mine. 'It's old-fashioned. Even the Sami people use snowmobiles these days, but for me, it's the safest way.'

I'm still holding on to his hand and he involuntarily tugs me closer, and I'm sure he's going to kiss me even though we've got our scarves pulled up over our noses, but eventually he blinks and pulls his gloved hand out from under my fingers.

'I'll set the *lavvu* up. Can you . . .' He hands me both the reindeer reins, and I tie them to a tree, put down food pellets, and then collect some lichen that's hanging from nearby branches because they deserve a treat after pulling us all this way.

I don't wander far enough to lose sight of Tav or run into a lynx, but when I get back, he's got the huge poles arranged in some kind of tripod formation, like a tepee on the banks of the frozen lake.

'Are you sure the Sami people won't mind us using these?'

'They're here for weary travellers.' He gets a huge fold of fabric from underneath his sleigh.

The reindeer nibble the lichen greedily out of my hands, making me laugh at their enthusiasm. I quickly leave it with them when I realise Tav has unfolded the fabric and is trying to spread it out over the poles by himself.

'Let me help.' I take half before he can protest and between us we tie it onto one of the poles and wrap it around the sides to form a tent, leaving the top open.

'Ventilation for the fire,' Tav says when he sees me looking at it, thinking we must've done something wrong.

'You make a fire *in* the tent?'

He laughs at my lack of exposure to the ways of the outside world and starts unpacking the sleeping bags, while I go off and gather some sticks for the fire, and when I get back, the *lavvu* already looks like a snug winter den, the kind of place you'd voluntarily spend a night under the stars.

He's thrown down woollen blankets and two winter-weight sleeping bags are unfolded on top of them, and the fact they're laid out side by side makes something inside me go all hot and fluttery. He's gathered some stones to build a fire-pit, and he arranges the sticks and sets a match to them, and the tent fills with the crackle of wood burning.

'Well, aren't you just a regular Bear Grylls.'

'What kind of bear is that?'

It makes me laugh so loudly that Mr Bean drops his lichen in fright. 'Believe me, no one's worked that out yet.'

The flap that forms the *lavvu* door is still open, but the fire offsets the cold night air coming in, and I'm impressed by how . . . easy . . . that was. Who knew you could fling a tent together in ten minutes flat? I mean, maybe everyone did, but I've never been camping before, so I didn't. Or maybe it's just how easy Tav makes it. *Everything* seems easier when he's around.

It's cramped and Tav, unsurprisingly, can't stand at full height inside. I nod towards the two sleeping bags. 'It looks suspiciously like we might have to huddle for warmth.'

'I was counting on it.' He gives me a wink and a cheeky grin that makes my heart melt so much I'm in need of a blast of cold air.

When I step back outside, there's a flare of green overhead and I stop and stare. They're not so much flashing and dashing tonight, but the sky has taken on a green tinge, brighter in some places than others, and getting stronger as I watch it.

I let out a long breath, still mesmerised by the splashes of light even after seeing them so many times now, but Tav barely gives it a cursory glance. He's building up another fire outside the tent, in front of a fallen log, and I look between the lights and him as he carries on working.

'Tav, stop.'

'Hmm?' He glances up at me from where he's crouched.

'Stop for a minute. Take a breath. Look up.'

I half expected him to ignore me and carry on, but he pushes himself up, looking towards the sky.

The green fades to a ribbon of pale yellow, like a dragon appearing from the corner of my vision and weaving across the sky.

Tav stands next to me; his hand is hanging limply by his side, so near that my glove brushes against his, and while I'm trying to persuade myself that it would be wrong to take his hand, his fingers close around mine.

Shades of pinks and purples have crept into the sky now and the lights above us have started their usual swirling movements, and every curtain of light that twists above us is spellbinding.

I've forgotten how cold it is. Our breath appears in front of our faces, but my whole body feels overwhelmed by every aspect of Tav filling my senses, his spicy almond cologne that blocks out everything apart from the spectacular light-show above us, and that feeling of being so incredibly lucky creeps up my spine again. I can't believe *this* is my life.

'Dance with me,' Tav murmurs.

I almost laugh at the thought. Dancing in the snow under the Northern Lights is so romantic, it's bordering on cheesy, and if I'd seen it in a movie, I'd probably make puking noises, but I also think of what he said the other night, about Dancer and after the accident, and my hands have slid up his arms and closed over his shoulders before I realise I'm going to agree.

His hands settle on my hips and hold me against him, and it feels like the kind of moment you need to be wearing delicate heels and a slinky, silky dress, not huge snow-boots and enough layers of clothing to rival that episode of *Friends* where Joey comes in wearing all of Chandler's clothes.

My head finds his chest and rests against it, listening to the thump of his heartbeat through his clothes, and Tav starts humming "December Song" by George Michael as we step aimlessly across the snow, enjoying the closeness and the peace.

I keep coming back to that word. I've felt nothing but peaceful since I came here.

I tilt my head up. 'I can't remember the last time I danced.'

His arms grow impossibly tighter. 'You're not going to punch me for suggesting something so tacky then?'

It makes me burst into such laughter than both the reindeer look up from their lichen-munching in annoyance. 'I'll try to restrain myself.'

'Good, because everyone should have a life that makes them want to dance occasionally.'

I'm pretty sure the extreme temperature is the only thing that's preventing me from melting right now.

'How about you? Do you do a lot of dancing in the moonlight?' I move my head against his chest, nodding towards the crescent moon, glowing above a mountaintop in the distance.

'Not as much as I used to. Everything feels different since you got here though. You make me feel like dancing again.'

I can't contemplate the depth of those words. It makes me want to hug him tighter than is physically possible, but if he notices me squidging up a bit closer to his body then he doesn't complain. It's a good job his hair is hidden under a hat because I'm not sure I'd be able to stop my hands winding in it and dragging his lips down to mine.

I stay silent instead, because silence has to be better than kissing Tav and doing something we can't undo. No matter how much I want to, there's still some sensible part of me saying I can't kiss this man when I have to go home in January.

Instead, I try to enjoy it for what it is – just a beautiful friend appreciating a beautiful, magical place. I'm humming along with "December Song" and although the Northern Lights are the most spectacular thing I've ever seen, they're not as important as enjoying his closeness.

'Is this how you seduce all women?' It was supposed to be a joke, but he instantly stiffens and I know I've said the wrong thing.

'I'm not the seductive type, Sash.' He stops moving. 'Sorry, this wasn't meant to come across as . . . I mean, I wasn't trying to . . . We should eat.' His arms drop from around me and he hurries over to stoke the fire and then goes to the sleigh and gets out a Tupperware container of warming chickpea curry my dad made this morning and a small pan, and some veggies to roast.

'I'm going to check on the reindeer.' I walk over to where the two lads are tethered, still munching their way through their piles of lichen. I stroke their sides and rub their noses when they sniff over my clothes to see if I'm hiding any more lichen about my person, but it's so impossible to take my eyes off Tav that it's a good thing they've both dropped their antlers by now or I would definitely have been impaled because I'm not paying attention.

I wait until he beckons me over and then go and sit on the log beside the fire and warm my hands over the flames. He's got a camping kettle in the fire, boiling water for cups of tea, and we take a fork each and share the curry straight from the pan.

The lights haven't faded yet, and I nearly miss my mouth with the fork a few times because I keep looking up at them.

'Trying to make the most of them before you go?'

The curry turns to concrete in my mouth and I make a noncommittal noise.

Neither of us speaks for a few moments.

'I don't do relationships, Sash. I've never wanted my life intertwined with anyone else's.' He's quiet for a minute and then he takes a deep breath. 'I was in a relationship when I had the accident. We'd been together for nearly two years. I thought we had a future together . . . But she'd left by the time I came out of the coma. Apparently she visited once, and then told my father to tell me – *if* I woke up – that she was sorry, but she had enough to deal with without having to cope with a crippled boyfriend too.'

I shift minutely closer on the log. That one little thing explains so much. No wonder he has a hard time opening up and refuses to let anyone do anything for him. He doesn't want to be an imposition on anyone else's life because someone left when it looked like he might be. 'That's horrific, Tav, but she was just one person. The wrong person for you, clearly. Anyone else would've stuck around and helped you through what must've been the hardest time of your life.'

'It's not about that. I never blamed her for leaving. We were young and my injuries looked lifelong at that point. She hadn't signed up for that. Even if she had stayed, I was in a bad place and would've chased her off anyway. I couldn't deal with anyone but myself and anything other than my own recovery. But it made me realise that I *had* to be independent. I had to be alone. I don't want to share my life with anyone. I rely on myself and expect nothing from anyone. To change now, after so many years, I'd need to be metaphorically knocked off my feet. Floored by something that can't be ignored. And I've never felt that.'

Why do I feel a sudden sting of disappointment? There can *never* be anything between me and Tav. I *know* that – we live in different worlds. But I'd be lying if I said I wasn't feeling *something* for him, and I thought he might be feeling something for me too. No one could blame him for closing off after that, but I thought he was starting to open up to me and that it might extend to *all* senses of the word, but he clearly isn't. 'Have you ever looked for love? Been on dates?'

'A couple of dates, here and there. Never more than that. I've never felt any chemistry or spark that would make it worth upturning my life for. It's taken me a long while to see myself as anything other than damaged and that doesn't make it easy to go on dates.'

That makes my breath catch for an altogether different reason, and something more magnetic than the lights above flickers between us.

He looks away sharply. 'How about you?'

'Nah. It goes back to that not feeling important thing. I dated a guy for a few years in my twenties, but towards the end, it

237

was a completely loveless routine. I spent most of the time feeling like an inconvenient afterthought to him, so I broke it off, and since then . . . Online dating with guys who are only after one thing, and a couple of dates where they only wanted to talk about themselves or barely put their phone down for long enough to order their food. And on one occasion, *my* food as well.'

Tav laughs. 'Oh no.'

'He insisted he was being chivalrous, even when I told him in no uncertain terms what I thought of that, so I tried to teach him a lesson by pretending to be allergic to peppers, faked an allergy attack to make him think twice about his actions, and left. I *may* have also stabbed myself with a biro and pretended it was an epi-pen.'

'Oh my God, you're amazing. I want to date you just for that. And I will never, *ever* order food for you.' He gives me a mock look of fright, making me giggle.

It's the most I've laughed about my love life in recent years.

'I've always thought that happily ever after begins with "happily" – you've got to be in the right place to find it. People use relationships as a bandage for an unhappy life and think love will fix anything, but I think you need to be happy yourself before you can share that with someone else.'

Something is making my eyes water, and I'm not sure if it's the cold air or him and his beautiful sentiments, but he's got a point. I've never really been happy with my life, and no relationship has ever worked out. Maybe the two things *are* connected. I've always gone into them half-heartedly, expecting disappointment, and on that front, I've never been disappointed.

'Will Mr Bean and Pedro Pascal be okay?' I ask as we get ready to go to bed. It's only 8 p.m. but trying to stay warm in this temperature takes its toll and neither of us can stop yawning.

He laughs at my worrying. 'Their fur is hollow so they've got built-in insulation. They survived the Ice Age, Sash, I *think* they can make it one night with us.'

'What about wolves?'

'Fire's burning, we're right here, and there are two of them. I'll put bells on the harnesses so we'll hear them ring if they get worried and move around. Reindeer can sense when a predator is nearby.'

I feel bad for leaving them out in the cold when the tent is warm and snug, glowing with the light from the fire while the smoke rises in a perfect line, up and out of the chimney at the top.

'Do you want . . . I mean, we don't actually *have* to huddle for warmth, we won't freeze to death if we sleep on opposite sides.'

'I'm going to pretend I didn't hear that. We *might* not freeze to death, but I don't want to risk it, do you?'

He laughs loudly. 'I can honestly say I do not.'

It's warm enough inside that we're able to take our coats and gloves off and get in our sleeping bags. Tav gets into his with ease, lies down on the blankets, and is enough of a gentleman to bite back his giggles as I try to get into mine with all the grace of a flamingo being thrown out of the pub at closing time, and tuck my water bottle down the front in an attempt to stop it turning to ice.

Once I've stopped wriggling around, he drags an open sleeping bag across to cover both of us, but instead of pulling back, his arm stays draped across me, and I can almost forget we're in a tent in the Norwegian wilderness, that there could be literally *anything* lurking out there, and it's minus-twenty degrees.

But it's also awkward. He's taut and unrelaxed and probably as hyper-aware of touching me as I am of touching him.

'This is . . . not how I expected to be spending tonight.'

Addressing the awkwardness head-on makes him laugh and instantly eases the tension. He shifts until he can slide his right arm under me, and I settle my head on it like a pillow.

His arm is outstretched in front of me, his palm open and

his fingers limp. The movement has rucked up the sleeve of his thermal top and the flickering of the fire picks out the deep white line of a scar on his palm that runs under the base of his thumb and down the side of his wrist. This time, I can't stop myself touching it. I pull the sleeping bag up so it keeps his arm warm, and then I unzip my bag until I can snake a hand out and let my fingers touch his inner forearm and graze gently up to the palm of his hand and down again, over and over.

He shivers and I don't think it has much to do with the temperature. After a few long minutes, my stroking has the desired effect because I feel him start to relax. His arm over the top of me gets heavier, and he exhales and snuggles closer. He uses his chin to push back the sleeping bag until his lips find my shoulder and press a kiss there.

'Thank you.' He says it so quietly that I feel the reverberation of the words through my top rather than hear them.

'What for?' I whisper into the darkness without letting my fingers stop as they trail across his inner wrist.

'Your enthusiasm. Your creativity. Your dedication to the Santa letters and everything you're doing.' His lips touch my shoulder again, higher up this time, closer to the bare skin at the nape of my neck. 'You're right: I am burnt out. I'm burnt out and I'm lonely, and I didn't realise either of those things until you forced me to.'

His voice is a low rumble that travels all the way down my spine and I let my fingers rub over the scar on his hand, my nails catching on his skin and dragging gently.

'I don't want to do this on my own anymore.' His voice is so quiet and muffled through the layers of sleeping bag that even the slightest movement would drown him out. 'You've invigorated me. Having someone to share this with. You've made me realise what's been wrong lately . . .' He sounds like he's only realising it for himself as he says the words, which isn't like Tav who carefully considers everything before opening his mouth. 'All year, I've been fighting against your dad. Having to adjust to him being in charge has been tough, and I haven't appreciated how much easier it's been to have someone to talk things over with. And you. You've changed everything.' His arm over the top of me squeezes. 'I've lost my motivation lately. I hadn't realised how demoralised I was getting from being alone. You've given me my joy back. Made me feel young again. Made Christmas fun again. Made *life* fun again too.'

I unzip my bag so I can get my other hand out and wrap both of mine around both of his, my fingers sliding in between his and curling over the backs of his hands.

'You're the first person who's seen *me* in a really long time.' His fingers tighten and cover mine completely. 'I can feel myself melting, Sash. I'm different than I was a couple of weeks ago. Anything feels do-able because you're here.'

I lift both his hands to my mouth and breathe into them until I can press a kiss to his knuckles.

'I don't want to go,' I whisper into his hands, holding his arms around me. It's the first time I've said it out loud and there's a freedom in admitting it to myself as well as to him.

'I don't want you to go.'

Tears. Instantaneous tears. No one has ever said that to me before. No one has ever cared whether I'm there or not, and I didn't realise how much I wanted someone to want me until he did.

I turn onto my back and he pulls his arm up far enough to lean on an elbow and look down at me. He wipes the tears away from under my eyes and his lips press against my cheek.

'What I said earlier about relationships . . . I was trying to convince myself it hadn't happened, but it's too late. I've been metaphorically, physically, *and* literally knocked off my feet by you. You got under my skin from that very first night when you ordered me into the house. To me, this is something that can't be ignored and I *really* hope you feel the sam—'

I surge up and smash my lips against his.

His skin is cold but it heats up under the frenzied kissing

as our lips move against each other's and his nose rubs against mine. His stubble scrapes across my jaw, creating a delicious tingle, and the arm across me slides under my ribs, his huge hand opening and pulling me closer to him, and I feel encased by his body, and at the same time, I can't get enough of him. My hands are everywhere. One clutches into his top while the other slides into his hair, knocking his knitted hat up and curling through the brown strands to hold him in place. It's a desperate, grasping kiss that sends lust jangling through my entire body, and if we weren't both entombed in separate sleeping bags, I'd have wrapped my legs around him just to get closer.

Every point of touch is such a hot and burning mark that I'm sure there must be steam rising from every spot where his body touches mine, until our foreheads are pressing together and we're both gasping for breath.

'Oh my God, Tav,' I wheeze.

'You feel the same then?'

I laugh and I pull his head down until I can kiss him again.

This might be the best night of my life.

We're off bright and early the next morning. Well, dark and early, seeing as the sun won't rise for a good few hours yet. The moon is still up as we set off across the frozen lake – the first time we haven't had a path to follow and have to forge our own way through the snow.

Tav leads Mr Bean on foot for a while before he gets into his sleigh and we ride across the white tundra, fast when the reindeer are allowed to set the pace, and it's another couple of hours until the sun is bobbing at the edge of the horizon, covering the world in a strange twilight-esque light.

We've come even further north than I'm used to, and there's a blisteringly cold chill in the Arctic air, and miles and miles of untouched snow stretches in front of us, undisturbed by even so much as an animal's footprint.

'We're not far now,' Tav calls to me. 'Keep your eyes out. An injured reindeer could've moved to anywhere nearby; there's no saying she's going to be in the exact spot she was last seen.'

It isn't long before Tav gets out again and walks beside Mr Bean, double-checking a paper map against my dad's handwritten instructions, his compass, and the intermittent GPS on his phone. Eventually he halts the reindeer and looks around, a bewildered look on his face. 'Well, we're at the exact coordinates.'

The snow is almost knee-high as I climb out of the sleigh and battle my way over to him.

'There's nowhere for a reindeer to hide in this; it's barren.' He checks the map again and gets a foldable walking pole out of his sleigh and wades off through the snow. 'I'm going to walk around and have a look.'

I stay with our reindeer to make sure they don't wander off without any trees to tether them to, and they scrape at the snow, foraging for lichen with their hooves and noses.

The sun has stayed below the horizon giving us pseudo-daylight, a weird mauvy light cast over the area, but it's easy not to lose sight of Tav because there's nowhere to go. I keep my eyes on him until he's a speck in the distance and then watch as he turns and goes the other way, looking for the injured reindeer.

'No sign,' he says as he arrives back from the opposite direction, having done a full circle of the area.

'Could she not have been as badly injured as they thought and walked off?'

'There aren't any tracks. It didn't snow last night, so hoofprints would still be visible.'

'Should we ask someone?' Even as I say it, I know what a stupid question it is. There isn't a soul around. The last other person I saw was Dad as he waved us off. 'Who told you about her?'

'No one, your dad took the message . . .'

We meet each other's eyes.

'And he was *very* keen for me to go with you,' I say slowly. 'It was like he'd planned it . . .'

'And for a reindeer to have been hit by a train, there'd have to be some form of . . . y'know, train *track* somewhere nearby, and there isn't. There are no roads and no trains anywhere in this region. I should have made that connection earlier . . .'

'Surely he wouldn't have sent us out here on a wild goose chase?'

'A night alone, the Northern Lights, sleeping under the stars . . .'

'Yeah, but it's also freezing and could be dangerous. My dad wouldn't be that sneaky and underhanded . . . Would he?'

Tav looks doubtful.

'I'm going to see what he's got to say for himself. Maybe we're in the wrong place.' I get my phone out and ring the number of the main desk, surprised when Freya answers.

'Is everything okay?' I ask quickly.

'Oh yes, fine, Sasha. I stopped by on my day off to see if Percy needed any help. He's in his grotto with Anja and Nils dressed up as elves. Lots of unexpected visitors for a Sunday morning.'

'That's good. About this reindeer . . .'

'Ah, yes. Percy said that if you phoned, I was to pass on the message that the man who found it rang again and said it had gone. Sorry, you've headed all that way for nothing.'

She doesn't sound in the least bit sorry, and I double-check everything's okay again before I hang up and pass on the message to Tav.

'Hmm.' He strokes his chin.

'Hmm,' I agree.

'I think we might've been set up, Miss Hansley.'

There's something about his Norwegian accent saying my name like that and it makes me go tingly all over. I should probably be annoyed at my father for what I'm ninety-nine per cent sure was some sort of scheme, but after last night . . . Worse things have happened than being sent out into the Arctic wilds with Tav.

'He's such a character.' Tav doesn't sound annoyed either. 'I used to look forward to him coming every year because he felt like a friend from the first time I met him. He's got such a vivacious and dynamic personality. You can't help but be cheered by his presence. No wonder he's the best Santa we've ever had.'

'He's so settled here. I've been here for three weeks and he's not once mentioned going anywhere or dashing off on his next hare-brained adventure.'

'He doesn't now. He used to, but since he bought the place last year, the only kind of dashing he's interested in is the "dashing through the snow" kind.'

'You know we should be mad at him for this little charade, right?'

'Yeah.' He grins so widely that his smile shows over the top of his scarf. His legs make easier work of the snow than mine, so he comes to stand next to me and his arm slides around my waist. He tugs down both our scarves and lowers his mouth to mine.

'But somehow I'm not,' he murmurs against my lips.

It makes me laugh into the kiss, and when we pull back, I wrap my arms around him and hug him for a moment.

'Are we going to tell him about this little development?'

'I think not, for now.' I tilt my head until I can catch his eyes. 'I don't want to give him the satisfaction.'

'We should do the sensible thing and head back . . .' Tav says, sounding as reluctant as I feel about the idea.

My younger self would think it was criminal to ignore the miles of untouched snow all around us. 'Do you want to build a snowman?'

'I thought you'd never ask!'

I bend over to grab a handful of snow and lob it at him. 'If you can't be a big kid at Christmas, when can you?'

'I'm glad you're coming round to my way of thinking.' He tilts his head to the side. 'Too many people absorbed the lie that when you grow up you have to stop liking fun things and start liking adult things, but the happiest people are those who embrace things they love without shame.'

Between us we build up a huge base, dragging in snow with our hands and piling it on, and then we roll a snowball for the head, lift it between us and rest it on the flat top of the body, and I feel like I'm playing a winter scene in *Animal Crossing*, and the snowman's about to come to life and offer me furniture. We keep packing snow on until the snowman is almost as tall as me, find broken branches for his arms, stones for his eyes, mouth, and buttons, and poke a twig in to make his nose. Tav pulls his hat off and places it on the snowman's head.

We finish by standing on either side of the snowman and planting a kiss on his cheeks and I snap a photo of the moment. I can instantly picture it in a frame on Dad's mantelpiece.

Mr Bean and Pedro Pascal look on uninterestedly, clearly wondering if we've both lost the plot. Maybe it says something about your life when a reindeer has to question your sanity, but none of it matters because I can't remember the last time I had this much uninhibited fun, laughed so much, and felt like I wouldn't be judged for it, not even by a reindeer.

With a few stops for leg stretches and rests for the reindeer, it's well after 5 p.m. by the time we get back and the North Pole Forest is closed to visitors for the night. Lights are glowing from inside Santa's House as we climb out of the sleighs, leave some food for the reindeer, and go inside to give Dad a piece of our minds about inventing fictionally injured reindeer and sending us out on wild goose chases.

'It's not funny, Perce,' Tav says as soon as he sees Dad standing behind the front desk inside the door. 'There could've been—'

'Oh good, I'm glad you're back.' Dad's face lights up when he sees us. 'I've got some wonderful news! There's been an offer on the North Pole Forest . . . and I've accepted it.'

Chapter 15

Dear Santa,
Can you take a selfie so I can prove to my friends that
you're real? I'll leave my phone beside the cookies and milk.
From,
Dean

The door shuts behind me with a loud slam, making us all jump as the horror of what he's saying seeps in.

'No!' I'm so shocked that I almost shout the word. 'You can't have.'

'You send us away for one night and sell the place while our backs are turned?' Tav says.

'No, of course not. I received the offer days ago and I've been mulling it over.'

'And you didn't think to mention it?' He folds his arms.

'I am the owner, am I not?'

I can see it stings Tav. 'Yes, but I didn't think you'd make a monumental decision like this without at least informing me. It's always been a partnership. We've never *not* discussed things before, especially something as big as this.'

'There has to be a mistake.' I step closer to stand next to Tav. 'He's winding us up to see how we'll react or something.'

I search Dad's face for some hint that he *is* winding us up, but he blinks seriously back at me.

'You can't be for real? It's not even on the market! It hasn't been valued. I never got around to getting in touch with an estate agent.'

'It's a good offer,' Dad says. 'It'll save us all the bother of estate agents and their extortionate fees.'

'But . . . but . . .' I stutter for words. Three weeks ago, I'd have been overjoyed about this, but now, it makes dread settle over me like a blanket and my face has still got pins and needles from coming in from the cold so I can't feel if there are tears rolling down it, but I'm pretty sure there are.

'I don't believe you.' Tav sounds hopeful rather than convinced. 'I don't believe you'd do something like that without talking it over with us.'

Dad winds his fingers through his curly beard. 'They wanted a quick turnaround. They were going to drop their price if I kept them waiting.'

'New owners who resort to blackmail and ultimatums to get their dirty hands in!' Tav smacks his forehead. 'Great! That's *exactly* the type of people we want to hand over to.'

'What are they going to do with the place?' Fear makes my voice come out choked and hoarse.

'They've given me their strongest assurances that they'll do everything they can to keep it the way it is.'

Tav scoffs. 'That sounds like a line trotted out by the most underhanded of property developers.'

'And you have faith in their "strongest assurances", do you?' My heart is pounding at a million miles per hour and I can barely hear over the throbbing sound of blood rushing to my head. This was the *last* thing I expected.

Three weeks ago, I expected a battle with Dad to get him to sell up and I didn't think he ever would, and now he's done it without a second thought, and it feels like the worst thing in the world.

'They seemed like decent people who are disillusioned with life and fed up with dead-end jobs and never making a connection with anyone. I liked them.'

'Did you check them out? Google them? Do due diligence? You can't hand this place over to any Tom, Dick, Harry, or Clive,' I snap. My dad is far too trusting. He could've been taken in by *anyone*.

'Who is it?' Tav asks.

'They've asked for their names to be kept out of it for the time being, but you can trust my judgement.'

'You've just sent us on a two-day journey to look for an injured reindeer that never existed! I'm beginning to doubt whether I can trust you on anything!' Tav sounds like he's barely holding his emotions in check.

I step closer to Dad. 'What about Tav?'

'The reindeer sanctuary isn't included in the offer. That's his property, not mine. This doesn't change anything for Tav. He can stay here and continue his good work.'

'All alone?'

'He's a big lad – he can take care of himself. He lived out here alone for a long time before I came along and he will for a long time to come.'

I feel like a snowball has hit me square in the chest and coldness is gradually seeping out from the point of impact. I cannot bear the thought of Tav being alone again, withdrawing again, going back to being hard and independent and not letting anyone in. 'And where will you go?'

'Back to the UK with you, of course.'

'Is that what *you* want?'

'It's what's sensible. You were right, Sasha. Not once in my life have I done the sensible thing, so I've got to start somewhere.'

'But not with this. Of all the things you choose to be sensible about . . .'

Dad does a "ho ho ho" at what is quite possibly the *worst* timing ever.

'But we have all these ideas.' I reach out to touch Tav's arm but he steps away and it makes the stone in my stomach grow into a whole peach. He must blame me entirely. 'All this stuff we want to implement. The social media stuff. What about the bookings? I thought you were glad about more visitors coming?'

'Yes, Santa's very pleased.'

'What about all the stuff we've been doing? The letters? Nils and Anja coming back to work? There's so much more to do. You can't back out on it now.'

'It was word of the letters spreading on social media that attracted the new buyers. They *love* the idea, and the added bonus of so much exposure lately made it a much more attractive prospect to purchase.'

I groan out loud. This is, literally, *all* my fault.

'I let Tav down last year, Sash,' Dad says. 'I blazed in and saved the North Pole Forest from the brink of going under with my grand plans to restore it, and then my silly heart started giving me gip. Tav deserves to see this place go to someone young and enthusiastic, not a sentimental old codger like me. It's what we all want.'

I glance at Tav. He won't meet my eyes, but I can see the hurt in every taut line of his face and the worry lines that crease his forehead. My mind is flooded by images of how much damage a new owner could do, someone who doesn't understand what it means, who doesn't care about the small things that matter to Tav, someone chasing profit rather than magic.

'From reading the room, I'd say neither of you are too happy about this.' Dad clears his throat and looks at me. 'I thought you'd be ecstatic. Didn't you want me to sell?'

'No!' I sigh. 'Yes, at first, but now? No. Maybe. I don't know. I know it would be the sensible thing, but . . .' I look over at Tav, who still doesn't lift his eyes from the floor. 'The sensible thing has seemed like the less attractive option lately.'

'I've never done what you wanted. It's about time I did. I know you were worried about broaching the subject with me so I wanted to save you the trouble. I thought you'd be proud of your daft old dad taking the initiative for once.'

'I can't believe this.' Tav shakes his head. 'You sell without even talking it over and you won't tell me their identity. There's no reason to hide who they are unless they're up to something. I thought we were friends, Percy. You know what this place means to me.'

'No, I don't, Tav. You've never told me.'

'Well, I've told Sasha. I'm sure she'll be happy to pass the info on. This is all about *her*. Her demands. Her control. Her ultimatum in exchange for coming here. Let her tell you. It doesn't matter now. It's too late.'

'Tav . . .' I start, reaching a hand out towards him.

'Don't,' he barks as he brushes past me. 'You came here saying you wanted to make it more attractive to buyers, and you've succeeded. You've even roped me into *helping* you, and you've got exactly what you wanted. It's gone. You can swan off back to England and never have to worry about it again. I *knew* this wouldn't end well. Trusting people never does. I'm going to take the reindeer back to their stables. *Don't* follow me.'

The whole house shakes with the force of the door slamming behind him, and I stand there staring at the wreath on it clanging back and forth like a pendulum swinging from side to side, watching it for so long that I don't blink until it finally stops.

'Why are you crying? I'm doing what you wanted me to.'

'Exactly. Want*ed*. Things have changed, Dad. You're blinder than I thought if you can't see that.'

'It's nice you're so worried about Tav, but I assure you he'll be fine. He might be standoffish at first but he'll soon get to know the new owners and become fast friends.'

'It's not about that. God, do you have any idea what it takes for him to trust someone? He *trusted* you. I think he was starting to trust me as well, and now he feels like you've betrayed him. Because of me. I thought we could save this place. I built his hopes up. I made him believe me when he was trying to protect himself because he *knew* something like this would happen. I don't think we can ever come back from this.'

'Sasha . . .'

'Don't!' I snap and stalk out the door, slamming it shut behind me too.

I'm hoping Tav will still be out there, waiting like he was the other day, but I know full well he'll be long gone, along with the reindeer and their sleighs.

I make it as far as the steps down from the porch before I collapse onto them, my shoulders heaving with sobs – the shuddery, snotty, gasping kind that make you glad there's no one around to hear the awful noises you're making because they'd definitely think there was an injured hyena in the vicinity.

The North Pole Forest is eerily silent tonight, and my tears fall onto the snow and turn to ice. It feels like an earthquake has just happened and the tectonic plates are still shifting under my feet and leaving the world shaking.

I try to be reasonable. This *is* what I wanted. I *shouldn't* care this much about a place I'd never even heard of last month. The more I keep repeating that in my head, the harder I cry. I *love* it here. In the space of a few weeks, I've gone from not wanting to come here to not wanting to leave. And when I think of Tav . . .

I bury my face in my hands and let the tears fall. I don't know how long I sit there before the sound of hooves on snow reaches my ears, and I look up to see a reindeer plodding up the road towards me.

'Hello, darling.' I recognise Rudolph Number Three-slash-Clive by his singular antler. He moseys over and I have to duck to avoid the antler as his furry nose twitches up and down my coat until he reaches my pocket. He's found the lichen I still had from earlier, and he waits expectantly for me to give it to him. I pull it out to hold on my open palm and laugh through the tears as his fuzzy lips tickle over my hand.

'This is all my fault,' I say to him, stroking his side as he chews. 'If I hadn't come here insisting my dad sell up, this wouldn't be happening.'

Rudolph carries on chewing.

'And now Tav hates me. He let me in, he shared parts of himself with me that he's never even told my dad and he's known him for years.' I'm so upset that it doesn't even matter that I'm talking to a reindeer. 'I really believed we could save this place. With the letters and the social media aspect . . . But Tav's right. We've got people talking so much that it's attracted the wrong kind of attention. I've inadvertently done what I set out to do before I realised I didn't want to do it anymore.'

I pat his side when he drops the lichen on the ground and lowers his head to pick it up.

'Typical Dad. Always doing the right thing at the wrong time.'

I'm torn between my head and heart. My head is trying to be sensible and say this is a good thing in the long run, because every reason I wanted my dad to sell in the first place is still valid. But my heart . . . Oh, my heart. My chest physically hurts at the thought of leaving, and of how much I've hurt Tav. Images of my dad's happy face when he's wearing the Santa suit fill my head. It's the first time I've ever seen my dad happy, truly happy, since before my mum died. How can it ever be the sensible thing to walk away from something that makes him so happy?

'Maybe it'll all be okay,' I say to Rudolph. 'Tav's upset now, but maybe these new owners will do exactly what they say they will. Maybe they're completely genuine and they'll love it as much as we do, and they'll respect Tav and value his input, and they'll have even more ideas than us, and it'll be the best thing that ever happened.'

The reindeer looks at me doubtfully.

'Yeah, I know, I don't believe it either.' I sniff so hard that I'm glad there's only a reindeer to hear me.

He gives a huff and walks away.

I watch him disappear down the path through the trees towards Tav's cabin.

'Just another thing that's gone wrong,' I say to the empty street.

I should've left well alone. I never should have come here.

Chapter 16

Dear Santa,
Can you ride a unicorn instead of a reindeer? And will
you knock on my window to wake me up because I've always
wanted to see a unicorn.
From,
Charlotte

A couple of days have passed and Tav's avoided me, but today . . .
today, we *have* to work together, and he can't get out it.

The North Pole Forest is busy. It's literally brimming with
people. They're everywhere as I step out of Santa's House –
admiring the lights and decorations, and queuing up to get in
for a tour with Anja, who's standing outside in her elf costume
and trying to organise the biggest tour group yet.

Despite everything that's happened between us, I still smile
when I see Tav coming towards me. 'Hi.'

He grunts and marches straight past.

'Tav, I didn't want this.'

'Believe me, none of us wanted *this*.' He turns around to face
me. 'And yet, none of it would be happening without you.'

'I didn't know Dad was going to do that.'

'He only did it to please you.' He sighs and his eyes flick to mine and then swivel away. 'Let's get on with the task at hand, all right? We started it so we'll finish it.'

He sounds so down. There's no emotion on his face, no joy in his voice, no mention of *nisse*, no cheeky glint in his eyes. Even his jumper is plain and not festively patterned.

I've been so focused on studying him that I don't realise I haven't responded until he holds his phone up. 'I'm going up to the cabin to meet Osvald, you stay here and intercept Freya. Text me when you've got her, as planned.'

I give him a sarcastic salute because he sounds so cold and hard, almost military in his approach to having to do one tiny job with me.

He stalks away, heading up the hill towards the cabins, and I stand there staring after him.

What did I expect? Him to run into my arms and forget all about it? My involvement has cost him the North Pole Forest *and* caused one of his closest friends to commit what must feel like a huge betrayal.

I sigh and attempt to focus because getting this wrong will be one more reason for him to hate me.

I'm dodging tourists as I walk towards the post office, skulking nearby to catch Freya on her round, and of all the things that have gone wrong lately, I half expect her not to turn up, but sure enough, at 10 a.m. on the dot, she trudges up the road, pushing a cart brimming with colourful envelopes.

'Sasha!' She seems surprised when I jump out from behind a holly bush. 'Everything okay?'

'Yes!' I rethink. 'Er, no, actually. I need your help. Can you come up to the house for a minute?'

She glances indecisively at the cart she's pushing. There are so many letters now that they no longer fit into even the biggest bags. I unlock the post office door, take it off her and wheel it inside, and then she unloads the two heavy bags from her shoulders to mine, and I throw everything inside to be dealt with later and shut the door.

Got her, by the post office, walking up now, I text Tav.

'How are you?' she asks.

'Fine,' I say breezily.

'I haven't seen you for a few days, and I saw Tav yesterday and he looked so down that I thought one of his reindeer must've died, but he assured me they're in good health.'

'All on top lichen-eating form.' I try to sound cheerful to push away the image of Tav being so sad.

'Only I couldn't help noticing things seem a bit . . . frosty around here?'

I laugh at the turn of phrase considering *everything* is covered in multiple layers of snow. 'Everything's fine. Just busy.' I nod towards the third group of tourists we've had to sidestep while they stop to take selfies.

The house is in sight, I text Tav again.

I see you. A typically curt response.

Passing the house, I text him back as we get closer. *Three steps from position.*

Two steps from position.

He replies, *Look up.*

I nudge Freya and incline my head across the road, and that's it. Her eyes lock onto the eyes of the man standing next to Tav at the base of the hill. I've never *heard* the sound of glitter before, but I'm fairly sure a twinkling thread weaves across the road between them, and if I didn't know better, I'd be certain an elf just peeked out from behind the roof of the nearest cabin.

Freya's breath catches as Osvald lifts a hand and offers a nervous wave, his face obliterated by a smile that starts slowly and widens so much that it's soon brighter than Boris Johnson's swimming trunks.

My eyes meet Tav's and instead of looking away like I expected, he gives me a smile, his eyes soft, his face missing the pinched look of earlier.

Freya's eyes have filled with tears. 'How did you . . .'

'Christmas magic.' I smile as I hand her a tissue, and shield her while she turns away to blot the tears before Tav and Osvald cross the road towards us.

'This is Osvald,' Tav says when they reach us, and Freya takes a deep breath and turns around to meet him.

'And this is Freya, postwoman extraordinaire and friend of the North Pole,' I say.

Osvald shakes both our hands, but he can barely take his eyes off her.

'Some elves told us you two should meet.' The emotion in both of their eyes is making me emotional and my voice wobbles when I speak.

'I've been looking . . .' His voice sounds jittery and nervous. 'I came back last year but I couldn't find you. It was only when I saw something online about Santa letters that I thought it might be a good place to start.'

'I've looked for you every day,' she says, and then folds her arms and looks between Tav and me. 'And you two . . .'

'It wasn't us, it was the *nisse*.'

Tav produces a card from his pocket and holds it out. 'And I happen to have a coupon here for a free festive meal at the restaurant in the local village. They're expecting you both for lunch.'

'You're trying to make me skive off work, young man.' Freya scolds him but takes the coupon with a huge grin.

Osvald offers her his arm and she takes it carefully and they walk off down the road, chatting as they go, so bewitched with each other that they forget to wave to us.

'Don't wait until next Christmas to swap numbers!' I call after them.

Tav's standing next to me, close enough to touch, which is a good few metres closer than he's been in the past couple of days.

I look up at his face. 'You don't think he's a serial killer then?'

He laughs out loud and then looks like the laugh has caught

him off-guard, but he hasn't instantly run away, so I'm taking that as a good sign.

'Can we talk?' I say quickly, hoping to grab him while his heart's still melting as we watch their silhouettes disappear into the distance.

He shakes his head. 'Don't beat yourself up about what's happened. I knew it was going to go wrong. I knew better than to get my hopes up.'

'Yeah, but it's my fault.'

'It's not your fault, Sash.' He finally takes his eyes off the distant road and looks at me. 'Well, yeah, okay, it is your fault, but it's my fault for believing in it. I knew it was impossible to save this place, and for just a little while, I let myself dream. I let myself believe in your plans.'

'I thought you thought nothing was impossible at Christmas'

He shrugs. 'Some things are beyond even Christmas magic.'

'I don't know how to fix it. I'd do anything to change this, Tav. If there's any way—'

'Leave a bowl of rice porridge out for the *nisse* on Christmas Eve and make a wish. It's as good a solution as any.'

I *should* smile at the childlike simplicity of his answer, but he sounds like a man who has completely given up.

He nudges his arm gently against my shoulder. 'I know you feel bad, but none of *this* would be happening without you either, Sash.' He indicates the many visitors. 'The good and the bad. And honestly, we don't know who these new owners are yet. They *could* be absolutely genuine in wanting it to stay as it is. And you've given us the best chance of that happening. Look at this place. It's *alive* again. It's buzzing with guests because of you. *That* makes buyers unlikely to pull it down without at least investigating the idea of keeping it open. That's a good thing.'

'But . . .'

'It was going to come to this one way or another, no matter how nice it was to think otherwise for a little while, but that wasn't reality. There's nothing we can do. Your father is the owner and has every right to accept an offer made to him. I can't be angry at him for that. I'm not angry with either of you – I'm angry with myself for letting *anyone* in when I know how these things end, always.'

'That's it? What about us?'

'What about us? You're going home and I'm staying here. There *is* no us. Whatever happened was . . . I got carried away with sparkly Christmas magic and the feeling that maybe anything is possible if the stars align and you're in the right place at the right time. Your enthusiasm got under my skin and I let myself get drunk on possibility, on Santa magic and the Northern Lights and whatever else has been zinging around here lately. Maybe there *is* some sort of hallucinogenic in the water supply.'

I'd laugh at the throwback if he didn't sound so completely and utterly defeated.

'I told you I don't want my life intertwined with anyone else's because it gets too complicated. If this isn't absolute proof of that then I don't know what is. You only run into trouble when you start thinking you need other people. Being alone has always been what's best for me. This has done nothing but prove it. So thank you for that – it's a lesson I'm not going to forget again.'

'Don't say that. The worst thing to come from this is the fact it's done *this* to you, and—' I'm cut off by my phone ringing, and Debra's name flashes on the screen.

Talk about bad timing.

Tav indicates for me to answer it. I don't want to but there's something impossible to ignore about a phone ringing and vibrating in your hand, and a few of the visitors are giving me irritated looks. I reluctantly accept the call.

'Sasha! Where on earth are you? I've been to your house three times but you're never in!'

'I'm in Norway,' I say distractedly.

'Norway?' Her voice gets distant as she must pull the phone

away from her ear and bang it. 'Bad line, I think. There's no way you said Norway. You never go *anywhere*; you're certainly not going to make a trip like that.'

I bristle and go to snap a response, but Tav starts walking away and I reach out and grab his sleeve, making him stop. I shouldn't have answered the stupid phone. Deb can wait, but if I let Tav go now, we'll never be able to reopen this conversation.

'What do you want?' I bark, hoping to get her off the line before Tav pulls his sleeve out of my grasp.

'Oh! Great news! My sister-in-law's got a new job so you can come back to work for me. Isn't that fabby?'

Fabby. Even the word makes my cringe. She'll be on about holibobs any second too.

Tav looks down at my hand on his sleeve and tries to tug it away, but I flap my phone around, trying to make a "halt" gesture with both hands occupied and my mind reeling, and not just from use of the word "fabby".

'What?' Tav mouths.

I hold the phone away from my ear. 'Debra offering me my job back.'

'Wow.' He sarcastically elongates the "o" and makes a scoffing noise. 'Unbelievable. You got everything you wanted and then some. Talk about being handed life on a silver platter. Lucky you, Sash. I hope you'll be very happy.' This time, he rips his sleeve out of my grasp and stalks away.

'Tav!' I yell after him.

'What?' Debra says through the phone. 'What's a tav? Is it a breed of dog?'

'And when would I get to keep the job until this time?' I say into the phone as I chase after Tav, who can cover ground a lot faster than I can. 'Until someone more important than me comes along? Someone you like better?'

'Oh, I'm sure we could work out something a little more permanent,' Debra is saying, but I can't concentrate because Tav spins around and comes back, and I pull the phone away from my ear again.

'You know what the saddest thing about this is? It's that you think *that* is how friends treat friends. She couldn't give a damn about you. After months of hard work for her, undoubtedly more work than she ever did, she still didn't have any loyalty to you. You don't treat employees like that and you definitely don't treat friends like that. You don't work with someone for months and then fire them because someone else wants their job and then call them back when that someone else has found something better. If you *want* to go back to that, you deserve to be as unhappy as you've been up until now.' He takes a breath and softens. 'No matter what's happened here, you are *brilliant*, and you deserve a job that recognises that. Don't settle for less than you deserve, Sash. I'm not sure I'll able to sleep at night knowing you're back there working for Ms Holibobs.'

I burst simultaneously into laughter and tears, which frightens a few nearby children.

'No, Debra,' I say into the phone. 'Thank you, but no.'

I hang up and breathe a sigh of relief. I thought I'd be overjoyed to have my old job back, but even thinking about it set my nerves jangling, and Tav somehow understood that and said exactly what I needed to hear at the exact moment I needed to hear it.

He gives me that gentle smile again, and that's it. I leap on him. I throw my arms around his neck and drag him into an enforced hug, giving him no choice but to catch me.

His arms come up around my waist, holding me secure, but he's not open and relaxed like he's been when I've hugged him before. It's not like I expected anything different, but I press my face into his neck as I speak into his shoulder.

'Thank you for making me feel valued. Thank you for making me realise what it's like to matter to someone. To be important in someone's life. I'm changed for meeting you, no matter how this end—' I stop abruptly when I realise something and push

261

myself off him as the idea rolls through my mind like a snowball, picking up size as it gathers speed.

It takes me too long to think about it, but once the idea is there, that's it. 'This isn't over! Taavi Salvesen, this isn't over!'

He raises an eyebrow. 'It isn't?'

'I don't want to go back there. I want to stay here. Right here. With you and your nine million reindeer—'

'Twenty-three.'

'And your *nisse* and your letters and your Christmas magic and your height and your voice and—'

'We don't always get what we want, Sash.'

'No we don't, but we've got a bargaining chip.'

'What's that?'

I grin at him and then take off running down the road. 'My dad is Santa Claus.'

'I counter!' I yell as I blaze past the queue and slip-slide headfirst into the grotto. 'I counter their offer!'

'Sasha, children!' Nils hisses. He's dressed in his red and green striped elf costume and helping out in the grotto while Anja is still covering the house tours.

'Oh-ho-ho, my elves are getting overexcited today,' Dad says to the little boy on his lap. 'Why don't you tell Santa what you want for Christmas while they get themselves under control?'

The boy reels off a Christmas list so long that I'm convinced he's here on behalf of his entire school while I stand there waiting, hopping from one foot to the other and trying to contain my excitement.

'Now, what's all this?' Dad says when the boy and his parents are safely herded out.

'The other buyers. I counter their offer. A seller has a right to receive and review all offers, and you've just received another offer. Well, you will have, when I figure out how to do it.'

'A verbal offer?' Nils suggests.

'Yes, that!' I give him a thumbs up. 'I want to buy the North Pole Forest and I must have some first right of refusal because I'm your daughter and Santa grants Christmas wishes. I'm making a verbal offer, right here, right now.'

'Can you afford to do that?'

'The house. The house back in the UK. I'll sell up and move here. I'm willing to throw everything into this. I believe in it.'

'You can't be serious, Sasha. You would give up *your* security for this?'

'It's all I have. I don't have savings. I don't have a great salary because I don't work in a hotel like you think I do. I don't know how much the house is worth, probably less than your offer, but there's something special about this place. About what we can do here. I can't give up on it. You don't really want to sell, you're just trying to make me happy, but the only thing that's made me happy in years is being here. And I know you feel the same. I know you're happy here.'

Dad's eyes shift to Tav, who's come in the grotto door. 'Happy with someone else too, Santa wouldn't wonder.'

'He's already accepted the offer,' Tav says quietly.

'Don't say that.' I spin around and point a finger at him before turning back to Dad. 'I'm *not* giving up on this. It's not too late. Anything is possible at Christmastime. Sellers can pull out of transactions. And you can say you've been coerced into it, or accepted without the agreement of your business partner, therefore making it invalid. Property sales fall through all the time. Have you signed anything yet?'

'Well, no, but . . .'

'There you go!' I grab Tav's hand in excitement and hold it between both of mine. 'This is not over. I said we could save this place and we *can*. What we just did with Freya was so special. That's the kind of thing that doesn't happen in real life, and it's a true privilege to get to share in people's lives like that. The same with the letters. What children write to Santa deserves to be read and cared about. I meant what I said earlier – meeting you has changed my life, Tav. You made me see what's important. I don't want to go back and work for someone who only cares about their spray tan and designer footwear. I want to stay here and do something that makes people's lives better, with some*one* who makes the world better just by being in it.'

I don't realise I'm crying until he encircles me in his arms and squeezes me tightly.

'I wondered how long you'd leave it before telling me about the hotel,' Dad says.

I smack at Tav's side. 'You weren't going to tell him.'

'*He* knew?' Dad sounds surprised. 'I only know because I follow you on Instagram. You're always posting photos of the dogs you're walking. At first I thought it was part of the hotel service but I quickly realised . . . And then realised what an awful father I must've been that you didn't feel you could tell me.'

'It wasn't that—'

'It's okay, Sash. It doesn't matter. Christmas is not the time to focus on mistakes, but on the good that can come of them.' Dad strokes his white beard. 'I thought you wanted me to go home?'

'You *are* home. I've known that from the moment I saw you. Whatever you've been searching for in the past twenty-four years, you've found it here. I still think the temperature is dangerous, I still wish we were nearer to a hospital, but what I was most worried about was you trying to do everything on your own. Things will be different now. We can afford to take on staff—'

Nils cheers.

'We've got visitors. We've got a great online presence and bookings stacking up for next year. There is so much good we can do here and I can't walk away from that.'

'And if we fail?' Tav says. 'You'll have lost your house, your security, your—'

'We won't.' I shrug out of his arms far enough to look up and meet his eyes. '*You* are the only thing I can't bear to lose,

Tav. You're the best person I've ever met. You've made it feel like home in the middle of nowhere. I've never left where I live now, and I've never felt anything like what I feel when I'm with you. Maybe it's time to try something diff—'

Both his hands slide up my jaw and cup my face and he lowers his lips to mine. It's just a peck seeing as we're not alone, but it still makes my knees decidedly jelly-like.

'I didn't know you felt like that, Sash.' Dad waggles a finger between me and Tav. 'Or like *that*. What Santa's elves get up to behind his back, eh?' He does a "ho ho ho", perfectly timed for once. 'I'll see what I can do about the offer. I don't think it'll be a problem.'

I grin at Tav and I can literally see his shoulders rise as the weight lifts from them.

This is the answer to a question I never could have imagined asking just a few short weeks ago, but now seems like the most important thing in the world.

They were both right – there's something special about this place.

Chapter 17

Dear Santa,
Can I have a doll that will eat, drink, walk, do my home-
work, and clean my room?
From,
Ruby

It's December 24th, a couple of days later, and we're in the middle of a busy morning. We're closing in an hour's time seeing as Norway's main festive celebration is on Christmas Eve, and the last thing I expect is Tav to call with a reindeer problem.

'Careful, I don't want to frighten her,' he says when he hears me approaching.

I squeeze through the trees behind the post office until I find Tav's footprints and follow the trail to the fence that divides our land from the overgrown back area of the outdoor pursuits company, the one he mentioned ages ago.

Tav's on his knees in the snow, trying to calm down a female reindeer with both her antlers caught in the broken wire fencing, wrapped around and trapping her in place. When she sees me coming, she backs up and starts bucking and twisting, only serving to tighten the wire trapping her.

Tav murmurs to her soothingly. He's got one arm through the fence, the wire digging into his forearm as he tries to reassure her. 'She's terrified and if she pulls much more she's going to rip the antlers out or cause herself some other serious injury.'

'What do we do?'

'There's no way of untangling this. I need to cut her loose wire by wire.' He uses his free hand to dig in his pockets for a set of keys and chucks them to me blindly, and I pick them up from where they land in the snow. 'There's a toolbox under the desk in my cabin. Can you go and get it? I can't risk leaving her, especially with so many people around, and judging by the size of her stomach, I think she's pregnant. So at least we know what Rudolph Number Three has been up to on his jaunts around the forest and why he's so keen to get out all the time.'

The one-antlered male reindeer is standing nearby, looking worried. 'Aww, Clive, you've got yourself a girlfriend. You're going to be a daddy.' I still have lichen in my pocket and hand him a clump, but he drops it without interest, too concerned over the new female reindeer's welfare.

I recognise her as the one I saw him with ages ago, and the one who comes by the kitchen window to critique my cooking skills.

'It's a big metal box with a handle. There are reindeer ropes nearby. Can you grab a couple of them too? I can't let her go after this, I need to check her over and find out if she's got an owner. If not, she can stay with us.'

It feels good to be doing something useful, and especially good that Tav has actually *asked* for my help. I dart around tourists as I run up the main road of the North Pole Forest to the tiny path towards the reindeer sanctuary, weaving through trees and jumping over snowdrifts like it's an Olympic event and it still feels like it takes me hours to reach Tav's cabin.

The desk is piled high, and I skid over to it so fast that I ram into it with my thigh and send a stack of papers flying, fluttering down around me like a papery snowstorm as I sink to my knees and stick my head underneath. I pull out the huge metal box tucked into one corner, grab two ropes that are hung on the wall above, and run back out the door. It's only when I go to close it that I realise the mess I've left of papers all over the floor. I drop the things and dash back, gathering them up at super speed and shoving them onto the desk. Tav will understand them not being in order.

And then I catch sight of my name.

I pull the sheet out of the haphazard pile and scan over it. It's a bullet point to-do list, signed by my dad at the bottom, and the date at the top is the day I arrived.

The first point is *Pick Sasha up from airport* and in brackets underneath is – *Something exciting that she won't be able to back out of. No reindeer. Too dull.*

I immediately think of the huskies. That was planned? That was set up as something I wouldn't be able to back out of? What?

Sasha is your number-one priority. She takes precedence over all other jobs.

I'm a job? I blink at the paper. Half of me doesn't understand what I'm reading and half of me already knows.

Get her anything she wants.

Make her feel important. I've never made her feel important in my life and I want her to feel that here.

Christmas magic. I've failed epically at making Christmases magical for her. Let's make a real effort with Christmas magic.

Get her involved. I don't think she makes many connections in her life – make her feel a part of something.

Outdoorsy stuff. I don't think she likes the outdoors much and she needs to get more fresh air.

Am I ten? I feel like a child sitting there while my dad scolds me for having too much screen time. Why has Tav got a printed-out sheet with all this stuff on it? Why is my dad sharing this with Tav?

The memory of Tav saying he gets jobsheets from my father every week flickers across my mind. That's what this is.

These are his instructions. For dealing with me.

I scrabble out another page, dated the following week this time.

Remind her of childhood Christmases. She used to love Christmas but she doesn't anymore. I think that's because of me. My dad's added a hand-drawn crying Santa face underneath the printed sentence.

Give her a wishing jar. She would've loved that as a little girl.

The post office was a brilliant idea. Nothing can invoke the spirit of Christmas more than a few Santa letters. Make sure Sash carries on reading them.

Tears splashing onto the paper is the first thing to tip me off that I'm crying.

None of this has been real. My entire stay here has been carefully orchestrated by my dad.

And implemented by Tav.

I don't need to read the rest of the commands on the second page to know what each one will say. Every single thing we've done together hasn't been spontaneous and fun – it's been part of his to-do list. Every aspect planned to precision. As instructed by his boss. The heading on the paper may as well read "Operation make Sasha into the daughter I wish she was'. Why else would my dad be writing these? Some underhanded way of making me more like him? I've never been the daughter he wanted and he's finally seen a way to manipulate me into changing?

I feel like I've been hit by a submarine. I thought Tav was honest to a fault, but nothing that's happened between us has been genuine. He's been following instructions.

I feel like I'm part of one of those magician's tricks where they're poking swords into a box but something's gone wrong and every bullet point on that list is a further stab.

He was *told* to do everything he's done.

Shaking my head to clear it reminds me of the reindeer and I scramble to my feet and grab the toolbox and ropes and shove the two pages into my pocket. I've already wasted too much time, but I'm sure she'll understand. She's a woman. She's probably been lied to by bulls too.

'I knew this fence was going to be a problem,' Tav says when he hears me approaching. 'If the outdoor pursuits place won't replace it, I'm going to have to do it myself.'

The reindeer is calmer now and I creep forwards and set the box down within Tav's reach, and he digs around blindly until he finds a pair of small clippers.

'Thank you. I don't know what I'd do without you.'

'Oh, I think you do,' I mutter.

He gives me a questioning glance over his shoulder but doesn't have time to concentrate on me at the moment, and that's fine, because I don't know how to process this information yet.

It changes *everything*.

I thought he liked me. I thought we had a genuine connection. But everything he's done is part of his job. Every little thing was on a list. From the very first moment I met him, he was following instructions. Everything was a set-up. Everything was manipulated.

'What can I do to help?' I ask because the reindeer bucks and starts pulling again at the sound of the snip as he cuts through the first wire.

'Nothing for now. It's a one-person job.'

I sit down next to Rudolph-slash-Clive and pick up the lichen he dropped earlier. This time he takes it out of my hand and chews it, like he knows Tav's got the situation under control and is feeling a bit better about it. All I can think of is the folded pages shoved in my pocket.

Tav cuts the wires entangling the reindeer's antlers piece by piece, painstakingly slow and calm. Every movement is precise and calculated, being careful not to stress her out more than she is already. He murmurs to her the whole time, stopping to stroke her side when she gets impatient. An expert at keeping people calm in unusual situations.

270

When most of the wire is cut and bent away, Tav manages to get his arm through the fence and sling a rope around the reindeer's neck, and he beckons me over to hold it while he cuts the last tangles of wire and frees her. I expect her to run away, but she stands quietly, patiently waiting while Tav cuts away enough of the fencing to make a big enough gap for her to get through, offers her lichen from his pocket, and then tugs the rope gently, encouraging her to cross to our side.

And she does. She trusts him now. She knows he's trying to help, but I keep hold of the rope while he quickly examines her. 'Definitely pregnant. Given the number of times we've seen her around, and the fact she has no notches on her ears to show she belongs to a herder, I'm guessing she's wild, maybe orphaned or abandoned by her own herd. She can stay here. It might keep Rudolph-slash-Clive in a bit too, seeing as it seems he's only been sneaking out to meet up with his girlfriend. Do you want to name her?'

'How about you tell me the truth?'

He looks at me with a raised eyebrow. 'Quite an odd name for a reindeer. I was thinking more along the lines of Blitzen Number Five or something a bit more traditional.'

'I didn't mean the reindeer. I meant you, Tav.'

'The truth about what?'

'Your job, for a start.'

'What?' He looks confused. 'Sash, you're not making any sense.'

I sigh and pull the folded pages from my pocket and open them out. 'I found your jobsheets, Tav. So has *everything* between us been part of your assignment or just ninety-nine-point-nine-nine per cent of all things?'

'I don't know what you're talking about.' He wraps the reindeer's rope around his wrist and holds out his hand and I pass them over.

He's pale anyway but I can see the colour drain from his cheeks and he shakes his head as his eyes scan over the pages. 'Okay, I know what this looks like, but you've got the wrong end of the stick. You can't honestly believe—'

'Believe? It's right here, printed off in black and white. It's probably on a spreadsheet somewhere! I've just read everything we've done together in bullet point list form, planned to precision *before* we actually did it.'

'Sash, *I* haven't read these! I glanced at the first one solely to get your flight time to meet you at the airport—'

'In a pre-decided husky dog sled!' I shout, upsetting both reindeer.

'Well, yeah, because your dad said you liked dogs so I thought it would be a nice touch, *not* because I read this!'

'What the hell are these doing in your cabin then? Filed neatly with all the other to-do lists he sends you every week. *Clean Santa's windows, shovel the pathways, change the lightbulb in Mistletoe Cabin, fix the toilet flush in igloo #12, oh, and don't forget to make Sasha fall in love with you!*'

'You're in lo—' He stops himself when he realises that now is *not* the time to comment on that ill-timed remark that I didn't intend to say aloud. Instead he shoves a hand through his hair. 'They weren't filed neatly, they were face down on my desk with all the others I ignore every week. God, Sash, I don't read these things. I told you I've been fighting against your dad all year – struggling with him taking over and no longer being my own boss. Yes, he puts one of these through my door every Monday morning, more often if the mood catches him, and I never read them because I *hate* being told what to do. I've worked here for fifteen years. I built the place. I have a *very* good idea of what needs doing without his input. I know he's trying to help, but I hate the implication that I'm not on top of things.' His hand swings down, like the pages are too heavy to hold up. 'Didn't you notice the two piles? One face down for things I'm ignoring, one face up for things that need dealing with.'

I hesitate. 'Well, admittedly I didn't see which way they were facing . . . I knocked into your desk and sent them flying . . .'

I meet his eyes, and I *want* to believe him, but I shake myself. 'It doesn't make any difference which way they were facing. You're trying to distract me with minutiae. Facts are facts, Tav.'

'I know how bad this looks, but it *isn't* how it looks. I don't like your dad's approach. I don't need to be micro-managed. I glanced at the first one and knew straight away that it wasn't something I was going to have any part in. You can't manipulate people into having a good time. I didn't want anything to do with this. I didn't want anything to do with you. I had enough to do without being lumbered as caretaker of some condescending tourist who didn't want to break a perfectly manicured nail.'

'Wow. Nothing like a bit of honesty.'

'I don't mean now, Sash.' He rolls his eyes. 'That's what I thought you'd be like, and that changed the moment you ordered me into the house on the first night. I'm trying to explain that when I got those sheets, I was angry. I ripped them from the letterbox and slapped them face down on the pile of things to ignore because I was annoyed at your father for adding to my workload with frivolous tasks that were never part of my job description. I didn't want to do a crash course in adult-babysitting. I wanted to get on with the endless list of jobs I already had for myself. I didn't need his patronising work notes telling me what needs to be done.'

'You've already said you looked at it.'

'Yes, I saw the priority bit, but his priorities and mine are different, and quite frankly, I didn't give a toss what his were. Mine are the reindeer and fixing everything that needs fixing around here in some sort of logical order. I didn't want to look after you as well. I didn't expect to get on with you. And that wishing jar thing . . . I don't even know why he put that on there because I put one of those in *every* gift basket, without fail. One for each person in each cabin.'

I glare at him. 'Now you're trying to make me feel special by making me feel non-special?'

'You're the most special person I've ever met. You've turned my world upside down. How can you *not* know that? Every rule I've lived my life by went out the window when you ordered me into the house. That one simple gesture punched a hole straight through my walls. It was the first time anyone's ever *not* accepted "I'm fine" as my brush-off answer.' He takes a step towards me with one hand held out, and I take a step backwards.

'You've been making me feel special – exactly as it's written here.'

'I haven't been *making* you feel special. You *are* special.'

I hate him for always knowing exactly what to say to make me melt, but it's not that simple this time.

'You are special and I don't think you have enough people in your life who tell you that,' he continues. 'Until the other day, I was working on the assumption you were leaving, and I wanted you to go back with a bit more self-worth than you came with.'

I'm crying again because I want it to be true so badly, but no one can argue with cold, hard, printed in Times New Roman facts. 'Everything I thought was so special about you was pre-planned, Tav. The coincidences. The stuff we have in common. The songs you sing that remind me of my mum – did he tell you what her favourite songs were? Even Shakin' flipping Stevens. That was her favourite Christmas song and I thought it was a sign from the universe that you started singing it, but was it because he told you?'

'No, it wasn't.' He looks at the paper and then slaps it with the backs of his fingers, his voice sounding panicky. 'It doesn't say anything about songs on here. He never mentioned anything about that at all. This doesn't change anything, Sash. It's just words on a piece of paper that I promise you I didn't even read.'

It makes the tears fall harder. 'It changes everything. Everything that's been so perfect since I got here, everything that's felt like it's meant to be has been because it was designed that way. Everything

I liked about you. Your childlike joy, your belief in *nisse*, the matter-of-fact way you speak about flying reindeer. I thought you were an adorable big kid, but all your joy was faked to give me some weird nostalgic childhood Christmas experience. You're a grown man. You don't believe in elves. No one does. And I wish more people did, and I thought you were that person.'

'That's not true.'

I shake my head. I *can't* believe him. There are too many coincidences between this list and how the past few weeks have gone. 'Why is my dad doing this? I know I've never been the daughter he wanted, but what did he think he was going to get from this? That it would somehow turn me into being outdoorsy and adventurous?'

Tav's quiet for a moment, thinking it over, and even in the midst of this, with two reindeer and a distressed woman shouting, I appreciate that about him. 'He feels guilty. He got reflective after the heart attack. Thinking over mistakes he's made in his life. The way things have gone between you is his biggest regret. I don't think there's anything nefarious in these, Sash. He was trying to make up for the Christmases he failed you.'

'Or did he know it would come to this? Did he painstakingly plan to make me fall in love with this place, knowing I could come to the rescue by selling the house?'

The chatter of tourists and the laughter of children filtering across the forest brings into sharp focus the juxtaposition of how hopeless I feel. I've never felt less Christmassy, and *that's* saying something.

'I can't believe he's capable of that. He'd be a different man than I thought—'

'Ho ho ho!' My dad's rumbling laugh approaches through the trees. 'What's going on out here then? Anja said something about a trapped reindeer.'

I let out an audible groan. Dealing with Tav is one thing, but trying to handle them both together *and* this revelation is too much.

275

Like Tav can sense that, he tugs the reindeer's rope and starts walking off, beckoning for Rudolph to follow him.

'You two need to talk.' He holds the pages out to me as he passes, and when I snatch them from his hand, he waits until I look up at him, his blue-brown eyes uncomfortably open and honest, and for just a second, I suspect he's telling the truth.

But the moment sputters away when the Arctic breeze rustles through the forest and flaps the papers in my hand, reminding me of quite how ridiculous this situation is.

Tav sighs. 'I'll take the reindeer back and give her a proper check-over. Come and find me when you're ready. We can sort this out.'

He vanishes from view between the trees with both reindeer in tow and Dad looks in the direction he went with a puzzled look on his face. 'Has something happened?'

'You.' I shove the pages at him. 'You've happened.'

'You can't honestly think he reads these?' He almost "ho ho ho"s again as he reads over them, clearly not getting that this is also *not* the time for a jolly Santa act. 'He indulges me by not telling me where to shove them because I'm a daft old fool and he's a gent. Can you imagine being able to tell a man like Tav what to do?'

'Then why do you send them?'

'To feel like I'm earning my title as owner? The truth is I've been pretty useless since last year. When I took over, I had so many grand plans, but they all fell through because of my health. I've let him down. These lists are me trying to make myself feel worthwhile. I thought if I could curate his endless list of tasks into some kind of logical order, it might be less overwhelming. It's selfishness really, to make myself feel like I'm making a contribution to the place.'

Even though I understand that, and I can easily imagine how frustrated my dad is by the limitations of his old age, it doesn't make *this* any better. 'None of that explains this. From the very first second you phoned, I've felt like my decisions were being pre-decided for me. On that phone call, you'd decided I was coming here before I'd even answered the call. You must've written these lists beforehand too. You sounded so ill on the phone. A fragility that magically disappeared as soon as I agreed and hasn't been evident since I got here.'

'I wanted to see you, Sash. I *may* have been exaggerating a little because I was terrified you'd say no and I'd die before I got to see you again.'

The honesty makes my breath catch because I was terrified of the same thing. 'You should've just said that.'

'I didn't think you'd come. I wouldn't have blamed you for telling me where to go. I've missed every important event of your life. I've never come back when you've asked me to. You had every right to refuse when the shoe was on the other foot.'

He shivers, making me realise I've forgotten how cold it is. 'You shouldn't be outside in only a Santa suit. Come on, the post office isn't far.'

I'm taller than his shrunken form now and I slip my arm around his shoulders, rubbing his back as we head along the narrow path back to the building.

Inside, I turn the heater up to maximum, make him sit down in the back office, blanket him up, and pour him out a hot chocolate from the flask Tav brought me earlier, and I'm once again grateful for his thoughtfulness, but the idea that maybe that was on a list somewhere too prickles at my mind. It impacts on *every* aspect of my time here.

Dad's still clutching the pages in his hand. '*This* was because I wanted him to know some of our history and I was too embarrassed to admit it out loud. He knew things were strained because I talked a little, but it was easier to write it down.'

'But you can't plan people's lives like this. You basically paid him to spend time with me. I thought he liked me, but it was because his boss had instructed him to. I've never been a priority in anyone's life, and I thought Tav was different.' I perch on the edge of the oak desk and sip a hot chocolate that does nothing to warm me up.

'I didn't tell him to spend time with you, Sasha. That was all him.'

'You told him to make me feel important!'

'Yeah, in a butler-ish way. I didn't want you to want for anything this Christmas. I wanted someone to attend your every need. I know you don't like the outdoorsy life and he's an excellent guide when it comes to things like that.'

'That is *not* what's written on those pages. It goes a lot more in-depth than being some sort of wilderness guide.'

'He doesn't read them. He gave it a glance and told me not to be so patronising. Everything he's done has been his own choice. I might be the owner, but I'm not his boss in a traditional sense. I don't have any authority over him.' He fiddles with his empty cup. 'All I wanted was to give you a nice Christmas. The North Pole Forest makes me feel like a child again. I wanted you to experience that magic. A way of making up for lost time. Tav *is* the magic behind this place, and I wanted him to share that with you. A childhood Christmas, like the ones you missed out on.'

'All I've ever wanted for Christmas was to be important enough for you to spend it with me.'

It seems to take the wind right out of Dad's sails. 'And you never felt like you were.' He says it as a statement, not a question. 'It wasn't because of you. I was battling my own demons, my own grief.'

'But you never thought about mine. I was twelve. I'd lost my mum. I needed a father around, not halfway up a skyscraper somewhere in Saudi Arabia wrestling Komodo dragons. I needed us to grieve together. I know things were different without Mum, and Nan was great, but she didn't know *our* lives. So many times I wanted to reminisce with the only other person who was actually there, to think of the Christmases we used to have, to remember the good times. I needed to matter more to you than your next great adventure.'

'I haven't been on adventures. I've been running away.'

'From what?'

He puts his cup down on the chair arm and takes the Santa hat off his head to fiddle with the white pompom on the end. 'From the fact I killed her.'

'Mum? It was an accident. It wasn't anyone's fault.'

'But if I'd been going slower or my reactions had been faster . . . I was driving and I walked away unhurt.'

'You had three broken ribs, organ damage, and internal bleeding! You were in hospital for weeks!'

'But I lived. She didn't.'

My breath catches and a lump forms in my throat. I had no idea he felt like that. No idea he'd ever blamed himself for the accident. He never spoke about it afterwards. He recovered from his injuries in silence. He barely left his room after my nan came to stay, and then he left for his first great expedition.

'When I'm doing something adventurous, it's the only time I don't think about it. That's why I've kept chasing adrenalin rushes. Because they're the only thing that's ever temporarily blocked out the feelings of guilt. Coming back to our happy family home, being still and quiet, in the places she loved but without her . . . I couldn't do it. And you're right. I was so wrapped up in my own grief that I never stopped to consider yours. I thought you were better off without me.'

'That's not true. It never even crossed my mind to blame you.'

'I blamed myself and I always will do. But this place . . . Coming here was the first time I wanted to stop running. I got the job as Santa Claus because it sounded like fun, but as soon as I set foot here, something changed. Something tethered me to this place. It's been like having a part of your mum back. The first time I came here, I felt like she was with me. I couldn't wait to come back for the next festive season.'

I look upwards and pinch the bridge of my nose, trying to stop the tears from falling. 'Mum would've adored it here.'

'And him. Can you imagine how much she would've loved Tav?'

I smile at the thought. She *really* would.

'Tav's a big part of the sense of peace I feel here. Someone so centred and grounded. I still don't know what happened to him, but I've got an idea because of the connection I felt with him from the first time we met, and because he doesn't hide those scars nearly as well as he thinks he does.'

I have to stamp down the all-too-familiar urge to find him and hug him. I didn't realise the importance of him opening up to me. Was that carefully constructed too? And maybe the point is that I can never tell. I will *never* know if anything Tav did was genuine or because it was his task of the day.

'And now I've let you all down.' Dad puts the Santa hat back on his head and then takes it off again. 'You, him, and your mum. I wanted to do something to make her proud, and instead I've meddled and tried too hard and it's all gone pear-shaped. Don't let this change things between you and Tav.'

'It's a bit late for that.'

'I know Tav. He can't fake *anything*. I've never seen him like he is around you. There's nothing about that that's false. You've metaphorically swept him off his feet. He's in a daze whenever you're nearby. He puts his head on your shoulder every time you sit next to each other. I've known Tav for years and I've never even seen him close his eyes. Never seen him relax. He only sits down once in every three blue moons.'

It makes me think of the other day when Tav flopped down beside me on the living room sofa and rested his head on my shoulder and Dad walked in and couldn't hide his surprise.

'Don't let this interfering old fogey ruin what's happened between you two. You've changed him. You've made him stop and realise that he *is* worth taking care of and that he can't keep going and going forever. Before, I think he felt quite unimportant, like part of the furniture here. This job defined him. He *is* the North Pole Forest. But you've seen *him*. You're the first person to realise that he's a person too – he's not just a job, and he'd be missed if he was gone, because of *him*, not because of what he brings to the North Pole Forest.'

'This changes everything, Dad. It changes his integrity. No matter what he did or didn't read, I thought we had some mystical connection, that he *got* me, but he knew everything about me upfront.' I pace the room, treading on envelopes that have fallen from a nearby mail bag.

'What are you going to do?'

'I'm going to go home.'

'What? Sasha, you can't . . .' Dad gets up out of the chair, reaching out a hand like he's trying to stop me.

'This was all just a fantasy. These pages prove that. Girls like me don't do things like this. We're meant to stay where we are. Do run-of-the-mill jobs for people who don't appreciate us. We don't step on a plane at a moment's notice and sell our houses on a whim. We don't believe in magic because it isn't real.'

'Sash, no.'

'Yes, Dad. This isn't real life. It never was. It's a Christmas story. A fairy tale. A magical forest deep in the Arctic Circle where elves dart out of sight and reindeer stick their noses in your windows and "dashing through the snow" is a regular occurrence. But every fairy tale has to end sometime. Accept your other offer. Or don't. Keep it. You're in a good position now. You and Tav can take on staff and not go chasing reindeer around frozen forests in the middle of the night. But I have to go back to real life and get a proper job and pretend the last few weeks didn't happen, because that is what a sensible, rational person would do.'

'Sasha, don't let it end like this.' My dad looks absolutely distraught. The broken look on his face is almost enough to make me doubt my convictions.

'I'm glad we've had this time together.' My teeth are nearly cutting through the inside of my cheek as I try to keep my emotions in check. I clap my hands on both his upper arms and then bend down to give him a stiff hug, because I'm going to burst into a fountain of tears if he hugs me back. 'It's been good to reconnect. I wish you'd told me everything you've just said years ago, and I'm glad you've found something that makes you happy, but for me, this is absolute proof of what happens when you step outside of your comfort zone.'

'You find something wonderful?' Dad pulls back, sounding hopeful.

'You get hurt.'

Chapter 18

Dear Santa,
*Can you bring me a pair of rollerblades that don't crash
so much? The ones you brought me last year are defective
because they keep crashing. Can you bring some plasters too?*
From,
Blake

Darkness has long since fallen by the time I've trekked back up
to my cabin, packed my suitcase with clothes that were never
really mine but have been more comfortable than anything I
own, called a taxi and dodged tourists who thankfully couldn't
see my tears in the fading light.

Not good for business to have people walking around the
North Pole Forest sobbing to themselves.

The cab driver barely speaks English, but from his stilted
Norwegian ranting, I ascertain that he isn't happy about being
called on Christmas Eve and wants a big tip.

When we pull up at the airport, he opens the door, half yanks
me out of the car, throws my suitcase out behind me, and speeds
off at approximately seven times the speed of light.

It's a million miles from the husky dog sled that met me here
nearly four weeks ago.

I realise it was a mistake as I stand there and look up at the darkened building.

And not just because the airport is closed.

Oh, holy night. Who the heck closes an airport just because it's Christmas Eve? Do people not need to travel on holidays? I look at the completely deserted car park, and walk around the side of the building for a glimpse of the runway. The plane I came in is parked up and, judging by the layers of snow, looks like that may well have been the last flight it actually went on.

So, evidently not, then. This is such a tiny airport that the plane is chartered on a personal basis, and it's not in use tonight. There are signs on the closed door, and I'm hoping one of them might give me a number to call to arrange a flight out, but they're all written in Norwegian and I can't understand a word.

Could this day get any better?

As if on cue, a flash streaks across the sky and I look up to see a now-familiar wave of green weaving across the sparkling navy darkness. Instead of making me as happy as it has until now, it makes me lose control of the emotions I've been barely holding in check throughout the cab ride.

It's the first time I've seen the Northern Lights without Tav next to me, and I let out a sob so loud that it's probably attracted the attention of every wolf and grizzly bear from here to Greenland.

Great. What am I going to do now?

I turn away from the lights and look up at the silent building again, like it might provide some clues about what to do when you're stranded at an airport in minus-twenty degrees on what's supposed to be the most magical night of the year, and one thought obliterates all others.

I don't want to go.

I wouldn't want to go even if the airport was open.

I love the North Pole Forest more than I've ever loved any place before. I didn't think it was possible to fall in love in a few short weeks, but I am – with the myth of Santa, letters from children, *nisse*, and reindeer.

And then there's Tav . . . the thought of this being *it*, that image of him walking away this afternoon being the last time I ever see him . . .

A sob comes again and tears spill from my eyes. This is a huge mistake. Coming here has been the craziest, most spontaneous, ridiculous thing I've ever done in my life, and I've never enjoyed anything more. For the first time ever, I've woken up every morning excited for what the day will bring. I've looked forward to every moment. I've been happy. And the prospect of staying here, of actually living here and getting to continue sharing the magic of Christmas every day . . . It feels like something I've been waiting for my whole life.

What the hell am I thinking in wanting to give that up over a few words on a sheet of paper?

As I'm trying to figure out the best way to get back there, the sound of a car engine reaches my ears, getting louder, and I watch the road as a truck roars into view, shining red as it passes under every streetlamp.

The roads are gritted but the truck is going so slowly that I could walk faster, and it's weaving enough to make it a good thing that the roads *are* deserted, because if they weren't, they soon would be.

And it looks oddly familiar . . .

My heart jumps into my throat when I recognise the garland twinkling along the dashboard and the wreath hung on the front grille. It's my dad's truck from outside the house! He must've realised the airport would be closed and come to rescue me.

And given how carefully he's driving, he is a case in point for re-testing elderly drivers because it doesn't look like he can drive well enough to still have a licence and he clearly knows that.

Eventually the truck comes to a halt at a safe distance away and clips a snowdrift as it stops, sending a shower of snow spraying across the pavement, and I'm so relieved to see him that I pick up my suitcase and start running towards the truck and come to an abrupt halt when the door opens and a very familiar-looking pair of boots hits the ground. I follow the boots up long, long legs, a wide expanse of charcoal grey coat, to a pale-looking stubbled face.

'Tav!' I half-laugh in relief and then let out a sob when I realise the magnitude of him being behind a wheel. 'You drove?'

'Not sure you could call it driving.' He slams the truck door closed behind him and holds on to it on unsteady legs and shows me a trembling hand. 'Just give me a second.' He looks truly shaken up by the experience.

'You haven't driven for eighteen years!'

'Some things are worth facing your fears for. Turns out *that*,' he jabs a thumb towards the truck, 'wasn't as terrifying as the thought of letting you go.'

I have my hands over my mouth as the enormity of that sinks in. I know he was destroyed by the accident he was in. I know he hasn't even sat inside a car in the two decades since, and the thought he'd do that, for me . . .

'And yes, I *do* know it's not smart, but the roads are completely empty, I've gone at the speed of a sloth on sedatives, and I did a few practice runs in the car park before I left, but nothing else was fast enough to catch you.'

'Airport's closed.' I point up at the dead building behind me.

He bursts into relieved-sounding laughter. 'Thank God for that.'

And it finishes me off. If I thought I sobbed earlier, now I *really* sob. There is snot and tears everywhere, and I don't have any tissues on me so I end up digging in my suitcase and trying to retain my dignity by drying my face on a sock.

I can tell his legs are shaking as he pushes himself off the festive truck and walks over to me. 'Please don't go, Sash. You're the best thing that's ever happened to me. We've got something special here – I *know* you feel that too. And I know you don't believe me, but I didn't read them, and I know I can't prove that but I'll spend the rest of forever trying.'

'Tav . . .'

'Meeting you has literally knocked me sideways. Who I was before I met you feels like years ago, not less than a month. You've made me feel loved, cared for, and safe. I've never shown vulnerability to anyone and from the very first night, you've made it okay for me to need help occasionally. You've *forced* me to accept help. You're the only person who's ever touched my scars – emotionally *and* physically. I didn't want my life entwined with someone else's, but . . . I want to be tangled up with you forever.'

There are tears rolling down my cheeks again, and he holds both his hands out and I slip mine into them, my gloves rubbing over his as his fingers tighten.

'I've never left Norway, but if I hadn't caught you tonight, I was going to apply for a passport the moment the offices reopen after Christmas and turn up on your doorstep in Britain as soon as they'd let me. You are worth a car *and* a plane journey, and that might not mean much to some people, but it's a lot to me, and I know you know—'

I use my grip on his hands to pull him down far enough to silence him with a kiss.

Tav's surprise quickly turns to gentle and protective carefulness. One hand squeezes mine and the other slides around my waist, pulling me against his body and holding me there.

'As responses go, I quite like that one,' he says, muffled against my lips and making me giggle.

I kiss him again, feeling light-headed and tingly, which I'm not sure is from kissing him or being outside in the cold for so long, but I'd like to think Tav's solely responsible.

His lips leave mine and press along my jaw and down, pulling my scarf aside until he can kiss my neck, just under my ear, and I have to hold on to him tighter because I go hot and flushed all over.

His laugh vibrates there until he pulls away, his hand tucking my hair back, his fingers tangling in the twisted mess of my side plait, his thumb rubbing over the shell of my ear, lifting my mouth to his for a peck that turns into more, until neither of us can catch our breath and his forehead rests against mine.

'I was going to come back.'

His whole face lights up as he stands up to full height. 'You were?'

'Not just because the airport's shut.' I slide my hand up his jaw. 'Because I've fallen head over heels for you too. God, Tav, the thought of leaving you . . .' It makes me shiver and he pulls me impossibly closer.

We look up at the lights, neither of us speaking, both his arms wrapped tight around me, blanketing me with his body, my hands curling into his arms, tight enough to let him know I never want to let go of him again.

It's such a special sight, like Mother Nature is putting it on just for us. It feels like we're the only two people in the world. The only two people who have ever seen *this* formation of these beautiful lights, and it reaffirms that I've made the right decision. Leaving would be a mistake, but staying never will.

'I can't believe you did that.' I nod towards the truck. 'Are you okay?'

He nods against my head, slowly, like he's not quite sure. 'Yes. Because some things are worth stepping outside of your comfort zone for. But I'm not doing it again, I can tell you. We're walking back; someone can come and collect the truck another time.'

'I thought it was two hours away and there'd be a coroner involved!'

'I promise I'll look after you.' He grins at my apprehension. 'Come on, there are blankets in the truck for extra warmth and your dad's waiting on tenterhooks to know if I caught up with you.'

'You sure he's not just waiting to see if you smashed his truck up on the way?'

'Nah.' He glances back at it. 'Probably, anyway. He's different since you came, Sash. More settled, somehow. I know it's through his own choices, but I think *you* were what was missing from his life. You coming here has changed everything. For all of us.'

He tugs me across to the truck and opens the door to pull out an armful of Christmas blankets, soft and fleecy as he wraps one and then another one around my shoulders, and I pull it up to my face and breathe in the soft, pepperminty smell of Dad's festive-themed fabric conditioner as he shrugs a blanket around himself.

He takes my suitcase with one hand and drops the other arm around my shoulders, tucking me against his side as we walk back through the trees, the Northern Lights dancing above us.

The North Pole Forest is lit up. Even though it's closed to visitors, it seems like every fairy light in Norway is twinkling here tonight, and although the lights above are fading now, the occasional pink-edged green streak still skips across the sky.

After we get through the gate and start walking towards the house, I see Dad pacing back and forth across the road, dressed in his Santa costume.

'Ho ho ho!' He shouts when he sees us. 'Here's Santa's two best elves.'

'Dad, you shouldn't be outside at night without proper layers on – it's freezing.'

'Oh, nonsense. Santa's used to a bit of cold.' He smiles and points to us, still quite a way away. 'I knew I could rely on him to catch my favourite daughter.'

'You also knew the airport would be closed, didn't you?' Tav calls.

'I might've had a teeny tiny inkling.'

'You could've shared that with me *before* I got in the truck; I'd have taken the reindeer.'

'I think you needed to do that as much as Sasha needed you

to,' he says. 'Now, enough about that, you're just in time to meet the new owners!'

'What?' Tav and I both stop dead in our tracks and the whole world falls apart.

There can't be new owners. He *must* have rescinded the agreement. He never mentioned it again, but I assumed . . . I glance up at Tav who's gone decidedly ashen. This was *not* part of the plan.

This can't be happening. We've come this far – he can't sell it from underneath our feet, not after all this.

'Ah, yes, here they are now.' Dad indicates to the empty road behind us, and we both look round.

There's no one there.

I meet Tav's confused eyes, wondering if my dad is quite all right. The road remains empty.

'Dad, I really think you should go inside, maybe we should phone a doc—'

'It's you two, you blummin' great pair of idiots. *You* are the new owners. Both of you.'

'Us?' The confusion I'm feeling is mirrored on Tav's face. 'What about the offer?'

'There's something I need to tell you about that.' Dad ums and ahs, twisting his hands together. 'There was no offer. It was a little bit of a test. I wanted to be sure you loved the North Pole Forest as much as I did before I handed it over to you, Sash. Both of you. I know Tav hasn't been happy here lately, not until you arrived anyway, and I had to be sure that it was *really* what you both wanted.'

'Dad! That's not okay. We're going to have to do something about your compulsive lying.'

'You can't hand this place over to us, Perce,' Tav says.

Dad waves a dismissive hand as we approach him. 'The paperwork's already with my solicitor. What you and Sash have done here is phenomenal. I know how much you love it, and I know that you both bring something to it. It wouldn't be the North

Pole Forest without you, Tav, but the one thing you need is a partner in all senses of the word. I can't do that, but Sash can. It's the perfect solution for all of us.'

'I haven't sold the house yet,' I say, even though my stomach fills with butterflies at the prospect of this being permanent, of somehow owning a part of this incredible place. Of getting to stay.

'You don't have to. That's not part of the deal. The thing is, when I bought this place, I bought it for you, Sasha – for the little girl I knew who loved Christmas. I know I'm part of taking away that joy in recent years, and when I came here, I thought this was the one place where you might rediscover that childhood magic. I knew you'd love it. Admittedly I didn't see *this* coming—' he waggles a finger between me and Tav '—but that makes it so much better, because the North Pole Forest thrives on love. Falling in love is true, real life magic for any time of year. Combine it with Christmas magic and you've got a whole forest of happiness.'

'But you can't—'

'There's no point in protesting. It would be your inheritance anyway, but I don't like all that morbid stuff. Much better for you both to take over now. I won't be around forever. I'm nearly eighty and I've had a heart attack, you know.'

'You do seem to forget that sometimes.' Tav pushes a hand through his hair, looking bewildered and like he can't quite believe it.

I squeeze the hand I'm still holding and he looks down at me. Our eyes meet and he smiles slowly, and all the doubts fall silent while the butterfly wings double their fluttering.

When we've been smiling at each other for an abnormally long time, Dad clears his throat.

'And what are you going to do?' I ask him.

'I'm going to continue playing Santa for as long as my new bosses will have me, and in the off-season, I might pay a little visit back to Britain. Maybe it's time to face some old ghosts.

But not tonight. For tonight, there's hot chocolate on and mince pies in the ov—'

The smoke alarm rings out across the forest and Dad groans.

'I'll get it.' Tav laughs as he runs towards the house. 'Like father, like daughter.'

Dad pulls me into a hug before we start following him indoors. 'Welcome home, Sash.'

I still can't get my head around it, and I'm fairly sure I should be quite angry with my dad, and he's probably lucky it's Christmas Eve because it's a scientific fact that you can't be angry with a man dressed as Santa Claus on Christmas Eve. Especially when he's answered all of the Christmas wishes I didn't even know I'd made. The one thing I've always wanted – a family and a home.

Chapter 19

Dear Santa,
Can I have a dinosaur for Christmas? We've got a garden
for it to play in and I'll take it for a walk every day.
From,
Marie

When I wake up on Christmas morning, Tav's asleep beside me, and I lie there for a while, appreciating the softness of his breathing, the warmth of his skin, and the weight of his arm draped across me. We stayed in a spare bedroom in Dad's house last night, and at Dad's insistence, we left some sweet rice porridge with a knob of butter out for the *nisse* and hung our empty stockings above the hearth.

I feel like a child again as I slip out from under Tav's arm and creep down the stairs, and even though I *know* there aren't really porridge-eating elves who stop by on festive nights, I still squeal in delight when I find the empty bowl on a table by the fireplace, and a set of sparkly footprints leading to the tree, made from stencils and spray snow.

'They were pleased with the offering then?' Tav appears in the living room doorway, leaning against the doorframe with an adorably dishevelled "just woken up" look.

'You can't honestly think . . .'

'Can't I?' He gives me a wink and then yawns and rubs a hand over his eyes. '*You* made it for them last night.'

'I was keeping Dad happy.'

'Or you want them to be real . . . You want to believe in— Hold that thought.' He disappears into the hallway and the front door opens as he sticks his head out and then comes back, beckoning me to follow.

'I'm told something that's important to Brits is a white Christmas.' He throws the front door open again.

I squeal. 'It's snowing! On Christmas Day!'

I've gone right back to being a child here. I always used to wish it snowed on Christmas Day. Dad nicknamed me Bing one year because I was always singing Mr Crosby's most famous song.

I barely have time to shove my feet into the snow-boots by the door as I dash outside, stamping them down until they're on properly. Tav's laughing as he follows me out, clearly indulging the Brit who's never had snow at Christmas before.

I spin around with my arms thrown wide and try to catch snowflakes on my tongue. This is not the sleety rain we have in Britain. These are huge, flat, fluffy flakes, like someone's tipping a bucket full of bunnies' tails onto us and I have to look up to make sure someone *isn't* on the roof with a snow machine because it's too perfect to be real.

It's too early for daylight yet, but the streetlamps illuminate each falling flake, and when I've caught a few more and watched them melt in my rapidly freezing hands, I look back at Tav, who's standing at the top of the wooden steps outside the house, his eyes shining with amusement as he watches me.

There's something so intimate and relaxed about seeing him out here in his pyjamas, thermal layers on under a plain sage green T-shirt and tartan-patterned wide jersey bottoms, unevenly shoved into his own boots.

I grin at him and do the same "come hither" gesture he did

earlier and he's smiling as he pushes himself off the post he was leaning on and steps onto the road, his legs long enough to avoid the steps altogether.

I grab his hand and make him spin in overexcited circles with me, and then I can't keep my hands off him as they rub up and down his arms, brushing snow off his top, knowing we can't stay out here for long because we're not wrapped up well enough.

His hands hold my waist and he lifts me up, holding me high and then lowering me down until I can wrap my arms around his shoulders, and he pulls me tight against him, spinning us both around as the snowflakes fall.

I press a kiss into his neck and he uses his chin to nudge my head up until our lips can meet.

My mouth crushes against his, surrounded by the scent of his shampoo blending with ice-covered pine branches and the crisp scent of freshly fallen snow. I lose myself in him for long minutes, his closeness warm enough to shut out the Arctic chill.

If kissing in the snow isn't the epitome of winter romance, then I don't know what is. I could very well have stumbled onto a movie set. It's the most perfect Christmas Day ever and it's only 8 a.m.

'Ho ho ho, Santa's glad to see his favourite elves having fun.' There's the sound of footsteps and hooves on snow and Tav puts me down when we see Dad heading up the road towards us, still dressed in full Santa gear, and leading Rudolph-slash-Clive, who comes across and hoovers over me, and then huffs, disappointed by the general lack of lichen pockets in traditional pyjamas.

Dad tugs his harness and offers him a consolatory snuffle of food pellets from his hand. 'Thought he could do with a bit of exercise and manly companionship. His new missus has taken an unfortunate liking to Pedro Pascal.'

'Where on earth have you been at this time of day?' I ask.

'Around the world, of course. It was Christmas Eve. My busiest night of the year.'

'Dad, you're not actually Santa.'

Tav laughs. 'He's been out for his early morning walk, Sash. He's just winding you up.'

'Of course I am.' Dad offers me a wink. 'Or am I? All I'm saying is you've never seen me and Santa in the same room together . . .'

'That's because Santa isn't—'

Dad cuts me off by tugging the reindeer between me and Tav, making me jump aside to accommodate his single antler.

'Merry Christmas to all, and to all a good night,' he calls as he walks back towards the reindeer stables, "ho-ho-ho-ing". 'Get some hot chocolate on, will you? Santa's had a hectic night!'

'Now you're here for good, you'll have to take charge of him.'

'Dad?' I snort. 'It's a grand idea, but good luck in trying.'

Tav laughs. 'The reindeer. He likes you.'

'I like him. I like quite a few things around this place.'

He lifts my hand to his mouth and kisses the back of it. His hair falls forward and he doesn't take his eyes off mine, the intensity in them so hot that's it's completely at odds with the snow falling around us.

'Can I ask you something?' He holds my hand against his face, my fingers tingling with the soft prickle of his stubble. 'Have you checked the wishing jar?'

'I keep forgetting.'

'Can I run up and get it?'

I rub my arms in an attempt to warm up as I watch Tav easily navigate the hill up to my cabin, and when he comes back and deposits it and the tiny key in my hand, it doesn't look tampered with. I unlock it and pull out the piece of paper. It's blank.

'Okay, how did you do it? I *know* this is trickery, and it's very sweet, but now I'm going to be working here, you have to let me in on all your secrets.'

'All I want to know is what it said.' He clearly isn't going to elaborate on any tricks of the trade.

'A happy family Christmas.' I look up and meet his eyes. 'It's come true from the moment I arrived, Tav. I know Christmases can never be as they were again, but this is the closest I've ever had. Something has felt different this year. Special.'

He encloses me in his arms again, wrapping around me completely, and I hug him back, still grasping the wishing jar in one hand.

'Right, one good old-fashioned family fun day coming right up.'

'Chevy Chase isn't about to turn up with a tree on the car roof, is he?'

He laughs. 'No, but Christmas movies are a good place to start. I know Christmas Day is your big celebration, but it's a quiet day here, for family. Some cooking, eating, reading . . . Sitting around in the warm house with the Christmas lights on, doing absolutely nothing but enjoying the cosiness with the people you love most.'

'Sounds perfect.'

He reluctantly unfurls himself from around me, but I pull him back when he starts towards the house. 'Thank you.'

'What for?'

I consider it for a moment. 'Letting me in.'

He beams like he physically can't stop himself. 'Thank you for stepping outside your comfort zone. Well, flying, dog sledding, and reindeer-sleigh-riding outside of your comfort zone. It's inadequate to say I'm really glad you did, but I'm *really* glad you did.'

'You sure you don't mind sharing your North Pole Forest with me?'

'You've given it back its heart. I'd got lost with it, lost what it meant to me, what my goal was when I started. You've reminded me of that. It wouldn't be the North Pole Forest without you.'

I melt into his arms again and we stand there cuddling as the snow coming down gets heavier.

'You know it's freezing, right?' he whispers against the top of my head, his stubble soft against my hair.

I laugh like I somehow hadn't noticed. 'I know. Just enjoying the best Christmas ever for a moment longer. It only comes once a year.'

'It's the first of many.'

I laugh because he makes me feel more important and more loved than I've ever been, and when you make a Christmas wish, who knows, maybe someone does listen and somewhere in a distant forest that twinkles with Christmas magic, it really does come true.

Acknowledgements

Firstly and always most importantly, Mum, this line never changes because I'm *always* eternally grateful for your constant patience, support, encouragement, and for always believing in me. Thank you for always being there for me – I don't know what I'd do without you. Love you lots!

I also want to give a big shout-out to some Facebook groups that have supported me tirelessly this year and are an absolute pleasure to be part of. If you're looking for book-loving groups filled with readers who will be good for your soul (but terrible for your to-read list!) then I highly recommend joining The Friendly Book Community, Heidi Swain and Friends, Chick Lit and Prosecco, and The Socially Distanced Book Club. Thank you so much to all members and admins of these wonderful groups who put in so much effort to make little communities that are a joy to belong to!

The biggest thank you to an amazing author and one of my very best friends, Marie Landry. I look forward to talking to you every day. You never fail to make me laugh and feel loved, and you are *always* the highlight of my day! I love you more than I hate a certain moustache!

An extra special thank you to Bev for always writing lovely

letters, always taking the time to ask about my writing, and for always being so encouraging and supportive and kind!

Thank you, Charlotte McFall, for always being a tireless cheer-leader and one of the best friends I've ever had.

Thank you, Jayne Lloyd, for being a wonderful friend through good times and bad, and for the emails that always make me smile!

Bill, Toby, Cathie – thank you for always being supportive!

All the lovely authors, bloggers, and readers I know online. You've all been so supportive since the very first book, and I want to mention you all by name, but I know I'll forget someone and I don't want to leave anyone out, so to everyone I chat to on Twitter or Facebook – thank you.

Thank you to all the team at HQ and especially my fabulous editor, Belinda Toor, for always knowing exactly what each book needs!

And finally, a massive thank you to *you* for reading!

Keep reading for an excerpt from
*The Little Christmas Shop
on Nutcracker Lane . . .*

JAIMIE ADMANS

The *Little*
Christmas Shop
on
*Nutcracker
Lane*

Chapter 1

My phone beeps with a text message and I look up from the nutcracker bunting I'm painting. Hopefully the guy I'm seeing telling me he's missing me and he's sorry I've got to work late again. It's not serious yet, but maybe it could be one day. After so many disappointing relationships, it's nice to be dating such a reassuring man for a change. He's always texting to ask where I am and what I'm doing.

Can't wait to see you tonight. That's odd. I'm not seeing him tonight. *Wear that purple lingerie set I bought you. It looks sexy on you but it will look even better on the bedroom floor.* Again, odd. I don't own a purple lingerie set. *Nia's working late again. Thank God for this shop she's got. We'll have all night without her constant needy texts.*

It instantly makes sense. Oh, great. Not only am I dating another cheater, I'm dating a cheater who thinks "it'll look better on the bedroom floor" is original or even slightly seductive *and* thinks my texts are needy. I thought I was being romantic. I thought he liked me because he's always texting to find out what I'm up to. I should've realised it's because he's carefully scheduling his purple lingerie appointments.

A few seconds later, my phone beeps again.

Hah! Had you going, didn't I? Ha ha ha ha ha ha ha!

Does he think it becomes funnier with the more "ha"s he includes?

It beeps again. *Obviously I was joking. Nia? Nia?? Nia???*

I wait until he's added an abnormal number of question marks and then text back. *Oh, go schnitzel yourself, twatspangle. Enjoy your night with Ms Purple Lingerie. You won't be getting to see my lingerie ever again, purple or not.*

I delete the last bit before I send it. My lingerie is mostly a sort of off-greyish colour because I accidentally washed it with a black T-shirt. The mention of it is not going to make him fall at my feet and question his life choices.

I should probably feel sad, but we'd only been seeing each other for a couple of months. It wasn't serious. And there's become a sense of inevitability about it now. Every relationship is the same. Boy meets Girl, Boy is cute and funny, Girl does everything by the book and presents herself as most perfect specimen of normality she can muster – ie: Boy doesn't know Girl bleaches arm hair and plucks out occasional hag whisker. Things seem to be going well for Boy and Girl, and then . . . Boy cheats on Girl. Repeat *ad infinitum*.

My phone beeps again. *Sorry, Nia.*

At least he sent it to the right person this time. And had the decency to apologise, which is more than can be said for the last three cheating boyfriends.

I put my phone down on the desk and pick up one of the blank nutcracker silhouettes I'm painting and lift it away from the string it's attached to. 'What am I doing wrong?' I ask it.

It doesn't answer. Maybe it's the answer in itself – talking to wooden Christmas decorations.

Strings of tiny, flat nutcracker soldiers are laid out in front of me and I move along the desk as I put a coat of primer on each wooden figure so they've got plenty of time to dry overnight, and tomorrow I can start painting in the details like faces and brightly coloured clothing.

Maybe it's a good thing that it's ended. Now I won't have to worry about working late and not spending enough time with someone and can concentrate entirely on the shop and making it the biggest success it can be. Having my own shop on Nutcracker Lane is what I've wanted my entire life. It's good that I won't have any distractions. I keep repeating that to myself as I move from one hand-cut MDF figure to the next, trying not to let my mind wander to the text message. It's not like it was a serious relationship. Just a guy I met on a dating app a couple of months ago, chatted a bit with online, and have met up with a few times since. I didn't really think it was going anywhere, but I *did* think I was the only woman in his life. Another lie.

Tears blur the workbench in front of me and I try to blink them back as the tip of my brush dunks into the white primer. It's not even *him* – it's the fact that it's happened again. Yet another guy who can't be satisfied with just one person. Is it me? Am I not good enough for them? Other men get married and stay in committed happy relationships and their eyes don't wander. And yet, even when I meet someone who seems like one of the good ones, I repel them like water on oil paint. This makes it the fifth guy who's cheated on me in the last five relationships. That is not a promising ratio. And I'm the common denominator.

Maybe it's time to give up on love forever. I don't know why I keep trying when it's becoming clear that *every* relationship is going to end the same way.

I shake my head, sniff and wipe my eyes, and hum "Little Drummer Boy" as loudly as I can. Painting nutcrackers always makes me think of this song. No use dwelling on it. Another unfaithful man is not worth any more tears – not when it's December tomorrow and Nutcracker Lane will open to the public for the first time this year and my decorations will be for sale. This is something I've dreamed about my entire life and Stacey and I have spent the past few years trying to make it happen. Sharing a Christmas shop with my best friend. Yet another cheating boyfriend makes no difference to how amazing that is.

It's late by the time I've got the strings of nutcracker bunting finished and transferred to the little workshop in the back room behind the main shop. I should've been painting out the back, but this is my first year, and I wanted to watch from the window as the other shop owners finished their final preparations before tomorrow and left one by one. I wanted to watch the last of the Christmas lights be turned off as the sky gradually darkened above us.

The clear roof has always been my favourite thing about Nutcracker Lane – the way you can watch the skies and experience the weather. Even though it's warm and dry inside, the rain still patters down and the snow still blankets us, unlike the fake layers of felt snow that are piled up around the edges of the lane.

I pull on my red coat, tug my bag over my shoulder, and turn the lights off in the back room. One final walk through the shop floor reveals there's nothing else I can tweak or change. I've been here every day for the last month, transferring stock from my garden shed-slash-workshop, rearranging tables and display units, setting out everything *just right* and then setting it all out again in another formation until it really is *just right* and Stacey yells at me to stop fiddling.

I want it to be perfect. My own shop on Nutcracker Lane is what I've always wanted, and I'm desperate for nothing to go wrong. I could easily spend another hour carefully rearranging the wooden snowman family that is standing near the counter or displaying the array of hand-painted baubles and hanging decorations that are set out in wicker baskets on a table, but even I know that I'm tweaking for the sake of it, and the shop already looks like the cosy little Christmas haven I always imagined my shop on Nutcracker Lane would be.

I set a hand-painted "'Twas The Night Before Christmas" glittery plaque straight on the wall and then have to do it again because it was straight anyway and now it's wonky, and I adjust the gingerbread-house earrings on a mannequin in Stacey's side of the window. It's going to be amazing working here with my best friend. Going halves on the rent and sharing the shop space – her Christmas jewellery on one side, my Christmas decorations on the other, a window each, and one counter and till between us. We've done craft fairs at the weekends for years, but this is the first time either of us will have an actual shop for the season.

I give one of the retro Nineties-style foil garlands hung across the window a final fluff-up, hoping that my nostalgic display will encourage the feeling of walking into a homely cottage and not a shiny, flashy shop. My decorations are handmade and old-fashioned by modern standards, but I want them to invoke the feeling of Christmases gone by, before every decoration had to sing and dance and be controlled via a smartphone app.

I step out onto the honey-coloured crazy paving and bend down to turn off the multicoloured lights wrapped around the tree outside the door. There's an identical one outside every other shop doorway on the street, each one decorated in the owner's choice, usually displaying some of the goods. Ours is covered in hanging wooden stars and gingerbread men I've made, and acrylic holly leaves and candy canes that Stacey's made.

Every shop on Nutcracker Lane is identical – all large redwood log cabins with fake snow draped across their slanting roofs and a three-foot-tall Christmas tree in a red Santa's sack planter outside the door. The shopkeepers are allowed to decorate their own cabins in any way they choose, and each one has a wide double window and a sign nailed above the door displaying the name of their shop and a slogan. I wood-burned ours in my shed at home and it reads *Starlight Rainbows. Handmade decorations and jewellery.*

I lock up and slip the keys into my bag and turn around to

take in the 11 p.m. atmosphere before the place fills with shoppers tomorrow morning. Well, hopefully. It's been many years since Nutcracker Lane was as packed as it used to be when I was little and my grandma used to bring me here to visit Santa, see the lights, and buy a new decoration for the tree that year, and of course, make a wish on the magical nutcracker.

It's deserted at this time of night. Even the Victorian-style streetlamps that line the lane on either side and emit a warm orange glow in the evenings are off, but there's still the faint whiff of peppermint from the production of peppermint bark in the sweetshop next door today.

The only thing that's unusual is the empty shop directly across from me. I can never recall seeing an empty shop on Nutcracker Lane before. Getting a shop here is more difficult than scoring an invitation to afternoon tea at Buckingham Palace with the Queen. Not that I'm likely to manage that either, but since I started making decorations and selling them online, I've applied every year to rent a shop for the season, and this is the first year I've been a successful applicant.

It's odd to see the log cabin opposite completely dark inside, with nothing in the windows and no sign above the door, not even a Christmas tree outside. Were they really that short of applicants this year? I know things have been deteriorating, but an empty shop is unprecedented. A shiver runs down my spine, and not just from the chill in the air as a cold breeze blows through the lane. Is this a sign of things to come? Is Nutcracker Lane really going downhill so fast that they can no longer fill all the shops?

I turn away and start walking towards the exit. Even with the lights off and the log cabin shops shut, the lane still looks festive. Without any gingerbread baking in the Nutcracker Lane bakery, the balsam scent of the Christmas trees mingles with the faint peppermint from earlier, making me wish I could stay here all night and breathe it in.

'Goodnight, Mr Nutcracker.' I approach the supposedly magical giant nutcracker. When I was little, I thought he was the most magical thing in the world – even better than Santa. He was the talk of the town. *Everyone* knew about the magical wish-granting nutcracker on Nutcracker Lane. He's old. I don't know how old, but he's carved of solid wood, and his mouth and the lever at his back to operate it are his only moving parts, unlike modern-day nutcrackers that are all pins and dowels and glue. He's an older version of the nutcrackers we see everywhere today, with eyes and a moustache carved into dark brown polished wood, and inlaid cherry-stained wood to make his rosy red cheeks, instead of being painted on like they are these days. He has the same white furry beard, long and slightly threadbare now, and his once-bright soldier's outfit, painted in shades of yellow and red, is faded and chipped after so many years of cracking nuts. He holds a carved candy-cane wand and his black boots are encased in cement and buried in the floor to prevent him being stolen.

He's the main attraction of Nutcracker Lane, and he stands proud, over eight-foot tall, in the middle of the big court inside the entrance. He's surrounded by a wooden fence, Astroturf, and white-spotted red mushrooms with little wooden doors on their stems to make up an elf garden.

Next to him are a few large plastic cases of various nuts – walnuts, hazelnuts, and a fake nut alternative for allergy sufferers, and there's a sign up that reads – *Nutcrackers are brimming with magical powers. It's long been said that if a wish is made at the exact moment a nut is being cracked, when the stars shine bright and the wind rustles his beard, and you can almost hear the sparkling of Christmas magic in the air all around, the nutcracker will grant the wish. Try it!*

Surrounding the nutcracker's feet are a bed of broken nutshells where people can throw them, ready to be composted after Christmas, and there are steps up to the handle so even little ones can reach, although a far more popular position is on the shoulders of parents, the way my granddad used to lift me up to crack a nut and make a wish.

The poor old thing might need a fresh coat of paint and some wood filler, but he's stood here for as long as I can remember – if anything, he's the most reliable man in my life. He's here every year without fail. Every year as strong as stone, like an old friend you look forward to catching up with in the festive season, who brings a smile to your face when you remember them throughout the year.

This old nutcracker has seen so many years go by. Things aren't how they used to be, but he's still here, watching over his lane, even though wish-granting is a thing of the past now, and it's been a long time since Christmas magic sparkled around here.

'You're the kind of man I need, Mr Nutcracker,' I say to him as I go to walk away. 'Goodnight.'

And for the weirdest moment, a chill goes down my spine as the breeze through the lane suddenly picks up and ripples his beard. It's a crisp, clear night and I look up and see the stars twinkling through the glass roof and a crescent moon glowing to the east.

I glance back at the nutcracker, half-expecting him to have moved, what with the similarity to the sign about the stars twinkling and the wind rustling his beard.

I turn around and walk back towards him. 'I know when the universe is trying to tell me something. And I suppose a wish couldn't hurt . . .'

I go through the gap in the fence surrounding him and pick a walnut from one of the nut-vending machines. I reach around him to pull the lever up and open his mouth, put the nut in, and pull the lever gently back down.

I look up at his cheery, red-cheeked woodgrain face. A face I've looked into many times and always felt was smiling back at me. I was fifteen the last time I made a wish on him, and my last wish was that one day I'd get to work on Nutcracker Lane, and even though I am now working here, it's taken twenty years to come true, and determination not to give up even when every application for a shop has been rejected, so I don't think I can quite credit Christmas magic for that one.

'Ah, what the heck . . .' I pull the lever until the nutcracker's jaws touch the walnut shell. 'I wish to finally find Prince Charming. A prince like you, Mr Nutcracker. A strong, dependable, handsome man who will be loyal and charming and kind. Is that too much to ask?'

The breeze whispers through the lane again and the walnut splits. I take it out of the nutcracker's smiling mouth, throw the shell into the nutshell garden, and pop the kernel into my mouth. 'Goodnight.'

A cloud passes over the moon above and for just a moment, it looks like he winks at me.

I shake my head at myself as I walk away. Apparently break-ups cause hallucinations now too. It reminds me that I'm alone again, and I decide to take the long way round and pop into the 24-hour supermarket on the way home. Never mind magical nutcrackers and walnut wishes, there's only one thing that'll make me feel better in this situation – Ben & Jerry's. Several tubs. And one of those gigantic tubs of chocolates they bring out for Christmas.

In 65,903 calories' time, yet another cheating man will be nothing but a distant memory. It won't matter that I'm alone again because it's Christmas and Nutcracker Lane opens in the morning, and it's my first year here. It's going to be the best Christmas ever.

Dear reader,

Thank you so much for reading *The Post Box at the North Pole*! I hope you enjoyed a festive escape to snowy Norway and enjoyed getting wrapped up in Sash and Tav's story, as well as all the Santa letters!

Seeing the Northern Lights is a lifelong dream of mine, and I thoroughly enjoyed getting to live vicariously through Sasha while writing this, and had so much fun doing all the research into Norwegian traditions, reindeer, life in that part of the world, and of course, delving into Santa's mail bag! I want to go and visit Santa this Christmas now, even though I'm much too old for it!

If you enjoyed this story, please consider leaving a rating or review on Amazon. It only has to be a line or two, and it makes such a difference to helping other readers decide to pick up the book, and it would mean so much to me to know what you think! Did it make you smile, laugh, or cry? Would you write to Santa even as an adult? What would you write in your Christmas wishing jar? What do you hope *Julenissen* will leave under your tree this year?

Thank you again for reading. If you want to get in touch, you can find me on Twitter – usually when I should be writing – @be_the_spark. I would love to hear from you!

Hope to see you again soon in a future book!

Lots of love,

Jaimie

Dear Reader,

We hope you enjoyed reading this book. If you did, we'd be so appreciative if you left a review. It really helps us and the author to bring more books like this to you.

Here at HQ Digital we are dedicated to publishing fiction that will keep you turning the pages into the early hours. Don't want to miss a thing? To find out more about our books, promotions, discover exclusive content and enter competitions you can keep in touch in the following ways:

JOIN OUR COMMUNITY:

Sign up to our new email newsletter: http://smarturl.it/SignUpHQ

Read our new blog www.hqstories.co.uk

https://twitter.com/HQStories

www.facebook.com/HQStories

BUDDING WRITER?

We're also looking for authors to join the HQ Digital family! Find out more here:

https://www.hqstories.co.uk/want-to-write-for-us/

Thanks for reading, from the HQ Digital team

If you enjoyed *The Post Box at the North Pole*, then why not try another delightfully uplifting romance from HQ Digital?